I0583285

Redeemed
in
Crimson

T.K. DRAKE

SINCLAIR AFFAIRS BOOK ONE

Redeemed
in
Crimson

T.K. DRAKE

Redeemed in Crimson

Copyright © 2025 by T.K. Drake

All rights reserved.

No part of this publication may be reproduced or transmitted in any form or by any electronic or mechanical means, including information storage and retrieval systems, without written permission from the author, except for the use of brief quotations embodied in book reviews.

The characters, events, businesses, organizations, incidents, and places in this book are fictitious or a product of the author's imagination. Any similarity to real persons, living or dead, is coincidental and not intended by the author.

The moral right of the author has been asserted.

Contact Info: www.tkdrake.com

Cover design/formatting: Sandra Maldo (@smaldo.designs)

Editing: Jenny Sims (Editing 4 Indies)

979-8-9995185-0-7 (paperback)

ASIN: B0FJ2F8VQV (ebook)

First edition: August 2025

10 9 8 7 6 5 4 3 2 1

To all the good girls who never got their chance to be bad.

Author's Note

Thank you from the bottom of our hearts for taking the chance on a brand new author and reading Redeemed in Crimson! When we started this journey one year ago, we set out to write our perfect book boyfriend and merge our love for reading romance with our untapped creative energies. Neither of us could have imagined the roller coaster of emotions that creating Sloane and Ledger took us on! We've laughed, cried, laughed until we cried...and spent more time together as best friends than we have in a decade. This book healed something in us that we've been chasing for our entire lives, and we're so grateful to everyone who's helped along the way.

Redeemed in Crimson is book one in a five book series but can be read as a standalone.

Content Warning

This is a sexually explicit, dark romance featuring themes some readers may find triggering, including but not limited to: stalking, exhibitionism, group sex, blood play, anal sex, hidden cameras, references to birth control tampering, etc. Please read at your own risk.

Our hero is obsessive and possessive of his FMC and we guarantee an HEA.

For specific questions or concerns, please contact tkdrakeauthor@outlook.com

Chapter One

Sloane

"I will never understand why you insisted on bringing this god-awful chair all the way from home. A pink velvet chair belongs in a teenage bedroom, Sloane, not your first college apartment. This is a chance to refine your home design skills before you get married and have an entire house to decorate yourself."

And I'll never understand why you bothered having a child, Mother, but you don't hear me criticizing your decisions.

I turn, eyeing the only piece of furniture I've ever picked out for myself. "Fine, Mom, we can take it to Goodwill and donate it if you don't think it matches the space."

"Well, nothing is *really* going to work in this space. The building's orientation does not allow for any good natural light during the day, and the layout of the bedrooms is abysmal. I'm not sure why you picked this complex to begin with. And we aren't taking the chair back home. Your father already went to the trouble of bringing it all this way. Especially after he almost threw his back out carrying all your books," my mother says, continuing the overarching theme of my life—that no decision I ever make is good enough.

Not for a lack of trying.

Hobbies, clothes, hairstyles, boyfriends. They've all been carefully chosen in an effort to keep Janice Johnson happy. The only things that have come close to succeeding have been my choice of college (her alma mater) and my current boyfriend of three years, Dean Christensen.

Maybe my parents can adopt him, and they can live a peaceful beige existence together.

Wishful thinking, although I doubt I would be missed at all in this scenario. It might take a month or more for anyone to notice I was gone. At least until my parents host another party or event that requires my attendance, in a nice dress, on Dean's arm, making small talk and listening to jokes about when we'll finally get engaged.

My mother's scoff from the front door of the apartment brings me out of my daydream world, where my parents and I don't know each other. "I think you have the wrong apartment, dear. This is 121 Bedford Street. Are you sure you aren't looking for another address, perhaps something on the east side of town?"

Looking toward the door, I see that Jan has physically blocked a petite brunette with bright blue highlights from entering.

"Allie! Thank God you're here," I greet my roommate, who I met last fall in speech class. She single-handedly saved me from an hour of utter boredom and icebreaker questions by suggesting we make up increasingly outlandish stories about ourselves to pass the time. We stayed close after that and even had a few of our introductory-level drama classes together. Those classes were really what kept me from breaking down during my freshman year—the only light-heartedness I felt among the business classes my parents forced me into.

"Sloane, I've missed you so much." Allie gives me a look that says she can't believe she's finally met the infamous Janice Johnson, and she's even more impressed than she already was that I'm such a well-adjusted, relatively normal human.

I know, aren't I impressive? Can you believe she spawned me? I try to convey with a look, but Allie is already in the apartment and moving toward what we agreed would be her bedroom.

"Oh, I'm so sorry, dear, you must be Andrea. Sloane has told us so much about you, but she didn't mention what...fun hair you have. Scott, isn't this hair just the quirkiest thing you've ever seen?" my mother says, clearly looking to my dad for backup on the unsavory character who just interrupted her monologue on my shortcomings.

My dad is too engrossed in golf highlights on his phone to offer more than a dismissive, "Of course, dear."

"It's Allie, ma'am, and I'm so glad you like my hair," Allie says with a casually dismissive wave as she heads into her bedroom.

Watching her leave, my mom turns back to me and opens her mouth to no doubt spew some sexist, homophobic, or otherwise offensive nonsense, but I'm saved when a timer goes off on her phone and she's redirected. "Oh, it's already half past five. We need to leave to meet Dean at Marchetti's for dinner."

My gaze snaps up to meet hers as she gathers her things, my dad already standing to head to the car. "I didn't know you were planning to meet Dean. I made plans with Allie to see some of our friends from class once we finished settling things here."

"Don't be ridiculous, Sloane. Of course Dean would want to see you the first day you were back in town, and surely, you knew we wouldn't leave without seeing our favorite guy. Just because he had a prior commitment this morning and missed the actual moving doesn't mean you aren't his top priority," my mom says.

"His prior commitment was golf with his fraternity brothers, Mom." I sigh. Not that I'm surprised at the fact that I'm not his priority. I don't think I've ever been anyone's priority. Certainly not for something as insignificant as moving day.

The drive to the restaurant begins with instructions on how I should conduct myself this semester, as well as the organizations and activities I'm expected to participate in. A few reminders are thrown in about how I'm the only child my parents have and how I have the sole responsibility for our family's reputation.

"When did Dean say he was supposed to meet us? I thought we agreed on six o'clock?" Mom asks after being seated at a booth in the back corner of the cozy Italian restaurant.

I start to tell her that he hasn't responded to my text, letting him know we finished with the moving truck and were on our way, but I stop when I hear Dad defend his tardiness.

"It's only six twenty, Janice. He's been golfing all day. Cut him a little slack."

My father, ladies and gents, always wanting the absolute best for his daughter.

"I know, I know—but we need to get checked into our hotel. We'll need a good night's sleep tonight after all that moving if we're going to make the first service at Sloane's church tomorrow morning."

Oh crap. I forgot I told her about that church. My parents are religious with a capital R. Finding a church was a requirement of theirs if I was going to go away to college, but to be honest, I'm a little churched out. And with the extra classes they insist I take every semester, I really just want to sleep in on Sundays. I told them I had been attending a church called "Calvary" last year and have just rolled with that ever since. I even told Dean I was going regularly, and because he's either sleeping off a hangover on Sundays or golfing, he's never called my bluff.

In the past, I've wondered why my parents don't expect Dean to attend church if it's so important to them, and the only answer I've arrived at is the patriarchy. Or just general misogyny? He's golfed with my father for years, and I'm convinced he's more like a child to them than I am. If both of us were hanging off a cliff, they would save him, I'm sure. He and his "golf career" are way more important.

"There he is!" my dad bellows, breaking my thoughts about how I'm going to explain to my parents why literally nobody at that church will know who I am.

"Scott! Janice! How are you?"

Dean walks in wearing a pair of khaki slacks and a light blue golf shirt, skirting right past me to greet my parents. He definitely doesn't look like he's been out golfing all day. It's scorching hot outside, and while I'm sporting a lovely new sunburn from moving things from the truck, he shows no signs of having been out in the sun.

"I'm so sorry I'm late. I finished at the course early and decided to freshen up a little before meeting up with my favorite people," Dean says, smiling widely.

He shakes my father's hand and half hugs him, then gives Mom a huge bear hug. A little shoulder squeeze is the only acknowledgment I get after he greets my parents.

Before I can feel too bad for myself, Dean wraps his arm around my shoulders and pulls me closer to him. His heavy arm on my sunburn hurts. I *really* want to ask him to move it, but I can only imagine what my mother would say about that, so I grin like a happy, lovesick girl.

It's not that I don't want to touch him at all. It's just that something seems off. I'm not pleased with him blowing me off this morning to go golf with his buddies, so that could be clouding my judgment. But he never responded to my texts, he's late to eat dinner with us, and despite him saying he freshened up, he doesn't look like he just hopped out of the shower. He always lets his dirty-blond hair air dry, so it looks a little damp for an hour or so. But it's perfectly dry and combed to perfection. So neither has he just come from the course nor has he just "freshened up."

I have plenty of time to ponder where exactly Dean has been all day throughout the course of our two-hour dinner, during which *zero* of the conversation requires my input. In the past, it bothered me to be excluded from any of the stories being told or plans being made at these dinners, but now, I'm relieved that my mind can wander. Not for the first time, I consider my own hopes and dreams for my life while conversation flows around me with plans I have no say in. I zone back in briefly when I hear Dad say, "The Hendersons down the street plan to sell in a few years."

I look up to see Dean giving me a winning smile. "Well, that would be perfect. Close enough to have built-in babysitters, babe."

Knowing that saying anything contrary to the "Sloane Master Plan" would be seen as grounds for admittance to a mental facility, I smile and nod, ready to go back to imagining a life where my free will matters.

Finally, after dessert, two rounds of coffee, and my dad leaving an awful tip for a server they ran ragged, we make our way back to the car. Dad and Dean make plans for another round of golf tomorrow morning, leaving Mom and me with plans to go to church alone. The drive back to my apartment takes longer than usual thanks to traffic, and I spend the time gazing out the window while my parents continue talking about what a saint Dean is.

I'm contemplating the pros and cons of being dramatic and throwing myself out of the moving vehicle once traffic clears, if only to ruin my parents' plans for a few weeks and force them to think about something other than themselves, when a red and black monstrosity of a motorcycle comes to a stop beside our car. It's beautiful. I don't think I've ever taken notice of a bike before—unless it was to listen to my mom go on and on about how dangerous they can be, how only hoodlums ride them, and how I better *never* consider getting on one myself.

But this is different. Beautiful, huge, and overall intimidating, to be honest. All black and red swirls, designs that look threatening and enticing and sinful. Sitting still in traffic with no end in sight, I commit every detail of this bike to memory, thinking of a world where I could hop on and speed off to do whatever I wanted. I've probably been staring, entranced, for a solid five minutes when I first take notice of the rider. A giant black combat boot leads to a long leg, slightly bent...*Jesus, how tall is this man?* I'm not sure this is a man. This giant machine seems too small for this...creature. Troll? Viking? I have to assume this is a man, but I've never seen one this big. It could still be a troll since I can't see a single inch of skin...until the visor on the troll's helmet opens, and it looks like a man for sure. And he's staring right at me.

Chapter Two

Ledger

Fuck, I need to get my dick wet. Tonight. Preferably multiple times. How long has it been? Two weeks? Has it really been two weeks since I fucked anyone? No wonder the fights tonight didn't do anything to relieve this energy. I just beat three men to a pulp and...nothing. Nothing I do lately seems to calm me down. I've spent the past two weeks helping Mom organize Dad's old office, and all it's done is solidify the fact that I'm the family fuckup.

It was all going fine until we found his journals. Mom, content to let sleeping dogs lie, wasn't interested in reading them at all. I was going to put them in a storage box and forget about them until I dropped one and saw my name. How does she not care to see what he said? I couldn't help myself. I'd always been second best. My older brother, Henry, was—is—the perfect son. He did everything he was supposed to do and more. The golden boy. Smart, athletic, classy, kind, perfect. And the perfect brother too. He's the only reason I'm still here today and was more of a father figure to me than Dad ever was. Then there's my little sister, Margot, who could also do no wrong. I suppose if you have a baby girl when you're nearing fifty years old with more money than God, you're required to treat her like a princess. Hell, we all treat her like a princess. How could we not? Okay, so both my siblings are incredible people. I've always wondered why my father's approval meant so much when everyone else in my family made me feel nothing but love and support.

I thought I was fine after three years of Dad being gone, and years of therapy at Henry's insistence. But damn, does it make me feel like shit when I read how much of a disappointment I was with all the fighting, drugs, and women. Well, maybe he should've been a little concerned, but it still hurts to read. I'm not a complete menace anymore. I cut the drugs out a long time ago, and I used my trust fund to start my own business, a very successful one at that. Granted, it's a sex club, and I wouldn't have dreamed of doing that while Dad was alive. It would've been just another thing for him to be disappointed in, like the fighting. Well, fuck him because my club is the most successful club in the Southeast, and I'm a damn good fighter.

I've just always had this energy that takes extreme measures to burn off. The drugs helped for a bit, but I was losing myself in that. The sex helps for a moment. The fighting helps. Over time, both have had to become more aggressive to get that release.

That's why I'm currently trying to figure out exactly how much debauchery I want to get into at the club tonight. I usually have my pick of women coming in, and it has nothing to do with the fact that I own the place. I keep that fact pretty well hidden. I have my pick of women because I'm a fucking wet dream and I know it. I know I sound like a narcissistic asshole to admit that, but it's true. I'm six foot five with more muscles than you can count and tattoos that cover every inch of them from the waist up. I'm not the man you take home to Mom. I'm the one you let pound the life out of you at a sex club. That doesn't mean I don't respect women. I would never lead anyone to assume I'd be open for more than a fuck. If I ever meet someone outside of the club, I make sure they know my expectations. But hooking up at the club is presumed to be just that, a hookup. And that's exactly what I plan to do tonight.

I'm lost in my thoughts of the club when I hit what appears to be a giant fucking traffic jam. Normally, I would either lane split or ride down the shoulder to the nearest exit, but Mom has been riding my ass hard about how dangerous this bike is and how she needs me around to give her grandchildren. *As if.* But considering the fighting and fucking, the least I can do is respect her wishes and be as safe as possible on the bike. I even wear a helmet now. I slow and eventually come to a dead stop, still a fucking ways away from my exit to the club. If anything, this just gives me more of a chance to consider how I'm going to expel this energy racing below my skin like a parasite. Jesus, I'm starting to sound like a philosopher or some shit. Maybe I need a track day, or a weekend in Amsterdam, or someone new.

I'm contemplating whether I think my sobriety can handle Amsterdam or if it would be worth it to test it in a couple of weeks on the anniversary of my sperm donor's death, when I see her. A sedan has pulled up next to me in traffic, driven by a plain-ass Mr. and Mrs. John and Jane Doe. In the back seat, though, is the most beautiful pair of eyes I've ever seen. Also, possibly, the saddest. She's blankly staring at what appears to be nothing—maybe the taillights of the car in front of me—but she isn't really seeing them. Shit, definitely the saddest. Just a blank stare, like nothing gives her any pleasure. Maybe she isn't always like this, and it's just boring John and Jane in the front seat making her evening horrible.

I'm considering breaking my own rules and lane splitting just to get away from her melancholy gaze when she sees me. Well, not really. It's like she doesn't see me at all, and instead all she sees is my bike. Granted, my Ducati is a perfect machine that I've had hand-painted and customized to my exact specifications, but I've never been so outright ignored. I look back up to see that her eyes have completely changed. Gone is the blank, sad, beige girl stare. Instead, her eyes are alight with beautiful fascination. I might as well be invisible. Perhaps I should step aside so she can have an unobstructed view or offer her some alone time with the bike. Her eyes are almost hungry, like all her problems would be solved if she just got on and rode off. I can empathize. That's exactly how I feel when I ride.

She finally seems to notice my...leg? Not usually the first thing women notice about me, but okay. Her gaze travels upward, looking almost confused. Like she doesn't quite know what she's looking at. As if she hasn't seen a man before. Or maybe she just hasn't seen a man my size before, which, if she doesn't spend her time around professional athletes or mountain men, I guess I understand. It's almost as if she's trying to figure out if I even am a man. As her gaze travels up my torso, I decide to go ahead and help her solve her puzzle.

I flip my visor open just as her gaze finally reaches my helmet, and we lock eyes. If I still gambled—which I don't, because how many addictions does one man need—I would've bet that her eyes would be filled with lust. That's always been what I've gotten from women. Not respect, not admiration, not love. Lust. And I've been happy to provide satisfaction on that front without any strings attached. But this little enigma trapped in the sad beige sedan looks at me with...curiosity? Wonder? Like she envisioned something else under the helmet and is surprised I'm *just* a man. I'm trying to think of the last time any woman looked at me like this, if ever, when traffic eases, and just like that, she's gone.

I'm still thinking of just how much my enigma's eyes changed from haunted and hopeless to hopeful and adventurous, all just from looking at my bike, when I finally make it to the club.

Rendezvous is my pride and joy, and I've grown it from scratch into the premier sex club in the region over the past two years. I've been fortunate to have a great team to help me, and now the day-to-day operations don't require anywhere near as much energy as they used to. That doesn't mean I don't still love to play. If nothing else, I created this club as an outlet for my desires and energy. Walking through our employee entrance is like coming home. Immediately, my floor manager and best friend, Jack, lets me know that two of our regulars who I've played with in the past are at the bar, along with a few new women and couples mingling in the lounge.

Passing through the exhibition hall on my way, I feel pride seeing every window filled with the scenes I imagined when I was dreaming up this place. Different options for whatever could strike someone's fancy. As I stroll, I wait for the familiar curl of desire to start at the base of my spine, for the urge to join a group or find a willing solo partner for the stress relief I so desperately need tonight. And...nothing? Fuck. This can't be right. Maybe I took a shot to the head today during one of my fights? No, I know damn well none of those weak-ass punks got even one good shot in.

Deciding to shake off whatever this funk is, I make my way to the lounge to see the new women Jack was talking about. They're standing together at a high-top table and immediately make eye contact, both looking the kind of perfect that you buy at a plastic surgery office. While the redhead looks like she showed her doctor a picture of a classic pinup model for inspiration, complete with full lips and unbelievable curves, her brunette companion looks like she hasn't eaten more than a leaf in years. I don't discriminate. I never have. I like pussy in all shapes and sizes. The more variety, the better. These two might be exactly what I need to get my head back in the game tonight.

"Good evening, ladies. What brings you in tonight? Looking for anything in particular?" I ask even though it's obvious exactly what they're here for.

"Oh hello, handsome," Pinup says. "What would you recommend?"

The brunette's eyes zero in on mine, and she runs her hand down my chest.

Ew...

Well, that's interesting. I can't say that I've ever been actively turned off by a woman's touch.

I lock eyes with Pinup, and they're...wrong? *How can eyes be wrong, you stupid fuck? Get it together.* I shake my head as if I can physically clear my brain fog and look back at Brunette. Her eyes are wrong too. Okay then, blindfolds it is for tonight. I can work with blindfolds as long as they're down.

I grab a strand of Brunette's hair and run it between my fingers. This seems wrong as well, and I can't for the life of me figure out why I would give a damn.

"Hello? Are you okay?" Brunette is looking at me like I'm crazy. "I asked if you wanted to go find an empty room?"

Before she can finish that sentence, I fake a phone call and apologize for having to leave before practically running out to my bike.

What in the actual fuck is wrong with my dick right now?

Obviously, I'm just tired. Everyone said turning thirty would make everything start to hurt, and this has to be the first sign since my birthday just passed. It's not even eleven o'clock. More people will be arriving throughout the night, and someone could spark my interest. Something just isn't clicking for me tonight, though, so I decide to pack it up and head home. Alone. Again. To my custom, luxurious, empty fucking house.

Chapter Three

Sloane

"Where are we sitting?" Mom asks as we make our way into the sanctuary. It's way too early to deal with her, but I'm on my best behavior this morning, hoping she doesn't question too much, like why everyone I know is either coming back to town next week or out on vacation.

"I tend to sit in the back. And before you give me any grief, that's where my friends like to sit. I would pick the front. You know that."

Phew, good one, Sloane.

"I just wish I could've met some of them. I guess your dad and I will just have to come back soon when everyone is back for school."

Dangit, I did not see that coming. We make it through the service, and I use some of my best acting skills to make sure it looks like I've definitely sat through this before. Multiple times. Definitely.

After the service, they list off some announcements, and I flinch when they mention sign-ups for a play.

I love acting. I love plays and drama classes. I had to fight hard for my parents to add them to my course load last year. Hard, hard. And now, I know. I just know Mom is about to say something about me signing up. The problem is that I don't plan to return to this church. At least not until my parents are here on a Sunday and I have to pretend again.

"Sloane! Did you know they were putting on a play? You can finally put some of those drama classes to use, missy!" They've barely dismissed us before she's dragging me to the table where they have the sign-up sheets. "Oh, this is so perfect! Your dad and I can come see you perform. You know he always thought those classes were stupid, but once he sees that you're using them for the Lord, he'll get off my back for letting you take them! This is so great!"

I'm at a loss for words. Not that she would let me get any words in either way. Before I know it, my name is on the cast list, and I have a packet of information in my hands. A beautiful woman, a little older than Mom, is reading off details to a group of us.

"Hi, everyone! My name is Blanche, and I'll be in charge of this year's Christmas play. We'll have practice every Thursday night from six to eight o'clock. We do a little something every year, but we're wanting to amp it up this year. Give it some more pizzazz, if you will. We'll meet this Thursday night to start assigning roles. If you aren't going to be one-hundred percent committed, please don't sign up. We need reliable volunteers if we're going to make this work. If you have any questions, I'll be here all morning. If not, I'll see you Thursday!"

Mom and I make our way to the car in silence. I still haven't said a word when Dad calls.

"Scott, guess what?" Mom answers the phone via Bluetooth so that we can all be involved in this conversation. As if that's really necessary.

"What's that?" my dad responds, obviously barely paying attention even though he's only been on the phone for thirty seconds.

"Sloane is going to be in the Christmas play at church! I told you those drama classes would come in handy!"

"That's good stuff. Hey, listen, we're almost done at the course. Are you going to be ready to leave soon so we can get back home? We have a long drive." Wow. Dad's interest in my life astounds me, even now.

"We're leaving church now. We can just meet you and Dean at the clubhouse and leave from there. I'm sure he can give her a ride home. See you soon." Mom hangs up and starts making plans for their next trip. I kinda want to play a game and see how long I can go without saying a word. How long would it take anyone to notice? A day? A week? A year?

Turns out, it's less than an hour. Apparently, it's rude of me not to verbally say goodbye to my parents. I watch them drive off with Dean's arm around my shoulders. The picture-perfect daughter with her picture-perfect boyfriend. Dean leads me to his truck and gives me a kiss. It's a nice kiss. The kind of touch I've been craving all weekend after a month away from my boyfriend. Too bad that's all it is. A kiss. I've tried to insinuate taking our relationship further, but he always stops me. It's not like we're still in high school. Shouldn't every college-age guy want to have sex with his girlfriend?

"So what's all this about a play?" Dean asks as I'm buckling my seat belt. "I know you like those drama classes, but you don't want to put too much on your plate this year."

"Well, Mom saw the sign-ups and volunteered me. Besides, it's just a couple of hours on Thursdays. It shouldn't be a problem."

We spend the rest of the short drive back to my apartment discussing schedules. Turns out, Thursday is one of the only nights he has free time. Go figure. His classes are pretty solid until one o'clock, followed by either golf practice or workouts until five o'clock. Then he has study hall from six to eight on Monday and Wednesday nights. That doesn't include the time he'll spend with his fraternity, which in the fall semester is pretty much Friday night through the weekend.

My schedule, on the other hand, isn't bad this semester. I have one class on Monday, Wednesday, and Friday from ten to eleven and then two classes on Tuesday and Thursday from nine to noon. My other classes are online, so I can fit them in at any time. And although my parents are insistent on a million and one other activities, they really won't know if I participate.

When we pull up at the apartment and I see Allie's car, I sigh internally. I just know Dean is going to freak out when he sees her, but it's best we get this out of the way.

I open the front door of the apartment, ignoring Dean's comment about needing a spare key for himself. "Allie, I'm home," I yell toward her bedroom. As I flip on the kitchen light, I realize I didn't need to bother announcing my presence. She's already in the living room, and holy crap, she's not alone. She is super not alone. She's contorted, with one guy thrusting into her mouth (Guy number 1? Brown-haired guy? Why do

I feel the need to name him?) while she bounces on top of another (I guess that makes him Guy number 2). It takes me way too long to figure out what's happening in front of me. Intercourse. Sex. Copulation. *Fucking, a word that sounds so taboo to my good-girl brain that I immediately dismiss it, even inside my own head.* I'm mesmerized and paralyzed, watching the three of them. I've never given any thought to anything other than straight-up missionary sex, to be honest, because that's what was vaguely described to me in the censored, church version of "sex ed" I got in my small-town school's health class. But Allie looks like she's getting her fair dose of pleasure, and I am...I don't know what I am. Am I turned on right now? Dean finally breaks my perverted paralysis.

"What the hell is going on in here?"

Allie, to her credit, doesn't miss a beat.

"Oh, hi guys," she says, "I didn't think you'd be back until later. We're almost done. Or at least I am."

She giggles and Guy number 2 underneath her groans, "Trust me, I'm not far behind you."

Guy number 1 grunts his agreement, and I realize he's shifted, and both Allie's hand and Guy 2's hands are on what I can only presume is Guy 1's penis. Dick. Cock? Have I ever even thought of the word cock?

Dean finally realizes I'm not going to move on my own and pulls me out of the room. "Were you just going to stand there and watch them? How are we ever going to sit on that couch now? We need to call your parents before they get too far and arrange somewhere else for you to stay. It's going to be hard this close to the school year, but I'm sure we can..."

"Wait," I say, "I'm not going anywhere."

"Are you serious, Sloane? They are having sex out in the middle of the common area like some kind of heathen group of Godless people!"

"I am serious, Dean! I like this apartment, and I like Allie. Everyone is doing...that at our age. It's normal, and I'm sure she won't do it again now that we had that embarrassing episode," I say, not believing for a second that this is the last time I'll see more of Allie than I want to.

Dean is pacing, seemingly more disturbed by the fact that I'm not disturbed than he was by what was happening in the living room. "You shouldn't be seeing things like that before we're married."

"Before *we're* married?" I ask, more disturbed by that statement than I've ever been by, well, anything.

Dean sighs. "You know what I mean, Sloane."

I'm beyond ready for this entire encounter to be over, and to be alone so I can get ready for my first day of class tomorrow. So I do what I always do and agree with Dean. "You're right. I'm sorry that happened, and I'll talk to Allie, but please don't mention this to my parents. I just got settled here. The location is great, and I really don't want to have to move again just as the semester starts. Please."

He looks at me for a long few seconds before finally leaning in, kissing me briefly on the forehead, and agreeing. "Fine. I know you're tired, and I need to go anyway to get ready for my week. I won't say anything, but if it happens again, you have to tell me so we can involve your parents and get you out of here."

Finally, I'll have a moment to breathe. "I will. I promise. I'll see you sometime this week?"

"Maybe. It all depends on how practice goes and how much rush week prep I need to do for the frat. I'll text you if I can. Bye babe, love you," he says, and then he's gone.

Of course. Who cares whether I'll need any support the first week back? Sloane will be fine. She always is.

A couple of hours later, Allie knocks on my door. "Sloane? Can I come in?"

"Sure," I say, hoping this isn't an awkward conversation.

"I'm so sorry about earlier. We were in the moment, lost track of time, and I really thought we would finish before you came back."

She does look sorry, and I can only imagine how hard it would've been for someone in her...position to keep track of time, so I really don't harbor any bad feelings about earlier. "It's really fine, I promise. Only, would you mind wiping the couch down?"

Allie looks at me for a beat before we both burst out laughing. "I already thoroughly cleaned it, I promise."

She's turning to leave my room when I stop her. "Allie, can I ask you a question?"

"Sure. What's up?"

"Are you dating *both* of those guys? Are they also dating each other? I guess I don't have a lot of experience, and I'm just curious how that all works. If it's not too intrusive of me to ask."

Her face softens as she realizes I'm clearly an innocent, naive girl just trying to understand her relationship status. She sits down in my desk chair to face where I'm sitting on the edge of my bed.

"Oh no, I'm not dating either of them. Those are our neighbors from down the hall. I met them while you were at dinner with your parents yesterday, and we all hit it off. It's not exclusive, although I definitely wouldn't mind a repeat of today." She giggles.

I smile, but I'm more confused than when I asked my question. "Is it...does it not bother you to...do that with them without knowing them very well?"

Allie gives me another, slightly more somber smile. "I think viewed from the lens of what you've told me about your upbringing, sex might seem like a very serious, very permanent kind of activity," she says, "but Sloane, it really doesn't have to be. I have a birth control implant in my arm, and I always use condoms. I get tested regularly, so no, it doesn't bother me. It's a fun, sensual, fulfilling activity that I enjoy doing with all kinds of people. I hope it doesn't bother you that I bring people home sometimes. I promise to stay in my own room in the future." She gives me a wider smile.

When she says it like that, it sounds fun. Not forbidden and scary and dangerous and overwhelming.

"Of course it doesn't bother me," I say. "Thanks for explaining. I think I'm going to turn in for the night since I have class in the morning."

"Sounds good," she says. "I have an early morning too." She turns to leave my room before saying over her shoulder, "Sloane, I hope you know that if you have any other...questions about anything, you can always ask me. I don't mind."

I'm lucky to have a roommate like her. "Thanks, Al. I appreciate it."

I feel like I've barely laid my head on my pillow before my first week of classes has flown by. It's already Thursday night and time for my lovely Christmas play practice, *which I don't resent at all*, and which I have plenty of time for. *Sigh*. It's fine.

Today's practice appears to be dedicated to setting expectations and assigning specific roles. I can see from the way Blanche is running things that this is far from her first time managing a production. She leads us into smaller groups, working through casting, handing out schedules with the next few months mapped out, and explaining holes we still have in case anyone knows more people willing to volunteer. By the end of the first hour of rehearsal, she announces that the next hour will be a meet-and-greet time for us to get to know each other. I've been cast as an angel, and the hour flies by as I get to know some of the others in my group.

Near the end of the rehearsal, Blanche makes her way around to our group. "Girls! I am so happy to see you all and have you here with us. My angel group is one of my favorites every year, and I think you're all going to have so much fun together!" Her energy is infectious, and I can't help but smile.

"How long have you lived here?" one of the other girls asks.

Blanche smiles the biggest smile I've seen yet. "Well, actually, I live in the city, but my sons—well, speak of the devil! There's one of my boys now!"

I turn to face the direction she's looking, and...what is in the water here? It's another troll? And by troll, I mean a chiseled god of a man. Another huge, viking-esque not-troll with curly hair that's almost black, longer on top than on the sides. He's got some stubble as if it's been a couple of days since he's shaved, but not enough to cover what has to be a jawline he paid for. Normal men are not carved like that. It wouldn't be fair to humanity if they were. Have I mentioned he's also huge? I mean, I'm not that short, and he's...he takes up so much *space*. He finally gets close enough to our group for me to see his eyes, and they're gray. The smokiest gray eyes that make me want him to light a cigar and blow the smoke in my mouth and...

"Sloane?"

I startle, realizing three things at once. One, my mouth is hanging open, and judging by how dry it feels, it's been that way for a while. Two, I am *staring* at the troll. Three, he sees me staring and so does Blanche, who has clearly been trying to get my attention for a while.

I shut my mouth.

Blanche smirks, obviously amused by my complete inability to function as a normal human being at this moment. "Sloane, I was just saying, this is my son Ledger."

Chapter Four

Ledger

I sigh as I walk into my mom's church. There are a million things I would rather be doing right now, but when Mommy Dearest asks you to play Satan in the church Christmas play, you play Satan in the church Christmas play. It's not that it's bad casting. It's pretty spot-on, honestly. Do I want to be here every Thursday night for two hours? Absolutely not. But I'm the only one of my siblings living in the same city as my widowed mother, so Thursday nights from six to eight belong to Blanche Sinclair.

The closer I get to my mother, the more I notice the stunning young lady she's talking to. Average height, platinum-blonde hair. She's wearing a sundress, so I can't make out the exact shape of her ass, but I can tell that she's got a nice set of tits. The closer I get, the harder I start to pray that she's not some young college student.

Pray. Interesting...must be the location.

She looks young but not inappropriately young. What is it they say? Half your age and add seven. That puts me at twenty-two? Younger than I've fucked in a while, but not too young—old enough to drink, at least.

I'm still considering if twenty-two feels a little young now that I'm officially thirty, when a stunning pair of green eyes locks with my own. The *right* eyes. Well, I'll be damned. It's my sad beige girl. And she is, without a doubt, the most beautiful woman I've ever seen. I only caught a glimpse of her eyes when I saw her last weekend. I didn't notice how her long blonde hair fell in wavy layers, framing her perfect, heart-shaped face. I didn't notice her thick curled eyelashes or how her freckles ran over the bridge of her little button nose. I missed her perfectly pouty pink lips. Lips I would love to see wrapped around my cock.

I definitely missed the full glory of the set of tits spilling out of the top of her dress. You can tell she's trying to dress modestly, and on a woman with an average chest, that dress would cover everything. As it stands, she's showing enough cleavage to confirm how well those creamy breasts would swallow my cock. I need to snap out of this before I'm at full attention standing next to my mother in this church. I force my gaze back up to her eyes. Those gorgeous green eyes stare up at me with a loaded expression. Once again, it's not lust—it's like she's in awe of me. It makes me wonder what expression she would make with my cock in her mouth while tears were falling down those rosy cheeks. Seriously, what is happening right now?

"Sloane, I was just saying, this is my son Ledger. He's going to be our devil this year, so you'll probably have a few lines together at some point." My thoughts are broken with my mom introducing me to Sloane. *Sloane*. That *name*. I keep repeating it in my head.

Sloane. Sloane. Sloane.

I somehow manage to function enough to remember how human interaction works and hold out my hand to shake. As soon as our hands touch, it's like someone has set me on fire. My blood feels like it's boiling, while at the same time, chill bumps form across my skin. I haven't felt butterflies in my stomach from touching a girl's hand since middle school.

As I'm shaking *Sloane's* hand, I can't help but notice how her full, luscious tits slightly bounce with each shake. My train of thought takes me straight to an image of just how much they would be bouncing as I ram into her over and over, *and there is my dick*. Fuck! *Fuck. Fuck. Fuck.* I really don't need a dickprint right now. For the first time in over a week, really? Now? I've never been more thankful to have picked up one of Mom's play brochures to strategically place in front of my traitorous crotch.

"Ledger, Sloane will be our lead angel." Either Mom knows me well enough or she has picked up on my blatant staring at the girl's chest because she adds, "She's a junior this year working on her bachelor's degree." Was that her way of warning me that this is, in fact, a young college girl? Damn. How old are juniors? You turn twenty-one in your junior year, so I guess she's twenty going on twenty-one. Well, fuck. Okay, new rule—as long as they are drinking age...in England.

I should really leave this girl alone. I just turned thirty. That's ten years. I sigh internally and pull myself together.

"It's really nice to meet you, Sloane. You are the most beautiful angel I've ever seen." I watch her rosy cheeks turn a dark shade of red. I shouldn't stir the pot more than I already have, but I pull her tiny hand to my lips and gently kiss her knuckles. Our eyes meet, and I swear the world stops for a moment. A moment when I can see waking up to those beautiful eyes every morning. A moment when no other woman ever exists but my beautiful green-eyed angel. A moment when someone actually looks into my eyes and sees *me;* chooses *me.* This tiny hand needs a massive diamond or maybe a tattoo she can never take off, so everyone always knows she's mine. *If she were pregnant, everyone would know she was yours.* I'm lost in this fantasy, still holding her hand, thinking about which cut of diamond she prefers and if she will want three kids or four, when I realize it's been much longer than socially acceptable to hold hands with a stranger. Mom clears her throat.

"Well, everyone, I think that's enough for today. Next Thursday, we'll start working through our scripts. Have a great week, and please shoot me an email if you have any questions."

My angel smiles at me, and just as I think she's going to leave without saying anything, she says, "You are the most beautiful troll I've ever seen." She blushes again as she gives me one last look and turns to walk away.

Did she just call me a beautiful troll? Is that some new church slang for the devil? There's a first time for everything, I suppose. I grab my mom's tote to take to her car and follow the crowd of volunteers out to the parking lot. I'm barely outside when I watch Sloane get into a car with someone. A guy? It never crossed my mind that she might be in a relationship. From the moment I realized she was my sad beige girl, my brain just registered her as mine. *Mine.* There's that word again.

Anger starts bubbling to the surface of my mind, and that's when I realize something else. Throughout my time with her, I felt a sense of peace. True peace. I felt it the first night I saw her too.

I make a mental note of the car's tag number and head to Mom's SUV.

"She's beautiful, isn't she?" Mom asks as I load her car.

"She's very young, Mom. I didn't know your matchmaking had gotten so desperate that age no longer matters as long as you have a daughter-in-law soon."

At least she has the decency to blush a bit at being called out. "Well, not just the daughter-in-law, you know. I'm also very interested in a whole brood of grandchildren."

"I'll see you on Sunday for lunch, Mom. Try not to scare off Sloane with your ideas, or you might be short a lead angel."

She gives me one of her Blanche Sinclair smirks and drives off.

With nothing to do for the rest of my evening, I climb on my bike and head home, definitely not thinking about my angel. My Sloane.

Dean Christensen, twenty-one, senior in college, five foot eleven, blood type: O neg., previously treated for chlamydia twice, heavily into online sports betting, and with quite the sealed juvenile rap sheet. It looks like Dean started causing problems young, with some small thefts from convenience stores as a preteen, a stalking episode in his teens, and even an alleged arson that looks like it was targeted at an ex-girlfriend of one of his friends.

None of this is public record, with his daddy's money in a pretty small town going a long way to ensure the picture-perfect public image of his son remained intact. Sloane's parents must not know any of this, right? No parents would ever willingly let a guy with this many psychopathic tendencies anywhere near their precious little girl. Although it does look like Sloane's dad and Dean's dad may have some business deals in the works. Maybe she isn't actually with him, and it's all a front to appease their parents. Or perhaps she's madly in love with him and they are fucking right now.

Nope, we are not doing this tonight, Ledger.

I know it's useless to get myself worked up over assumptions. It's better to gather details and work with facts. I'll slow down and make sure I'm as thorough as I need to be.

Along with fighting and all the other ways I was an abject disappointment to my father, the time I spent locked in my room tinkering with my massive bank of computers always drove him crazy. To him, business was the only real way a man could be successful, and everything else was a waste of time. I'm as personable as the next guy, but schmoozing old businessmen never appealed to me. I was lucky to have an older brother to take the brunt of that, and Henry never seemed to mind toeing Dad's line. I just couldn't. I would rather spend twelve hours hacking into Dad's financials to prove I could, go to the tattoo parlor for one more sweet hit of pain, then find a new girl *or three* to fuck. Rinse, repeat.

All that time spent at my computer has paid off over the years in different ways, either by giving me a heads-up when partners were planning to fuck me over when opening my club or giving me the tools needed to find out everything I could about my *future wife*.

Seven hours later, I feel good about what I was able to accomplish overnight. First off, Dean won't be a problem. He can remove himself quietly from Sloane's life, or I can methodically end his life as he knows it and ensure whatever career plans he has are over before they can even begin.

He's been back to school for less than two weeks, and I already have footage from his frat's security cameras showing him snorting enough coke to kill a horse, tracking info from his truck showing him at an establishment known for giving "happy ending" massages to college students, and a two-minute clip of him giving a beverage cart girl what looks like an underwhelming fucking just this past week at the golf course. It looks like he was the third of seven of his friends in line for her, and even if Sloane and her family were going to forgive everything else, having sex at a public golf course just isn't classy. Come on, man.

With Dean comfortably filed as "not a threat" in the back of my brain, I move on to my princess baby angel. *Sloane.*

Her online trail was much more satisfying to follow than that shitstain Dean's, and I can't remember the last time I had so much fun. It didn't take long for all of her publicly available information to be saved in its own folder on my computer. Her social media posts, high school pageant photos, report cards, doctor's visit notes, immunization records, dental records, etc. were all safely backed up on all my servers. *No records of any birth control prescription or implant,* my caveman brain helpfully highlights. My favorite find so far—*second favorite, says my lizard brain*—is a little blurb from her local newspaper showcasing her preschool's Christmas pageant fifteen years ago. The picture was a black-and-white version of my angel as a little angel, center-stage in the play. It's currently printed out and framed on my desk, and I hope our girls get her blonde hair.

Am I getting a little ahead of myself? Should I dial any of this back?

I'm known to be obsessive, but this feels different. I've never cared to see a woman for more than one night. I guess the saying is true—when you know, you know.

As fun as learning all about my angel's past was, getting to know her now and planning for the future made my night even better.

For her safety, I downloaded software to her phone to mirror it to one of the burners I keep on hand just in case. It's best to track her and keep tabs on any messages Dean sends her, because at this point, I could not trust that fucker any less. Reading through her texts is bleak, and her parents are shitty. I mean, I thought my dad was bad, but these two narcissists might just take the cake. *Your days of believing that you're nobody's priority are numbered, sweet girl. I promise you that.* The photos from her camera roll show some of her current life, but a lot are screenshots of her hopes and dreams. Her online inspo boards are helpful, too, with fairly recent updates showing that my girl has a classic taste in diamonds, a fondness for ragdoll cats, and, in a clear sign we are truly meant to be, a very similar taste in architecture to the house I'm currently sitting in.

Her kitchen and bathroom preferences are a little different, but with a rush order of marble from Italy and a dozen people hand-beading wallpaper, it'll be an easy fix. By the time she moves in, everything will be perfect.

I didn't spend much time on her internet browsing history, mainly because coordinating massive home renovations in the middle of the night across multiple continents does take time, even for me. What I did prioritize, however, was the history of her private browser tabs. And what I found convinced me she's even more perfect than I imagined. My Sloane is a virgin, but she has *a lot* of questions and interests when it comes to sex.

Her porn history isn't terribly adventurous, and the short amount of time she spends watching tells me that she's either ashamed of her curiosity or afraid she'll get caught. But while her searches started innocently enough, with "couples in love" and "first time sex," my good girl seems to have gotten dirty fast. Her recent searches have been rougher and darker. She's perfect, and I'm going to make her so, so happy.

I've finished adding myself as a contact in her phone and updating my name to "Devil." I snap a selfie of myself thinking about her, and make that my contact photo. I'm considering changing the contact to "My Devil" when my angel wakes up and unlocks her phone.

Why is she awake at five o'clock? Her phone history shows my girl is not necessarily a morning person, with most of her phone activity not starting until it's time to get up for class.

I can't wait to see how cute she is when she wakes up grumpy in the morning.

Today, she seems to be a woman on a mission, opening a private browser for her porn site of choice and immediately searching...*wait. Baby, what are you doing?* "Tall dark-haired man," "Man on motorcycle," "Older man," and "Tattooed man." Is my girl trying to find porn that looks like me?

She settles on a video that appears to have been produced to seem amateur, featuring a tall, tattooed man and a much shorter woman, neither of whom is as attractive as she and I. They've pulled over on a bike and parked on the side of the road. They're frantic, as if they can't get each other's clothing off fast enough, and the man sits the woman on the bike and rucks up her dress, drops to his knees, and starts eating her pussy like he's starving.

I wonder if she's touching herself right now. *Fuck it.* I pull my cock out, and it's the idea of her getting off to this scene that we're watching together, even if she doesn't know it, that has me rock hard. It won't take me long at all, especially with how long it's been since my dick has shown any interest in anything.

Just as I think the woman in the video is about to get off on the *less handsome imitation of me*'s tongue, Sloane...fast-forwards the clip? What is she looking for? She stops forwarding briefly to watch the moment the man flips the girl over and starts roughly fucking her doggy style over the side of the bike.

Is this what you're looking for, Angel? You'll get this and so much more.

But then she's forwarding again until she stops toward the end of the clip, as the camera zooms in to catch the man's last frantic thrusts before he stills. With this angle, you can hear his animalistic grunts and see his balls drawing up as his dick pulses with the force of his cum filling the woman. He slowly pulls out to show a frankly impressive amount of cum flowing out of her well-used pussy.

I can feel my own orgasm approaching at the thought of filling Sloane up when she... fucking fuck me. She's rewinding to watch him fill her up.

Jesus Christ. My perfect, perfect angel. She watches twice more before the thought of her being obsessed with this part of the clip is too much for me, and I come harder than I have in a while. Ever? Thinking of how badly she wants this and how I'm going to be the only one to ever give it to her. I'm recovering and reaching for a tissue when I realize that the last time through was apparently enough for both of us to finish, because my good girl has closed the tab and locked her phone again.

I hope we came together.

It's one of the last times we'll ever be apart for our climaxes. I've never been so sure of anything in my life.

Chapter Five

Sloane

Did I just call that beautiful, perfect man a troll? I didn't. That didn't happen. I'm almost positive I didn't say that out loud. I would be completely positive if it wasn't for the look on Ledger's face. He didn't seem offended necessarily. Just taken aback and confused. And was there a hint of amusement as well? I didn't stay around long enough to see. I turned myself around and marched out of that building as fast as I could while trying to look normal.

"Hey, S, you okay? You look like you're about to pass out," Dean asks as I climb into his truck.

"I'm fine," I insist. "It was just a little stuffy in the church, something about the air being out. It should be fixed by next week." I guess I'm becoming a pro at lying where this church is concerned. Also, would it kill him to remember that I hate being called "S"?

Dean turns onto the road and goes in the opposite direction of the burger joint we had discussed eating at tonight after my practice. It takes a few more turns for me to realize we're headed back to my apartment.

"Why are we going back to my place? What happened to dinner at Jesse's?" I'm not going crazy. We had this conversation. He was the one who brought it up. I remember because I thought it was a strange option considering how he's all about making sure I maintain a healthy diet.

"Did you not get my text, babe? I have a big assignment due next week, and this weekend is pretty much a bust with it being the first weekend all the guys are back. You know how they're going to want to go out."

"No. No, I definitely didn't get a text."

And no, I definitely didn't know he was going to be "busy" with the guys all weekend. I used to get upset that I was never invited to his frat house for their busy weekends, but I'm used to it by now.

"That's weird. I bet the service in the church is bad or something."

The service in the church is fine.

"Anyway, I picked up a salad from that Greek place you like. It's in the back. I really hate to cancel on you tonight." Dean grabs my thigh right below where my dress stops and squeezes it. "I feel like we've hardly seen each other since you got home. I miss you, babe."

"I miss you too, and I'd rather have the salad anyway," I lie. I was kinda looking forward to some hot, greasy fries. That's what I get for spending three years going on and on about how amazing salads are.

I place my hand on top of his, and my mind immediately flashes back to Ledger. The way he kissed my hand so gently.

Lost in my thoughts, I pull the hand I'm holding up a little higher. What would it feel like to have that beautiful man stroking the inside of my thighs? Inching higher. Higher. Higher. Until...

I snap back to reality when I hear a breathy, "Mmm, why are your panties wet, Sloane?" I realize it's Dean's hand touching me, and he's reached the apex of my thighs, stroking me right where I wanted Ledger to stroke. Except this feels wrong.

"Oh my God! What are you doing?" I clamp my legs together and shift in my seat until his hand is back in safe territory. I didn't even realize we had made it to my apartment.

How long have we been sitting here?

He looks at me with a hunger I've never seen from him before, and my alarms start going off. I've wanted to go further for years. I've wanted him to look at me like that, to touch me. So why am I about to have a panic attack?

"Babe, look, I know we both want to wait until marriage, but you know it's going to be me you marry. What if we...?"

"Dean, no!" I cut him off before swinging the door open and hopping out.

"Wait, Sloane!" He's around to my side before I can take a step toward my building.

I think my entire body is shaking when he puts his hands on my shoulders. "Hey, I didn't mean to freak you out. I just saw how wet you were for me and got carried away. Look, let's just think about it, okay? You know how much I care about you, right, babe? I just want to show you how much I love you."

Wet for him? Oh. Oh right. I was imagining that Viking with the piercing gray eyes trailing his tattooed hand up my thigh.

My breathing has slowed down, and I'm no longer shaking. "Okay, I'll think about it."

"I know I'll be thinking about it." He winks at me and then reaches into his truck to grab my salad. "You don't know how long I've wanted to get a look at those tits."

I grab my salad, give Dean a quick kiss on the mouth, then make my way up to my apartment.

"Allie?" I yell as soon as I open the door, making sure she knows I'm coming in. Although if I'm being honest, I don't think I would mind seeing what sexual escapades she might be up to.

When nobody answers, I make my way to the kitchen table and plop down with my salad. Man, I really wanted those fries. Maybe I should just order some. I scroll through the food delivery app for a good fifteen minutes, practically salivating over the greasy food on the screen, before I decide to just cut my losses and eat the salad.

When I've finished, I put on a corny romance movie and curl up in bed with a blanket. It's only nine, and I really should work on some of my classwork, but I'm so sleepy. I guess working yourself up into a sexual frenzy over a man who probably thinks you're a crazy college weirdo and then almost having a panic attack when your boyfriend runs his fingers over your panties for the first time in three years can take a lot out of a girl.

I'm dreaming of riding on the back of a black-and-red motorcycle with my giant biker troll, holding his thick torso for dear life. We pull over, and he lifts me effortlessly to sit facing him. My thighs wrap around his waist as he unstraps his helmet from his chin, and he's...Ledger?

I jolt awake, sitting straight up, disoriented, drenched in sweat, and hornier than I've ever been in my life. It's only been a couple of years since I even started touching myself, and I've never felt anything like this pure, scorching need.

Am I having a heart attack? This feeling can't be normal...

These are the last thoughts that I have before I'm on absolute autopilot, one hand in my panties and the other pulling up the only porn site I know. I'm not even sure what I'm searching for, just that I'll know it when I see it...

This one. This man and woman on a motorcycle.

This won't take long, and as much as I like watching him eat her out while thinking of what a mouth would feel like on me, it's not what I'm here for. I briefly fast-forward to watch him enter her for the first time. *Wow, that's a stretch. Why do I instinctively know how good that would feel, even if I've never felt anything there before?* I'm too close, and I need...I don't even know what I need.

I keep forwarding, past positions that don't even seem physically possible, and then I hear noises coming from this man that speak to some base instinct deep inside my brain. He's grunting, he's frantic, and then he stills, and I realize I'm watching him come deep inside her. I rewind, and I can literally see him pulsing as cum starts leaking out from where they're joined and...

That's all I need.

My finger works my clit as I come harder than I ever have, hard enough to feel lightheaded and like I might actually pass out. I reach lower, feeling exactly how wet I am, and even though I've never really explored touching myself there much, I imagine all this liquid isn't just mine, but instead, I think of my own tall, tattooed troll taking me over his bike. I realize far too late that I imagined Ledger the entire time I was watching, and I desperately wish this was his cum leaking out of me. Before I can question where these thoughts are coming from, I fall asleep again, exhausted from my efforts and dreaming of gray eyes.

The last week has been one of the weirdest of my life. Weird seems like the wrong way to describe it when, in reality, everything has been going my way. Friday, after I woke up in a post-orgasmic fog, I got lucky when someone pulled out of my favorite parking place, closest to my class building, right as I was looking for a spot. Then when I got home and I was scrounging around for something to eat in the fridge, a knock on the door revealed a delivery driver with practically the entire Jesse's menu in his hands—an odd gesture for Dean since he usually isn't so thoughtful, but maybe he's highly motivated since he's thinking about advancing the physical aspect of our relationship.

As if. What the heck, Sloane. I should be excited about the idea of my boyfriend touching me...right?

Regardless, the weekend continued in the same weird way. I think back to Saturday and how odd the entire day was.

Allie and I went to a new romance bookstore opening in the city and browsed for hours, followed by dinner at our favorite café. We had just finished and asked for the check when the server said it had already been taken care of.

"Do you think one of the neighbor guys is following you and trying to impress you?" I asked because this was definitely well beyond the scope of anything Dean would deign to do, no matter what he thought his reward would be.

Allie looked just as confused as I felt. "No. Like I said, we aren't serious, and they didn't know I would be here today."

We went home, trying not to think too much of it but wondering if we needed to be more concerned. The girls in horror movies never worry about being followed, and they always end up tied up, or worse, in the villain's basement. Nothing was amiss at first at home, but when I opened the door to my bedroom, I screamed. A giant pink gift box sat pristinely on my bed. Nothing else was moved, and there were no signs of any forced entry. Nothing.

"What is it?" Allie screamed as she ran into my room, brandishing a giant knife at the box in case a murderer hid under the sparkly gift wrap and large bow.

"It's okay, I think," I said, trying to convince myself. "Stay here with the...giant knife, just in case."

Reaching for the box, I slowly grabbed one end of the bow and unraveled it until it fell away. "Okay." *Deep breaths.* "We're gonna pop the top off the box in three...two...one!"

I flipped the top off the box, and both Allie and I screamed bloody murder, waiting for the inevitable jump scare that didn't come. We slowly approached the box and peeked inside to see a ton of books. I reached inside, realizing it was upward of twenty-five books, each wrapped neatly in the branded pink tissue paper from the romance bookstore that we visited earlier.

Opening the first, I realized it was a special edition of one of my favorite hockey romances. The next book I unwrapped was one from my TBR, which I had written down in my notes app.

Allie got in on the fun once we realized it was only books and no murderers in the box. By the time we reached the bottom, we were surrounded by fifty books. They were all either from my online to-be-read list or the notes app on my phone, plus editions I had in my hands at one point or another in the bookstore. The only one I had never seen before looked intriguing, with a tall, dark biker on the cover. Not a genre I would usually choose, but my mind flashed back to my dream the night before, and I decided to read this one next. Assuring Allie that I had no idea who ordered all these books for me, we agreed to keep our eyes peeled for anything else and went to bed.

The following morning, I lazed about and slept in, only for another package to arrive containing an assortment of pretty pens and notebooks I had added to my online cart just the night before. I immediately opened the app to see if I was now sleep-ordering things, because really, Sloane? But there were no recent orders, and all these items were deleted from my cart.

Okay, weird, but thanks, I guess, creepy fairy godmother.

I had just settled in to organize my new items on my desk when a knock on the door revealed food delivery for Allie and me from our favorite Sunday brunch place, including mimosa supplies. *Is that even legal? To-go mimosas?*

Finally, the school week started, and I assumed things would go back to normal. But instead, I kept getting lucky parking spots. My coffee was paid for by the time I finished ordering every day, even when I went to different coffee shops. Packages of things I either wanted or needed kept showing up, seemingly ordered by my very observant fairy godmother. I knew at this point it wasn't Dean, because he would absolutely be bragging nonstop about how thoughtful he was and how much credit he deserved. I decided to just bask in my luck and enjoy it while it lasted.

Now, it's already Thursday, and time to attend rehearsal. I'm kind of excited. Maybe nervous? Blanche has been nothing but nice, and her stories already have me wanting to ask her more questions about her life. And knowing Ledger will be there, well... I'm not sure if I really have the time to unpack those feelings right now.

I prepare myself for what I assume will be a couple of hours of boredom, but as soon as I walk in, I realize I have severely underestimated Blanche Sinclair.

The church hall has been transformed with professional lighting, and all the volunteers have begun picking up their script packets and moving into color-coded groups. Moving to the table at the front, where all the scripts are organized alphabetically by last name, I find mine and see that I'm in the pink group.

My lucky week continues.

Based on the map of the rehearsal space that Blanche has included, group pink is actually meeting in the...nursery? I make my way out of the noisy, crowded hall and down a back hallway. It appears the pink group will be the only ones meeting in this wing, and I'm the first one here.

The darling nursery is decorated in all pastel hues and has a fresh, clean scent, with a lingering aroma that tells me it's for the littlest babies. I walk over to one of the cribs lining the wall and see that someone has prepared it for the next time this room is in use.

A tiny onesie is lying in the crib, and I pick it up to get a closer look, smiling when I see it's covered in a tiny motorcycle print. Just as I'm considering how often motorcycles seem to be popping up in my life lately, the door to the nursery opens, and I turn to see...Ledger? Ledger is in group pink? *And currently staring at me with a look as if he wants to...eat me? Tackle me? Tie me up and hide me in his troll cave?*

Ledger slowly closes the door behind him, stepping farther into the room. "Sloane, hi. *Is that for our baby?*"

He's staring at me, and I realize I'm still holding this onesie and gawking at him like a crazy person. But we're alone in this room, and it feels like he's taking up so much of it. Was he this huge when I met him? I feel like my dream didn't do him justice.

He's holding a motorcycle helmet. Oh my God, does he have a motorcycle? Do they make motorcycles that big?

I realize he's now close enough to smell, and he smells *so good.* Fresh and manly, with the leather of his jacket and a hint of cologne that has me salivating. I realize, far too late, that I can smell him so clearly because he's approached slowly and has bent down to my eye level.

His hair is damp, as if he's just showered before coming here, with a curl falling across his forehead. We lock eyes, and he reaches for me, gently placing his forefinger under my chin to close my mouth, which has been hanging open this entire time.

My mouth now firmly closed, his eyes are still on mine as he brushes the thumb of the hand still cupping my chin across my bottom lip. His eyes track his own movement before he realizes how close he is and stands up to take a step back. "Are you okay?"

I finally come to my senses, and I'm able to squeak out, "Did you just ask me if this was for our baby?" I place the onesie back in the crib and clear my throat.

I turn around, and really, at this point, someone just needs to spray me with a water bottle before I climb this man like a tree. He places his helmet on a side table and takes his leather jacket off, revealing black tattoos that I'd only had glimpses of extending the entire lengths of both arms.

He's rubbing the back of his neck and has the decency to look a little sheepish, but all I can see is how the movement makes his bicep flex and how the thick veins running under his forearm pop. "I'm sorry, I meant to think that, not say it out loud."

My eyes snap back to his in time to see him wink at me, and I'm about to offer my womb to him on a platter when he continues, "I think we might have my mom to thank for this lovely setting."

"What do you mean?" I ask, already planning the best way to covertly send Blanche the world's biggest fruit basket as a massive thanks for forcing her son into my proximity.

Ledger sits on one of the rocking chairs in the corner and stretches his boot-clad legs out in front of him, taking up even more of the room somehow. "Well, I'm not sure if you've opened your script yet, but it looks like she's gone a little avant-garde this year with the play."

I quickly grab my packet, scan the script, and blush furiously as I realize what Blanche has done.

"So we...?" I start to say.

"Are a group of exactly two, and have all of our scenes in the play consisting of just the two of us?" he finishes. "Yes. It seems my mother has re-imagined certain aspects of the story, including a contemplative Lucifer discussing some of the more philosophical points of Christmas with an un-fallen angel."

Chapter Six

Ledger

Sloane is doing the super-cute thing where she blankly stares at me again, and I *think* this is in my favor. I *think* it means she's thinking about all the time we're going to spend secluded and alone working on this play, and I *think* she likes the idea.

"Angel?" I say, enjoying the fact that her eyes immediately meet mine. *She already knows her nickname. What a good girl.* "Are you okay?"

"I'm fine. I think I'm just tired after an odd week," she says.

I stand and move toward where she still stands stock-still in the middle of the room and rest my hand lightly on the middle of her back. Fuck me, she's so tiny compared to my hand, and so warm, and she smells like coconut and vanilla. I gently lead her toward the rocking chair I just vacated. Sitting her down, I drape my leather jacket over her lap, enjoying the way it dwarfs her, almost like it's an actual blanket. I stay kneeling in front of her, thinking about how glad I am that while she's relatively petite compared to me, she has perfectly sized hips. *I wouldn't want my inevitably huge babies to hurt her any more than necessary.*

"Tell me about your odd week," I say, continuing to kneel in front of her so that we're eye to eye even with her sitting in the chair. As much as I try, I can't resist giving her a tiny smirk as I wait to hear how she'll characterize all the little conveniences she's experienced this week.

Just a taste of how her life will be once she understands that she's mine.

She cocks her head when she sees my smirk, raising one eyebrow and looking at me like she's trying to see inside my brain. *Look as hard as you want, Angel. The sooner you understand where we stand, the sooner we can move you in and start our life together.*

"Well," she begins, "my luck started out last weekend with someone bringing me food and sending me books and quite a number of things that have been languishing in my online shopping carts and wishlists." She gives a soft smile, and I wonder which delivery she's thinking about. Maybe the luxury cashmere cat pajama pants that she's been eyeing for at least six months, based on her search history. Or perhaps the certificate that a donation had been made in her name to the county humane society as a result of my seeing her search how to help them after a small fire at one of their kennels. She doesn't need to know they have operating costs covered in her name for ten years. We'll save the dedication of the Sloane Sinclair animal shelter until after she's changed her last name.

"Then, toward the end of the week, my boyfriend, Dean, came over with my favorite snacks, and we cuddled on the couch and watched movies all night," she says, and a wide grin splits her face when she sees my entire demeanor change.

I'm unable to control my reaction to that mental image even though I know from reading her texts and tracking Dean's truck that he was nowhere near her apartment. She sees the few moments it takes me to get myself under control, and it seems to amuse her when I try to affect a neutral mask and move the conversation past her lie. I've seen her school records, and I know exactly how smart my angel is, but I didn't necessarily expect her to catch on to my scheming so quickly.

I manage to growl out, "Well, I'm glad you had such a great week."

"Thank you," she says too sweetly, still giving me the grin that tells me she suspects far too much when it comes to my machinations in her life this week.

I realize now that it's almost eight o'clock and likely that the rehearsal in the main hall is wrapping up. Sloane has the same realization and stands to gather her things and leave.

She gives me one more look like I'm a puzzle that she can't wait to solve, and tells me she'll see me next week. *It'll be much sooner than that, baby.*

Once she's left, I wait until her phone gives me the notification that she's driving, and I know she won't read any texts for at least twenty-five minutes.

I snap a picture of the motorcycle onesie and send it to her.

Me:

> I think you forgot something, Angel.

Feeling like I've had an incredibly successful night, I carefully roll up the onesie, tuck it into the pocket of my leather jacket, and head out to my bike for a ride filled with thoughts of Sloane and the next phase of my plan.

Angel:

Ledger? How did you get my number?

Oh, I'm in. I'm setting a countdown right now, but I give myself less than a month until my angel is begging for my cock.

The kitchen renovation is in full swing. I'm going to have to bring more people in to make sure this gets finished quickly so that they can start working on putting in space for a nursery. I've taken many precautions throughout the years to make sure children haven't been the result of my sexual encounters, so I didn't buy this house with a nursery in mind. I think if we knock out a few walls, we can add one close to the primary bedroom, though. I'm sure Sloane will want the baby close by for a while.

I'm lost in a fantasy of her growing large with my baby when I get a call from Jack. Oh shit, the club. I haven't thought about the club in days. I've been filling my time monitoring my future wife.

"Jack, what's up, man?"

"You okay, Boss? I've been trying to get in touch with you about the upcoming events at the club." *God, I hate it when he calls me Boss.*

I look at my missed calls, and lo and behold, there are several from Jack.

"My bad, I'm actually headed there now. If you can hang tight for a couple of hours, we can iron everything out when I get there." *Fuck.* I wasn't planning on going to the club tonight. I think I forgot I owned a sex club. *Double fuck.* How is Sloane going to feel about owning a sex club? She hasn't ever even had sex. I don't know if she's ever touched a dick before. Her being curious and watching some rough porn doesn't equate to wanting to have any involvement in my kinky enterprise.

I guess I can sell the club and focus on my more respectable companies. I can do that for her. But I have to at least tell her about it, and I don't know how she'll take that. She doesn't actually know anything about me. And just because I know *and adore* everything about her, doesn't mean she will reciprocate those feelings when she learns about who I really am. When she learns that I'm not some churchy guy from a suburban family. That I've done almost every drug on the market at some point. That I've fucked more women than I can count. Will she care that I've nearly killed some of the biggest, meanest men in the ring just to take out enough aggression to function like a normal person? Will she be comfortable being alone with me when she sees what my opponents look like after a few rounds in the cage?

She'll have to be.

She is *mine.*

I pull up at the back of the club and discreetly make my way to the office, trying my best to avoid seeing any of my regular play partners, then shoot Jack a text letting him know to meet me as soon as he gets a moment. While I wait, I look around at my office and the lack of personality. Two comfortable brown leather chairs face my desk, and a matching couch is positioned against the wall behind them. I don't bring anyone here for fucking purposes, but I wanted there to be enough seating for the staff to be comfortable when we have meetings or if they need to just vent.

I'm proud of my club. I built this from the ground up, so it's almost like a child to me. People can judge all they want, but I'm proud of providing a safe space for people to explore their kinks with other consenting partners. Exploring one's sexuality is an integral part of the human experience. I obviously know this, but how do I get this across to my innocent little virgin angel? Will she ever be able to trust that I'm nothing but completely devoted to her?

"Boss!" Jack flops into a chair, breaking my train of thought. "Are you staying long tonight? Your favorite twins are in the lounge, and they're waiting for you. When I saw them, I made sure to tell them you were coming in so they wouldn't wander off somewhere."

Dammit, Jack. I'm about to go off on him when I remember that just a couple of weeks ago, that's exactly the thing I would've wanted him to do. Jack and I have been like brothers since childhood. He's seen and knows about every dark part of me, and not long ago, getting lost in a set of twins is how I would've preferred to spend my nights. He doesn't know about Sloane. He doesn't know I'm getting married soon. More accurately, he doesn't know that I saw the most beautiful woman in existence, went home and stalked her for seven hours, and determined that she's going to be mine. So instead of whacking him over the head with my computer, I just respond, "Not tonight. Actually...not ever. I've met someone."

"Oh shit! In all my years of knowing you, I've never seen you in a relationship." His face goes from astonishment to pride. "I'm happy for you, brother. Truly! And let's be honest... that just means there's more for me."

I meet his grin with one of my own before he continues, "So tell me about the woman who's stolen my best friend's heart."

I spend the better part of thirty minutes telling him everything appropriate that there is to tell about my girl, starting from the first time I saw her on my bike and ending with how I'm slowly renovating my house to meet her exact tastes. I leave out how I know what her tastes are and the fact that I've only known her for two weeks. Then we get into the details of the upcoming event we're planning next weekend.

While we always stage events for our members, we also try to host a fun event at least every other month, open to everyone, to attract new people. Next weekend, we're hosting a Ladies' Night, offering full access to the front room of our club, including the bar and dance floor, as well as limited tours of the other floors. They can't participate with anyone until they've officially joined and are properly vetted and tested. But they can see what they're missing out on.

After ensuring everything is in order, we proof the flyers our marketing team has been working on and give them the all-clear to go out. It may seem too late to advertise, but we've found that if we send them out too far in advance, people tend to forget. I assure Jack I'll be here for the big night and head out with one person on my mind.

When I get settled at home, I check to see when Sloane last opened her phone, and it was just a few minutes ago, so I know she's still awake.

Me:

Angel?

Almost immediately, I hear a ding.

Angel:

> Devil?

I look at the security cameras I had installed in her apartment and find her curled up in her pink chair, reading one of the books I sent to her.

Me:

> What are you doing up so late?

Angel:

> Reading one of the books you definitely didn't have anything to do with

I can tell it's the one I picked out for her about the biker. Of course it is. I'm on the verge of proposing to her right now.

Me:

> Tell me…what are you reading about?

Angel:

> It's about a biker…

Me:

> Interesting. Do you have a thing for bikers?

Angel:

No? Yes? Maybe?

Angel:

I've never been on one, but I think I may want to. It looks so freeing.

I know, sweet girl, I know. I also know all the things you want to do on that bike. My dirty angel.

Me:

Yes, it is freeing. You name the day, and I'll take you for a ride.

Angel:

Wait. Really, really?

Me:

Really, really. Just let me know when you want me.

Me:

Read your book, Angel. I'll see you soon ;)

If she only knew that I'll be watching her until she falls asleep. We both have a big weekend coming up. Hers is filled with football game activities that come along with the fall semester, and mine is filled with devising a plan to have my girl find out her current asswipe of a boyfriend is cheating on her without totally breaking her heart. Before too long, my phone beeps with words that almost bring me to my knees.

Angel:

> I hope so. You'll be on my mind until then. Sweet dreams.

Two weeks fly by between prepping the club for Ladies' Night and plotting to make my future wife available to date. Every day, I start my mornings with a sweet text to Sloane, and we text back and forth until she falls asleep each night.

We've discussed what she's reading, her classes, her parents, my parents, my siblings, and her childhood friends. I told her I own a nightclub, then quickly changed the subject to avoid discussing the details. We've ventured into more controversial territories, such as politics, religion, and our overall outlook on life, and we share nearly all the same opinions. Over the past few days, particularly, we've both opened up more about our hopes and dreams for the future. Sloane is incredibly bright but not quite sure what she wants to do career-wise. Without showing my hand and telling her she could do whatever she wanted, I gently encouraged her, and we chatted about the different paths out there. We even discussed her relationship. To my absolute pleasure, I can tell she doesn't love him. It would've broken my heart to have to hurt my angel too much by outing what a douche her current boyfriend is.

I haven't stopped sending her little treats, and although she hasn't called me out on it, we both know it's me. It's as if acknowledging it would break our fragile game of flirting and pushing the boundaries of an innocent friendship.

It's Thursday, and after being absent from the last practice, I'm dying to see her.

I know that Sloane expects the dickhead to pick her up from practice tonight. I also know, from keeping tabs on him, that he's standing her up to try to get his dick wet. I'll be here to be her very own Prince Charming, coming to sweep her off her feet on my handsome steed. Well, as long as she counts my bike as a steed. I even picked up a pink helmet for her, complete with cat ears.

After a long practice of flirting and laughing and talking about anything but our lines, I walk my lead angel to the front of the church.

"Do you want a ride home?" I point her toward my Ducati. "I brought the bike tonight, and I have an extra helmet for you."

I can see her hesitate. She wants to come with me so badly. "Actually, Dean was supposed to pick me up."

"Well, where is he?" I look around the parking lot as if I don't already know exactly where he is right now.

Sloane is holding her phone up to her ear, and I can hear that it keeps going to voicemail.

"Angel, you can't wait out here in the dark by yourself. I'll make you a deal. If he shows up within fifteen minutes, you go with him, but if he doesn't show up before then, you let me take you for a ride and a quick bite to eat."

Sloane nibbles on the corner of her mouth for a few seconds before sticking her hand out. "Deal."

I set a timer for fifteen minutes and stand there, basking in my victory. Hiding my excitement, I put my arm around her shoulders and pull her toward me before lowering my head to her hair and getting a good whiff of *her*. Coconut and vanilla. "Come here, sweet girl. You should never accept a man being late to pick you up." I lower my arm from her shoulders to the small of her back and use my other hand to tilt her chin up to look into her eyes. "You deserve so much more than that."

She slowly nods while we keep our eyes locked on each other. I watch her throat bob as she swallows. Her lips slightly part. I lower my head to hers, and I'm inches away from feeling her lips on mine when that damn alarm goes off. I grab her hand and kiss her knuckles again instead. She shudders, and I decide to push her a little further.

I tuck the strands of hair framing the left side of her face behind her ear and lean over to run my nose up the side of her throat. "That means you're mine for the night," I whisper, before taking her small hoop earring between my teeth and giving it a slight tug. I watch as her skin pebbles with goose bumps.

"Are you cold?" I ask. But before she can respond, I wrap my jacket around her shoulders and lead her toward my bike.

When we get close enough to make out the details of my custom paint job, she freezes in place.

"It's you...you're the man I saw on the bike that night." She looks like she's just seen a ghost. "Did you know it was me? I swear you looked right at me before we drove off."

I walk back over to her and place my hand at the small of her back to lead her up to the bike. "I realized it was you the moment I saw you standing with my mom. You have the most beautiful green eyes I've ever seen, Sloane. I wouldn't have forgotten those eyes."

She looks like she's about to cry. I know she isn't used to being praised like that, but she'll have to get used to it. I tug at her hand, then place her brand-new pink helmet on her head. Perfect fit. "Come on, sweetheart." I lift her effortlessly onto her seat before getting on in front of her.

Grabbing her hands and wrapping them around my waist, I give her the whole safety spiel. "Hold on to me right here. Our helmets are Bluetooth-connected, so we should be able to hear each other. If you need me to slow down or stop, just let me know."

"Okay," she manages to get out while she squeezes me harder than I thought possible for her little body.

I tap her leg twice, letting her know that we're about to take off, and have to restrain myself from trailing my hand higher up her thighs. We ride for the next hour, taking backroads and wrong turns to prolong what seems to be the most joyous night of her life. I almost feel bad about what I'm about to do.

We pull up and park at the diner I've tracked her soon-to-be ex to. As I help her down and remove her helmet, I'm rewarded with the biggest smile I've ever seen on her face. I meet that smile with one of my own before taking her hand and leading her to the diner. I really do feel *slightly* bad about what's about to happen. I can tell the moment she spots him because she freezes in place.

There he is with that girl I saw following him around. I may or may not have had a hand in making sure he noticed her social media profile, then kept tabs on their DMs. The opportunity basically fell in my lap when I saw that she was asking if he was available tonight after he had already agreed to pick Sloane up. I knew who he would choose.

"Dean? What are you doing here? You asshole! You left me stranded after my practice because you're on a date?"

Dean looks like he's just seen a ghost. It takes him all of ten seconds to notice me standing behind her before he starts to flip the script. "*Me* on a date? Who the fuck is that, S?" He points at me like I'm not one therapy session removed from knocking him out cold in one strike.

"*That* is Ms. Blanche's son who had the *decency* to make sure I got home safe after my *boyfriend* left me stranded."

I'm watching this narcissist's gears turn. I know he's full of it, but looking over at Sloane, I can tell she's about to buy whatever load of shit he tells her.

"S, I'm so sorry babe. We have a last minute test to study for and I got carried away and completely lost track of time."

No baby, don't fall for it.

She does.

I stand back and watch as she leaves with him. I guess the other chick knew what was up because she didn't make a fuss the whole time Dean referred to her as just a "study buddy".

It breaks my heart to see how defeated she is. As she goes, she turns back and apologizes for leaving. I'm the one who should be apologizing. Next time, there won't be a way for him to lie his way out. Next time, she'll leave with me.

Chapter Seven

Sloane

You have *got* to be kidding me. At least ten packages of all shapes and sizes are on the doorstep of my apartment, ranging from my favorite skincare brand to the local bookstore.

"Are you developing a shopping addiction?" Dean asks, giving me a distasteful look. The idea that anyone else would ever send me gifts has clearly never once crossed his mind.

I manage to grab almost all of the packages in one go, and Dean makes himself useful and grabs the couple I can't quite fit in my arms. "No, babe, I don't have a shopping addiction. There were good sales, so I stocked up on some essentials and also got a head start on my Christmas shopping."

"In that case, hopefully at least half of these are for me," he says, "especially after how poorly you did choosing my gifts last year."

Rolling my eyes, I don't even bother giving him a response. Instead, I wave at Allie, who is sitting at the kitchen counter working, and then head toward my room to deposit the first armful of boxes. The "poorly chosen" gifts he's referring to were custom golf gloves with stitching that was the wrong shade of blue, and a voucher for the two of us to learn to ski during a trip we had planned on taking with his family to Colorado. Unbeknownst to me, he canceled the trip so he could instead golf with some hotshot CEO and "network".

I'm planning my weekend, hoping to spend lots of time with my e-reader and maybe catch up on schoolwork, when I hear Dean yell from the kitchen, "What the actual fuck is this, S?"

My mouth drops open when I walk back into the main living area and lay eyes on Dean holding what appears to be a hot-pink sex toy. It not only has a portion clearly intended to penetrate but also another shorter arm that looks like it would sit right on top of a clit. Allie has her hand over her mouth, trying not to laugh while Dean gets redder and redder in the face.

He's obviously not going to handle this like a reasonable adult or give me a chance to get a word in edgewise. "Are you serious? You've been declining every one of my advances because you're getting yourself off like some whore with a sex toy?"

This seems to be enough for Allie to stop thinking the situation has any humor at all. "Are you serious, asshole? Using a sex toy doesn't make you a whore, and even if it did, it's really none of your business what Sloane does with or without toys. And stop calling her S. She fucking hates that!"

If I wasn't already a certified member of the Allie fan club, that alone would be enough to make me want to join.

Dean is clearly not going to let this go, despite the fact that it's been a very tense couple of days for our relationship after the episode at the diner. "You're way out of line talking to me like that. This has nothing to do with you, and honestly, why are you even here? A normal person would see that we're having a discussion and leave us alone."

His rudeness toward Allie is enough to snap me out of my disbelief that he's *still holding the dang toy* and waving it around for emphasis. He seems to realize this fact at the same time as I do and drops it like a poisonous snake onto the counter.

I sigh heavily. "I think you should go, Dean. I have absolutely nothing to say to you right now, and I told you I wanted a quiet evening at home before you invited yourself over."

"You're seriously kicking me out?"

"Yep," I say, popping the 'p' because I know it annoys him. Allie comes to stand beside me, and I know she's considering whether she should get her knife.

Looking between us, Dean must decide this fight isn't worth his time today because he turns around and leaves without another word. I hear his truck fire up and peel out of our parking lot, and I breathe a heavy sigh of relief.

"Look...I know it's none of my business, and I won't keep pressing this issue, but if I don't say this at least once, I think my friend card would deserve to be revoked," Allie says. "You deserve a helluva lot better than him. I think you're starting to see that, and I'm going to be there every step of the way to ensure you get a man who deserves you. He ain't it, girl."

I smile, knowing that she truly believes that. "Thanks, Al. I appreciate you. I think I'm going to take a bubble bath, order some Thai, and enjoy a nice quiet evening with my book."

She gives me a devious grin that I know too well at this point.

"Allie...?"

"Well, there's a really hot nightclub in the city that's having Ladies' Night tonight. The DJ is someone I've been wanting to see for a while, and the drink deals are amazing. Look at this flyer! My friend Mel has a condo a few blocks away, and she already told me we can crash at her place after!" Allie's face looks so genuinely excited that I find myself reaching for the flyer.

It looks like a nice enough establishment, although I'm not sure what kind of nightclub would name itself Rendezvous. The security measures taken to keep women safe are outlined in big print at the bottom of the flyer, and it's clear the club has put a lot of thought into making this an evening that's fun and truly for the ladies.

I'm not sure if it's my incredibly tenuous relationship with my boyfriend, my desire to reward Allie for her steadfast support, or just a need to do something I usually wouldn't do that has me saying yes. But I must say it out loud because Allie lets out a cheer and immediately launches into detailed descriptions of what both of us are wearing. She pushes me toward my bathroom, telling me to "shave *everything*, just in case."

What on earth have I gotten myself into?

Before heading out for the night, we do a fit check. I'm wearing a white halter-neck bodycon dress that hugs my curves so well I'm almost in disbelief it's me in the mirror. The V cut dips lower than anything I've ever worn while also holding up my braless breasts. It's also shorter than anything I've worn, making my legs look incredible. I really owe Allie for letting me borrow this. On the other hand, she went for a blue halter dress that's shorter than mine, with sequins hanging from every inch. The dress matches her hair perfectly, and I don't know how, but she pulls it off.

We pull up to a club downtown, and a man in a tux opens the door for us. This is not what I was expecting. Allie hands the man her keys and grabs my hand as we walk inside.

"This is so exciting! I've never been here before, but I've only heard good things. The member fees are way out of my price range, but tonight is free for visitors!" I've never heard of a club charging a member fee, but I nod along like I know exactly what she's talking about.

Who am I kidding? The only club I've been to is a country club, and those definitely have membership fees. Maybe it's a normal thing.

As soon as we step inside, we approach a hostess stand with a woman whose name tag reads "Maria." She's built like a model with a face to match and long black hair that's pulled half up. Allie hands her the flyer, and Maria pulls out two wristbands.

"Welcome in!" she says, greeting us as she checks our fake IDs. Allie explained earlier she's had these on standby for weeks, knowing one day Dean would be enough of an asshole to warrant using them. Maria does a double take but eventually gives them back and wraps the wristbands around each of us.

"These indicate you are a guest. This means you're allowed three complimentary alcoholic beverages from the bar but also prohibits you from participating in anything beyond the first floor. Guided tours of the other floors will be available throughout the night. Your number is twelve, so listen for it to be called. If you want to tour, go to the bar and wait for the guide. If you're interested in joining, please let me know, and I'll add your information to our membership inquiry list. Have a great night, girls!"

We sit down at the bar, and Allie orders us both a vodka soda. I've actually never had a drink before. Dean drinks all the time, but I've been warned how unbecoming it is for me.

While we wait for our drinks, I look around. It's dimly lit, with dark walls and blue neon lights illuminating the dance floor. A DJ is on stage, and a large group of people are dancing erotically to the music. The dance floor appears to be polished black concrete, while the area around the bar features actual hardwood. It's classier than any bar or club I've seen in movies. I guess that makes sense why they charge a fee? For the upkeep?

The bartender hands us our drinks, and I hesitate but eventually take a sip. It really just tastes like soda. "Mmm, this is better than I thought it would be."

"I thought you'd like it! I never see you drinking at home, though, so I didn't know for sure."

"I'll be honest with you, Allie. This is the first alcoholic drink I've ever had."

Allie's eyes open as wide as they can, and she gasps. "What? You've *never* had a drink? How is that even possible? Your boyfriend drinks like a fucking fish!"

I shrug. "Ugh, I don't want to think about that asshole tonight."

"Touché! Cheers to that!" Allie holds up her drink, and I clink mine against hers, then chug it down before slamming my glass down on the bar. Allie laughs before following suit, and before we know it, we're halfway through drink two.

My mind wanders to the biker troll who has been occupying my thoughts for weeks. Trying not to overspeculate about why Ledger's texts have been less flirty than normal since the night on his bike, I go to pull Allie onto the dance floor when we hear the announcer call out for group eleven to come to the bar.

"Hmm, I guess we should just wait here since our group is next," Allie voices my exact thoughts.

"I don't even know what we're taking a tour of."

Allie gives me the most devious smirk I've ever seen and chuckles under her breath.

Again, what on earth have I gotten myself into?

Chapter Eight

Ledger

I'm sitting with Jack in our VIP section overlooking the club's first floor. Ladies' Night seems to be going well. Although I'm too far up and it's too dark to see any details of our guests, I can tell by all the glowing "visitor" wristbands that there are at least one hundred newbies between the bar and the dance floor.

I give myself a mental pat on the back and walk back over to the lounge chair where Jack's sitting with a half-naked brunette perched on his knee. I may be a one-woman man now, but I don't think Jack will ever be tamed.

"Well done, Jackie." I wink at him, calling him the nickname my mom always uses.

My mom and his were best friends, and when she passed away, leaving her five-year-old with a father who was hardly home, Mom basically adopted him.

He rolls his eyes at me before giving the nameless brunette a little smack on the ass. She gets up and walks toward the bar. "Maria texted me earlier that there have already been twenty new member requests. We're only an hour in and have almost reached our goal."

"That's fantastic. I guess I should look into giving everyone another raise, huh?" I give him a huge grin, already knowing what he's going to say.

"Hell yeah, you should! And you can start with me." He winks at me before standing and taking a sip of what looks like bourbon. He sets the glass down before excusing himself. "I'm going to go find an empty room with, um, well, I don't know her name, but that woman I just had on my lap." We both laugh as he walks out.

Alone at last, I pull up my GPS app, which I've linked to Sloane's phone, and almost choke on air when her location dot is right on top of mine. That can't be right. I refresh the app, but the dot remains. That still can't be right. I want to call her, but I've never done that, so I resort to texting.

Me:

Angel?

I'll give her five minutes to respond before I make that call. While I'm waiting to get a response, I start scanning the first floor for any sign of my girl, but it's useless. It's too dark. After a minute, I hear a ding and look down at my phone.

Angel:

Devil?

Me:

What are you doing tonight, pretty girl?

Angel:

You wouldn't believe me if I told you…

Oh shit…That's sounding a whole lot like my good girl is at a sex club.

Me:

Try me.

Angel:

Well…I'm at some club with Allie.

Angel:

Rendezvous, I think.

Fuck.

Me:

And what's my sweet girl doing at a sex club?

Angel:

Sex club??????

Angel:

What?????

Angel:

What in the world is a sex club????

Double fuck.

Angel:

OMG OMG OMG

Angel:

I just asked Allie, and she confirmed!

Angel:

WTF do I do???

Angel:

LEDGER!

Angel:

I had no idea! I didn't even know what a sex club is!!! I still don't think I know! It just looks like a normal club!

Okay, I need to pull myself together and respond before she has a panic attack.

Me:

> Sloane! Calm down. Go to the bar and wait there. I'll come and get you before anything happens. Don't go anywhere with anyone.

I'm so concerned with getting to my girl that I don't realize she hasn't responded. I'm standing at the bar, looking around like a madman, when she finally sends a text back.

Angel:

> Oh sorry! I'm already starting a tour of the back of the club. We're about to have some time to look around by ourselves.

Sigh. I know exactly where she is. Time to go explain to Sloane that I own a sex club. I could try to hide it, but the moment someone calls me boss, she'll have questions.

I head to our second floor, and as soon as I step into the VIP lounge section, I see her. She's across the room, sitting with Allie and the rest of their small group. They're about to go back to the exhibition hall. I take three quick steps toward them when something from a deep, dark recess of my brain makes me stop.

What if I let her look?

That's...interesting. It goes against my immediate instinct to shield my angel from everything she's about to see back there. Some people come to Rendezvous thinking they're kinky, but thinking it and seeing it in person are very different things. We've had people come through to experience something they were *sure* they were into after reading about it or seeing it in porn, and then the reality is just not anything they're comfortable with.

Ultimately, I decide to let my girl look to her heart's content. I meant it when I told myself I would sell this club without a second thought if it's truly something she isn't comfortable with me continuing. There are a million other things I could fill my time with, like watching Sloane, managing every aspect of Sloane's life to make things easier for her, and being a stay-at-home dad. My options are endless at this point, especially since I don't need to make another dime in my life for our great-grandchildren to live comfortably.

Taking one more deep breath, I watch the bouncer for the exhibition hall scan the wristbands of the group. Allie leans in to say something to Sloane, and then they're beyond the doorway. I turn toward my office, ready to follow them every step of the way. Sending a quick text to a friend who's here tonight, just in case Sloane likes what she sees, I move quickly to keep an eye on my angel.

Luckily, all of my monitors stay on 24/7, so there's no need to wait for anything to boot up once I hit my office.

It might sound like a massive invasion of privacy to video the happenings at a sex club, but unfortunately, it's necessary. Every person who enters the exhibition hall signs an agreement that they understand they're being filmed—not for profit but strictly for security. Of course, the private rooms for the highest levels of our membership are not video monitored, and anyone who plays in those areas understands that while we have highly trained bouncers employed to keep the peace with discretion, we can only do so much to police disagreements. Luckily, these have been few and far between. The exhibition hall does not require the same level of vetting as the higher tiers of membership. Although background checks are conducted for those entering the area, video monitoring enables me and a select few members of my security team to monitor the space and maintain a six-hour rolling record of any unacceptable behavior.

For now, I'm going to enjoy knowing not only exactly what my girl is watching, but also her reactions to each scene. I've been so focused on not dying of multiple heart attacks since I saw her location earlier that I don't even remember what I saw on the schedule for the hall this evening. It appears that my employee has completed the cursory description of the hall, and the group is now free to roam. Allie must have decided to leave Sloane to her own discovery time and has wandered off. I don't have to worry about any men approaching Allie because this small group is all women. *Jack really does need a raise for making tonight such a safe space for ladies.*

The exhibition hall is laid out, well, to be frank, a little like a zoo. A wide central hallway is lined on both sides by large picture windows from floor to ceiling. This glass can be one-way or two-way, depending on the performers' preferences. There is limited seating available in the center of the main hallway. However, if patrons prefer to engage with a scene more intimately, there are hallways between each room that lead to individual seating areas behind. The degree of separation between the performers and the audience is customizable, with some preferring glass barriers and others encouraging audience participation. Everyone who makes it here is tested, and thinking about explaining all of this myself to my angel fills me with pride.

Sloane has stopped now in front of one of the rooms closest to the hall entrance, and I see that it's occupied by some of our regular expert Shibari practitioners. This is a fairly basic demo, likely to appeal to the guests without overwhelming them. The man is just finishing up a beautiful diamond chest harness on the woman, and she's turned toward the hall with her breasts perfectly displayed by the rope and a glazed look in her eyes. He caresses her and whispers in her ear, likely telling her to look at the crowd gathering to watch them. After a few minutes of this presentation, he spins her back around and goes to work on her lower body, beginning what looks like a pair of diamond shorts to finish off the look.

My angel is enraptured. Her breathing is already a little heavier, and although I can't see her pupils, I'm sure they're dilated at this point. If Sloane is able to see the beauty in Shibari and isn't at all scared of the idea of a man tying a woman up like this, well, I think we might have even more fun ahead of us than I had ever dared hope.

The next scene is one that I don't think will hold her attention for very long, and my instinct is correct. This is our most experienced dominatrix, Miss X, putting her long-term submissive through the wringer. He's locked in a chastity belt and tied, wrists together and elbows to knees. He has a spider gag in his mouth and a blindfold on, while Miss X slaps his painfully purple balls with a riding crop. I know them well enough to know he's in heaven right now and likely begged her for this tonight, but to the newcomer, this is a lot. Sloane takes a respectful pause—*my sweet girl doesn't want to offend anyone with her disinterest*—before wandering across the hall.

She stops next at a scene I'm particularly curious if she'll enjoy. My brother, Henry, is here tonight—a rarity that he deigns to grace us with his presence. Luckily, Henry's play here never involves his nudity. I would hate to have to introduce my wife to my brother after she'd already seen him naked. Instead, Henry sits, wearing a 1950s-style smoking jacket and slippers, and reads a leather-bound book while seated in a wingback chair.

In his mouth sits a pipe, and I can smell the sweet tobacco he favors just from looking at him. His right hand holds his book, and his left hand holds a glass of liquor as he ignores the naked woman kneeling at his feet. Her knees are on a velvet tufted pillow between his legs, and her head is bowed.

If I know him, and I do, she likely has a pulsing plug in her pussy and/or ass, but every time she reacts, the odds of him letting her come get smaller. He once told me that he has an algorithm for determining whether they're allowed to climax, and it's really up to the math. It's complex, involving the submissive's behavior, the state of the stock market, the weather, and, bizarrely, the number of eggs his chickens have laid that week at his estate. The last time I asked, the odds were slightly in the submissive's favor as long as it had rained within five days of the scene. He's an odd one.

Sloane stops in front of a scene that I know she has at least a passing interest in, based on my kinky angel's porn viewing history. Beyond the glass is a trio I know well who go by Ace, Jay, and Bea when they play here. It looks like they're just getting started, and Sloane is so close to the glass that her forehead is almost touching.

Bea is fully naked at this point, but Ace and Jay are still clothed. Their ties are off and are being put to good use, with one acting as a blindfold and the other a short leash for Bea. She's sitting on Ace's lap in an armless chair, and her legs are spread open and hooked on the outside of his knees. He has wrapped her leash taut around his hand and pulled her neck back so that her head rests on his shoulder. I can't hear what he's saying, but it looks like he's whispering a constant stream into Bea's ear, while she writhes against him. Suddenly, Ace must give some sort of signal to Jay because Jay drops to his knees and licks one hot stripe up the entirety of Bea's cunt before stopping on her clit. Her scream echoes throughout the room, and Sloane takes a half step back, startled at the animalistic, primal noise.

Oh, Angel. That's nothing compared to how you'll sing for me.

Despite the brief relief, Bea obviously didn't come, although with so much buildup, it wouldn't surprise me if she was close. Jay stays on his knees but ignores her pussy, instead starting at her right knee and trailing tiny, teasing kisses all the way up her thigh. He stops to nibble at her labia before ignoring her clit completely and starting the process back over at her left knee. This time, when he reaches her inner thigh, he bites down almost hard enough to draw blood, and Bea again screams, this time with more pain lacing her voice. Ace has brought his hand up and has her pebbled right nipple pinched hard between his thumb and forefinger, coinciding with Jay's bite. I smirk. I forgot how much these two love marking her.

I can't wait to see how Sloane enjoys being covered in *my* marks.

Finally, the men decide they've given Bea enough torture, and Jay lifts her out of Ace's lap. She clings to him like a koala, and he soothes her, petting her hair and reassuring her as he sets her down, still blindfolded and leashed, onto a low padded bench just a foot away from the glass. Her head hangs off the end of the bench, and Jay leans down to kiss her passionately while Ace trails his hands up and down her legs. Both of them have lost their clothes at some point, and I see Sloane's pouty lips part as she realizes what's about to happen. Without warning, Jay shoves his dick into Bea's throat, not stopping until his balls are at her chin. Ace takes his cue to spread her legs and sink into her cunt, causing a muffled scream to tear from her throat. At this point, there's no telling how long they'll last or how many positions they'll attempt, so I decide it's time for me to join my angel and see what she thinks of my club.

When I reach the hall, I see that Sloane hasn't moved an inch from her position, shamelessly resting her forehead on the glass. Her stance has widened, probably subconsciously trying to relieve any pressure on her little clit.

My poor Angel. I can't wait to give you relief, sweet girl.

I don't want to scare her, so I approach her slowly from the side until she notices me. She doesn't startle, as if she could sense me entering the room, and when she looks at me, I see that her pupils are completely blown. She has a deliciously hazy look in her eyes as if she's in the midst of a wonderful dream.

"Hello, Angel," I murmur. "How is your tour going?"

She looks back at the trio behind the glass, where Ace is sucking Jay's cock while Bea grinds on Jay's face.

"I had no idea places like this exist," she says, glancing at me with amazement. "They look so happy and in love. It's like some of the porn I've seen, but..."

"Better," I say. I know exactly what she means. The connection you can see and the way you can feel the love and trust from a live performance is unmatched. It's one of the reasons I worked my ass off to get Rendezvous up and running.

"Better," she agrees. I can see that she's flagging a bit, standing tall in heels that I know aren't the norm for her. I move behind her and pull her slightly back into me. I'm immensely pleased when she leans into my body and rests the back of her head on my chest. The hall has mostly cleared out, but I know one more couple who will be here for a while, confirmed by the text I sent earlier. I don't want to rush her away from the trio if she hasn't looked her fill, though.

I'm considering the best way to suggest we move on when she says, "Is this what you like?"

Well. I knew this question would come up between us at some point, and although I've decided not to hold back from her, I don't want to scare her off just yet. Honestly, there's nothing I *wouldn't* be into with her, but telling her about my enjoyment of mixing pain with pleasure might be a little too much up front.

Instead, I'll take her to an exhibit showcasing another of my favorite pastimes—giving a woman so much pleasure that she passes out. I just won't include the part where I want to make her pass out so I can fuck her unconscious body as roughly as I please.

Using my new position behind her, I lean down so that I can breathe my response directly into the soft, delicious skin below her ear. "If you mean a threesome with another man and a woman, yes, I have played this way in the past. I've never been in a committed relationship with two people at once, though, which is the case for this trio."

I feel her shiver at my hot breath on her neck, and I reward her with the softest kiss just below her ear. My reward, in turn, is the thrill of seeing my tiniest stimulation lead to goose bumps prickling across her neck and chest. My angel is so responsive. She'll do so, so well for me.

"Do you...like...I mean, do you enjoy...other men, in that way?" she asks quietly.

I smile, deciding to tease her a bit. "In what way?"

She bites her thick bottom lip, and it's only my absolute belief that good things come to those who wait that keeps me from pinning her down and trying my hardest to put a baby in her right here, right now.

"Do you...have you...dated other men?" my brave girl finally asks.

"No, I've never dated another man," I say, and I swear I feel a tiny sliver of disappointment tremble through her. *I need to file that away for exploration later.* "I have, however, fucked around with the occasional man in a group setting," I clarify.

My perfect girl whimpers. She whimpers with desire and leans even more heavily back into me. I band an arm across her waist to keep her upright and to hold her even more tightly to me.

I can sense that she has something else she wants to ask me, but I need her to say it. She needs to understand she has to ask for what she wants. *As long as she asks, she can have anything under the sun. One day soon, she'll believe me.* "Ask me what you want to know, Angel."

"Is this..." She gestures weakly to the trio, who are now in a cuddle pile on the floor, lazily kissing and rubbing each other in a heap of soft-looking blankets. "Is this what you want? Is this your favorite? Or is it something more like..." She gestures back toward the other end of the hall.

"I would struggle to deny you anything, so if you want to know what it's like to be shared between two men, I would consider indulging you, sweet girl," I say. "Although I feel a possessiveness over you that surpasses any other emotion I've ever felt in my life, so I'm inclined to keep you all to myself. One of my favorites is something you haven't encountered in the hall yet. But it is represented this evening if you'd like me to show you."

She's silent for a moment, and I wonder if she's rethinking any of this. Maybe she's overstimulated, and my whispering in her ear and practically salivating all over her neck are too much for her tonight. I stand to my full height and pull back just a touch, considering taking her back to my office for some water and a snack, when she follows my body to keep us connected. Sloane places her hand over my forearm, gives me a little squeeze, turns her head to look up at me with those beautiful green eyes, and whispers, "Please."

Chapter Nine

Sloane

"Please."

It feels less like a whispered word and more like a release of something I've kept tethered to my soul for my entire life. For some reason, whatever this is, I trust Ledger with it implicitly.

He stares at me as if he can see things even I haven't felt ready to face yet, and he must find whatever it is that he's looking for because he finally lets out a ragged breath.

"My sweet girl," he says, "come with me."

Taking me by the hand, he leads me to the other end of the exhibition hall and down one of the hallways leading to the smaller seating area behind an exhibit. We find ourselves alone in a cozy room with comfortable-looking leather chairs and chaises facing a slightly raised platform. I sit on one of the plush chairs. On the platform, a curvy woman with long box braids is...*strapped ohmygosh*.

She's strapped to a padded table, her legs slightly bent and kept open by restraints. Her arms are by her sides, and her head rests on a U-shaped pillow. Overall, she looks comfortable, but

I can feel her anticipation. I realize I can also hear her shallow breathing because no glass partition separates us. A door opens behind us, and a man steps into the room. If I saw him on the street, I might guess he was an accountant or a professor.

Ledger steps forward to shake his hand. "Mark, it's nice to see you as always. Thank you for delaying a bit for me this evening, and for giving us the honor of an exclusive performance."

The man who indeed looks like a Mark gives us a broad smile. "It's our pleasure."

With that, Mark slips a remote out of his pocket, presses two buttons in quick succession, and the woman on the table lets out a muffled moan.

Mark smirks. "Melody has been a handful this week, so we're likely to be here a while."

Mark leaves us, heading to Melody and placing a tender kiss on her forehead. He stands at the head of the table, petting her hair and whispering soothing words as she begins to writhe against her bonds.

Ledger picks the chair up, with me still sitting in it, and puts me down front and center near the stage. Melody continues to writhe, and Mark has stripped himself down to slacks and an undershirt. He's much more muscular than I'd given him credit for at first glance, with scars running down one arm and a blackout tattoo on the oth...*ow!*

I look up indignantly to find Ledger staring at me with a serious look on his face, having pinched me for no reason.

"Do. Not. Check. Mark. Out."

"I thought you said you'd indulge my interest in multiple men," I tease.

Ledger's eyes darken as he grabs my chin. "I said I would *consider* indulging you, but I'm already starting to regret that."

Before I can even defend myself, a low moan sounds from Melody. Mark has placed a wand toy in an attachment on the table, and it looks to be sitting directly on Melody's clit. It takes less than thirty seconds for her to scream and for Mark to soothe her. He removes the wand toy for a few seconds while he coos reassurances, but she's still trembling slightly as he places the toy back against her sensitive flesh.

I uncross and re-cross my legs, watching Melody's shaking continue as she whines. Ledger moves to stand behind me and places his hands gently on my shoulders, pushing my long hair to one side.

"What's he doing to her? It sounded like she...like she..."

"She came, Angel. Hard, by the sound of it," Ledger says, his hot breath fanning across my neck and making me switch the way my legs are crossed again.

"But if she came, why did he put the toy back? Is he not going to have sex with her now?" I'm so confused by this sequence of events. None of the porn I watched ever deviated from the same general script. Even if the woman got off first, the man was never far behind. However, Mark looks completely calm, cool, and collected. He's totally tuned in to how Melody is reacting, but he's made no move at all to adjust the impressive bulge in his pants.

Ledger has shifted and his lips are practically on my neck now, giving me almost kisses that have his stubbled jaw tickling my skin. "No, he isn't going to *fuck* her now." His hands trail softly up and down my arms, and although my brain is fuzzy, barely formed thoughts start to race through my mind. *I'm going to have permanent goose bumps at this rate. If I pass out from overstimulation, will he have time to catch me before I hit the ground? I'm pretty sure even though I haven't touched Ledger tonight, this isn't right. I have a boyfriend. When was my last period? Could Ledger get me pregnant tonight? I wonder if he likes cats. I've always wanted a cat. I could have a Viking troll god of a husband and have his cats and his babies...*

"Angel!" Ledger gives me a nip on the shoulder and draws my attention back to him, then to the scene in front of us as Mark steps forward and twists both of Melody's nipples before releasing them. He slaps them in quick succession, then sucks one into his mouth as he twists the other. I draw in a ragged breath as Melody releases another plaintive cry, obviously coming again.

"Where did you go, Sloane?" Ledger murmurs, giving me a contemplative look as I turn to stare at him over my shoulder.

"I...this is a lot. I'm not sure what to think."

"Mmm." Ledger has his nose in my hair and his mouth on my temple now. "Well, Angel, you asked me what I liked earlier. I think what I like might end up being just the thing to calm your thoughts."

"I don't understand."

"Look at Melody," Ledger whispers, grazing the curve where my neck meets my shoulder with his lips.

I look up to see her trembling in earnest, as Mark has bent and spread her legs more, allowing him access to her...pussy. *You'd think in a sex club I could say the dang word in my own head without hesitation.* He toys at her entrance with his finger while the wand continues to buzz on her clit. He pushes two fingers into her without warning, replacing the toy with his mouth, and she screams again, all four of her limbs tugging at their restraints.

Mark keeps his fingers deep inside her, slowly lapping up the impressive amount of cum she's produced, and she shakes her head and whimpers as if to say she's had enough. He gives her one last lick before moving back and coming once again to stand by her head to pet and soothe her.

"She looks tortured but blissful?" I'm confused, though, about whether this is a reward or a punishment for Melody. "Is she in trouble?"

Ledger gives a little chuckle as he rounds the chair to come stand in front of me. Placing both of his hands on my face, he strokes my cheekbones as he finally answers the question I've had all night.

"She's not necessarily in trouble. Or at least, I wouldn't characterize it as simple as being in trouble. Mark derives his pleasure from her pleasure. And sometimes, if she's been a bit of a brat, he might take that principle to the extreme."

I look up into the smoky-gray eyes that have been nothing but captivating since the moment I first saw them. "What's the extreme?"

Ledger smirks as he presses a chaste kiss to my forehead, before walking behind me again and continuing the teasing, light strokes of his fingertips up and down my arms.

I'm about to ask him again what he means when Mark places the wand back on Melody's clit, along with what looks like a double-pronged toy in...both of her holes. I release a ragged breath, not even beginning to imagine what *that* would feel like, and watch as Mark finally pulls his hard...penis...out of his pants. He walks to where Melody's head is at the top of the table and taps her mouth until she opens to begin sucking him. He reaches down to pinch her nipple again, as she screams around his...*cock. I have to get used to saying the dirty words. I have to.*

Just as it's obvious she's coming for a *fourth* time, Ledger bites down *hard* on my neck and reaches around me to grip my thighs with his giant hands. I bow off the chair from the surprising pain and pleasure of his bite, but I can't get away from his grip.

"You wanted to know what I like. Well, baby...he's going to make her come until she passes out. And that's certainly something I've been dreaming about doing to you."

I think my brain may have frozen again. Instead of having a multitude of thoughts flittering past my consciousness one after the other, I have very few, and they're all moving slowly. I think about being spread out for Ledger, with nothing on my mind except how many orgasms I'll be conscious for. I think about feeling him everywhere and being so overwhelmed with his decisions about my pleasure that I can't feel anything else. I think about Dean with the girl at the diner. I think about a giant beautiful man on a motorcycle. And I think about the feeling of Ledger's strong, solid body standing behind me, gripping my thighs like he's afraid I'm going to hop out of this chair and never come back.

"Angel? Sloane?"

I realize I've been quiet for a very long time, and Ledger has come back around to face me. "Sweetheart, say something."

"You want me to pass out?"

He continues to gently stroke my thighs as if trying to calm a frightened animal. "I want to make you go out of your mind with pleasure. Making you come so hard you pass out would be an honor, if you reached the point you were comfortable with that."

"Why would you want that? Why would you care about my pleasure that much more than yours?"

Ledger fixes me with a stare so intense that if he took up any less than all of the space in my line of sight, I would look anywhere else. As it is, he's all I can see. He's everything. "I would care about your pleasure because...if you were mine, Sloane...well, I would care for what's mine in all ways. I would deny myself any number of things to ensure your comfort and happiness, and I would go to any lengths to show you just how much you deserve. Making you shake with the force of an orgasm, or cry when you think you can't take anymore, or allowing you a space where all you can do is feel and not think—that would be the greatest honor of my life."

The idea of anyone in my life putting me first, not just in a sexual context, but in any way at all, is foreign. The idea that he would want to solely focus on my pleasure is overwhelming and intoxicating, and *God, I want that so badly*. I don't think, no, I *know* for a fact that I've never really considered if that type of care would ever be given to me. A tear forms and as it falls and trails down my cheek, I know that if I don't allow myself to explore what Ledger is offering, I will never forgive myself.

"Show me."

Chapter Ten

Sloane

"Show me how you would pleasure me, Ledger."

He gives me another searching look, and apparently, my eyes have all the correct answers tonight. He gives me one more lingering kiss on my forehead before moving back behind me. Instead of standing as he was, he gently guides me out of the chair and to a sofa slightly to the side of the room. Our view of Mark and Melody isn't as clear, but I can see he's untying her now, and I assume they're done for the evening. Ledger sits down on the sofa and then surprises me by pulling me down on his lap. I feel what _cannot possibly_ be his _dick_ underneath me and wiggle.

"_Fuck_, Angel," he grunts, "Please don't do that or..." I swear I hear the words "babies" and "tonight," but he's mumbling so I really can't tell.

Without any more pretense, he pulls my back flush against his chest, rucks my dress up around my waist, and pulls my thighs apart so that my feet dangle over each of his legs. Shocked, I try to close my legs only to find that my own hands are on my thighs, keeping them spread, guided by Ledger's giant hands on top. He's barely touching me, only where his hands are too large covering mine, and the places where I can feel his skin on mine burn. His soft hands are not entirely smooth, leading me to wonder what kind of manual labor he does to have slight calluses in some places...*oh my God,* maybe he chops wood like those guys online. *Maybe he'll let me watch one day...*

"Angel!" Ledger barks, nipping at my shoulder hard enough to hurt and regain my attention. "That's three times you've zoned out on me tonight. I think you'll owe me three orgasms to prove I can keep your attention."

Before I can tell him that I'll take whatever he's giving, a low groan comes from across the room, causing my gaze to snap back, only to see that Mark now has Melody in the same position that Ledger and I are in, except...they're both completely naked. Melody is still covered in a sheen of sweat, having orgasmed four hard times by my count, and it looks like it's taking a lot of effort for her to keep her head up and off Mark's shoulder. She looks exhausted, blissed out, sated, and somehow still desperate. Her thighs are spread just like mine, and Mark's thick cock proudly stands tall between her legs. It gives her just enough pressure to grind against, and she's using small motions to coat him in her wetness, making them both glisten in the room's low lighting.

My body has a mind of its own, and I realize that I'm circling my hips in a similar motion, wishing that I had Ledger's bare cock between my legs so I could use it for friction. Ledger uses his hand placement over mine to bring it up, higher and higher until he's trailing my own hand down my neck. Faint, teasing touches that feel similar to when I touch myself but also totally new with the added pressure and heat of his skin on mine. He guides my hand lower, placing it on my breast, still covered by my dress.

"I've been staring at these perfect fucking tits all night, baby. I'm not sure who you had in mind when you put this dress on, but it damn sure better have been me."

I smile, biting my lip and looking over my shoulder to raise an eyebrow at his dirty mouth. "I wore it for me."

Far from displeasing him, my answer makes his smile widen. He leans in just enough to touch the tip of his nose to mine, and then he tilts my world on its axis by whispering, "That's my good girl."

Good girl? If my panties were wet before, they're soaked now.

Leaning back, Ledger nods to Mark and Melody. Placing his hand on top of mine again, he gently starts caressing my breast, alternating between a desperate kneading and almost painful pinching of my nipple. I realize I'm watching Mark do the same to Melody, and when Ledger switches our hands to give my other breast some much-needed relief, Mark's hands switch too.

Oh my God. Mark's hands are doing to Melody what my own hands are doing to me. Except she gets to rub herself all over Mark's cock, while I sit here humping the air like the horny, inexperienced girl I am.

Before I can even continue down this rabbit hole of negative thoughts, Ledger notices that I've realized what's going on.

"Do you see them, Angel? They're our avatars for the evening. Whatever you do to yourself with your perfect little hands, Mark will do to Melody with his mouth or his hands...or his cock."

I make eye contact with Melody and let out a ragged breath that ends in a moan I couldn't stop if I tried. For some reason, this seems to push her over the edge, and as Mark continues to twist her nipples in the same way I am mine, she comes again, her entire body tensing with what I assume is pain along with her pleasure.

Ledger grunts behind me as I tense myself, my hips lifting again off his to seek any pleasure I can find.

"Do you wish I were touching you right now?"

I can barely manage a whimper and a frantic nod.

"Do you want me to tell you what I would do to you so you can use those sweet little hands to bring yourself some relief?"

This question strikes me as wrong, and I shake my head. That's not what I want. I want his fingers inside me, his mouth on me, his cock and his cum inside me...A light smack on my outer thigh brings me out of this spiral and back to the present. I find that both of my hands are now on my nipples, petting, tugging, pinching at a much rougher pace than before because...oh my God, Ledger's hands are over both of mine now, guiding them like I'm a puppet on a string.

His mouth is on my neck, and then again at my ear. "I'll tell you anyway, sweet girl, because you need to know. You need to know what you're getting yourself into with me. Because once you're mine, and I've tasted you and been the first one to sink into that perfect virgin cunt, you're going to be stuck with me for life because I'm never letting you go. You need to hear exactly what I'm going to do to you so you'll know to run now if you want to."

"Please. Pleasepleaseplease."

I really don't know what I'm even asking for at this point. I think my brain, subconsciously, understands that I'll take whatever Ledger wants to give me.

"First, Angel, I'm utterly tired of seeing my tits covered in my presence. When we're at home, these are going to be out for my enjoyment all the time."

He unties the halter of my dress, letting my breasts fall free, then brings my hand to his mouth and spits on my fingers before bringing them back down to begin teasing my taut nipples. Movement catches my eye across the room, and I see Mark spit on his own hand before continuing to mimic my movements. *God, I wish Ledger's hand was on me instead. It's so much bigger and warmer and rougher than mine, and I need...*

Smack.

My head jerks from where it was resting, lying back on Ledger, shocked to see that Mark has gone rogue and given one of Melody's breasts a hard slap. As I watch, he does it again, twice in quick succession. She moans and grinds even harder against his dick, which looks almost painfully erect.

Ledger stops his constant up and down suckling of my neck, and I feel him smirk against me. "I think Mark got a little impatient there. What do you think? Should we indulge him?"

"Whatever you want, please...please."

At this point, I'm whiny, whimpering, wet, and thinking so hard about how to convince Ledger to put his dick inside me that I almost miss him picking up my forearm and directing my own hand to slap the absolute crap out of my boob. I shriek, trying to shrink back from the pain, only to find myself blocked by the same hard body that's been keeping me in place.

I'm rationalizing the pain and trying to regulate my breathing when four more hits follow, all to the same place. I'm drawing in a breath to scream when Ledger places our joined hands, wet again with his saliva, onto my reddening nipple to soothe the burn. It hurts—*damn, it hurts*—but as he brings our hands to my other nipple to continue tugging and pinching, I realize I feel an emptiness I've never felt before deep in my core.

I still don't have anything to grind against, and I'm out of my mind with this bereft feeling that I can't understand. I *can't* need anything inside me, not when I'm very used to life without it. I've made it twenty years. But I have to touch, and before I can overthink like usual, I reach down toward my clit. Mark reaches for Melody's, and her pleading gaze would *almost* convince me not to put her sensitive flesh through any more torture if I wasn't so convinced I would die without touch right this second. Just as I go to move my thong to the side and touch myself where I know I like it, Ledger's hand on mine halts its progress.

"Wait a minute, Angel. You haven't let me finish telling you my story yet."

I'm going to die via spontaneous combustion. It's going to be on the news. *God, everyone will know I died at a sex club. Unless spontaneous combustion burns hot enough to melt teeth too, and then maybe I could avoid identification via dental records?*

Smack.

"Sloane, at this point, you're convincing me that you're going to need ten orgasms a day to keep yourself out of that pretty little head."

"Please, I'm sorry...please."

"Shh, shh...don't apologize, love. It's my fault for not doing my job well enough. I was just telling you that while I love *this*, I think we can also do without it when you're at home."

Ledger reaches our hands down and hooks two of my fingers into the front of my thong, then he, *oh God*, he *pulls* and it's right against my clit and I'm going to...

"Come, Angel."

I detonate. My eyes are squinting, on their way to closing, when I see Mark slap Melody on the clit, and she comes again. My entire body goes rigid, my vision blacks out, and I've never come so hard or for so long.

"That's one, my sweet girl. I believe, if my count is correct, you owe me two more."

My eyes widen as I come out of my haze and realize his meaning. I squirm and try to get away, but he has one heavy arm around my waist and the other covering my hand until he lowers it and starts circling my clit. My fingers feel familiar yet foreign. I've never been brave enough to touch myself after orgasming before, too afraid of the sensitivity and the feeling of...too much.

But I don't have that choice tonight, as Ledger guides my hand in the quick cadence I prefer. *How does he know tha...*

Smack.

This time, he's brought my hand down hard directly on my clit, and that's all it takes for me to come again, harder, deeper, and with both more pleasure and more pain than the first. *Holy crap, I need to pee. I need to sleep. I need to hydrate.*

Ledger's deep voice brings me back again. "That's two."

His breath tickles my ear as he whispers, "You owe me one more, and you're going to give it to yourself while you finally put Melody out of her misery."

I'm still in an orgasm-induced haze, and I don't really understand his meaning until he takes my hand from my clit, stretches out my middle finger, and guides it inside me. It's...a lot, *too much,* but his hand on my wrist keeps me from removing my finger as his other hand guides mine over my clit again in slower circles.

"Watch, Angel."

I look up just in time to see Mark lift Melody effortlessly and drop her down in one smooth motion to the base of his cock. She's clearly too tired to scream, but she manages a long, low whimper. Her legs shake with pleasure, and I feel a deep heat in my core as I realize Ledger has added another of my fingers inside me.

I whimper, and I feel him smile against my neck. "What's wrong, sweet girl?"

Tears start to fall down my cheeks again, heavier than earlier, and Ledger pauses to remove my fingers and turn my head to look at him over my shoulder.

"Sloane, hey, baby...what's wrong? Do you want to stop? I have hot chocolate in my office and a fuzzy blanket for you if you—"

"No!" I interrupt him with as close to a scream as I can muster right now. "No, I don't want to stop. I just..." I take a deep breath and decide to continue tonight's theme of bravery and ask for what I want. "I wish that were us. I don't want my fingers. I want yours." I look up, and I hope whatever truth he's been seeing in my eyes all night continues to shine there. "I want you inside me, Ledger. I trust you. Please."

His face softens, the worry that had been there replaced with understanding and lust and *another adjective I want to be true but can't be so soon.* Placing the softest kiss to my forehead, he turns my head back to where Mark is still slowly rutting up into Melody, her head completely collapsed back on his shoulder now. With his lips on my temple, he takes my fingers and toys with my entrance. "My sweet girl. You'll get what you want soon enough. But not tonight. Tonight is about you giving yourself pleasure."

His pressure against my hand guides my fingers back inside, and he increases my pace as Mark does the same. My other hand is back on my clit, rubbing circles of varying pressure faster and faster, and when Mark reaches a big hand up to cuff Melody's neck and squeeze, Ledger takes one of my hands to do the same. I'm still pumping my fingers when he tightens his grip on my throat slightly, pushes the heel of my palm down on my clit, and says, "Watch, Sloane."

I see Melody's entire body go rigid, then limp, her head lolling back onto Mark's shoulder. From the way she's slumped, I realize from the back of my brain—*because all I can really think about is my third orgasm building deep in my core*—that she's passed out. Holy crap. And Mark continues to thrust furiously up into her, until he stills, and I see his cum start to spill out of Melody where they're connected.

Ledger returns his mouth to my ear, nipping my earlobe, and finally decides I've had enough torture tonight. His voice is lower and raspier than I've ever heard it when he finally gives me permission to fully let go. "Come for me, Sloane. Come for me so I can fill you up."

His voice alone would have been enough to finish me off, but the sum of the past few hours hits me like a truck, and I feel...*everything*. I feel like I'm so, so heavy, but also like I'm floating away. Every thought that's ever come through my head is gone, and all I am is a warm, soft, safe cloud of pleasure. Time stands still, and I have no sense of where or who I am until I finally focus on a pair of gray eyes looking down at me.

"That's three, Angel. How are you feeling?"

So good. So, so good. But I'm thirsty, and I also have to pee.

One of Ledger's dark brows arches. "You have to tell me out loud, baby. Although my life would be much easier if I could read your thoughts, for now, I lack that ability."

"I feel good. But I have to pee. Did I pass out?"

He chuckles before kissing me on the forehead and standing with me bridal style in his arms, as if I weigh nothing. "No, you didn't pass out. You did give me a hazy look and say over and over again that you love me."

He places me on my feet just long enough to grab a blanket and wrap me up tightly while I gape at him, mouth open in shock at what I apparently confessed post-orgasm. It's only when he reaches a finger out to press my jaw closed that I realize his mouth is upturned in a smirk.

"You liar! Don't tease me like that!" I punch his bicep, and his smirk turns into a blinding smile accompanied by a deep laugh, and I can't help but giggle too. "Not only do you tease me, but this blanket isn't even fluffy. I was promised a fluffy blanket."

Ledger picks me up again and walks toward a door I hadn't seen at the back of the room. "You're right. This blanket clearly fails to meet the fluffiness specifications you've set forth. But I did explicitly state that the *fluffy* blanket is back in my office."

"Your *office?*" I give what is meant to be a sexy smirk, but given how giddy I am from the three life-altering orgasms I just experienced, I'm not sure if the sentiment came across as intended. Ledger fights a chuckle while raising a single eyebrow.

"Carry me away to your *office*, sir."

Chapter Eleven

Ledger

Goddamn. I'm sitting here harder than I've ever been in my life, and I haven't even touched her sweet cunt. The fact that I didn't come in my pants just watching her writhe in my arms is honestly a miracle. At this point, I've pretty much trained my dick to last as long as necessary, but holding her in my arms while she fell apart had me almost losing control. Her soft, breathy moans are still undoing me. *If you were mine*, my ass. That girl has been mine since the moment I learned her name.

I look into Sloane's hooded eyes as I open the door to my office. She wants me. *I could take her right here, right now.* I put aside my intrusive thoughts and, instead, set her down on the leather couch and grab her promised fluffy blanket as well as some water. As I'm walking back, I notice that the gloss has left her eyes, and they're roaming around the room observantly.

"Ledger, where are we? This is a scenario room, right? I've...um...watched some things with casting couches and..."

I see the moment her eyes lock on the picture of me with my mom and siblings. Her breathing speeds up and her eyes go wide. Taking deep breaths, I motion for her to mimic me.

I wait until she's breathing normally before I drop the bomb. "Sloane, this is my actual office."

"Wait, what? You...You work here? Oh my God, are you some kind of sex worker? Ledger, what are you talking about?"

I rub my eyes and pinch my nose before I get too offended by the sex worker comment. I have to remember this is all new to her. Pulling a chair up in front of her, I remind myself that she didn't even know sex clubs existed two hours ago, and I'm about to tell her I own one.

"Sloane, I own this club." I pause to see her reaction, but she's frozen in place, clearly waiting for me to elaborate. "I built it from scratch two years ago. I'm extremely proud of what I've done to create a safe place for people to come and express their sexuality and kinks, so I'm going to pretend you didn't mean anything offensive by your sex worker comment."

I watch her face to see if I can get a clue about what she might be thinking, but it's still frozen. "Sloane?" I reach out to grab her hand and she doesn't pull away, so I give a little squeeze. "Baby, talk to me."

"I...I just don't know what to say. I didn't mean to offend you. This is all just so...different..." *Of course, my girl's first thought is to apologize.*

"Let's talk about it, then. What do you want to know?"

"Everything," she whispers, looking down at her hands like she's too ashamed to look into my eyes. I can't tell if that's embarrassment from her inexperience or disappointment in who she thought I was.

Fuck, I hate this.

I'm about to start telling her about the club when she gasps. "Oh God, Dean!"

Okay, so that was not what I expected to come out of her mouth.

"What?"

"Ledger, I'm still in a relationship! I just cheated. Oh my God, I'm a cheater—"

I cut her off before she can spiral down that path any longer. "Sloane! You didn't cheat on that piece of shit you call a boyfriend. You didn't touch me. And technically, you are the one who touched yourself. Also, he's been *actually* fucking other women since you've been together."

"What?" Her eyes cut to mine. "How would you even know that?"

How do I proceed with this? I'm not sure how well she'll take the truth. *Oh, you know, I'm basically a CIA-level hacker and have been stalking you and everyone you interact with since the moment I met you.*

"I'm very good with computers. I can find out anything and everything about anyone I want. I've been following that scum for weeks, making sure he didn't hurt you."

I let her sit for a minute to wrap her head around everything that she's just learned. God, sometimes I feel like such an idiot. This was the absolute worst time to bring Dean's cheating to light. This girl just walked past kink exhibition after kink exhibition, seeing things I doubt she has even imagined before in an establishment she didn't even know existed. She experienced her first orgasm that wasn't completely self-administered. And now I've dropped a bomb that destroys her reality even further.

She finally opens her eyes, but she's staring up toward the ceiling. "I don't understand what you just said."

"I really shouldn't have told you about Dean. It was..."

"No!" she snaps. "No, you shouldn't have." She's staring at me now, and a fire blazes in her eyes.

I start to speak, but she holds her hand up to stop me. "And regardless of what he has or hasn't done, I shouldn't have let that get as far as it did when he believes me to be committed to him. But *that* is not what I don't understand. What I don't understand, *Ledger,* is why you're stalking someone because of me."

Her eyes widen with a sudden realization. "It's not just him either, is it?" When I don't answer, she continues, "I knew it was you sending me all those packages, but I could never figure out *how* you were doing it. You hacked my phone, didn't you?"

I remain silent.

"*Didn't you?*" Tears well up in her eyes.

Now I'm the one who's frozen. I can't tell her that I fell madly and obsessively in love with her the first night we met.

"Sloane," I breathe out. "I...like you, a lot..."

I look in her eyes to make sure she's still with me mentally before continuing. "Do you remember asking me if I recognized you that night when we were stuck in traffic?" I don't let her respond. "Remember how I told you I recognized you by your beautiful green eyes?"

She nods, tears starting to fall down her face.

"Well, there was more going through my head that night than admiration of your eyes. I had never seen a person's expression change from such sadness to such joy in a fraction of a second. I saw life come into your eyes when you noticed my bike. Then when you noticed it had a rider, you looked at me like I was a mermaid or something. I've never had a woman look at me with anything other than lust, and it meant a lot to me. I wanted to ask you what was going on in that head of yours when you drove off."

"Well, you were way too large to be a man. I thought you might be a troll." She giggles.

I squint my eyes at her and grin. "A troll? Is *that* why you called me a beautiful troll the first night of practice?"

Her laughter stops abruptly as she gasps. "I really said that out loud?"

Deciding it's safe to touch her, I squeeze above her knee. "Yes, you sure did, you little menace."

Her laughter returns, and I watch her sad tears turn to happy ones. When she finishes drying her eyes, I take both of her hands in my own and rest them in her lap.

"I knew the moment I locked eyes with you at that first practice that I wasn't going to let you drive away again. I took your information from Mom and started looking into your socials. The more I found out about you, the more I wanted to know. So yes, I hacked your phone. And yes, I keep an eye on the people around you. I keep an eye on everyone I care about."

I watch as her body relaxes into the couch. We both sit there in silence for what seems like forever when she lets out a quiet, "Ledger?"

"Yes, Angel?" I feel like I'm waiting for a roulette wheel to stop on one of the fifty things she could be curious about from the past hour.

"Did you *really* send me a dildo?"

I choke on air. I had forgotten all about that. I look up to see her grinning.

"Have I told you what a menace you're being tonight?" I pause, watching her roll her eyes, then stand. Still holding her hands in my own, I give them a light squeeze. "Come on, let's get you home."

She allows me to pull her up and opens her mouth. I presume she is about to say something about Allie, so I let her know that her friend has already been taken care of tonight and knows that Sloane is safe as well.

I lean in close to her and whisper, "The two of you are also not going to be charged with having fake IDs."

I'm cuffing the back of her neck with my hand when she gasps and looks up at me with rounded eyes. I laugh and lean down to kiss the top of her head. She looks down and shakes her head before I move my hand to the small of her back and lead her through the back of the club to my car.

I've barely started driving when Sloane says, "So Dean, huh?"

I've been preparing myself to answer any of the questions she might have about the things she's learned tonight. Still, I have to admit, I'm a little relieved that we can spend the car ride bonding over mutual hate rather than having to tell her about my past fuckups. She'll eventually have to listen to that story, and I have no clue how I'll get her to stay once she has. We haven't even had sex yet, so I can't knock her up. Or maybe

I could sneak into her room at night with the famous turkey baster method. *I'm insane.* I could also act like a decent man and be there for her right now instead of plotting.

I grab her left hand and kiss it before resting both of our hands on her thigh. "Angel...I'm sorry—"

"No, no, it's okay. I think I hate him anyway."

I chuckle. "If you hate him, *why on earth* are you dating him?"

Sloane proceeds to tell me about how their relationship started. Apparently, their families had been close her whole life, and while she didn't actively have a crush on him, when he asked her to his senior prom, she was thrilled to accept. He was a popular senior who was good-looking, athletic, and whom her parents loved, so there wasn't really a question in her mind about beginning their relationship. Although he was sweet at first, things began to change when he went to college. She thought he was acting distant and weird, but he was also insistent that she join him when she graduated, so she didn't look too much into it. She didn't learn until she was already halfway through her freshman year what a trap she had gotten herself into.

Dean was close enough to monitor every move of hers, but with his golf team and frat commitments, she couldn't return the favor, so he got to do whatever he wanted, while she was pretty much forced to stay in. If she did anything against his will, like having fun, he threatened to tell her parents. By the time she realized all this, it was too late to transfer. She's in the middle of telling me about how he never wanted to move their physical relationship past kissing when I remember the chlamydia. *Oh Angel, you don't even realize what a favor he did you with that one.* Considering he's been fucking every willing hole for years except her's, I guess he has a "taking your wife's virginity on the wedding night" fantasy. *Well, had.* Apparently, he's been trying to take things up a notch for a couple weeks, but Sloane has been turning him down.

"Would you mind taking me to his place instead of mine tonight?" My hand on her tenses, and I guess she realizes how that sounded because she quickly elaborates, "And could you wait for me while I break up with him?"

I want to tell her no. I know exactly what he and his *frat bros* are going to be up to tonight. I was in a fraternity in college. I like to tell myself it was just an attempt to impress my father by joining as a legacy, but it's not like I didn't enjoy the parties and camaraderie that came along with it. That's how I know that the particular fraternity Dean is in has a very dark reputation.

My hand relaxes, and I give hers a little squeeze. "Sloane, do you remember how I said I was keeping tabs on him?"

She nods.

"Well…I don't know if you'll want to be anywhere near what's going on at his frat house tonight."

"Oh? Oh! I didn't think about there being a girl there right now. Don't worry about me. I'm a big girl, and I already told you that it doesn't bother me to let him go. I'm actually relieved."

I pause for a minute to figure out how I need to approach what I'm about to say.

Sighing, I just go for it. "It's not just a girl…" She gasps before I can continue, "His frat is known for their beginning-of-the-year orgy, and recent messages in the frat group chat have all but confirmed it's tonight."

I chance a quick look at her, only taking my eyes off the road for a second. She's in shock again. *Fuck.*

I hear her breathing get a little heavier. "Ledger?"

"Sloane?"

"Take me to that fucker's house."

The car has barely stopped before Sloane stomps toward the porch and bangs on the door. I watch as one of the frat members opens the door and then yells back into the house for Dean. He stumbles across the threshold looking thoroughly fucked up. She's yelling at him, but I can't hear what she's saying, so I quietly get out of the car and make my way up to the side of the porch with as much stealth as I can muster. He reaches out to grab her waist, and I watch as Sloane slaps him across the face. He staggers back, and you can see the moment he realizes what she just did. He starts to raise his hand, but before he can strike my girl, I've jumped up on the porch and grabbed his wrist.

"Don't you dare. Touch. *My*. Girl," I growl out.

Both Sloane and Dean snap their eyes to me. "Sloane, get in the car. We're leaving." She doesn't budge. She's just standing there looking between me and her ex. I realize my tone might have been a little harsh, so I soften my voice before repeating my request. "Please, Angel. I'm right behind you."

I take her hand in mine and kiss her knuckles. That seems to be enough for her to obey me. She turns and is walking back to the car when I start to twist Dean's wrist, letting him know just how easily I could break it.

"If you ever come near her again, I will ruin your life. Do you understand me?" I watch as fear grows in his glassy eyes.

His lips press together as he nods. "No, you fucker, use your words," I say, twisting harder.

"Okay!" he yells, "Ow! Okay, okay, okay!"

I let go, and he stumbles backward, rubbing his wrist. "I was tired of that uptight bitch anyway."

I spin around and punch him square in the face, hard enough to break his nose but not so hard he passes out. I want him to be aware enough to watch me drive off with Sloane.

He stands at the door staring at us with his hand holding his nose as I get in the car. I start the engine and look over at my girl, grabbing her chin to gently turn her head to face me.

"You okay, baby?" She looks fine, but I stroke her cheek to calm her down regardless. I can't stop myself. It's like my hands can't help but find her. My eyes almost roll into the back of my head when she leans into my touch. She's been single for all of ten minutes, and her body already knows who it belongs to.

She smiles, nods, then leans in to kiss my cheek. "Take me home."

It takes me longer than I would like to admit to remember that she's talking about her apartment and not the house I've renovated to her exact tastes. I could just go ahead and pronounce my love. Take her back to *our* house. Show her *our* owner's suite, which now includes a walk-in closet that's larger than her current apartment, stocked with all the clothes she could ever need. She actually doesn't ever *need* to go back to her current residence. I sigh internally. *She* just *broke up with her boyfriend of three years, Ledger. Give her a moment.*

It's not a long drive back to her apartment, but I do my best to prolong our time together. I can't help it. The mood has lightened, and I'm getting a personal concert as she sings along to the music. Laughing. Dancing. *Fuck, she's perfect.*

I pull her hand to mine and kiss it. "God, Sloane, I'm so glad you are finally free of that, what did you call him? Fucker?"

She bends over in her seat, laughing. "Me too! Oh, oh, I know! Let's celebrate by taking a ride on your bike! The ride you gave me Thursday night was incredible! That whole night was incredible! Well, not the end, I guess...wait! Do you think he was hooking up with that girl?"

I laugh. "Of course he was! Why do you think I took you to that specific diner?"

She freezes. "Wait, what?"

Oh no. Oh fuck.

She turns the music off and moves my hand from her thigh. "Please tell me you did not *purposely* ruin what was probably the best night of my life."

I'm going to have to turkey baste her.

Seriously, why is that the only thought in my mind right now? I'm trying to think of a reasonable way to answer without losing her, but nothing comes to mind. Not a single word because *I've built you a castle, and I didn't want you to be in a relationship when I brought you back to said castle to consummate ours* seems a bit extreme. Instead of giving her an excuse that will inevitably push her away even more, I just hang my head and breathe out, "I'm sorry, Angel."

We don't say another word for the rest of the drive. It's only a few minutes, but the silence makes it seem like an eternity. I stop the car, and she immediately hops out. Before she can make it to her door, I'm there. I have to try.

I take her face in my hands and pull her gaze to mine. In the dark, I didn't notice that she had tears welling up again. *Fuck.* We lock eyes, and I know she must feel exactly how *right* we are for each other. I use my thumbs to wipe away the tears that have started falling down her face. "Sloane, please forgive me. I'm so sorry."

She takes my hands in her own, and for a moment, I think she'll forgive me. I let myself fall into that fantasy. A world where she takes my hands and wraps them around her waist. I lean down and kiss her lips while I hold her tight. Soft at first, then, when those soft kisses become frantic, I pick her up and carry her to her apartment, not breaking our connection. She fumbles with her keys for a moment before finally unlocking the door. As soon as we enter the apartment, I close the door behind us, and her back is against it. I thrust against her, and she moans when she feels my solid length lined up perfectly. If the barrier of our clothes didn't exist, I would be able to fuck directly into her tight little cunt...

She throws my hands down aggressively, snapping me back to reality. "No, Ledger. Don't touch me. I can't do this right now. I just broke up with one lying asshole, and I'm not about to walk willingly into the arms of another." Tears stream down her face.

"Angel..."

She stops me when I go to wipe away another tear. "I'm not your angel, Ledger. Just, just leave me alone, okay?"

"No."

Her mouth drops open, and any sadness in her eyes turns to anger. "Excuse me?"

"I said no. I'm not going to leave you alone. I'm sorry for my lapse in judgment about the diner on Thursday night. I really am. But I'm not going to stop fighting for you. I'll give you some space to work through things. Two weeks. I'll give you two weeks. Then we're going to talk through everything like adults and move past it."

She's backed up to her apartment by now and takes a moment with her keys. She dramatically opens the door and steps in, but before she can slam it shut, she yells, "Fuck you, Ledger." There's that fire in her eyes again. *God, I love that fire.*

"Oh, I plan on it...*Angel.*"

Her mouth drops open, and she stares at me with wide eyes. It takes everything in me not to cross that threshold and fuck her *right now*. Instead, I walk back to my car and start to plan my week, already dreading that I've agreed to give my girl space.

Chapter Twelve

Sloane

I slam the door, letting out a guttural scream as I sink to the ground. A thud comes from Allie's side of the apartment before she races into view holding a...gun? What happened to her giant knife?

"Sloane? Jesus Christ, are you okay? Are you hurt?"

Standing, I show her that, physically, at least, I'm fine. "I'm okay, Al. Men just completely freaking suck."

Allie sighs and flicks the safety back on her gun. "Yes, yes, they do. Do you want to talk about it? Particularly if it has anything to do with the hickeys all over your neck?"

Pinching the bridge of my nose, I make a note to *throttle* Ledger the next time I see him. *Except he's probably into that.* "A full debrief tomorrow, for sure. If you have time, I'm going to order an obscene amount of snacks and alcohol for delivery. Maybe supplies for making a couple of voodoo dolls."

"I've always got time for you, especially to eat junk and talk shit about men," Allie says, giving me another once-over as if she's not sure I'm truly fine. "You're sure you don't need anything else?"

"I'm sure. Please go back to bed. We'll leave no stone unturned tomorrow during our debrief. Bring a colored pen set so your notes will be organized."

Giving me a salute, Allie turns to go back to her room, where I hear more than one muffled voice. *Glad she also had a fruitful night after our adventure. Although I hope hers ended on a better note than mine.*

I make my way into my bedroom, determined to at least get through my skincare routine before collapsing into bed. As soon as I have moisturizer on and finish flossing, I feel the full weight of the evening start to sink in. Lying down, it's obvious that sleep won't come easily tonight.

Of course, my first thoughts are of Ledger. I miss him, and that is *so freaking annoying* in the setting of what looks to be some world-class manipulation on his part. *Is it, though?* Another part of my brain unhelpfully supplies. Good to know I have an angel on one shoulder and devil on the other situation going on here, even in my own conscience. Damn. Speaking of conscience, regardless of how Ledger tried to spin things, I absolutely cheated on Dean tonight.

I take a deep breath and decide to think about just the facts of mine and Ledger's...relationship, friendship, whatever we have at this point.

We met with mutual lust, then became...friends, I thought. We certainly spent enough time together after his mother started trying to play matchmaker. While we were friends, though, he clearly became interested in me romantically, considering that he...stalked me, tracked me, and hacked my electronics to ensure every one of my whims, wants, and needs was immediately fulfilled. Okay, yes, it was very helpful and lovely stalking, but still, stalking. Clearly, he also spent time masterminding my breakup, and although I am still *so mad* at his methods, I can't deny the feeling of relief I have knowing that I don't have to pretend to have romantic feelings for Dean anymore. Especially now that I've seen his true colors. I don't want to dwell on what my life would have been like if I married him.

Ugh, even the thought is enough to make me want to dry heave.

I flip over to my other side, deciding that thinking about Dean is pointless since we're *obviously* over. Hopefully, I can avoid him for the foreseeable future. My dad is going to be mad about the business deals. *If he wants them that badly, he can divorce Mom and marry Dean himself.*

My last thought before I drift off into what is sure to be a fitful sleep is the same one I had when I lay down...I miss Ledger.

By noon, when I finally wake up, I feel disgusting, drenched in sweat from tossing and turning all night. An everything shower is how I decide to try to reset myself, and an hour and a half later, I at least smell better, even if I'm still feeling like I've been put through an emotional meat grinder.

Before I walk out of my room to find Allie, I decide to see how much damage is on my phone from last night. I haven't checked my messages since I was texting Ledger at the club, and while I'm hopeful everyone involved is giving me space, it seems unlikely. Sure enough, there's at least one new message from Ledger, but I save it for last, knowing that it's by far the most important.

Dean, luckily, isn't one of my missed messages. One is from my mom, asking what today's sermon was in church and telling me to send her my favorite verses the pastor used. That message is like clockwork every Sunday, so I'm not even surprised. It'll be worse if I don't respond, so I find the church's social media post from today. Thank God their team adds a cutesy post every week with the reference verses, so I can send it to Mom. The second unread text is from my dad, saying nothing, but containing a link to a men's conference where he's been invited to speak. The third is Allie's thread, asking if I'm okay and where I'm at. Her last message from last night said she had a ride and knew I was safe with Ledger, and that she'd see me at home. Finally, I'm unable to avoid Ledger's text thread anymore, so I take a deep breath before I open it.

Devil:

> Angel, I hope you're sleeping well. I handled last night poorly, and I hope I'll have a chance soon to earn your forgiveness in person. Please know that I meant every word I said, and that last night was, beyond a shadow of a doubt, the best night of my life.

I stare at the message for so long that my phone falls asleep, and I can already feel that my reaction to last night's revelations is...not normal.

I *should* be mad that the man who's been stalking me, *and spoiling me,* manipulated me into finding out that my long-term boyfriend is a general piece of crap who was also cheating on me. I *should* be at least a little hesitant at the fact that he owns and frequents a sex club because clearly there's a Grand Canyon–sized gap in our sexual experience, let alone life experience from our age difference. I *should* feel sad that my long-term boyfriend was cheating on me, because even with everything I've learned in the past twenty-four hours, Dean and I did have fond memories that will always be a part of my adolescence. And I really, really, *really should* be mad at the gorgeous bouquet sitting on my desk that was definitely not there when I fell asleep last night.

I should be mad, but I'm really not.

Allie and I successfully waste an entire day dissecting our experiences at Rendezvous, eating way too much junk food, and alternating between talking about how hot men are and how much we hate them. *She* had an even more eventful evening than I did, from the sound of it. I'm putting away my grocery order for the week that *someone* had delivered this morning, when I get a text from Blanche, of all people.

Unknown:

> Hi Sloane, it's Blanche! I hope you don't mind me texting you out of the blue on a weekend. I've gotten myself into a situation with the script for the play, and I was really hoping you might be available for brunch so I could get your opinion on it. Are you free? Would 12:30 at the Calico work?

Well. Brunch with Blanche was not on my bingo card for today, but she's been nothing but nice to me at play practices, and it would be helpful to get some insider info on Ledger and his family. Even if I am pretending to be mad at him. In for a penny, in for a pound.

Me:

Hi Blanche! I'm free at 12:30. See you then!

I have time to make myself presentable in a tennis dress and cardigan, with just enough light makeup to ensure that I'm put together enough to be in public. Heading out to my old car, I sigh and hope it's going to start this time. My parents had initially planned to buy me a *slightly* nicer car when I started driving in high school, but apparently, my choices of friends in school weren't up to their standards. When I chose not to end friendships at my parents' whim, this is how they retaliated. It's honestly not a bad car, with leather interior, heated seats, and comfort befitting, well, a grandma...as long as it'll start up.

After two tries, I'm successful, and I make the short drive through town to get to the café Blanche has chosen for brunch. The Calico, a staple in this town, is as cute as a button. The food reminds me of my own grandmother, and the decor would fit in her kitchen as well. I'm lucky again with my parking spot, and I head in to see that the predictable post-church surge of patrons has the café bursting at the seams with a line out the door. Wondering how Blanche and I are going to manage getting anything done with this much noise, I see her pop her head out of a door I've never noticed in the back of the building.

Deep breaths, Sloane...It's perfectly normal for your stalker's mom to lure you into a hidden room.

Chapter Thirteen

Sloane

"Sloane, darling! I'm so glad you could come on such short notice. Follow me!"

Blanche leads me through the unassuming door into what looks like a smaller, more intimate dining room that I had no clue existed. It's like a slightly more sophisticated version of a classic kitchen.

"Wow. I had no idea this extra seating space was back here!"

She smiles as we take our seats at a two-person table near a window. "Well, it's not exactly advertised. This room is primarily used by families who have lived in town for years and friends of the café's ownership group," she says.

After some standard small talk about how my classes have been going, I sense Blanche getting ready to talk business as the server takes our orders.

"Sloane, I have to be honest that I lured you here under false pretenses."

"Oh. Okay," I reply. "Is everything okay? If it's not the play...is Ledger okay?" Immediately, my mind goes to the worst possible scenarios.

Oh my God, he's been in a motorcycle crash. His club got raided by the FBI. He's an assassin, and he's been taken out on a job. He doesn't want to see me anymore, and I don't matter enough for him to tell me in person, so he sent his mom. Wait, has he told his mom about us? Is there even an us? For all I know, he takes all his women back to private shows at Rendezvous...

"Sloane? Sloane, dear, are you okay?"

I look up to see Blanche's concerned face, and her hand poised on her water glass as if she was seconds away from breaking me out of my trance by pouring it over my head.

"I'm so sorry. Sometimes my mind goes to the worst-case scenarios. Is Ledger okay?"

"That's quite alright," Blanche says with a kind smile. "And yes, Ledger is fine."

I allow myself a moment of relief before continuing. "You were just about to tell me why you asked me here today?"

Blanche shifts back into her more serious, business-like demeanor. "Yes. Yes, I was. I'll start by saying that I owe you an apology."

My eyes widen, and I sit back into my seat, shocked at her statement. "An apology? To me?"

"Yes. I must admit that, as a director, I've been involved in some mid-size productions, and I've become accustomed to having things done my way. Over the years, that desire for control has led me to...meddle, one could say, in my children's lives. While his siblings have been away for school or work, Ledger has stayed close, partially to keep me company. In return, I've tried my best all these years not to pry into his personal life. That was his one request of me," Blanche says, giving a wince as she takes another sip of her mimosa.

"You see, when I saw the two of you lock eyes that first day of rehearsal in the church, it..." She looks away with a wistful look in her eyes. "It reminded me of the spark between my late husband and me. And I just felt deeply that you being in my play was kismet, and you and Ledger were meant to be in this together. So I know I shouldn't have intervened, but an old, romantic biddy like me can't help it. And my Ledger has been lonely for so long and never really shown any interest in anyone, certainly not the way he looked at you when he first saw you. That's why I wanted to meet with you today—to apologize and to say I hope I haven't made you uncomfortable. I can adjust the practice schedule so the two of you won't be alone so much..."

"No!" I yell, surprising both myself and Blanche at the ferocity with which I decline her offer.

"No?" she says, the glimmer returning to her eyes.

I cough and sip my coffee, trying to decide how I'm going to play off my clear objection to having less alone time scheduled with her son. "I'm sorry for yelling. I just meant, no, you haven't made me uncomfortable at all."

"Hmm," she says, eyeing me with a loaded look. "I'm glad to hear it, dear. I would quite like it if we were friends. I miss my daughter when she's gone, and it's hard not having anyone young around me to shop and gossip with."

Phew, okay, so Blanche is not mad that I yelled at her, and she's not about to boot me from her play. Dodged a bullet there. "I'd love that."

A few hours later, Blanche and I have to-go coffee in hand, and we're completing a walking circuit through campus. We decided we didn't want to sit and take up a table in the busy café, and after a huge brunch, a walk was just what we both needed. When she discusses her husband, she's both nostalgic and practical.

"I loved Henry very much. From the moment we met, our relationship was...explosive, to say the least," she says, glancing to see if I'll give anything away regarding my relationship with Ledger. I simply smile, and she gives a little eye roll before continuing. "Well, he was quite a bit older than me."

At her glance this time, I decide to throw her a bone. "That's not so bad. Older men can be kinda...hot. Experienced," I say with a giggle.

"Exactly! Well, in any case, the rest is history, as they say. We were married quickly, and I threw myself into helping him run his company while keeping the home. And then the children came along, which was such an adventure. Of course we had lots of help, but I was very hands-on, even back then when it wasn't en vogue. Henry tried to be there as much as possible. He was an amazing husband, but as a father, I think his own experiences growing up clouded his view of what a healthy father-son relationship could look like," Blanche says.

"Was your husband's father very strict?" I ask, fascinated by a look into someone *else's* dysfunctional family dynamic for a change.

"Oh, very much so. Tragically, even." Blanche sighs. "And my Henry was really never able to connect with our children other than Margot. She was his princess from day one. Luckily, the boys felt the same, so they were never jealous that she and her father had such a different relationship than theirs. My Henry had such high expectations for his boys that I'm afraid Henry and Ledger never really stood a chance."

We find ourselves at a bench under a large shade tree on a corner of the quad at the center of campus and decide to sit before continuing our walk back to our cars at the café.

"I realize I never even explained what I was talking about with all my Henrys, and it can be so confusing. I'm sorry, dear. My Henry was Henry Jr., named after his beast of a father, and of course he had to continue the tradition of naming his heir after himself, so my eldest son is Henry III."

I blush deeply, remembering that while I haven't yet met Henry, I have seen him in quite an intimate situation. If Henry worked his entire life to live up to his father's expectations and run what sounds like a huge company, it makes sense that he enjoys wingback chairs, tobacco pipes, leather-bound books, and women on their knees before him. I try to take a sip of my cold coffee to cover my snort of laughter, but instead, I end up spraying it all over my lap.

"Are you alright, dear?" Blanche says with concern, pulling an honest-to-god *embroidered handkerchief* out of her purse to help me clean up my spill.

"I'm fine," I choke. "Just went down the wrong pipe."

"If you're sure," Blanche says, still looking at me like she's ready to perform CPR if necessary. After a minute of coughing, I finally quiet down and give her a thumbs-up. "Well, as I was saying, my husband had incredibly high expectations for our little Henry, and he tried his best to meet them. I'm afraid his adolescence was not as enjoyable or carefree as it should have been, with numerous lessons and obligations. I think he tried on his own to meet his father's expectations, but I think he also tried to deflect some of the pressure off Ledger."

I furrow my brow at that. "Did Ledger not meet expectations?"

Blanche sighs, and when she speaks, it's much softer. "He tried. He tried for so many years. When the boys were younger, they were inseparable, with Ledger trying to do and learn everything that Henry did. When Ledger started school, it became clear that despite his extreme intelligence, he wasn't going to be the excellent student that Henry was. And while Henry seemed to have quite a bit of patience for his father's business partners and their stuffy attempts to teach him boardroom politics, Ledger did not. Eventually, my husband seemed to give up on raising Ledger to have a role in the company, and left him to his own devices much more often."

"That's horrible," I say. "To exclude one child and make them feel less important."

Blanche's face shows her regret. "I know. It's the one thing I will never forgive him for—how he treated Ledger. I tried to help him in my own ways, ensuring that Ledger had his own outlets. He may not have had Henry's gift for studying, but he's an extremely talented musician."

"Really?" I exclaim. "He's never told me that!"

"Really!" Blanche chuckles. "He can play almost any instrument, but he loves the piano. And he may not have had Henry's knack for winning boardroom war games, but both of my boys are quite sporty. He played rugby all through high school and college."

His bubble butt makes so much more sense now. All those rugby players online look like you could bounce a quarter off their...

"And then, of course," Blanche continues, oblivious to the fact that I was totally checked out thinking about her son's ass, "everything changed when Henry was sent away to complete his studies at boarding school.

"I can't imagine how Ledger felt without Henry there as a buffer. He bought his first motorcycle with money he stole from his father's desk, started joining every street fighting club he could find, and finally ran into the wrong people who got him into drugs. Luckily, it was always recreational and never anything more, but it was so hard to watch him turn inward and embrace his demons more and more. With Henry away, my husband turned his attention to Ledger and Margot, and while Margot was his princess who could do no wrong, and Henry was the perfect heir he had trained in his ways, Ledger could never meet the expectations set for him."

Blanche pauses for so long I'm not sure she remembers I'm sitting next to her. "I'm lucky he's alive, Sloane. And I'm even luckier that he's forgiven me and not only has anything to do with me at all, but is also one of my closest friends. He's such a good man despite his childhood. He deserves all the happiness in the world, and I would do anything to give it to him."

She reaches out and places a manicured hand on top of mine. "I'm sorry for meddling. But now you know why I'm so invested in Ledger's happiness."

I feel tears forming in my eyes and squeeze Blanche's hand. I decide not to be coy anymore and give her what she wants. "I'm glad you meddled. Very glad."

With another smile, she takes a deep breath and then stands spryly from the bench. "Well, as refreshing as our respite has been, I think we'd better continue back toward the café, don't you think?"

I join her as we head back, realizing that time has flown by, and it's almost dinnertime. "I'm sorry for keeping you so late today," I say. "I hope you didn't have any dinner plans."

She turns to me with the biggest smile I've seen all day. "I didn't, but now that you mention it, dinner is a wonderful idea!"

Four hours later, I've been to Blanche's home and gotten the grand tour. "*The children didn't grow up here, but I've had this house for years. We moved here when all the kids were out of the house. We wanted something a little smaller and closer to the city.*" I've gawked at the fanciest library I've ever seen in a personal home. "*This is nothing compared to the family home where Henry lives now. I'm sure one day you'll get to see it.*" Best of all, I've spent hours poring over baby pictures of all of Blanche's children, but particularly one lanky, smoke-eyed boy. "*Wasn't he just the most handsome boy you've ever seen? Between you and me, I was concerned for a bit that he would never grow into how big his ears were, but then he shot up to six foot five during his sophomore year of high school and shocked us all!*"

I've just agreed to join Blanche in her family's box for the football game this Saturday when I realize I left my car at the café.

"Oh my gosh, we forgot my car earlier!" I exclaim, horrified that she'll have to drive me back across town just because I was too busy gossiping with her to remember I had a whole car I was responsible for. "It's been there all day. I hope they didn't tow it." *That would be awful to have to explain to my parents. Unless the tow truck company has already called them about it. Ugh.*

"Oh, not to worry, dear. I sent one of my assistants to retrieve it not too long ago. He should be back any minute."

Okay, an assistant did her bidding to go get my car. Play it cool, Sloane. Everyone has an assistant these days. I breathe a sigh of relief. "I'm so sorry you had to go to the trouble, but thank you so much."

"It's truly not a problem, dear. And I think I hear Andrew pulling around now. Grab your purse, and we can go meet him outside to make sure your car is unscathed."

Making sure not to forget anything in case Blanche thinks I'm a clinger trying to fully move into her mansion, we make our way outside to see a sheepish-looking Andrew and a car that is absolutely not my car. It's a freaking huge, gleaming luxury SUV that looks meant for a celebrity.

"Umm, Andrew," I say, trying to stay calm, "I think you stole someone's car. That's not mine."

"Well, the thing is, Miss..." Andrew starts.

"Just Sloane," I say with a smile.

"Well, Miss Sloane," Andrew continues, rubbing the back of his neck, "when I didn't see your car, I went into the café to ask if they had anything towed today. The manager asked if I was looking for a black sedan, and when I said yes, he gave me the keys to this and this note."

Andrew hands me a piece of paper sealed with wax, the logo for Rendezvous imprinted onto the seal.

I know you're still pretending to be mad at me, but your car was truly on its last legs. I couldn't help but ask one of my guys to take a look at it today, and he deemed it unsafe to drive. You have to be safe, Angel. At this point, that's nonnegotiable. So is the car. Nonnegotiable. Don't even think about asking for your car back. I've already had it crushed. When it comes time to tell your parents, I'll hand them twice the value for it. All your things are in this one, with your favorite air freshener plugged in, custom embroidery on the seats, and car snacks in the console. Insurance and registration are in the glove compartment. I also hate to tell you this in a note, but I'll be out of town for two weeks with a packed schedule of meetings. I'm dealing with permits and red tape while trying to get my next club open in New York. As much as I don't want to leave you, this will make it easier to give you the space you've requested and deserve. I already asked Mom to be available in case you have any emergencies. I'm sorry I'll miss practice. Don't talk to any other Devils. And Angel, please, please take the car.

Xoxo, Your Devil

I stare in shock at the note, take a deep breath, and decide there is nothing I can do at this moment except quell my murderous rage at Ledger's complete inability to refrain from being a creeper. Turning to Blanche, I see her slight grimace, no doubt wondering if she's going to reap the wrath her son just sowed. "Thank you for a wonderful day, Blanche. I think we're going to be great friends."

Obviously relieved, she smiles and gives me a hug. "I think so too, Sloane."

Heading for the giant SUV that I freaking hope I can drive, I turn back just before opening the door. "If you can forgive me for murdering your son."

Blanche's laughter rings out as I situate myself in the car, adjusting the seat and mirrors to accommodate my slighter build compared to Andrew's. It's nice, way nicer than any car I've driven, and as I'm basking in the mix of my favorite car air freshener and new car smell, I turn and see the custom embroidery that Ledger mentioned. It's a monogram in a classic font on the headrest of the passenger seat, and I stare at it in confusion. sSo? That isn't my monogram. First and middle initial sure? But S? What on earth...*oh my God. Ohhhh my God.*

He had my initials monogrammed...but with *his* last name. Sloane Olivia Sinclair. *Crap.* I'm gonna kill him. I also think I might love him.

Chapter Fourteen

Ledger

Mom and I stroll into our family's empty skybox hours before kick-off. She insists on being the first one to arrive to make sure everything is in order. Blanche Sinclair always has a theme, and while the food and drinks are usually catered, she personally decorates the suite because "Nobody else can do it the way I can, darling."

"What's the theme today?" I ask, holding up a wig with a grimace on my face.

"This week is 'let them eat cake' because they are a bunch of *peasants*," Mom looks at me like I'm dumb for having to ask and grabs the wig out of my hand, securing it onto her head in a single impressive sweep. "As happy as I was to hear you would be able to make it today, you can take yourself right back home if you're going to bring such negative energy. This is one of the biggest games of the year, and so help me, we are going to enjoy ourselves."

"Yes, Mother," I say as I start placing the extravagant decorations out.

This really is a big game. My alma mater has a few rivals, and while this isn't *the* big game of the year, it's the team we all despise the most. It helps that they haven't beaten us in over fifteen years.

Mom walks around, rearranging everything I've placed while humming a tune I can't quite catch. "I'm so glad that you were able to come home a week early. Did you get everything settled with your new *electronics* store?"

I choose to ignore the way she just insinuated my business isn't a totally reputable security company and smile. "Yes, Mother, I was able to get everything settled."

"Hmm, whatever you say, dear." Mom clears her throat before continuing. "I really wasn't expecting you this week, so I invited a new friend of mine. I hope you don't mind."

"Whatever you want, Mom. It's your suite."

What the fuck is that about? Of course I wouldn't mind. There's more than enough space in this suite, and I would be thrilled for my mom to spend more time with friends.

We spend the next hour finishing the setup and chatting about how the team's been doing this year. I love coming to games, but this has been the first one this season I've been able to attend. I'm even more thrilled that both of my siblings are joining us today. It's been quite a while since we've all three been together. I guess that's why Mom has it looking like the Palace of Versailles. In contrast to the pastels and shimmering golds around the room, I stick out like a sore thumb in my matching black slacks and sport jacket. Mom told me to dress up, and if her own creamy-yellow two-piece skirt suit with gold embellishment is anything to go by, I'll probably be one of the only guests in attendance not matching the color scheme.

As our guests file into the suite, I notice everyone is indeed wearing soft hues. Margot waltzes in wearing a knee-length muted pink dress that complements her blonde hair. Jack swaggers in sporting a pair of light khaki slacks and a light blue dress shirt. Henry is the only other one who didn't receive the memo, walking in wearing a dark charcoal-gray suit. It's tailored to him perfectly, which, at six foot six, it would pretty much have to be. He may have an inch on me, but due to our different workout preferences, I've always been bulkier.

"It would seem Ledger and I are the only two attendees today uninformed about the dress code," Henry says, greeting our mother with a composed hug.

Mom squeezes him hard and stands up on her tiptoes, kissing him on his cheek. "Oh please, like it would've mattered either way. I don't think Ledger even owns a color other than black, and you never show up in anything less than a ten-thousand-dollar suit."

I'm about to defend myself and let everyone know that while I definitely don't own any pastel clothing, I wear colors other than black, when the most beautiful woman in the world walks into our suite. *Sloane.* I'm completely caught off guard. So *this* is Mom's friend. I have indeed been giving her space while I was gone. I obviously had a tracker put in her new car, but unless the location is somewhere I have flagged, it won't alert me. That goes for her phone as well. I only have certain contacts and words set for alerts, and nothing has popped up. I clearly didn't think that my *mother's* number needed to be added to that list. Now I'm standing here, eyes and mouth wide open, looking like I've seen a ghost.

She's *stunning*. Her hair is pulled half back with a pale pink bow, matching the color of her dress. Her long platinum-blonde hair falls down her back in loose curls. Her silky pink dress is not quite floor length, but it hits well below her knees, showcasing the bottom of her muscular calves, which are enhanced by the strappy nude heels on her feet. The cowl neckline, low back, and slit up to her right thigh show just enough skin to maintain a tasteful look. She *actually* looks like a piece of cake. One that I would love to indulge in. *Let them eat cake indeed.*

Mom immediately walks over to greet her. "Sloane, darling! You made it! We are so happy to have you here. And I see you got my dress code memo. Oh darling, your outfit, *I die.*"

Sloane's cheeks blush to match the color of her dress as my mother continues to gush over her beauty. It's obvious she isn't used to compliments, and that breaks my heart a little every time I see her struggle to accept one.

I pull myself together and walk to her as suavely as I can. I'm no Prince Charming, but my girl looks like a literal princess today, and I can't help but try to match her energy.

"Angel." I take Sloane's hand in mine and gently kiss her knuckles. "You look stunning."

This time, her blush turns a shade darker than her outfit. "Ledger! I didn't think I would see you here. Your note said you'd be out of town for two weeks, and I thought—"

"Apparently, our boy was able to get back early." Mom cuts her off with a wink. "Well, I'll leave you all to it. The game is about to start, and I have a few more guests to welcome before we all take our seats."

I notice I'm still holding Sloane's hand in mine, but instead of letting it go, I interlace our fingers and lead her toward the seats. I should grab two in the front row since I'm sure she's never been in one of the boxes before and would appreciate the view, but I don't. *She'll be here for any game she wants to be for the rest of her life.* Instead, I lead us to the table seats in the very back. They're arranged behind the rest of the seats, and the counter blocks anyone's view of where my hands might roam. I help her into the seat against the wall and sit to her right, giving myself access to the side of her dress with that deliciously high slit.

As soon as we're both seated, I lightly wrap my arm around her shoulders and pull her body close to mine.

"If you didn't know I was coming today, who, pray tell, were you wearing that scrumptious dress for?" I whisper in her ear.

Her eyes squint. "I've already told you, I dress for myself. I never get a chance to wear something like this, and I thought, given the theme of the party Blanche, er, your mom was planning, this would work."

"Mmm, the only other person you're allowed to dress for other than myself of course," I say, lightly running my hand up and down her arm.

"*Allowed?* Since when have you had the authority to *allow* me to do anything?" she snaps.

"Since you're *mine.*" I notice how her breathing halts, her skin pebbles into goose bumps, and her pupils dilate.

Her mouth opens to no doubt protest my statement when Margot walks up behind us.

"And who is *this* lovely young lady?" She has a grin on her face that reaches from ear to ear.

She's never actually seen me with a woman. I dated around in high school, but I never brought them home. And I sure as hell haven't been with anyone longer than a night in the past decade.

"Margot," I say in a tone that hopefully reminds her to *behave*. "This is Sloane, she's my—"

"I'm his friend." Sloane cuts me off.

Margot's eyebrows bunch together, no doubt confused. "Oh, I'm sorry, I just thought...well, Mom mentioned something about Ledger's girlfriend, and while I didn't believe her at first, I truly haven't ever seen him with someone, and I thought..."

"Oh no, I'm not his girlfriend." Sloane giggles.

Something about that enrages me. Girlfriend seems like such an inferior title to what she actually is. Honestly, there isn't a word in the English language that does her justice. Lover, fiancée, even wife all pale compared to the hold she has on my soul.

"No, she's just *mine*. In fact, we were just discussing that. Isn't that right, *Angel?*"

We stare at each other for what feels like forever. The heat in her eyes is rising, and it's not from anger. I know if I pulled her out of this room right now and dragged us to the en suite restroom, I could have her. From the look in her eyes, she would let me take her against the wall raw and hard.

"Okay, weirdo." My sister interrupts the moment as well as my thoughts. "Anyway, Sloane, it's so nice to meet you! I know Ledger mentioned it earlier, but my name is Margot. I'm his sister." Margot tosses her things down in the seat below us, then sits in the chair beside me before calling Henry over to meet Sloane.

The moment Sloane sees Henry, her face turns beet red. He has no idea she saw him that night in the club, but I'm sure she's embarrassed, nonetheless.

"Hello, Sloane. It's very nice to meet you. I'm Henry. I hope Ledger hasn't slandered my name beyond repair. Lies, no doubt."

She laughs. "Hi Henry! I'm Sloane. I'm Ledger's—"

"Not girlfriend," Margot interrupts, causing more laughter to spill from me and the girls. If Henry is confused, he doesn't show it. That perfectly built wall never breaks for a moment. Instead, he just waits for the explanation I'm sure he knows is coming.

I wrap my arm around Sloane again, pulling her into me and giving the top of her head a gentle kiss as I see Jack sidle up beside Henry.

"Henry, this is absolutely the one and only woman I'm in a *very* committed relationship with."

Shock fills everyone's face except Jack's. "Oh shit! You must be Sloane!"

He all but yanks her to stand and gives her a gigantic bear hug. The shocked look on her face is something straight from the comics, causing Margot and me to start laughing again.

"This is Jack, Ledger's lifelong best friend," Henry explains. "And I assure you, whatever wild tales Ledger has told you about him are all very much true."

She smiles at that and returns Jack's hug. "It's very nice to meet you, Jack. It's very nice to meet *everyone.* I really have heard so much about you. I can tell you mean a great deal to Ledger."

At that, the game begins, and everyone takes their seat, leaving Sloane and me to sit alone in the back.

I move my hand to her thigh, playing with the hem of her dress. "So how do you like the car?"

"You mean the tank?" She shakes her head. "It's too much is what it is. But...it's very nice. I haven't gotten used to the size of it, though."

I smirk, sliding my hand up higher on her leg. "Oh, we'll get you used to the size, don't you worry."

"Ledger!" she whisper-yells, slapping me lightly on my bicep. "I'm talking about the car, not your, your *dick.*"

I remove my hand from her thigh and take her hand, guiding it to the bulge in my pants. "Oh? Does my little virgin really think she doesn't need time to adjust to all this dick?" I whisper into her ear. "If that's the case, we can go to that bathroom in the corner right now, and you can show me how you can take my cock like the good girl I know you are."

I pull back to look in her eyes, and just as I thought, her pupils are dilated. We stay locked in a trance for a moment before she lets out a breath and shakes her head.

"Really, thank you for the car. I don't even know how to respond to a gesture like that."

Acknowledging this isn't the time or place to deflower my maiden, I move her hand from my increasingly interested dick and give it a little kiss before throwing my arm around her and holding her tight to me. Before long, she has her head on my shoulder, and we're lost in the game.

Halftime is an event, I'll say that much. Between all the champagne and cake, everyone is either high on sugar, alcohol, or both. Everyone is in good spirits, though, even Henry.

Jack has his arm around Margot, and they're hunched over, laughing. "Come on, Henry, you were way better than that guy tossing the ball around down there."

Henry rolls his eyes. He was truly a once-in-a-lifetime talent, but Dad was insistent that he run the business. He let him have his fun in college, but going pro was out of the question. Besides, who needs to play on a team when you can own it instead? Or at least that's what Dad always said. When Henry graduated from college, Dad bought him the team that he was supposed to be drafted to. It was the first asset he sold when Dad passed away.

"Oh! You played here?" Sloane asks.

Before Henry can respond, Jack cuts in. "Damn straight he played here! There hasn't been a better quarterback since him! They went undefeated for two consecutive years, earning back-to-back national championships. He won the Heisman in that second year, but he should've won it both years if you ask anyone who knows anything. Hell, he's got records that have *yet* to be broken. He's the reason Ledger played here, albeit briefly."

Sloane looks at me with confusion. I keep forgetting she really doesn't know shit about me. "I didn't know you played football. I thought you played rugby!"

Well damn, I've certainly never told her that. It seems my girl has done some digging of her own. "Rugby was much rougher, which I preferred. I found football to be too constricting. But yes, when Henry left here with such a legacy, I was pretty much a shoo-in. I mean, I was a decent enough linebacker, and I thought it would make Daddy Dearest happy since he seemed so proud to watch Henry play here."

"Well..." She says, looking at Jack. "What do you mean by briefly?"

We all share a loaded look before I nod at Jack, giving him the assurance he needs to tell her what ended my collegiate career.

"Ledger was...a lot...at that age. Nobody could get through to him, and the coach at that time, well, he's known as the greatest for a reason. He didn't put up with *shit*. He absolutely loved Henry and was more than enthusiastic about another Sinclair boy joining his team. But he didn't expect that second boy to be such a stark difference to the first, erm, no offense, Ledge. They both tried, but it really wasn't working out." Jack pauses to look at everyone and stops on me, once again looking for permission to tell the rest of this story. I nod him on. "One game, Mr. Sinclair didn't show up, and it, well, it put Ledger in a bad headspace. The only reason he was playing in the first place was to impress that man. When the same man who turned down royalty to attend every one of Henry's games decided to plan a business dinner on that particular night, Ledger lost it. He was aggressive through the first half. Warning after warning went unanswered. At the beginning of the second half, the stupid special teams coach thought it a good idea to put him on kickoff. Well, long story short, the guy returning that ball still can't walk to this day. As you can imagine, he was kicked off the team immediately. Mr. Sinclair was furious. There was a huge trial, and he threatened to stand by and let Ledger go to jail. Blanche and Henry both did their best to persuade them, but it was actually Margot whose breakdown did the trick. The Sinclair family paid off the other guy, and nobody ever spoke of it again. Well, until today at least."

Sloane looks like she's about to start crying, and I can't tell if that's out of sympathy for me, the other guy, or herself at being the object of my desire. "Wow, that's so sad. I'm so sorry, Ledger."

I give her hand a little squeeze. "It's fine. I didn't love it anyway. I was able to join the rec league rugby team and had a much better time."

"So all of you are alumni?" She looks between the four of us.

Jack, being the showboat he is, speaks up before anyone else gets the chance. "The three of us guys are. Our smart Margot got accepted into Harvard, though. She finished her undergrad degree in business last year and is currently pursuing her master's degree in fashion in New York. Isn't that right, Princess?"

I roll my eyes at the nickname Jack adopted from us growing up. That's what everyone in our house called Margot as a child, and since he grew up with us, he wasn't exempt. The only difference is that Henry and I stopped when she declared herself a woman.

"Oh, the game is back on!" I hear Jack yell, grabbing Margot's hand and pulling her back to where their seats are. Henry joins them, leaving me alone again with Sloane.

When we sit back in our seats, she immediately snuggles up to me. I think about draping my arm around her again but decide to pull her into my lap instead. She wiggles around to get comfortable, eventually turning sideways so that she can lean her back against the wall.

I note that nobody can see us before I slowly slide my hand up the slit at her thigh. Our eyes lock, and her pupils dilate again. *She wants this.*

My touch gets higher and higher. "Do you want me to stop?" I whisper in her ear, nibbling at her earlobe before trailing soft kisses down her neck.

She moans just low enough for me to hear with the noise from the game being piped into the suite. "No, touch me, please. Please touch me, Ledger."

I move my hands from the outer side of her thigh toward her pussy. Before I even get to her panties, I feel her sticky, wet arousal on the inside of her thigh. "Mmm, baby, you're so fucking wet for me, aren't you? Have you been walking around like this since you touched my cock earlier? Did the thought of me taking you just behind that wall make you this fucking messy?"

She nods, and her eyes plead with mine. "Do you want me to make you feel better, Angel? Do you want me to finger fuck your messy little cunt just a few feet away from my family?"

I move my fingers closer to her pussy, slowly pushing her panties aside as I get my first full feel of her perfect, smooth cunt. It doesn't take me any time to find her swollen clit and start to circle it, making sure not to give it any direct pressure.

We both inhale as her head falls back against the wall. I move my arm from around her back to grab the nape of her neck, forcing her to look at me. I want to look into her eyes the first time I enter her. When her gaze meets mine, I move down to line up with her opening and thrust my finger inside her little hole. It's so *fucking tight.* I knew she was a virgin, but damn, this will be an issue. I can barely fit one finger in, and my cock is... well, let's just say I'm well endowed. Then there are my piercings on top of that. I planned on putting another finger in, but she's gripping this one so damn hard I can't make it fit. At this rate, we won't be fucking until next year.

I'm about to bring my thumb down on her clit again when everyone starts cheering. Both Sloane and I freeze. *Okay, nobody is watching, but by the looks of it, the game is over, and they're about to be if I don't move.* I slowly remove my hand and bring my finger up to my lips. *Goddamn, that's good fucking pussy.*

"Exquisite," I say, removing my finger from my mouth.

Sloane scurries to stand, and I help steady her.

"Next time, Angel," I whisper into her ear before my family makes their way over to us to celebrate our win.

Chapter Fifteen

Sloane

I haven't seen Ledger since Saturday. Four of the longest days of my life. Not that we haven't talked on the phone every day. And I don't mean just texts, although we definitely text all day long. But every evening, when I'm done with class and he's done with work, a food delivery will show up at my door from the same place he's eating, and we video chat. All night. He watches me get ready for bed. We talk while I take my nightly bubble bath and he begs me to tilt the phone down. I only tease, of course, which I'm sure will come back to bite me.

I go to sleep with him telling me stories about his life. Tales of his childhood growing up in the many estates their family owned. The extravagant vacations they would go on every year, where he and Jack would sneak off and cause havoc. Apparently, Jack all but shared their last name. He tells me about all the things he and his frat brothers got away with when they were in college, and about how he got his club up and running. He tells me so much about himself, but I can tell it's all surface level. Every story has a happy ending. I'm not sure if that's just to put me in a good mood before I fall asleep or because he simply isn't ready to discuss his negative experiences yet.

In addition to the constant communication, I'm still receiving packages daily, and this time, he's spoiling me. It's no longer just items on my measly wish list or saved for later. I'm getting entire outfits from brands I've only seen in magazines, complete with matching shoes and handbags. He insists I wear them even though I'm scared to death I'm going to mess them up.

Tonight is a particularly special night, though, and I'm relieved he sent me an outfit. While I wait for Allie to finish getting ready, I look in the hall mirror at the black luxury tracksuit and matching combat boots I'm wearing. I could zip the top jacket up to cover the bandeau bra, but it's for Ledger, so I'm going to be brave. My hair is pulled into a high, curled ponytail, and with a red lip stain, I look sexy as hell, if I do say so myself.

It's fight night at the underground arena, and Ledger is up for tonight's bout. A bracketed competition takes place each fall, and he's been picked to win again this year.

He mentioned his fighting a few days ago, and hearing about how he got started and his training regimen was enthralling. Sheepishly, he admitted that although it began as an outlet for his anger with his father, it's become one of his passions. His record speaks for itself. He's undefeated, and his next fight is tonight. I asked if I could come, and he immediately lit up with a resounding, "Yes please!" His only request was for me to see if Allie could join because he didn't want me to sit alone.

To no one's surprise, Allie was thrilled to be invited to the fight. It was like I was giving her an all-expenses-paid vacation the way she jumped up and down. She swears she was free, but judging by her reaction, any previous plans would've been canceled with no remorse.

She saunters out of her room wearing a pleather miniskirt and matching red bralette with fishnet tights. To complete the look, she has on a pair of black combat boots, but hers are much edgier than mine.

"Damn, girl! You look sexy," she says as she twirls my ponytail. "Are you sure we're leaving there together tonight? Because I'm pretty sure Ledger is going to fuck you into the nearest surface when he gets a look at what you're wearing."

"Ugh, yes!" I blush. "We're coming home and watching movies until we put ourselves into a sugar coma. And we haven't even really done anything yet. He *barely* fingered me Saturday, so no. No sex tonight."

"Whatever. I'm not going to be a cockblock if he tries, though." She wiggles her eyebrows at me as we make our way to my car.

"You look amazing too, by the way. Then again, you *always* look sexy," I say, tossing her the keys. She's the one who wanted to bring the tank tonight. She can drive.

Our drive consists of jamming out to our favorite hype girl songs, and as we pull up to the venue, I'm feeling sassy. I strut into the arena and start looking around for my man. He told me he would probably be in the locker room until his fight, but it's impossible not to hope I get a view of that perfect ass.

I shoot him a text letting him know we've arrived safely, then turn to Allie and start ranking the men we see.

Before I know it, someone is sitting beside me and kissing the top of my head. I jump before realizing it's Ledger. He's wearing black athletic shorts and a soft white shirt. I've never seen him dress so casually, and it *does something* to my insides. If I stood right now, I bet there would be a little puddle on the seat, and I'm pretty sure, despite never having even touched a penis before, I'm pregnant.

"Do I have some competition, Angel?" Ledger asks with a smirk, then leans over to whisper, "You look even better than I imagined in this outfit. *Fuck,* I want to rip it off you and take you right here. The next time you put this on, plan for it to be in a pile on the floor before we even leave the house."

Well, I can't say Allie didn't tell me so. My eyes go wide as they lock on to Ledger's, but the moment is broken by Allie's laughter.

"The rankings are for me, silly. We all know Sloane is taken by *the* Ledger Sinclair, and no other man could ever compete with his excellency." She fakes a curtsy, and we all start laughing.

"When are you up?" I ask as he slides his arm around my waist. *I hope he says never. I hope he tells me he's going to sit like this all night holding me close to him.*

"I'm the main event, baby, so I'll be up last. It's an easy win tonight, though, so I don't mind sitting out here with you until closer to my match." He looks over at Allie. "If that's alright with you?"

"Oh, it's definitely alright with me," Allie says, wiggling her eyebrows. "I already told Sloane, so I'll tell you too. I may be a lot of things, but I'm not a cockblock."

Ledger raises a single eyebrow at Allie before bringing his gaze back to me. "Good to know," he says with a wink, and I know for a fact he's thinking about testing the limits of that statement.

We sit together for an hour and a half while Ledger walks us through each contestant's strategies and what he would or wouldn't change. It's impossible not to laugh as Allie tells us which of the men she would screw and what *her* strategy would be with each of them *in bed*.

Before we know it, Ledger is up. He says goodbye with a kiss to my forehead and jogs casually to his side of the cage. I've had such a good time in the past couple of hours, I've forgotten to be nervous for him. *For him because someone has to since he certainly isn't.*

My worry is instantly put to rest when Ledger reaches behind his head with one hand and pulls off his shirt. My mouth hangs open. If I thought there was a puddle before, there's a freaking lake now. And I am *for sure* pregnant. With twins probably.

"Oh. My…"

"God!" Allie finishes for me.

I look over, and her mouth hangs open in a similar position to mine. "Jesus Christ, woman, if you don't fuck this man soon, then I'm going to."

"You stay away, ma'am." I laugh. "That man is *mine*."

And she's correct. Sleeping with Ledger has moved to number one on my priority list.

I look back at the man who has been infatuated with me for weeks. His muscles go on for days, and I don't think I've ever seen a better physique. I sweep my eyes from his chiseled arms to his proud chest to his *wow* eight-pack to his Adonis belt that leads... *oh Sloane, don't go there.* I can see the outline of his dick through his shorts, and although I'm a little jealous that everyone else can see as well, I'm proud knowing that it belongs to me. *Well, it* will *belong to me. Hopefully. One day soon.*

Getting my head out of the gutter, I bring my eyes back up to look at all his tattoos. I knew he was heavily tatted, but seeing the full picture is like getting to finally see a masterpiece. *Okay, so I'm technically too far away to make out exactly what that image is, but I know it's sexy.* While there isn't a noticeable thickness to his chest hair, I'm too far away to tell if it's completely smooth. Judging by the dark happy trail leading back down to that area I'm *trying* not to think about right now, I'm guessing he doesn't wax.

I think I've gotten myself mostly composed when he turns around, and *I melt.* I didn't realize a man's back could be so sexy, but you might as well add it to the list of aphrodisiacs: oysters, chocolate-covered strawberries, Ledger's back.

I'm lost in my head when the fight starts. I honestly don't know what I'm watching. Even though Ledger just spent the past hour explaining things to me, I know nothing about fights. All I know is that Ledger's opponent, *Bad Guy*, is punching at Ledger, and Ledger is avoiding the swings. That goes on for a few minutes until *Bad Guy* finally lands a couple of punches. I barely have time to grimace before Ledger starts landing hits of his own. Unlike Bad Guy's, all of Ledger's punches hit home. Within minutes, *Bad Guy* is knocked out cold, and the ref is holding up Ledger's hand.

Allie and I stand and do the obligatory *hug and jump up and down, screaming at the top of our lungs* thing for a respectable amount of time. When I finally let go of her to look back at the cage, a gaggle of other scantily clad women are cheering for Ledger as well. I think I'm about to cry when a couple of them approach him, but he immediately waves them off and makes a beeline straight to me. I feel stupid for even entertaining the thought that he would give them any attention. Like he hasn't stalked me every day like a madman for close to two months.

As soon as he's in front of me, I throw myself at him, jumping into his arms and wrapping my legs around his waist. His grin is contagious, and I match it immediately. "Great job tonight, baby!"

That must spark something inside him because his eyes slightly dilate before he grabs the back of my head and pulls me in for a kiss. The second our lips touch, I lose control. I wrap my hands around his neck and open my mouth to allow his tongue inside. The kiss isn't gentle, but it's not out of control either. It's an exploration for us both. Melting together for the first time. His lips are pillows against my own, as our tongues dance to a rhythm known only to each other. As the kiss deepens, I start to run my fingers through his hair, and *wow, it's so soft*. Just when I think I'll combust from the intensity in this kiss, he grabs the base of my ponytail and pulls my head from his.

"Mmm, are you sure you can't come with me tonight?" Ledger moves his hand to my face and starts rubbing my bottom lip with his thumb.

"Yes, I'm sure," I say.

At the same time Allie responds, "She's all yours," and we all look at each other.

I want him so *damn* bad, but I can't help the intrusive thoughts running through my head. *What if I'm not good enough? What if he realizes I'm the worst lay of his life and never speaks to me again? What if I fall madly in love, and this was all just a game for him to take my virginity?*

I snap back to reality before anyone notices how deep I've been in my head. "Allie and I are going to have a super girly movie night and eat a five-pound bag of gummy bears. It's locked in."

"Damn. Well, promise me a date tomorrow night. After rehearsal," Ledger says as he peppers my face with kisses.

"Yes!" Allie responds for me before we all break into laughter.

"I'm serious, Sloane. It doesn't have to be anything fancy since we'll be coming from rehearsal, but an actual date. I'll pick you up!"

I grab his face with both hands and give him a chaste kiss on his lips. "That sounds wonderful. As long as you let me pick the music in the car."

"Deal. Now let me go grab my bag and let's get out of here," Ledger says as he carries me through the back of the arena to his locker.

Once we have his things, we head out the back door into the parking lot, and since we parked on the other side, we have quite a walk to the car. He carries me the entire way like I weigh nothing, which greatly pleases my lizard brain.

"I'm driving!" Allie yells before we get to the car, letting Ledger know to take me to the passenger seat.

He sets me in the car and gives me another chaste kiss on the lips before stepping back, saying goodbye, and shutting my door.

"You're an idiot for not going with him tonight," Allie says as she starts up the car.

I turn our hype girl music back on, but wait to blast the volume. "You're probably right, but I'm going to be honest with you, Al. I'm scared. Not about losing my virginity or it hurting or anything, but I have zero experience, and he...well, he owns a damn sex club, for God's sake. Change of plans for the night. No more movies. You are going to give me any and every tip and piece of advice you have about sex. Because if the way I felt tonight was any indicator about how tomorrow's date is going to go, I may be in trouble a lot sooner than I ever thought I would be."

"Oh girl, judging by the dickprint your man was sporting, I definitely think you're going to be in trouble." Allie chuckles and turns the music up. "Let the debauchery begin."

Chapter Sixteen

Ledger

It took everything within me not to steal Sloane away last night. Had that fight not been a shoo-in, had I been required to unleash the more unhinged side of my personality in order to win, Sloane would absolutely be waking up in *our* bed this morning. No doubt with my head between her legs.

I look around the owner's suite, taking note of how much it's changed from the first time I laid eyes on my angel. I came back that night to a perfectly decorated house lacking any of the personality that makes a house a home, but as I look around now, I see life. It no longer sports the sterile nautical theme my previous interior designer chose, with shades of navy, black, and charcoal paired with leather furniture. Instead, it features a French cottage theme that I curated myself. Pulling from Sloane's inspo boards yet again, I personally picked out the fluffy cream bedding, white linen furniture, and gold-framed floral landscapes adorning the walls. I found the perfect Persian rugs in hues of blue and green to tie in the cozy blankets and throw pillows I have scattered throughout the room.

If she gets here and wants to change it all, I'll hand her the card. I just want to make her feel like it's a place that belongs to both of us. A place she can wake up every morning excited to get up and start her day, knowing she's exactly where she needs to be.

Tonight is the night, though. I have no sexual expectations, but after our date, I'm bringing my girl home.

We spend yet another practice secluded in our nursery, but there's a tension in the air that hasn't been there before. I'm going out of my way to keep our interactions PG. Sloane doesn't push it either, but we both want to. I can see the longing in her eyes, and I'm sure she can see the fire in mine.

Walking to my car, I help her in before getting into the driver's seat. As soon as I shut the door, I see her shiver, so I grab her hand closest to me and lace our fingers together.

"It's a little cooler out than I anticipated. I think it might rain later," I say, squeezing her hand. "I have heated seats, though. The controls are over on your side."

Sloane doesn't respond, but I can tell by the way she's staring at a bug that just flew into the windshield that her mind is working overtime. "Hey, what's going on in that head?"

"Oh, um…you really want to know?"

When I nod, she bites the corner of her mouth like she's unsure if she should speak her thoughts out loud.

"I'm just thinking that I definitely wouldn't want to get stuck in the rain because I don't think our relationship is ready for you to see how my hair behaves when it's been rained on. And I would probably start to chafe if my pants got wet. And between the wet dog look and the chafed thighs, I'm not sure you'd be so interested in any bedroom activities later, making this an overall unsuccessful date for you. And how, if it's a bad date, you might not want another one. And how I really want there to be another one."

I chance a brief look at her to see her head hung in defeat. She really thinks that I could walk away from her. Like she isn't about to walk into a house that's been fully renovated to her specific tastes. The thought that any moment spent with her could be "bad" is comical, let alone it being bad just because she doesn't put out. Or maybe she's worried she just won't be good, which would be impossible.

"Whoa, Angel. You're way too nervous right now. You're under no obligation to do *anything* with me tonight. Let's just enjoy each other's company, okay, baby? The only thing that would disappoint me is if you were too concerned with being what you think I want that you forget to be the only thing I actually want. Which is undeniably you."

This seems to calm her down, and her mood begins to lighten. I put on some music that I know will get her confidence up a notch or two and we make our way to a local barbecue joint.

"Oh wow! I've never been here!" Sloane says as we walk into the tiny restaurant.

She's looking around at the wooden walls lined from floor to ceiling with the college's sports memorabilia and signed pictures from players, past and present. I know for a fact that Henry has an autographed picture hanging in the small room off to the side of the building, but I'm not about to cause a scene dragging her over to see it.

"What? How have you lived here for over a year and *not* had this barbecue?"

"I've had it before, silly. I just haven't been to the original location. I mean, I've never been without either my parents or, erm, Dean, and they never wanted to come to this part of town.

Sloane's eyebrows pinch together as she studies the short menu. "Where is the rest of their menu?"

"The original location does ribs and ribs alone. You get potato salad, baked beans, potato chips, and bread to go with it. And if you want dessert, it's banana pudding or bust."

"Yes, please!" she says, laughing.

Before I can respond, our server comes to take our order. "We'll start with two racks of ribs, and then a side of everything, each. Oh, and go ahead and bring us two puddings."

We hand the menus back to the server and start to sip our ridiculously sweet tea.

"So, I have a question for you," Sloane says with a smile.

"Shoot."

"Everyone I've talked to in your family, including yourself, makes you out to be this big, scary Tasmanian devil who destroys everything in his path, but...I've only ever seen you be gentle and kind. Even yesterday in your fight, you were completely composed and in good spirits. I guess I'm wondering if...if that's just an act you put on for me."

I sit for a moment, gathering my thoughts. "Well, yes and no. I've definitely earned that reputation, but I've also worked very hard to overcome past traumas. On top of the fights and the club, which you already know about, I see a therapist regularly. The release I feel during fights and through, um, the club outlet, erm, helps tremendously, and I should pay my therapist triple what their rate is for the mess they've sorted out in my head. My mind is always on overdrive, and I mean it when I say that looking into your eyes that day on my bike was the first time I had felt peace in years. You've helped more than the other outlets combined, and tenfold at that, Angel. I know I can come across as obsessive, and honestly, I do struggle with that. But all the time I've not only spent with you but also thinking about you has done wonders. I've never acted like that around you because I've never felt *out of control* around you."

"Oh." Sloane's mouth is parted slightly as she stares at me in disbelief.

Our food arrives at our table before we can continue our conversation. I watch in awe as Sloane devours a whole rack of ribs as well as the rest of her sides. I don't think I've ever seen her eat so enthusiastically, and I feel pride in my restaurant of choice for our date. Sloane doesn't say a word until the last bit of her dessert is cleaned from the bowl. "Wow, that was amazing! Way better than the other location in town!"

"It's a classic for a reason," I agree as I sign the bill.

As soon as we're back in the car, "Mom" lights up the dashboard screen. "Hey, Mom. You're on speaker in the car. Sloane is here."

Sloane greets her with an enthusiastic, "Hi, Blanche!"

"Oh, hello darlings! I'm so sorry if I'm interrupting your night. It looks like the costumes were just delivered, and I'm about to get on a plane. Is there any way at all the two of you could swing back by the church, bring the boxes into the dress rehearsal room, and do an inventory check so I can let them know if there are any mistakes? I think you have a key, yes?"

I sigh internally at this slight delay. I'm beyond ready to bring my angel home, but there is no way I'm about to get out of helping Mom, especially with Sloane now involved in the discussion. "No problem. Yes, I have a key. We're leaving dinner now, so we should be there in twenty."

We all say our goodbyes as we make our way to *not home.*

"Okay, so we're missing one supporting angel, two donkeys, and a wise man costume. I think we have everything else," I say, looking down at the mountain of clothing strewn across the room.

"What is *this?*" Sloane questions as she holds up her angel costume from my pile. "What happened to a white sheet draped over you with cutouts for your arms and a halo headband?"

"I believe this is what Blanche Sinclair has you wearing on your 'date with the devil.' Although by the look of this dress, I'm not sure who's supposed to be seducing who."

Sloane continues to stare skeptically at the dress as I walk over to her. I grab a strand of hair and push it behind her ear, leaning in to whisper, "Go try it on, and we can put that theory to the test."

Her body shivers as my breath hits her neck, and a smirk forms on her face. "And what does the winner get?"

"Oh, I think you'll find that there are *only* winners in this game, Angel." I move both of my hands to cup her face as I lean in to give her a kiss.

The moment our lips touch, she opens her mouth enough to allow my tongue inside. I will never get enough of the way this woman tastes. Her minty gum is at the forefront, but underneath is a sugary sweetness. Tonight, it's surely from the tea or dessert we had, but I tasted it yesterday too. The girl has a sweet tooth like none I've seen, so it wouldn't shock me if she has the taste of candy permanently embedded in her.

I move my tongue in slow strokes around her own as my hands make their way down from her face, gliding down her body until I've reached her hips. I let myself explore her mouth a moment longer before I force myself away.

"Put it on. Let me see how hard I'm going to have to work to keep my hands off you in front of the entire congregation."

I watch as she walks into the bathroom to change and wait two minutes before she's calling for me.

I walk in to see her looking at herself in a full-length mirror. The second I see her, I know we'll never get through the play with that dress intact. The entire floor-length gown fits her body like a glove, with a thigh-high slit on each leg. The sleeves are full length, but their modesty is stolen when paired with the plunging V neckline. I don't know what Mom was thinking.

"Zip me?" she demands more than requests.

I step up behind her and make eye contact in the mirror before leaning in to kiss the bare side of her neck.

"You win," I say as I trail kisses down her spine. Slowly, I bring the zipper down as I kiss every inch on the way.

Chills erupt on her skin as she lets out a breathy, "That's the wrong way."

I don't respond, instead continuing all the way to the curve of her perfect ass. As the dress falls to the floor, so does her hair as she lets go of it to cover her exposed breasts. Standing back up to my full height, we lock eyes again in the mirror. Her breathing is heavy, and her eyes are dilated.

"Don't hide from me, Angel," I say, slowly reaching around and pulling her hands to her side so that she's standing in her white lacy thong and nothing else. I've never been so blown away by a woman's body, and standing here staring at Sloane has me forgetting what another woman has ever even looked like. Hers is the only one that has ever or will ever exist.

I spin her around in my arms to look directly into her eyes, then lean in for a kiss. I've held back with every other kiss we've shared, giving us time to get to know each other. This is not that. This is a demonstration of just how desperate my entire body has been for this woman for two months.

My hands scour Sloane's body as if the parts untouched will disappear. One palms her heavy breast, and I note how perfectly it fits in my hand. I knead her gently at first, but as the intensity of our kiss increases, so does my grip, and I know I can't continue without taking more than she might want to give. I bring a hand to the back of her neck and use every ounce of discipline I have to break our connection. We're both panting as I rest my forehead against hers.

"Sloane?"

"Ledger?"

"Tell me you want this. Tell me you want me," I say between breaths.

Her arms wrap around my neck. "I want you like I've never wanted anything in my life."

We stand there for a moment, lost in each other's eyes, our breathing the only sound in the room. I pick her up, and her legs instinctively wrap around my waist. I lead us back into the main dressing room to a red velvet bench sitting against the wall.

I set her on the bench and push her back gently so that she's leaning against the wall before kneeling in front of her. I grab her right leg and trail kisses from her foot to her panty line before repeating myself on her left side. When I reach her thong this time, I pull it down slowly until she's sitting in front of me completely bare.

"Goddamn, this is the most beautiful pussy I've ever fucking seen," I growl out.

Her perfect pink pussy is smooth and glistens with her arousal. I lean forward and inhale, breathing her in before bringing my attention back up to her face, where she's looking down at me with as much desire in her hooded eyes as I feel.

"There's no way your tight little pussy will be able to take my cock without it hurting like hell. I almost sent you some bigger dildos to work your way up to me, but I just couldn't deny myself the feeling of having your blood lubricate my cock as I fuck into your virgin cunt for the first time. So here's what we're going to do. I'm going to make you come three times before I fuck you. Once with just my mouth, once with my fingers and mouth, and once with just my fingers. Then I'm going to make you come on my cock."

"Ye...yes...please," she breathes out. The way her body shivers in this warm room tells me this first orgasm will be over before we know it. I bet I can get her in less than five licks.

Placing her legs on either side of my head and licking a trail from her asshole to her clit, I circle my tongue around the swollen bud. I repeat the broad circles three more times, starting right at the bottom of her clit and licking up with a twirl at the end, putting increasing pressure on her with each lick, and by the fifth lick, she comes undone.

Her hands grab my hair, pulling my face into her core with as much force as her little body can muster, so I keep twirling my tongue until her shaking subsides and her grip on my hair loosens.

"That's one." I look up at her with a grin.

I take one of my hands from her thigh and move it to her pussy, rubbing up and down a few times before lining my middle finger up with her opening and entering her. She's much more relaxed this time, and before long, I'm able to fit another finger.

"More, please," she begs as I stroke her G-spot relentlessly. I take that as my cue, and resume licking her clit. I swirl my tongue in circles around her until she's trembling. I know she's about to break so I bite down gently, causing her to *scream* as her release hits. I suck her whole bud into my mouth and continue thrusting my fingers until she comes down from her high.

"Two," I say, moving up her body and sucking a pebbled nipple into my mouth as her body continues to shake. I remove my mouth from her nipple and replace it with my hand. "We got you up to two fingers, but we have to make it to three if you want me to fuck you properly."

She nods, and that's all I need before I move my other hand from her thigh to her dripping pussy. This time, I don't tease, thrusting two fingers in hard and fast, finding her G-spot and applying as much pressure as I can at this speed. As her breathing picks up, I take my other hand from her breast and start working her clit.

"Oh my God!" Sloane yells as her body shakes.

"No God here, remember, Angel? You're on a date with the devil tonight."

The speed of my thrusting increases, and I barely have time to add another finger before she's coming undone.

Chapter Seventeen

Sloane

What. The actual. Fuck. I just peed on Ledger, and he's smiling at me.

"Oh my God, I'm so sorry," I say, hiding my face in my hands. "I can't believe I peed on you."

"That wasn't pee. You just squirted." Ledger chuckles. "And that, Angel, is the only way we were going to get you wet enough to take my cock tonight."

I am blissfully at a loss for words as he walks over to the pile of costumes to make a pallet. It only takes a moment for me to realize he's still fully clothed while I'm completely naked. "Hmm, I think you have too many layers covering your, erm, dick for you to put it in anything."

Ledger turns toward me with a smirk on his face. "Oh, does my girl want a little strip tease?"

I nod enthusiastically before he starts slowly undressing. He begins with his shirt, pulling it off over his head in that sexy way only the most attractive men seem to do. I admire the closer look at his muscled chest, noting the presence of just the right amount of hair to be masculine without obstructing his tattoos.

Next, he makes quick work of kicking off his shoes before pulling his pants down, leaving him in black boxer briefs. I notice the tattoos that dip below the waistband of his briefs before zeroing in on the massive bulge that's honestly a little scary at this stage of the game. I slowly work my eyes back up to meet his as he pulls that last piece of clothing all the way down. A desire radiates from him that makes my pussy clench at *nothing*, reminding me how badly she needs to be filled. I brave a look down, and *that thing is huge.*

His dick stands proud with a slight curve toward his navel. The few veins I can see are practically pulsing. It looks to be the same girth from the base up to the perfectly proportioned head, and is that...something shiny on the tip?

I stand and walk toward him to get a better look. I'm trying to walk seductively when I trip over one of the animal costume heads and fall right into Ledger, knocking him down as well.

His shocked face turns into a smile as his laughter fills the air. My absolute horror is short-lived when I realize we are wrapped up in each other's arms, skin to skin.

I trace my fingers over all his tattoos, memorizing every one of them so that if I never see them again, all I have to do is close my eyes. I notice that the only part of his chest without ink is the patch of skin over his heart. I gradually work my way from his neck to his chest to his abs, tracing both his tattoos and his chiseled muscles, relishing in the way they spasm at my touch. I lower my gaze to his beautiful dick and brace my hands on his thighs before looking back up at his face. His pupils are completely blown, and his breathing is labored.

"How bad did that hurt?" I ask, referencing the two silver bars in the head of his dick.

"The magic cross or the ladder? They both hurt like hell, but it was worth it for the pleasure they bring. And not just for me," he says with a wink.

I look back down, confused about what either of those are. I've only ever heard of a Prince Albert, and I don't even know what that looks like.

Lo and behold, there are seven bars on the underside of his shaft starting about an inch from his balls and continuing every inch all the way up.

I reach out to touch it, looking up at him for reassurance before continuing. When he doesn't protest, I run my finger down the ladder before wrapping my hand around his shaft, or trying to. My fingers barely touch.

"You're never going to fit inside me."

Ledger takes my hand from his dick and kisses it before pulling me close to him and looking into my eyes. "It will fit. It'll hurt like hell at first. But it *will* fit."

I search his eyes for any insincerity, but I find none. For two months, this gorgeous, tattooed Viking with a beautiful dick has been pursuing me relentlessly. He's shown more interest in me than everyone in my life, combined. I'm scared. If it were just the attention from an attractive guy, it wouldn't be a problem. It's that I actually think he's *incredible.* He's kind, and I know it's not just an act to impress me because I've seen the way he interacts with his friends and family. He's passionate, and his sense of humor matches mine. He makes me laugh every time we talk, and he seems genuinely amused with me as well. But most importantly, his soul seems to call out to mine.

I'm scared because I want to give myself to him, but I'm afraid this is all just a game. Everyone in my life who is supposed to love me has treated me as if I'm just a pawn to be used when it was most advantageous to them. That's all I know at this point. On top of that, I've been taught my entire life that my virginity was sacred. That I shouldn't give it to anyone but my husband.

The thought of that misogynistic teaching pulls me out of my head. If I'm going to lose my virginity, it might as well be to a man who knows what he's doing. What's the worst thing that could happen? *I fall madly in love with him, and he leaves me crying and heartbroken?* Ugh, at least I can say I lost my virginity to a sex god.

I press my lips to Ledger's and kiss him as passionately as I feel. It's the only way for me to express how badly I need him.

I crawl into Ledger's lap, wrapping my legs around him, pulling our bodies as close as possible. I can feel his hard cock against my stomach, the metal from his piercings a cool contrast to the heat of his shaft. Ledger breaks our kiss, running his hands up and down the length of my back. "This is your only chance to run, Sloane. Once I'm inside you, there's no turning back."

I nod.

"Words, baby," Ledger says, grabbing the sides of my face and staring into my eyes. "I need your words."

A breathy yes is all I'm able to say before he has us flipped over and is kissing me again.

He starts with my mouth, then trails down my entire body with kisses and nips until I'm shaking with desire. Moving back up, he takes a nipple into his mouth and gives a little nibble before moving to the other.

I'm impatient, pulling on his head to get his attention. "Ledger, please, I need more. I need *you.*"

"You have me right here." He smirks before going down farther and trailing a line of kisses to my core.

His hands have replaced his mouth on my breasts, and he massages them with the same rhythm as his tongue. He's licking my pussy everywhere but my clit.

"I need your cock!" I demand.

I have no idea where this has come from, but I sincerely feel like if he isn't inside me *right now,* I'll die. *Spontaneous combustion from acute lack of cock...*

Finally, I'm shaken from my thoughts by Ledger making his way back up my body, giving me one last tiny kiss to the tip of my nose before his hand reaches between us.

He lines his dick up with my opening and starts to slowly push his way inside.

The pain is sharp as his head enters me, and I squeeze my eyes together in an attempt to avoid grimacing.

"*Fuck*, you're so fucking tight, baby." As the sting subsides, I open my eyes, and Ledger seems to be in pain as well. He's trying so hard to hold himself back that he's shaking.

Do I want him to hold back?

Before I have time to second-guess myself, I place a hand on one of his cheeks. "You don't always have to be in control with me. Let go."

"I'll hurt you," he says, dropping his forehead to mine.

"You'll hurt me either way." I push my hips up, trying to force him deeper inside. "Fuck me like you want."

"Trust me, you don't want me to fuck you like I want," he says as he repeats the pattern of removing his head to rub against my clit, then bringing it back down to my opening, thrusting in just a little more each time. "I'd fucking ruin you, baby."

I haven't even felt the first ladder piercing, so it's going to be hours before he's fully seated inside me at this rate. I need more. I need *all* of him. His mouth is on my neck, kissing and sucking. His hands roam my body. He's everywhere. Everywhere except where I need him the most. Every rub against my clit has me growing more and more feral.

The moment he lines himself up to my desperate opening to, no doubt, give me a shallow thrust, I grab onto his ass, digging my fingers into him and holding him there with all my might. I need him. I thrust my hips up to meet him, trying again to force him deeper. "Ruin me, then."

He pulls back just enough to look at me, his eyes darkening as he growls, "I love you, Sloane. You're my woman, my queen, and I need you to remember that while I'm tearing you apart."

He thrusts completely into me in one motion, pulling a blood-curdling scream from my lungs. I thought the books were lying, but it really does feel like my body is ripping in two.

Before I can adjust to the pain, Ledger bites down *hard* on my shoulder, distracting me, and starts rolling his thumb across my clit. He's *so big*, and it hurts *so much*, but I can feel my body responding to his presence. I didn't think it was possible to get any wetter, but as he remains inside me, I relax around him, producing more lubrication, as if my body wants him as deep as possible.

"Goddamn, baby," he grunts as he begins slowly fucking into me. "I knew you would be exquisite, but this is beyond my wildest dreams." He pulls back to make eye contact again as he stops, seated deep inside me, like he doesn't even want to separate our bodies for the time it would take him to thrust. "*You* are beyond my wildest dreams, Sloane."

Tears of pure happiness join those that were already rolling down my cheeks from the pain as I stare back into Ledger's eyes. *He means that. He chooses me. He's been choosing me for months in a million different ways.*

He reaches down to wipe away my tears. "That's my good girl, taking my entire cock. I knew you could, Angel. It was made for you."

Ledger pulls almost all the way out slowly, and I feel every single one of his barbells across spots inside me that I had no idea existed. I release a ragged breath. "I had no idea anything could feel like this."

But he's not looking at me anymore. Ledger's entire world has narrowed to the point where we're still connected, just the wide head of his cock remaining inside me enough to spread my lips around him. He's as still as a statue, mesmerized. I lean up on my forearms to see what exactly he's looking at, and I realize it's *blood*. And a decent amount of it, too. I assumed the stories I'd heard were exaggerated, and I rode horses growing up, so I wasn't sure I would even bleed. *But I did. And Ledger looks...beyond feral.*

I'm considering whether I should say something to try to break him out of his trance when he reaches for his phone and takes a *picture* of my virgin blood covering his cock. I'm about to ask what the hell he's doing when he tosses the phone and leans back down to look in my eyes, sliding slowly *all* the way back inside me and holding himself there.

"Look at me," he growls, holding my face between his hands. "You are *mine*. This is *my* cunt that's bleeding all over my dick. I'm the only man who's ever going to be inside you. Nod if you understand, Sloane."

I nod.

"You're my woman, you're going to be my wife, I'm going to fill this perfect little pussy up with babies, and you're going to have everything you want every day of the rest of your life. Nod if you understand."

I nod, my pussy clenching around his hard length, feeling the piercings at the head of his dick touching my deepest places as he starts to thrust again, hard.

He feels my reaction and smirks, realizing that my pain is receding and that his words are music to my vagina's ears, apparently.

Who knew she was this into dirty talk?

"Is that what you like? You like me telling you what I'm going to do to you?"

I nod again, wondering if he's actually fucked the ability to speak out of me permanently.

He smirks devilishly. "In that case, I'll make sure to tell you every." *Thrust.* "Fucking." *Thrust.* "Thing." *Thrust.* "I plan to do."

And with that, Ledger stops holding back. He pulls both of my legs over his shoulders, bending me in half and knocking the air out of my lungs as he goes even deeper. He looks down again, no doubt seeing the blood smearing all over us both, and *growls.*

"You wanted me to ruin you, baby, so I'm going to fucking destroy this bloody cunt." He puts his mouth just under my ear and *sucks* as I moan with pleasure. Ledger keeps finding new spots to drive me higher. He keeps his promise, telling me every filthy thought in his mind.

"You're being my perfect girl right now, Angel. Goddammit. This is the wettest, tightest pussy I've ever felt, baby. You did so good keeping it all for me, keeping it nice and tight so I could rip it apart and claim it. *Fuck*. You look so beautiful split around my cock. You knew deep down I would be coming for you, didn't you, Sloane? Your soul was always meant for mine. I wish I had found you sooner. I would've been on your doorstep the day you turned eighteen."

I gasp as he picks up his pace, and his thumb finds my clit again. "Tell me, Sloane. Tell me who you were saving this pussy for."

"You," I rasp out. "I was saving it for you."

"That's my good girl. You're doing such a good job taking this big cock, baby. I know it hurts," he says, more frantic now as he alternates between looking at our connection and into my eyes. "I'm *glad* it hurts. It hurts because no one else has ever been in this tiny little hole, and no one ever will. It hurts because you're mine. My perfect sweet girl to fuck, aren't you?"

"Yes, yes, please. I think I'm going to..."

"That's right. Come on my cock."

I do. I do come, but it's so much *more* than I've ever felt. Having something inside me to clench down on, something so big, so deep, feels completely different from any orgasm I've ever felt in my life. It's as if I'm morphing into a new version of myself, someone who needs this *always* and will die if I don't get it. I'm floating for longer than I thought possible when I come back to feel Ledger slowing down his thrusts as he bends down to give me a filthy kiss, invading my mouth in a sensual mirroring of what he's doing to my pussy.

"That's a good fucking girl, coming on my cock like that, Sloane. Fucking *insane* little cunt. I'm going to have to keep my cock inside of you 24/7 to loosen you up for the things I have planned for us. You're doing so well."

I preen under his praise, my pussy fluttering around him at his words even though she's getting the workout of a lifetime right now.

Ledger moves my legs down off his shoulders, and I wrap them back around his strong waist. We're both slick with sweat from the effort, and I reach up to run my fingers through his damp hair, pushing back the lock that's always falling into his eyes.

He picks up his pace again, and the look in his eyes takes on another edge I haven't seen.

"That's four. I need one more from you, Sloane. Give me one more and I'll give you what you've earned. One more and I'll fill this perfect pussy up with my cum. I know you're not on birth control. I've seen your medical records, baby. You're not ovulating right now, but there's always a chance...so if you don't want me to fill you all the way up and pray to every god I can think of that I get you pregnant, you need to tell me to pull out right now. If you don't, I'm going to coat every inch of you in my cum and then I'm going to make sure it all stays inside you where it belongs."

Holy crap. He's not wearing a condom. I didn't even think *to insist he put one on. I'm sure he's clean with all the testing he requires for his club, but he's right...I'm not on birth control. How does he know when I ovulate? I don't even keep track of that...there's just never been a need. This is crazy, but...fuck it, I don't care. I want it all.*

"Sloane..." he groans, shaking with the effort as his thrusts become frantic. "Where?"

"Inside me." I don't even hesitate. I know exactly what I want.

"Fuck, baby." He's desperate now, alternating between growling in my ear and looking into my eyes. "You have to come with me. I need to feel you choke this cock with that tight little pussy so I can fill you up. Come for me so I can come inside you, baby."

He reaches one hand up to grasp my chin, holding my stare, then claims my mouth again. My sore lips are surely bruised from his attention but still want more. His other hand slips back down to my throbbing clit, and I'm so, so close.

"I know you want it. I'm going to keep you full so that you're dripping even when you're not with me. And I'm gonna put a ring on your finger, and a baby in you, and everyone will *fucking know* that you're mine. And you'll never forget because I'll always be inside you. I'm gonna keep you full, sore, and sated, baby. You just have to come for me. *Now.*"

Ledger slaps my clit, and I dissolve into pieces as he stills inside me while I clench around his throbbing cock. I can feel him filling me with his hot cum as I scream his name, and knowing he wanted to claim me this badly is intoxicating. He's kept my gaze as we both shatter, and his eyes roll back as he continues to come.

"Fuck, Angel. Fuck."

We lie joined as our breathing calms down. *I love you* is on the tip of my tongue. I want to tell him just how irrevocably in love I am with him. Instead, I close my eyes and lose myself in this paradise.

Chapter Eighteen

Ledger

Jesus fucking Christ, what was that? Sex has *never* felt like this. It's more than just the two-month chase or the months of celibacy. I knew that it would be incredible with Sloane, but that was unfathomable. I expected there to be a learning curve due to her inexperience, but that couldn't have been further from the case. After she adjusted to my size, her hips met mine thrust for thrust. Her moans and screams were the most beautiful composition I've heard. If it wasn't for how *goddamn* tight she was, and of course, the blood currently coating my dick, I would find it hard to believe she hasn't been doing this for years. Her body reacted to mine like we've been fucking for *lifetimes.* And maybe we have. Maybe reincarnation is real, and our souls reunite with each other in every life.

I rest my forehead on hers until my breathing calms, then brush away the strands of her damp hair plastered to her face and begin peppering kisses all over.

Before I kiss her lips, I pull back and look into her eyes, combing my fingers through her hair. "Are you okay, Angel?"

She swallows as she nods, but I push myself back onto my knees to see for myself. With a full view, I'm able to see the damage. She has bruises all along her neck and tits from my mouth and along her thighs from my fingers. The bite mark I left on her shoulder has started to swell, and there are small droplets of blood where I broke skin. I make a mental note to dress that wound, then bring my attention down to where we are still joined.

There is *so much blood*. I was expecting, *well hoping,* that there would be some, but this is excessive. I want to stay joined to her for eternity, but I need to make sure she isn't seriously hurt.

As I slowly pull my still semi-hard dick out, I feel every piercing tug out of her tight little hole, and from the way her body jumps a little each time, she does too. She inhales with a pain-laced squeak when I'm finally all the way out, and the look in her eyes tells me she's just as devastated from the lack of connection as I am.

"I'm just going to make sure everything looks alright, okay?" I say quietly.

There's so much blood that I can't get a good look, and I don't want to lick it off until I'm sure she doesn't have any open wounds. I reach down and tear a piece of cloth from the white dress that started the series of events leading up to this and gently wipe her pussy.

She's swollen and red, but no bruises are forming, and I don't see any tears. I let out a sigh of relief before moving my head between her thighs to clean the rest of the blood.

When she props up on her forearms to look down at me, creamy pink cum starts dripping out of her pussy, and I can't help myself. I lick from the bottom of her opening, gently shoving my tongue inside her to scoop out as much of our combined juices as I can.

"Jesus baby, your bloody cum mixed with mine is the best goddamn thing I've ever tasted," I say, grabbing the back of her head and pulling her in for a kiss. I twirl my tongue around in her mouth, and she moans when the taste hits hers.

"You're mine, Sloane. Do you understand me? *Fucking mine.*"

"I am." She nods. "But...does that mean you're mine too?"

"I've been yours from the first day I saw you. Everything that I am belongs to you." I take her hand and kiss it before moving it to my once again hard dick.

"This is yours," I say as I wrap her hands around my shaft. She squeezes hard enough for me to let out an involuntary growl. "I will never even think about another woman for the rest of my life. You've erased the memory of any woman from my brain. In fact, humanity as a species no longer exists. There is only you."

I move her hand to my chest and flatten it over my heart. "But more importantly, Angel, *this* is yours. I've never given my heart to anyone. I've never loved anyone romantically. But I love you so fiercely it burns. My heart aches every time I'm away from you."

Sloane sucks in a long breath, blinking in disbelief before she hones in on my eyes, searching for a lie in what I've told her. "I...I think I love you too, Ledger."

She brings her other hand to my chest as I reach behind her neck and pull her in for a kiss. What begins as slow and tender quickly becomes feverish. When she bites my bottom lip, I have to stop myself from laying her down and thrusting into her again.

"You have ten seconds to get dressed before we start round two," I say as I pull our bodies away from each other.

I watch her scurry over to her discarded clothes and begin putting her bra and panties on. I almost stop her from wearing the white thong home, but I decide I'd rather her leak that beautiful pink concoction of our cum and her blood on it until we get home and I can stash it away in a shadow box.

I look down to pull on my boxers when I notice the bloody handprint over my heart. *I need that forever.* The wheels in my brain start turning, and it takes me no time to decide I'm going to get that tattooed right where it sits over my heart, on the only patch of skin I've left blank. God, if I wasn't already convinced the universe made us for each other, this would do it. I snap a picture just in case any of it rubs off on the way home, then send an urgent message to my tattoo artist to come over later tonight before putting on the rest of my clothes. Luckily, the blueprint for my soon-to-be-favorite tattoo is dry, so hopefully it'll stay put for a couple of hours.

"I guess I'm not wearing this."

Looking up, I see Sloane holding the ripped white dress she was supposed to be wearing in this damn play. I take the dress from her and pocket the ripped piece that's stained with her virgin blood. "No, Angel, you were never going to be wearing that."

I add "lead angel" to the list of missing costumes and send the text to my mom before picking up Sloane bridal style and carrying her to the car.

"Let's go home."

With our fingers intertwined, we bask in the afterglow of our first time together as we listen to the radio. "Where are we going?" she asks as soon as we turn on the interstate headed to *our* house.

I give her hand a squeeze. "Home, baby. We're going home."

Her brows are pinched together as she turns her head to look at me. "This is definitely not the way to my apartment."

"I didn't say we were going to your apartment. I said we were going home." I lean over to kiss her head. Keeping my eyes on the road should be an Olympic sport with this goddess in the car next to me.

"I don't have any of my things! I don't mind going to your house, but I would at least like my toothbrush."

I bring her hand to my mouth and kiss it softly. "You'll have everything you need. And it's *our* house. Not my house. *Ours.*"

I can hear her breathing hitch, but she doesn't comment on the whole *our house* thing. Instead, she just mumbles, "Of course you have everything I need, you creepy stalker."

"Yeah, but I'm *your* creepy stalker."

"Yes, you are!" she says, laughing, before turning to me seriously. "You better not stalk anyone else, ever again."

"I promise, Angel. It's only you and me from now on."

I've barely parked my car before I'm jogging around to Sloane's door to open it and scoop her into my arms. Her eyes have been wide since we turned into the driveway, and all she's been able to say is "wow". I've been waiting for weeks to give her a tour of her new home, but right now, I need to get her in a warm bath.

Her "wows" continue to our en suite bathroom, and if she doesn't stop craning her head to look around at everything, I'll be treating a sprained neck as well as a swollen pussy tonight.

"I'll give you a tour of everything later," I assure her. "We've got a nice hot bubble bath to get to."

The mention of a bath relaxes her. "If you insist."

I carry her through our bedroom and smirk when I notice the surprise on her face.

"Is this your room?"

"Ours," I correct her.

I set her down on the bed before going to run the bath. When I walk back in, I'm confused by the frown on her face. "What's wrong?"

"It's just, this doesn't really seem like your style, and...I was just thinking, it kinda seems like this may have been decorated by another woman. Like maybe an ex of yours or something."

Fuck. I didn't think about how that would look. I was so focused on making this room *hers* that it never crossed my mind. Of *course* she would think another woman decorated this.

I walk over to her and start removing her clothes. "I renovated this entire house to meet your tastes, this room included. In fact, this is the first room I've had that *hasn't* been decorated by a woman. And by woman, I mean either my mom or an interior designer. I just wanted you to feel at home when I finally got you here. I picked out everything myself," I say with a proud grin. I grab her face and turn her attention to me. "I've never brought another woman into this house, much less this bedroom. You're the only one, baby."

I wipe away a tear that's falling down her cheek, then finish undressing her before picking her up again and carrying her into the bathroom. I set her gently into the warm water before turning off the faucet.

"Are you going to join me?"

The large clawfoot tub is more than large enough for both of us, but I don't trust myself tonight. "No, Angel, tonight is just about me taking care of you. Plus, your pussy is too sore to take me again tonight, and if I get in that tub with you, that's exactly what it would be doing."

She laughs. "I can't argue with that."

The next hour is spent taking care of my girl. Using the coconut soap she loves, I suds up my hands and run them over every inch of her body, making an effort to be especially gentle over the bruised areas. When I get to her beautiful pussy, I take extra care running my fingers through every crevice. She shivers as I trace my soapy fingers over her clit, and it takes all that's within me not to push this further.

When she's squeaky clean, I squeeze a dollop of her shampoo into my hands and lather her hair with it, spending more time than necessary washing and conditioning, then grab a heated towel and wrap her up in it. Motioning for her to have a seat at the vanity, I find some soothing bruise cream I bought just in case I got a little too *bitey* with my angel. *Nobody can accuse me of not knowing myself.* I apply it gently to her neck, being extra careful where I broke her skin. I can't help but gently wrap one hand around her neck when I'm finished. Her eyes, which had drifted closed while I alternated applying the cream and massaging the back of her neck and shoulders, pop open and meet mine.

"You weren't paying attention to me," I pout, sticking my bottom lip out dramatically.

Sloane leans into my hand, and I give her a tiny squeeze, watching her pupils dilate. *If I don't stop right now, there won't be enough bruise cream in the world for how sore her pussy will be.* I ease my grip, and she rises just enough to press a soft kiss to my pouting bottom lip. "I'm sorry, dear. It won't happen again."

"Dear? Is that what you've settled on to call me?"

She smirks. "I'm still workshopping nicknames for you, honey. You've got so many for me, and I feel like I need to catch up."

"Hmm, how about Your Majesty, Your Worship, or even just Master?" I suggest with a wink.

"Hmm, how about loser or weirdo or just dork?" she teases.

"Touché," I say, smiling at how proud I'll be for her to call me anything she wants as long as I'm hers. But I can see how sleepy she is, so we need to continue her routine so she can rest.

"Is this everything you need?" I ask, picking up a leave-in conditioner spray to coat her hair.

She nods.

I brush her hair before handing her a case and solution for her contacts, and then a pair of prescription glasses.

"See," I say as I give her a pink toothbrush.

"Yeah, I know, I know. I don't need anything," she says, rolling her eyes.

I walk into her closet to grab a pair of cozy pajamas for her and make my way back into the bathroom. She's flossing when I come back in. "Before you rush to conclusions, I bought these for you." I kneel as she finishes flossing, pulling the silk pajama pants up her long, smooth legs. Unable to help myself, I kiss up as I go. Helping to pull the pajama top over her head, I'm satisfied that they fit perfectly. *Easy when you have them tailored to her measurements.* I kiss the top of her wet head and walk to my closet to change into something comfortable as well.

I'd like nothing more than to hold her in my arms all night with nothing between us, but I don't think my dick could stand the torture of feeling her skin against mine.

When I walk back into the room, she's lying under the covers in her pink-striped pajama set, wearing glasses, with a long, wet braid hanging over her shoulder. It's the most beautiful she's ever been. My mind flashes with thoughts of her in a thousand different pajama sets. Or out of them, with a ring on her finger, a big belly...*Getting a little ahead of yourself there, Ledger.* But it feels like destiny. This *must* be how Armstrong felt on the moon, or how Beethoven felt writing his Ninth Symphony. I feel like a complete, actualized being instead of a jumble of atoms making my way through life. I climb in beside her and pull her into my arms.

"I didn't know which side you slept on," she says, nuzzling into my neck.

"This is perfect," I say, kissing her before holding her tight against me.

She lets out a contented sigh and continues to observe the room around us. "I still can't believe how beautiful this room is. You said you picked everything out yourself?"

I give her a sheepish smile. "Well, really, love, I would say you did."

Her brow furrows for a minute as she studies the space. "It does look a lot like..."

Her eyes pop open as she turns to face me fully. "Please tell me you didn't create my dream bedroom from my inspo boards."

"I didn't create your dream bedroom from your inspo boards. I created your dream *home* from your inspo boards, Angel."

And I have to admit, I've really outdone myself. The house is an early 1900s property situated on a hundred acres of land. Sloane's vision gave me the chance to take the interior of the house back closer to its original spirit.

The wall to the right of the bed faces the back of the property and has huge windows allowing a relaxing view outside to the trees. French doors lead out to a balcony large enough for a two-person lounge, and I can't wait to watch sunsets over the forest with my girl in my arms. Opposite the bed, Sloane's luxurious yet understated taste led me to add frame molding to the wall, with a hand-painted wallpaper displaying English countryside landscapes. I wonder how long it will take her to notice that the house in the background of the scene is this one, and a couple who look suspiciously like us are strolling along with no fewer than six children following along. *The painter promised to come back if we made it past six...*

I turn the lamp off on my nightstand and roll back over to cuddle up to Sloane. Breathing in the scent of her shampoo, I smile. I've never been this relaxed. Or happy. Or satisfied. "I love you, Angel."

"I love you too, Devil."

When she finally dozes off, sleeping soundly in my arms, I shoot a text to my tattoo artist, giving him the all clear to head this way.

Chapter Nineteen

Sloane

I wake up to something warm and wet between my legs and a heat rising in my core. Before I have time to realize what's happening, a tongue plunges inside me, and I moan as I arch off the bed. A sheen of perspiration covers my entire body, and I'm shaking uncontrollably. I imagine he's been down there a while, judging by how close I am to coming undone.

He replaces his tongue with two of his fingers thrusting in and out as he works his mouth up to my clit, sucking while he twirls his tongue around the sides. When he reaches his other hand up to pinch my nipple, it's enough to push me over the edge. I hear myself screaming out his name as I spasm out of control, but Ledger doesn't let up until my orgasm has completely ebbed, and I've collapsed dramatically onto the mattress.

I feel his body crawling over mine before a head of black tousled hair pops up from under the covers. "Good morning, my love," Ledger says before stringing a line of kisses from my shoulder up to my mouth. "I wanted to let you sleep in as late as possible since your class got canceled, but I just couldn't help myself. Did you get enough rest?"

"Mm-hmm." That's the only noise I can manage with his lips mere inches from mine. I lean up, closing the distance between us, and he meets me for a lazy kiss. I can't help but moan when I taste myself on his tongue.

He effortlessly flips us over so that he's beneath me. "Angel, you're still swollen today, but don't think I won't push it if you keep moaning like that. I barely kept my control last night."

Grinning up at him, I wrap my arms around his neck and plaster my body to his. We have a layer of clothes between us, but the feeling of his body against mine is equal parts intoxicating and comforting. I want to tell him to lose control, and that I want every dark piece of him, when his phone starts ringing. He lets it go through the first time, but when it starts again, he groans and reaches over to his nightstand.

"Ugh, morning, Mom," he grumbles, still tracing his fingers up and down my spine. "Is there a reason you're interrupting my sleep?"

The phone isn't on speaker, but I'm so close I can hear her response. "Good morning, dear. I was just calling to double-check the costume inventory. You said we're missing one supporting angel, two donkeys, and a wise man? Although if I'm being honest, I think two wise men are unbelievable enough. Maybe we can start a whole new denomination that only puts out two wise men at Christmas."

The moment a laugh slips out of me, I cover my mouth and look at Ledger with wide eyes.

"Oh! I'm sorry, I didn't realize you had company..." She draws the last word out in an obvious search for explanation.

"It's Sloane, Mom," Ledger answers as I feel my face flush.

"Beside you...while you're sleeping...in your bed?"

"Yep," he responds.

"Oh, thank God! I thought we would *never* be able to start rehearsals as a group. Hi, darling!"

I'm mortified. I'm the color of a tomato right now and borderline hyperventilating, but I somehow manage to choke out a weak, "Um...hi, Blanche."

"So those were the only missing costumes?" She repeats her question.

"Those and Sloane's angel costume," Ledger says, giving me a little spank. "There's no way she's getting up there in that dress."

"Oh darling, I was never planning on it, but I do believe it served its purpose quite well."

Ledger and I look at each other with matching expressions of shock. But Blanche hurries off the phone before either of us can say anything.

"I can't believe you just told your mom that I'm in bed with you! She's going to think...we've had sex," I say, dropping my voice down to a whisper for that last part.

"Oh, I'm sure she's counting on it. She's been trying to stud Henry and me out for years in hopes of getting some grandchildren. I'm afraid we were toast the moment she saw us lock eyes."

Ledger stands with me in his arms, and when I wrap my legs around his waist, I feel his growing erection. I give him a knowing look, and he just says, "Can't help it, love," with a shrug as he carries us into the bathroom to get ready for the day.

This is all so new to me. This life where I wake up with a man between my legs, feasting on my pussy. Where he casually tells his mom I'm in his bed, and it's totally fine. Where we stand at the his-and-hers sinks in the en suite bathroom to the room he personally decorated just for me, brushing our teeth and getting ready for the day. It's domestic, like we've shared this routine for years. And I love it.

When I'm finished getting ready for the morning, my phone dings with a text from Allie. *Crap, I forgot to check in with her.* I'm thinking of what excuse I can give as to why I didn't check in when I see she's just sent me: An eggplant, a devil, and a thumbs-up. Before I can reply, another text comes in. *Ledger sent me a text last night letting me know you would be staying there for a while, but girl, if I don't get details soon, I might combust.*

"You hacked Allie's number from my phone, didn't you?" I ask, looking over as Ledger reaches for something from a drawer.

"Of course," he says flatly before closing the distance between us so we're only an arm's length apart.

"I need to talk to you about something, Angel." He's holding something, but his hands are too big to see what's inside. "We didn't use protection last night. First, I want to apologize. I had hoped that we would be heading for an intimate evening soon, and I should have initiated this conversation much earlier. I do want you to know without a shadow of a doubt that I'm clean. I get tested regularly, but I had a panel taken the night after that first rehearsal and haven't been with anyone since. You're also the only person I've ever been with without a condom. I know you aren't ovulating right now so the risk of you getting pregnant is low, but I wanted you to have this just in case."

"Oh!" I say, taking the object from him. It's the morning-after pill. I'm not sure how to feel about this. On one hand, I'm glad he respects my body enough to give me this choice, but my lizard brain was extremely turned on by all his talk of filling me with babies last night. *You do* not *need a baby right now. Sloane. Take the pill and be done with it.*

"You don't have to take it if you don't want to. I just wanted you to have the option. Trust me, the thought of filling you up with babies makes me feral."

Well, there goes all my reasoning. Lizard brain for the win.

I swear I see his eyes darken when I shake my head and hand him back the box. "Mmm, baby, does that mean you don't want to go on birth control?"

"I don't know. I've never thought about it before." *Considering I was basically born and raised to be a virgin sacrifice to my husband, it's never mattered before now.*

"Well, you've got a little while to think it over, but I'll only be fucking you raw, so if you want prevention, that's your only option. Now that I've had you bare, there's no way for me to backtrack and wear a condom. Every time I look at you, I need to know that your pussy is stuffed so full of my cum it can't help but drip out. I'll be dripping out of you so often now you'll confuse it for your own wetness."

Well, damn. I swoon. Literally, I'm falling. I think I had been leaning toward Ledger the whole time he was talking, and without knowing it, I lost my balance.

Ledger catches me and laughs. "Easy, girl. Let's give you a tour of your new house."

He starts by showing me another section of the bathroom that I hadn't noticed earlier housing a shower room with rainfall showerheads. I've never seen so many nozzles and buttons, but Ledger promises it's intuitive to operate once I know how.

He then leads me into a closet larger than half my apartment filled with so many clothes I can't make sense of it all. There are sections for purses, shoes, and lingerie, all filled with pieces I recognize as my favorites, joined by designer items. We dress in matching cozy pajama sets before exiting back into the bedroom.

"Alright, so you've seen your entire owner's suite, where do you want to go next?" Right on cue, my stomach lets out a loud growl, and his laughter starts again. "We can start with the kitchen."

We make our way into the kitchen and *wow*.

He's obviously followed my classic French Country taste to a T in here as well. This is the most gorgeous kitchen I've ever seen. Huge windows face the woods behind the house, allowing lots of natural light. Wooden beams run the length of the ceiling, obviously original to the house. A huge island dominates the space, with plenty of room to entertain.

Ledger hands me a cookbook titled *Breakfast* filled with all the breakfast recipes saved on my social media. "We have all the ingredients and appliances for any of these recipes, and I am your humble sous chef," he says with a bow.

I flip through the book, astonished at its quality and organization. "Ledger, I'm a horrible cook. I can try some eggs and bacon, but I burn that half the time."

His eyebrows are pinched together in pure confusion before he responds. "Angel, you have 12093 recipes saved across your social accounts. What do you *mean* you don't cook?"

"I don't know, they looked good! I mean I've always wanted to *learn.*"

"How did I miss that?" he mumbles to himself as he rubs his temples. "Pick out one of those recipes. We are going to learn together because I sure as hell can't cook either. And choose something easy. I don't want to burn the house down before you've gotten a proper tour."

Laughing, I pick out an easy enough-looking breakfast casserole. I call out the ingredients we'll need, and we get to work. It takes us longer than I'd like to admit to get the oven on, and twice the necessary dishes are dirtied. However, after an hour and a half of hard work, we have a beautiful, albeit slightly burnt casserole and some berries for breakfast. Ledger pours us both a glass of orange juice before taking a seat at the breakfast nook beside me.

"Bon appétit," I say as we take a bite. It's honestly not half bad. The eggs are slightly chewy from being baked too long, but it tastes great.

"Mmm, I only got one piece of shell in that bite," Ledger teases.

"Hey, you were the one in charge of cracking the eggs, mister." I laugh. "But luckily my bite was shell-free."

"It's perfect, love. Seriously, the best breakfast I've ever had," Ledger pauses and runs his hand up my thigh, giving me chills. "Well, second best." He stops right before my pulsing core and gives my upper thigh a little squeeze. "Anyway, baby, you have twenty other cookbooks in the cabinet. Go pick something out for lunch."

I look back over at the mess we've made in the kitchen. "Can we just order in? I think I'm a one-recipe-a-day kinda girl."

"Oh thank God." Ledger exhales in relief. "Now let's finish up so I can show you the rest of your new home."

Chapter Twenty

Ledger

"Alright, where do you want to start?" I ask as Sloane and I put our dishes in the sink.

"What's your favorite?"

I grab her by her waist and spin her around to face me. "Our bedroom," I reply, grabbing her hips for emphasis.

"Well, I've already seen that, silly," she says, wrapping her arms around my neck and looking up at me with those beautiful green eyes.

"Hmm. I think we should go back up and spend the rest of the day making sure you got a good look at everything, *especially* the ceiling above our bed," I whisper in her ear.

Her pupils dilate, and I know I could easily whisk her back upstairs and sink deep inside her. Unfortunately, I decide to be a responsible man and not take advantage of her still swollen pussy. I do, however, take advantage of her slightly parted lips and lean down for a kiss before lacing our hands together and leading us into the living room. "Come on, love, we can start downstairs."

I lead her through the living room with floor-to-ceiling windows made cozy by a large plush sectional, where a grand piano sitting in the corner catches Sloane's eye.

"Your mom mentioned that you play," she says as she walks over to the piano and sits down, running her finger gently across the keyboard cover.

Following her over and resting my hands on her shoulders, I run my hands through her long, silky hair. "I do."

"Do you play often?"

"It's been about two months. I find myself with much less free time lately."

Every room of the house seems to make her happier and happier, and when I show her the formal dining room, she lights up at the mention of her hosting family events.

She gives my large home gym a cursory inspection but squeals in delight when she sees that half of the space has been transformed into a luxurious yoga area for her to enjoy. "I can't wait to watch you work out while I stretch." She giggles, and I have to stop myself from giving her a different kind of stretch right now.

Our double office seems to please her as well, especially when she notices her pink chair and pink computer. She flounces down in the plush office chair and spins around until I'm sure she'll need help walking.

Finally, I lead her up the stairs to show her all of the bedrooms available for our future children. In the center of the rooms is a large, open space that will be perfect for a playroom or a game room when the kids get older.

"How many kids do you think we're going to have?" Sloane chuckles as I explain to her that if we need more space, we can always add on to the house.

"As many as you'll let me put in you, baby. If it were up to me, you'd stay pregnant." I look down at my wife-to-be, playfully shaking her head at me. "Which leads me to this room."

We walk into the last room upstairs, sitting adjacent to our own. You can access it from the hall as well as our bedroom. The nursery. I had to have some walls knocked down and reconstructed, but it's the only room in the house that's still a blank canvas.

"What's this?" she asks, walking around the empty room.

I walk up behind her and wrap my arms around her waist, pulling her taut against my body. "Well, it's nothing right now," I whisper into her ear. "But whenever you're ready, we're going to decorate this for all those babies we were talking about."

I have my arms wrapped around her waist, rocking us both side to side as I start telling her all my ideas for the room, when she quietly asks, "Ledger, why are you doing all this for me? You've only known I exist for like, two months."

I spin her around and stare into her eyes, searching for an answer I'm afraid to ask. "You told me you loved me. Were you lying?"

"No, I mean it. I love you. I've never felt like this, but it's just happening so fast."

I shrug. "When you know, you know."

She starts nibbling the inside of her mouth like she does when she really wants to say something but doesn't quite have the courage. "What's really bothering you?"

"What if I move in here, and in a month or even a year, you get tired of me? Where do I go then? I just pack up and..."

Before she can finish, I grab her face in my hands and kiss her as passionately as I can, trying to show her just how much she means to me. "Baby, your name is on the deed. When I say this is our house, I mean *our* house."

This seems to ease her worry because before I know what's happening, she's jumping into my arms. "I love you," she says, nuzzling into my neck. "Thank you for all this."

We spend the afternoon cuddled up on the couch watching a marathon of our favorite movies. We're on our third when our food delivery arrives.

"Wow, when I said you pick, I didn't think you would pick *everything*," Sloane says, reaching for a french fry.

I continue laying everything out on the coffee table and hand her a paper plate. "I didn't know what you'd be in the mood for, so I just got all your favorites."

"Well, I'm definitely a fan. I'm going to let you pick from now on."

I chuckle, handing her a drink. "Got it. Just order everything I can think of for every meal."

Sloane stops eating and looks over at me with a much too serious look in her eye for this conversation. "Ledger, seriously, no. I know you well enough to know that you'll actually start doing that."

"Hey, just making sure my girl gets fed properly."

After we're done eating, the movie has finished. Sloane is about to drift off to sleep, so I sneak up to our bathroom to draw her a bath.

"Come on, Angel," I whisper to her when the bath is ready. "Let's go take a bath and get in bed."

She immediately perks up. "*We?* You're going to join me tonight?"

"Yes, love, I'll join you tonight." I pick her up and carry her bridal style to the bedroom, remove her clothes, and set her down in the warm water. Her eyes don't leave me as I strip. I climb in behind her, but before I can wrap her in my arms she spins to face me.

I watch her eyes land on my new tattoo, the one of her virgin-blood-covered handprint on my chest. My tattoo artist did an excellent job detailing how every drop splayed across my heart, the color an exact replica of the photo I took when the blood was still fresh. It's the only color on my body, and it stands out against the black patterns beautifully.

"What's this?" she asks as she traces her hand over the tattoo. Her touch is so light I barely feel it through the clear cellophane wrap covering the fresh ink.

"You don't remember marking me up last night, baby?"

She shakes her head, so I clarify. "You got some of that precious blood on your hand last night then touched my chest. When I saw it, I snapped a picture and texted my tattoo artist to be on standby. Then when you fell asleep last night, he came over and put your mark on me permanently. Too bad I can't use your blood as lube every time I fuck you. That was the sexiest thing I've ever seen, you bleeding all over my dick. I guess we always have your period—"

She cuts me off by slamming her mouth into mine, kissing me feverishly. I return everything she gives, our tongues and teeth clashing together until she pulls back, breathless. "That is both the weirdest and sexiest thing I've ever heard." Then she slams her lips back on mine.

I pull her into my lap as we lose ourselves in this kiss. Our hands explore each other's bodies as if this is their only chance. My dick is rock hard between us, and I thrust myself toward her so that it slides between her legs. She moans when she feels my shaft slide across her clit and begins rocking back and forth to get more friction.

"I want you," she breathes, breaking our kiss and resting her head against my chest.

I was going to give her one more night, but fuck it. I've never been so horny in my life. I slide my hand between her legs and rub gentle circles on her clit. Her breathing and moans increase in volume, but as I go to insert a finger, she winces. I move my fingers back to her clit and continue my circles.

"One more night," I say, just as much to myself as to her. "We'll give your sweet pussy one more night to heal, baby."

I continue circling her clit until she comes undone in my arms.

As soon as she's gotten her bearings back, she reaches down into the water and starts stroking my dick. "Let me take care of this for you."

Her touch is electric. Just her light grip alone has me ready to burst. I place my hand over hers and guide it up and down the way I like. It doesn't take my girl long at all to get the hang of it, and I'm so close to losing it. I pick her up and sit her on the edge of the tub, pulling her legs apart before reaching down and finishing myself off. I line my dick up as jets of cum shoot out against her opening.

My dick jerks one last time, and I pull back to look at my masterpiece. I groan in pleasure as I see most of my cum sitting in her pussy. I use one finger to gently push it in deeper before scooping what missed her hole and pushing it in as well, then give her clit a gentle kiss before lowering her back down in the tub.

I wash her body and then my own as we sit in silence, both still in the haze of our orgasms. I get out of the bath and dry off, then help her out and hand her a towel as I go to her closet to grab her pajamas. When we are finally done getting ready for bed, Sloane looks down at what I've laid out for her.

"Um, Ledger?" she asks, breaking the silence.

"Yes, love?

"Can I sleep in one of your shirts tonight?"

I give her the biggest grin. "Absolutely," I say, grabbing an old cotton shirt of mine.

I walk it over to her and put it over her head. "Only one rule, though, baby. No panties. I don't want anything in my way if I wake up hungry in the middle of the night."

Her eyes darken with lust. "You promise?"

"I promise, Angel," I whisper before pressing a kiss to her forehead as she cuddles up to me, and I turn off the lamp. *My paradise.*

I wake to the sound of Sloane moaning. Before I realize what's going on, my dick is at full attention, ready to service the woman writhing in my arms like a cat in heat. *Down, boy, it's just a dream.*

The more she moans and pleads, the less discipline I have to keep my hands off her. *She needs this. She's literally begging me to help her. Just your fingers. Just her clit. You don't even have to go anywhere near her tight little hole.*

I move my hand to her swollen bud, and *Jesus Christ,* she's soaking wet. I can't help myself as I move my fingers lower to the source of her arousal, and *fuck,* she's dripping. She arches her back, forcing her ass into me as I slowly slide a finger inside her, the extra pressure causing my cock to pulse. He *needs* her.

Rolling her onto her back, I easily slide another finger inside her drenched pussy, thrusting in and out before daring to add a third. Whatever she's dreaming about has her soaking wet, and because she's asleep, her pussy is relaxed enough that I can fit three fingers inside her with ease.

She lets out a groan in protest as I remove my fingers to spread her legs, and sit on my knees between them. I run my dick up and down her pussy, growling as my piercings run over her folds.

I need more.

Just the head, I tell myself as I push my head against her opening, and to my surprise, it slides in effortlessly. I allow myself only a moment. I know if I stay any longer, I won't be able to help myself. I'm about to pull back when I hear her soft little voice.

"Please, Ledger, more."

I freeze. It's still too dark to see if she's awake, so I reach over to turn the lamp on and see her glossy green eyes staring back at me.

She wraps her legs around me and tries to use them to pull me in deeper. "Please don't stop. I'll be fine. You can just be gentle."

Can I be gentle? "Gentle" isn't really my thing. I don't know that I've ever fucked gently. I've only ever, well, *fucked*.

It only takes another breathless "please" before I'm sliding inside her pussy. *Almost* effortlessly. She's still tight as fuck. I rest one hand on the headboard to support my weight and use my other hand to explore her body, stopping to grab one of her heavy breasts.

I'm stroking in and out of her as gently as I can, and it's the perfect mix of torture and euphoria. I usually go straight into fucking hard, but this is so much more. While I still want to go harder and faster in a natural search of release, this pace allows me to feel her pussy grip around me in a way I haven't before. Instead of screams of pleasure laced with pain, she's moaning my name in worship.

I help her take her shirt off before leaning down to kiss and suck every inch of her body from her navel up to her neck, never breaking rhythm.

"I love you," I whisper into her ear before claiming her mouth with my own, matching the rhythm of my tongue with the thrusts of my cock. She wraps her arms around me back, now holding me as our bodies come together in a dance of passion and intimacy.

I can tell she's getting close when she starts to flutter around me. I break the connection of our kiss and move my hands to grab her face, forcing her to look at me. "Let go for me, love."

As soon as she nods her head, I start thrusting into her slightly harder and faster than before, maintaining the same angle on her G-spot and pressure to her clit, doing everything I can not to let go until she can milk it out of me.

Each thrust brings her closer and closer, and before I know it, she's coming undone. Her body shakes violently, and her eyes begin to close as her orgasm threatens to take over.

I'm still cupping her face in my hands, so I move one to her breast and pinch her nipple while growling, "Look at me when I make you come."

The pinch is all she needs to explode, milking my cock empty in the process.

Well, I'll be damned. I think I just made love for the first time in my life. *And I'll be even more damned.* It was phenomenal.

I drop my forehead to hers. "*Fuck,* I love you so much, baby."

"I love you too," she says as she runs her hands through my sweat damp hair. "So, so, so, so much." She punctuates every "so" with a kiss.

I roll us over to where she's on top of me and fall asleep with my cock buried inside the woman I love.

Chapter Twenty-One

Sloane

I'm not entirely sure what I was expecting a Halloween party at Rendezvous to look like, but *this* is beyond anything I could have imagined. Jack is clearly in his Roaring 20s era, based on the fact that the entirety of the club is dripping in art deco excess. While there wasn't a dress code, per se, all the waitstaff are dressed accordingly, and crystals drip from almost every surface. It's incredibly decadent, and based on the dancing going on already, people are truly indulging this evening.

Ledger, predictably, already had our outfits ready for tonight, and we're both on theme and on brand for ourselves as a couple. He decided to flip our roles from the church play, meaning he's looking exceedingly dapper and not really all that angelic in an all-white suit, while I'm wearing a pair of devil horns and a black-beaded mini-dress.

He interrupts my awe-filled perusal of the main club space, suggesting we go find the man of the hour and offer our regards before heading to the exhibition hall for the more salacious activities he's planned for the evening. *Not that he would tell me anything.*

Ledger moves to continue into the hallway leading to the exhibition space he's picked for us tonight, but before we get there, we run into Jack.

"Jack! You've outdone yourself, brother. I don't want to know what this is costing us, but whatever magic you're working with the special events is clearly paying off," Ledger says, bringing Jack in for a hug.

"Thanks, Boss. Something about the theme nights really brings out my creative juices," Jack gives me a quick wink, and I roll my eyes already knowing he's about to try his best to rile Ledger up. "And hello, Sloane, dear, you've never looked more ravishing."

Jack takes a step toward me, reaching for my hand to bring it to his mouth for a kiss. I'm not sure what's gotten into me tonight, but I decide to give Ledger a little tease. "Mmm...good evening, Jack," I say in the most seductive voice I can conjure, enjoying the feeling of Ledger tensing behind me.

Ledger takes Jack's hand from mine and twists his arm around in what appears to be a painful grip. Turning him, Ledger gives Jack a little shove back toward the dance floor.

"That's quite enough out of you for the evening, I think," he growls, leveling Jack with a stare that would make many men piss themselves out of fear. Jack, however, simply smirks, shakes out his tux jacket, and gives me another wink before roaming back into the crowd.

Sensing that I need to get Ledger out of this growly, possessive mood, I decide to play up how excited I am to return to the exhibition hall. And I *am* excited. But I'm also nervous since Ledger mentioned tonight would feature a different set of exhibits from the last time I was here.

"Baby," I whisper, barely loud enough to be heard over the music flowing from the dance floor. "Can we go to the exhibition hall now?"

Ledger angles his head to look down at me, and the cold look in his eye transforms into something softer but no less predatory. *I'm just the prey now, rather than Jack.* "Of course we can. It's almost time for the scene that I'm most excited for you to see, so we won't have as much time to wander as the last time you were here."

I give him a soft smile. "Whatever you want, pumpkin."

"Pumpkin? You've settled on pumpkin now?" he half-heartedly groans, smiling as we make our way upstairs. "I thought you had settled on babe since you won't call me husband and you didn't like daddy when you tried."

I roll my eyes at him as we stop just outside the exhibition hall doors. "Well, 'tis the season, you know. It's fall vibes."

He's looking at me fiercely now, with a dark possessive look I've come to *love*, because it means he's *this close* to losing his control. That has led to many orgasms over the past week. Not too bad for Sloane, I must say.

He leans down until we're eye to eye, his stormy grays already blown wide with lust. "I might not be either of those things currently, baby, but I'll be both before you know it, so I suggest you start wrapping your head around calling me both. Sooner rather than later." He gives my bottom lip the briefest of touches, then brings his gaze from my lips back to my eyes. "Nod if you understand."

I nod. God, he's mesmerizing. I'll call him anything he wants. I'm honestly ready to just get on my knees for him right now, but the doors open behind us, signaling the start of the evening's festivities. Some scenes are already underway, giving the exhibitionists time to ease into things before the voyeurs arrive.

"See what I mean about this evening having completely different offerings than the last time you were here?"

And boy, do I. We're walking at a moderate pace, without time to stop and really take in any of the scenes, but it's obvious the Halloween spirit is alive and well in the hall. We pass what appears to be a priest/sinner role play including a confessional booth, a vampire-themed knife play scene, and...what looks suspiciously like a classroom at a wizarding school, with a dark-haired professor sitting at a desk and multiple female students mixing things in cauldrons as he berates their progress. I lift a brow questioningly at Ledger.

He sighs. "*That* is a scene we have a monthslong waitlist for. It'll go on for hours, then devolve quite rapidly into, well... Let's just say they all get very bad marks and have to serve *detention.*"

I giggle, thinking that sounds pretty fun. However, I'm such a good student that it might upset me to receive a bad grade, even in a kinky scene. As we continue, I'm about to ask Ledger if I could find an old uniform to wear and work on "homework" in our home office one day when he turns to me, giving me a contemplative look.

"This is something that I think you'll like, based on our experiences last time. But if you don't, the safe word we discussed is applicable. You'll let me know immediately if you want to stop playing?"

He's so earnest with my comfort, always, but he's never once put me in a situation I didn't love. "I trust you, and I remember my safe word."

He opens a door in the hallway, and we walk toward the viewing room for the scene he's excited for me to see. We didn't miss anything, as voyeurs continue to make themselves comfortable and select their seats. Ledger leads me to a slightly raised, roped-off area to the right side of the room, with an armless leather chair and a padded railing facing the stage.

When a group of people enter the stage and a hush falls over the crowd, I feel Ledger watching me as I try to tease out what's happening. I realize the stage is set up like a...locker room of some sort? Faux lockers, chairs, and a few benches are placed throughout the space. Now that I'm paying more attention, I realize that the group is all dressed as hockey players, clearly just having finished a game.

They're all joking with each other, re-enacting plays from the "game," and stripping their gear off in a way that looks too natural to be a scene. *Is this a real hockey team? What is happening?* It's only seven guys, so not a full squad, but they must have picked the seven hottest players for whatever this is, because holy crap. No man is as otherworldly as Ledger, but these men are damn close. Tall, muscled, glistening with sweat, and providing a buffet for the eyes. Light hair, dark hair, tats, no tats, chest hair. They look rugged too, like a few have been in hockey fights and have the scars to show for it. I let out a sigh that Ledger notices, and he pulls me into his lap to whisper hotly into my ear, "See something you like, Angel?"

While I've been distracted, the hockey players have continued stripping and are now walking around in various stages of undress. Two of them stand particularly close, with one toying with the edge of the towel wrapped around the other's waist. I'm about to ask Ledger if this is going to be a male orgy because, *yes please,* when a door opens and a woman comes into the room. She's looking at her phone and not paying attention to where she's going, until she walks right into a tall, muscled chest and lets out a startled squeak.

"Oh my gosh, I'm so sorry! I'm looking for my dad's office, and I took a wrong turn! Let me just..." She starts to back away, but Muscles has a gentle hand on her arm.

"Your dad? Are you Coach's daughter? Emily, right? He's been talking about you coming back from college for the summer all week. He's so excited to see you."

Emily flushes. "Yeah, that's my dad. He told me to meet him here, but clearly, I have the wrong room."

A man with curly black hair who could pass for Ledger's sibling steps up behind her. "Maybe you're exactly where you're supposed to be. Coach told us you were coming and wanted us to make you feel welcome."

"Oh, that's nice of Dad...Oh!" she exclaims, and I realize Curly's towel has dropped to the floor, and his erection is fully pressed against her ass.

"Do you want to stay with us and let us welcome you home?" asks Muscles, who has also dropped his towel and is sandwiching her between him and Curly.

Emily's chest is heaving now, and my brain finally catches up to what my eyes are seeing. "Ledger...are they all going to...?"

"Yeah, baby," he growls in my ear, "they're all going to fuck her."

Chapter Twenty-Two

Sloane

I watch as the team makes quick work of Emily's clothing, and all towels are dropped, removing any pretense of what's about to happen.

Muscles is apparently in charge, at least for now, because he sets Emily down on one of the benches, kneels in front of her to pry her thighs apart, and immediately starts licking her pussy. Her head drops back, and Curly's dick fills her mouth, while their teammates surround them to get involved however they can. So many hands are on her body, plucking her nipples, using her hair to guide her mouth back and forth onto different men. I realize I'm actively grinding on Ledger's thigh, trying to get friction.

"Do you like that, Angel? She's got fourteen hands and seven cocks at her disposal for pleasure. Is that what you want?"

All I can do at this point is whine. I'm too entranced by the scene in front of me and the feeling of Ledger's hard body behind me to respond. Too late, I realize he was *not* asking a rhetorical question, as he stands me up and bends me over the railing in front of us. My flapper dress is flipped over my hips before I can ask what he's doing, and I've gotten two quick smacks on each ass cheek. I'm catching my breath—because *damn*, that *hurt*—when he sees the surprise I wore for him.

"You little *whore*," Ledger rasps out affectionately, and I feel pleasure straight down my spine at his endearment. My pussy also responds, with another gush of wetness from my already soaked core. "You've been walking around my club all night in this tiny fucking dress wearing crotchless goddamn panties?"

He drops to his knees behind me and sticks his tongue deep into my pussy, sucking like he wants to get as much of me into his mouth as possible.

"I knew you were my good girl, but I didn't realize you were my dirty little slut too."

He rises back up to press his wet mouth to my neck while one hand lazily comes around to play with my clit. "Did you want someone to see? Were you hoping Jack would smell you when we walked in and reach under your dress to grab your ass, only to pull back a *wet hand* because there was nothing to keep you from dripping down your thighs? Or did you want to lean over just enough for a stranger to see how easy it would be for them to walk up and stick something in your pussy? Hmm?"

I really hope he isn't expecting an answer because speech is not possible for me right now. He's still speaking roughly right into my ear, and rubbing tight circles on my clit. I feel like I'm going to come or combust or both any second now. Before I can fall apart, Ledger stops rubbing, immediately killing my orgasm.

"Fuck," I yell, unable to hold back my frustration. "Please, Ledger, please, please let me come, I'll do anything," I sob, hoping he'll put me out of my misery.

"I love hearing you beg, baby. And you're right, you'll do anything I want because you're my good girl. But the answer is no. Sluts don't get to come when they want to. I decide when you come, and you're nowhere near desperate enough. But I do need you to do something for me. Start getting this nice and warm."

I don't get a chance to ask what he's talking about before I feel the blunt end of something at my entrance. He gives me half a second to realize what's happening before pushing what feels like a moderately sized dildo all the way inside me. It doesn't fill me up as good as Ledger's cock, but it's enough to get the job done. Breathing out a sigh of relief, I start to mindlessly ride the dildo before I get another harsh slap on the ass.

"Stop, Sloane. When I want to fuck you with something, I will. I told you, you're just keeping this warm for right now. Don't move."

I freeze, contemplating if it's worth it to get more spanks just to feel some relief and friction with a little movement, but Ledger is already one step ahead of me. He rests his hand on my clit, barely applying any pressure, and nips at my ear. "This could've been any man in here tonight, with you flashing your pussy like a little whore, baby. You don't have any comparison, but this dildo is a slightly above-average-sized cock. Do you like it? Or would you have preferred for someone to bend you over the bar and put the neck of a beer bottle in this needy cunt? Maybe a champagne bottle, befitting the theme of the evening? I think the bar is usually stocked with cucumbers for garnishes...would that have made you happy? You just wanted anything in this pussy, didn't you?"

"No...not anything...just you..." I gasp out, desperate to say the right thing to make him do anything more than the static, possessive hold he has on my clit.

"I don't believe you," he whispers in my ear, "because you haven't stopped dripping since this scene started. I think you're jealous of your little friend Emily up there. She's taking all those cocks beautifully, isn't she? Pay attention, Sloane. Look at what they're doing to her."

He's right. The team still surrounds Emily, but now she's leaned back against one man while he fucks up into her from below. Her head is thrown back with another cock in her mouth, and her nipples are being plucked while someone rubs her clit. Ledger finally takes pity on me and rubs harder against my clit once...twice...then he pinches it, and I'm finally over the edge, clenching on the dildo and struggling to stay upright. Ledger pushes me against the railing and spreads my feet further apart before coming to stand between them.

"That's a sweet little slut...coming all over another cock in my club." He starts to move the dildo in and out of me at a leisurely pace, and I can feel my cum seeping out around it and running down my thighs. "But one cock isn't enough for you, is it, baby? You need two, like Emily."

I raise my head to see Muscles step between his teammate's legs, his hands gripping Emily's thighs to push them back as he watches the man underneath spread her open on his cock. Muscles bends forward, and I gasp, realizing he's aiming for the hole already occupied.

Trying to imagine what *that* stretch would feel like, I clench around the dildo that's still deep inside me...only for him to start talking again, his voice deep and strained against my ear.

"That's right, Angel. If you want to be my good little slut and get off on other cocks, you've got to get one thing straight. There's no way anyone else is ever going to be in your pussy without me being there too. Relax for me, baby. Take a deep breath and let it out..."

Breathing like he commanded, I'm asking what he means when I feel a familiar pressure at my opening. Ledger has the wide head of his cock *right there,* but I'm already stretched around the dildo. He starts to push in alongside it, and the searing pain has me crying out.

"Ledger, please stop! Please...it hurts."

"Shhh...you're doing so good, baby. Relax and let me in. You want to be my good girl? You're plenty wet. Let. Me. In."

He's underneath the dildo, and I know he did this on purpose so I could feel every single ring of his Jacob's ladder. But there's so much more pressure than usual. I'm so much more full. I'm considering screaming my safe word when I hear a low moan from the stage and look up to see that both of Emily's men are seated to the hilt inside her. The view of her, stretched wide around them, is enough to make me push back into Ledger, helping him along as he works his way into me.

He growls and sinks his teeth into the juncture between my neck and shoulder. Keeping his head in my neck and giving me slow, deep thrusts, I'd almost think he was losing control if I didn't know him so well. "Fuck. That's my *good fucking girl.* Pushing back to take all this dick. You were made to take my cock, baby. Fucking wetter and tighter than any pussy I've ever felt...*goddamn.* Who do you wish this dildo was? Hmm? The TA from your bio class who spends fifteen minutes after every lab talking to you about the master's programs? That barista at the café who knows your order and always puts a little heart by your name? Is this what you wanted? You wanted to be stuffed full of cock?"

I have no response but to scream, shattering again because Ledger has found my clit and pushed me right over the edge. My poor pussy clenches around both dicks inside me, and I'm clamping down so hard and stretched so far that it's half pain, half pleasure, and I see white as I ride the tidal wave of my orgasm. I'm vaguely aware of Ledger praising me through it, and fucking me through it, giving me shallow thrusts as I realize he hasn't come yet. Finally, he pulls out of me first, then gently removes the dildo, and pulls me flush against him, my back to his chest.

"You're fucking like a pro already, baby. But you're not done for the night. Bend back over."

I slump over happily, comfy on the padded bench and blissed out, hoping for a nap in my near future. A high-pitched whine steals my attention, and I glance up to see Emily has been flipped over and is riding another of her hockey studs...leaving her ass in the air as the biggest guy on stage thumbs her hole.

"Warm this up for me, Sloane. You're so good at it," Ledger coos, before I feel something much smaller enter me. It feels like...metal? And it's slightly flared, but short, and not enough to really give me any pleasure. It's nice and cool, though, which is soothing to my poor pussy since she feels like she just went nine rounds in a boxing ring.

"Good job, baby. You can't help but get wetter, can you? As long as there's something behind you, you'll bend over and take it. Such a good slut. So good."

I preen under his praise, enjoying my pussy massage, when I feel warm liquid drip onto a place where nothing has ever been. I freeze, but Ledger is undeterred, slowly spreading the liquid with his thumb.

"Ledger, what..." I try to stand and question him, but he stops toying with whatever is in my pussy to pin me down to the railing.

"You want to be my dirty girl, right? This is your next step, and I promise you'll like it. Just relax and let me in this tight little asshole like you did for your pussy. Just keep breathing for me."

I take a deep breath and relax, as his long middle finger breaches the tight ring of muscle. It's an impossible feeling to reconcile, and as he passes his second knuckle, the sensation morphs into deeper pleasure than I've ever felt. Ledger feels the moment I relax into him, too.

"Oh yes. That's it. What a good girl, letting me play with this little asshole. You're doing so good for me, baby. Now, you get your reward for warming your toy up."

He pulls his finger out of me, and I barely have time to wonder at how good *that* felt before he's pulling the warm metal out of my drenched pussy, and slowly pushing it in to replace his finger in my ass. It's tapered but still a little thicker than his finger, and I groan at the stretch.

"Shhh, baby. Remember how good it feels once it's in. You have to breathe, Sloane."

I realize I've been holding my breath, so I let out one big whoosh of air as he pushes the plug all the way inside. I *know* it isn't very big, but damn, does it feel monstrous inside my virgin asshole.

Ledger is silent for longer than he has been all evening, his thumb gently rubbing over the flat base of the plug, sending little shivers up my spine each time. Finally, he's looked his fill, and he reaches around to gently tap my chin and draw my gaze to him over my shoulder.

"You need to know that I'm eventually going to fuck you there. Every single inch of you will know my tongue and my cock. Every hole is going to be mine and only mine. You mark my words baby. But do you know why I'm not fucking it tonight?"

He doesn't give me a chance to do anything but stare at his nearly black eyes as he thrusts into me in one long, deep slide, filling up my pussy completely again and connecting us in a way that will always leave me breathless.

"It's because it's gonna take years for me not to want to fuck this perfect little pussy, baby. *Fuck.*"

His eyes roll back into his head briefly before they snap right back to mine, looking at me with the intensity I've come to crave from him. He grips my jaw with one hand and my hip with the other. His thrusts grow more and more frantic, and I realize he's on the very edge of his control.

"Fucking *crazy* pussy. Will never get over this. *Fuck.* So tight and wet for me, my perfect, sweet girl. You know why else I won't be fucking your ass anytime soon, Sloane?" His hand moves from my jaw to my neck, holding me in place while his other hand snakes around to my clit. "I can't put my cum anywhere but your pussy, baby. I've promised you babies, and I intend to deliver. All my cum is going in this sweet little cunt until every bedroom in that big house is taken. Now, I need you to come so I can fill you up."

His words go straight to my core as my orgasm crashes into me with wave after wave of pleasure. My pussy clenches around his dick, bringing him right along with me.

Chapter Twenty-Three

Ledger

Sloane's body slumps onto mine after milking every last drop of cum from me. The scene continues as I take her into my arms and walk toward my office. Bringing someone back to my office is new to me. I never get too rough in my own club, so I usually only participate in brief aftercare in the exhibition hall.

It's different with my angel, though. I could have lost control tonight, watching her give in to her pleasure so perfectly. She's intoxicating, a siren calling me into the depths of my most depraved thoughts with her song. It took every ounce of willpower I had to keep myself in check...but now seeing her soft and sleepy, I just want to scoop her up and cuddle her until morning.

When we make it into my office, I lay her on the couch, then grab some water and a warm rag to clean her up.

"How are you feeling, baby?" I ask as I run a brush through her tangled sex hair.

"I'm feeling great, but I think one dick might be enough for a while." She smirks up at me. "Especially when yours is basically the equivalent of two."

"That's good to know because I'm the only one you'll ever have." I grab her chin and tilt her face to look at me.

Her eyes narrow. "Oh really? What was all that talk earlier about sharing me?"

"That was all talk. I've never had a problem sharing a woman and even enjoyed it. But just thinking about another man touching you makes me want to cut off his hand." I finish with her hair and kiss the top of her head. "You're all mine, baby."

She lets out a contented sigh and reaches for me, pulling me to sit next to her on the couch. "I think I could sleep on this couch for twelve hours straight."

Too far apart for my liking, I pull her onto my lap and nuzzle into her neck. "Well, if you're ready for bed, I would much prefer to take you back home so you'll be comfortable. But I was hoping to show you off in the club a little more. Maybe grab a drink and hit the dance floor. What do you think?"

She runs her fingernails through my hair, drawing a growl from deep in my chest. "On second thought, you're right. All we need tonight is this couch and twelve hours..."

"Ledger!" She giggles. "Don't you dare! I'm way too sore for any more of *that* tonight. Meeting people sounds good. But...you won't leave me alone with anybody I don't know, will you?"

I kiss her temple and pull her to her feet. "Of course not. I wouldn't let you out of my sight for anything."

With wide smiles on both of our faces, we leave my office and head back out into the club to enjoy more of our first Halloween together.

I'm describing to Sloane how Jack and I decided on the name Rendezvous when a grating voice interrupts me.

"Ledger! Darling, it's been far too long. And to think, our old group was just talking the other day about how you must be out of the game. I'm so glad to see that's not the case."

I turn to see a tall brunette walking toward us. Lenora is a particularly enthusiastic member of the kink community and has frequented our club since we opened. As usual, she greets me with a kiss on each cheek.

"It's nice to see you. Never out of the game, but I have been preoccupied lately. Lenora, this is Sloane, my girlfriend," I say, beaming down at the woman who is so much more to me than just a girlfriend. *I need to propose to her so I can at least call her my fiancée.*

Lenora turns her head to look down at Sloane and smiles. "Slooooane, what a lovely name. How nice to meet you. I can't believe you've managed to snap up *our Ledger,*" she says as she kisses Sloane's cheeks the same way she did mine.

"Yes, well," Sloane says, placing a hand on my arm, "I'm not so sure which of us did the snapping."

She *laughs.* "Well, you don't have to tell me just how *snappy* he can be."

Sloane squeezes my arm hard, and I realize Lenora has a hand on my other arm. I immediately remove her hand and band my now empty arm around Sloane's waist. "It's nice to see you, but Sloane and I need to get going."

She's upset by this, although she hides it well. "Do the two of you want any *company* this evening? I saw you watching the hockey scene. I know how much you love to share, Ledger, and I sure do miss that decorated cock of yours."

I frown at her, removing her hand again. I can feel Sloane trembling when I fully wrap my body around hers. "Actually, Lenora, *that* is a game that I'm fully out of. Sloane will be my wife soon, and I'm fully faithful to her."

I can feel Sloane's body relaxing as Lenora's face falls. "Well," she says, "I'm sure everyone will be disappointed to hear that."

Smiling again and kissing Sloane on the top of her head, I turn us to continue on our way. "Feel free to spread that news far and wide. It's only a matter of time before a ring is on her finger, but until then, I certainly want everyone to know I'm spoken for."

As soon as Lenora is out of sight, Sloane tears my arm from her.

"Angel, what's wrong...?"

She barely lets me begin my question before she hisses out, "Have. You. Slept. With. Her?"

My face falls. For a man who has trackers and cameras on her and has become a veritable expert in her moods over the last couple of months, this was clearly a massive blind spot. But now I see exactly how stupid it was of me not to prepare her to run into some of my past partners.

All I can manage to say is, "Yes."

There is no other excuse I can give her. There are dozens of women we could have run into tonight, and it was beyond irresponsible of me not to have warned her about them. I'm older and more experienced, and she was a virgin last week, for Christ's sake. *Fuck.* I was just so excited to come with her tonight. She plasters a fake smile on her face and meets my very concerned eyes. "Okay! Good to know!" she says, sounding slightly manic. "Let's go to the bar!"

"Are you sure? You seem..."

"No! Let's go hang out with all your sex club friends. We can even play a little game. I can point at random women, and you can tell me if you've put your dick in them or not," she says before stomping off toward the bar.

I follow after her, trying not to cause a scene. When I reach her, she's sitting on a high-top chair, facing the dance floor, and slurping down a shot of something clear. "Sloane, baby," I say, placing my hands around her waist.

She wiggles out of my grip and looks out at the dance floor. "So, *baby*, how many of the women here tonight have you fucked?" she asks before pointing out each woman individually.

When I refuse to indulge her, she huffs and practically runs to the dance floor.

My beautiful girl instantly gains the attention of every man in the crowd. I watch as a guy who looks to be in his mid-twenties approaches her. To my displeasure, she allows him to wrap his arms around her and starts moving with him to the beat of the song.

The moment I remember she's wearing crotchless panties, I forget about not causing a scene and march toward the asshole holding my girl.

"Get your fucking hands off her if you want to keep them," I growl as I rip her arms from around his neck and pull her from the dance floor.

"What are you doing? Let me go!" Sloane screams, struggling against my grip.

As soon as we are clear of the crowd, I pick her up and throw her over my shoulder. She kicks and screams the whole way to the car, but I don't say a word until we're both buckled in.

"What the hell was that?" I say calmly. "You get mad at me and go dance with a random man? To what? Make me jealous?"

"You know what? Yes!" she yells. "I wanted you to feel a fraction of what I felt knowing that there was every likelihood that you had fucked dozens of women in that club tonight. How would you feel if Dean came up to you and commented about how much he missed my pussy? What if it wasn't just Dean? What if I didn't even remember how many men had been inside me?"

I'm gripping the steering wheel so hard that my knuckles turn white. The thought of anyone else touching my angel makes me want to throw up.

"How would you feel, *Ledger*, to watch me kiss the cheek of a man who had made me come? Would you wonder for the rest of your life if it was better with him?"

I can barely breathe, let alone speak. Because she's right. I've always preferred a woman with more experience, but I wouldn't be able to stand the idea of another man making her come.

I remain silent as we pull into the garage. I open her door and help her out before going to draw her a bubble bath. When I make my way back downstairs, I find her sitting in the living room, curled up in a ball, sniffling and wiping tears from under her eyes.

Picking her up, I cradle her in my arms and walk her into the bathroom. I pull her dress up over her head and take off her underwear, then pick her back up and lower her gently into the warm bath where she sits, pulling her knees to her chest.

It's taken an hour, but I've finally cooled off enough to remember how to speak. I kneel beside the bath and put both of my hands on her knees.

"Sloane, your feelings are absolutely valid, and I'm so, so sorry for putting you in that position before preparing you first. But baby, I *need* you to know, there is only you and there will only ever be you. All of the faceless women before you were just a means to release. I will *never* think of anyone but you, love. I swear to you, I wouldn't be able to remember what it was like with another woman if I tried. Sex with you is by far the best I've ever had. I can't begin to comprehend how hard it will be for you to believe me. I couldn't talk for an hour just thinking about you with one other man, and I'm a selfish asshole for being glad I never have to when I have as much experience as I do."

She's still not looking at me, but I can see tears trailing down her cheeks. Seeing her in pain breaks something in me, and I have to cover my eyes with my palms to hide from the shame of what I've done. "Please don't hold my past against me. I love you, baby, please don't shut me out now." I try to say more, but my voice cracks as I fight back tears of my own.

"I love you too," she whispers as she takes my hands from my face and brings them to her mouth to kiss.

We stare into each other's eyes until all our tears are gone. "I'm sorry, Ledger. You've never been anything but honest with me about your past, but I guess experiencing it was different than hearing it. I just got so jealous. I've never been enough for anyone, and well—"

I cut her off with a kiss. "You're *everything* to me, sweet girl. I will spend the rest of my life proving that to you."

After a few more minutes of letting her soak, I pull the drain on the tub and guide her into the shower. I adjust the temperature and ensure the pressure is on the setting she likes best. When everything is to her liking, I pull back to allow her some space, but her soft hand grabs my wrist before I can get very far.

"Join me?"

My sweet, sweet Sloane. We're both emotionally raw, but she still wants to be near me. I'll take that as a massive win and thank my lucky stars she has such a kind heart.

I strip, noticing the heat rising in her eyes as I reveal myself to her, including her handprint over my heart. I'll cover every free inch of my skin in her marks if she'll let me.

Grabbing her favorite shampoo, I thoroughly wash her hair and massage her scalp. After I'm finished, she relaxes and leans back into my chest. Before I can ask if she's ready to get out and get ready for bed, she turns around and looks up at me. She lathers her hands with soap to wash me, starting with my chest, but quickly gets distracted and heads toward my already half-erect cock. It feels like I'm always at least half hard around her, and being in the shower with her naked, wet body is more than enough to have me wanting her. But tonight has been a lot, and the last thing I want is to do anything else sexual while she's emotionally drained. I'm about to tell her we should really be getting to bed when she slowly drags her fingertip through the precum beading at the tip of my cock.

She brings that finger to her mouth, sucking as if she's savoring my taste...*Jesus Christ*...I'm not sure I've ever been this hard in my life.

"What are you doing, Angel?" I rasp out, not sure if this is real or if I'm in a dream.

Sloane is almost bashful looking at me, and I feel my chest seize up with lust when she says, "Can I taste you? I've wanted to, but I've been nervous since I obviously don't know what I'm doing."

I cup my hand under her jaw and bring her lips to mine for a soft kiss. "You don't have to be nervous, baby. Anything you do will be amazing. I've honestly been too obsessed with your pussy to even think about you sucking my cock. You don't have to—"

She cuts me off by dropping to her knees and pressing a soft, teasing kiss to my head. I suck in a breath, feeling like this is going to be over embarrassingly quickly. My angel on her knees for me is a sight that's already seared into my memory as one of the best moments of my life. Before she can go any further, I grab a small towel from the heated shelf next to the shower and place it down on the floor so her knees won't bruise on the hard tiles. She gives me a small smile, then focuses all her attention back on my dick like it's a prize she's won.

Trailing little kisses down the underside of my shaft, she teases each rung of my ladder before reaching the base of my cock and wrapping her hand around me. At least, most of the way around. Looking back up to meet my gaze, I see determination in her eyes as well as nerves.

"You're doing so good, baby. Lick your way back up."

My girl is smart and does as she's told. I'm about to tell her to just suck my tip into her mouth when she surprises the hell out of me by taking my first few inches and sucking *hard,* hollowing out her cheeks and using the tip of her tongue to tease my slit. Nothing can prepare me for the feeling of her hot little mouth combined with her tongue, and when her eyes meet mine, shining with tears and loaded with forgiveness, love, and understanding, I find myself unable to hold on or warn her about what's happening.

I roar out my orgasm, pleasure racing up my spine as I fill her mouth with more cum than I think I've ever produced at once. My chest heaving, I lean over to put one hand on the shower wall and reach down with my other to cup Sloane's cheek as I try to catch my breath. I'm stroking her jaw when I realize her cheeks are puffed out, and when I meet her eyes with a questioning quirk of my eyebrow, my perfect little troublemaker smirks and opens her mouth to show me the cum she pulled out of me in less than a minute.

I huff out a laugh and drop to my knees in front of her, slamming my mouth to hers and moaning as I taste us together. After she swallows the rest of me down, I pull back to look in her eyes. I see pride there, like she knows she did a good job, but she clearly doesn't understand the extent to which she's just rocked my world.

"My love," I groan out, taking her face in my hands and leaning down to press my forehead to hers. "That was...*God.* That was the best blow job I've ever had. I'm slightly embarrassed."

She gives me a little smile and a quiet laugh. "The best? Really?"

I know she finds this hard to believe, but damn, it's the truth. "Really, baby. That's the fastest I've ever come in my life. Even when I was a horny teenager desperate for anyone to touch my dick, I've never lasted less than a minute. You hold that record by a wide margin. I'm still catching my breath. Holy hell, Angel."

She must see the truth in my eyes because I finally get a sweet giggle out of my girl. "You did come, like, super fast."

I give a mock huff of indignance when she starts laughing in earnest, before joining her, belly laughing on the floor of the shower.

I take her face again in my hands and try to convey how damn much I love her with my eyes.

"Thank you for that gift, baby. You have no idea how much I cherish you and every one of your firsts. I love you. I love you so much, and I promise to do everything I can to continue to grow and be a better man for you."

She must see the truth in my eyes because she leans in and gives me a chaste kiss. "I love you too. Now dry me off and take me to bed."

Chapter Twenty-Four

Sloane

It's been almost a month since Ledger brought me here. *Home.* I'm having to shut that thought down more and more with every passing day even though he's adamant about this being *our* place. Even though I've spent every minute outside of class with him either laughing, talking...or fucking, it still feels too good to be true. I'm happier than I've ever been, especially knowing I have a whole week of bliss with Ledger for Thanksgiving break. We're cuddled up on the couch reading when my phone dings with a text notification from my mother.

Mom:

> We decided to come for Thanksgiving. We will be there Monday. Please make sure your apartment is presentable. We can't wait to see you and Dean.

"What's wrong, baby?"

He reaches out and gently tugs my bottom lip from between my teeth with his thumb, running it back and forth to soothe where I've bitten down too hard. "You're scaring me, Sloane."

Taking a deep breath, I exhale and tell him about the text in one long rush.

"*MyparentsarecomingtotownforThanksgivingbreakandIneed togobacktomyapartmentsotheydon'tknowwelivetogether.*"

"Mind repeating that for me? Maybe a few words at a time?"

I jump up and pace around the room, his gaze following my every step. "I'm sorry. I know you'll be mad, and I don't want to go. But I haven't told them I broke up with Dean, let alone told them about *you*. It's out of the question to drop all this on them at the same time I tell them we're *living in sin!*"

"Sweetheart, I think you're right that we need to meet your parents and give you a chance to tell them about Dean, but I don't see why that should keep you away all week. Maybe you can spend a night at your apartment, have dinner and tell them about Dean, then bring them here the next evening. We can even have the guest suite ready for them, play some board games, eat dinner together...what? What's wrong?"

I can feel the tears forming in my eyes, my breathing shaky as I try to make him understand. "You have *no idea* what they're like. They aren't just going to accept us. And if they know we're living together, they'll yank me back home so fast you wouldn't believe."

He practically growls on an exhale as his eyes darken. "Nobody. And I mean it. *Nobody.* Is taking you away from me and our home. I *promise* you that. Let's just have you spend a night there, get them up to speed with everything, then we can all come back here..."

"No! No, Ledger. You'll understand more when you meet them, but this is not a fight I'm willing to have with them right now. It's too much, and as much as I want to just ignore them and live my life...they're still my parents, and I have to respect them. It's not worth it to rock the boat so much at one time. I'm going to pack, and I need to be at my apartment when they get into town."

I turn to leave, but before I can get away, he wraps his arms around my waist, pulling my back to his chest. "Don't go," he says, leaning down to trail kisses from my shoulder to my ear. Spinning me in his arms, he drops his forehead against mine. "Let's go for a ride. I want to take you somewhere."

All I can do is nod as I try to get my breathing in check, but it's enough for him to pick me up and carry me to the garage. It takes no time to get our riding gear on, and before I know it, I'm being lifted onto the seat of my favorite bike...the sleek black-and-red beauty that caught my eye months ago.

We've gone on enough rides that I'm used to being Ledger's backpack. I wrap my arms around him and squeeze him tight before running my fingers up and down his washboard abs. My touch usually results in us pulling off the road somewhere safe and out of sight for a quickie, and I love that I have that effect on him. But today seems different. He grabs one of my hands and interlocks our fingers, holding it against him before returning it to the handlebar, his attention locked on the winding road in front of us.

After an hour of unfamiliar turns, we pull up to a beautiful estate, well away from the hustle and bustle of the city. If the unusually silent ride wasn't enough of a tell, the palpable tension building around Ledger would be enough to know that this place must be important.

He picks me up off the bike and sets me on the ground, then proceeds to take off my helmet. I'm about to ask where we are when he finally breaks the silence. "This is where I grew up."

"Wow...this is beautiful," I say as I look around, taking everything in.

"Yeah," he says, scratching the back of his neck as he looks down at his feet. "It's Henry's now, but we are all welcome to come and go as we please. I haven't been back in...well...years, probably."

"Oh..."

I'm at a loss for words. He's told me stories of his childhood, all of them positive, but I know from Blanche that it wasn't always so. And I can tell by his demeanor that being here must be hard. Instead of asking one of the hundred questions I have about what we're doing, I grab his hand and lace our fingers together, letting him know he's not alone anymore.

Immediately, he pulls me against his chest, crushing me against his body before scooping me up. "Come on, I want to show you something."

We walk at least half a mile before he sets me down on a wooden dock overlooking a lake behind the enormous house. I take my shoes and socks off and pull up my leggings so I can put my feet in the water. "Is this where you used to bring all your old girlfriends?"

I hear him chuckle behind me as he follows suit, removing his shoes, and before I know it, his body is wrapped around mine. "No, baby, I never brought girls home. You're the first person I've brought here. I used to come to this spot when I was feeling sad... "

I lay my head back on his shoulder, waiting for him to continue.

"Dad used to bring Henry and me here to fish when we were younger. Before Jack came to live with us and before Margot was born, when it was just the two of us. It stopped when I was around five, but those are some of the only fond memories I have of him. When I started kindergarten, things changed. I was...different...than Henry. He was so polished and perfect, and I wasn't. Soon after, Jack moved in, and then Margot was born. Things were never the same.

"He already had his perfect son in my brother, and then he had a baby girl to gush over, taking his attention and most of his patience. Jack entertained me for the most part, but the hole was still there. I guess I found that acting out was the only way to get any attention and started causing more and more trouble. It created a cycle of toxic behavior for both of us until there was no way out...I was his disappointment, and boy, did I live up to it. If he was going to be ashamed of me, I was going to give him a reason to."

Ledger's voice breaks, and I can hear the evidence of pain. I want to turn around and wipe the tears I know will be falling down his cheeks, but he squeezes me tighter.

"I always talked a big game about hating my father...I still do. But...but I used to come here and remember. He would toss us in the water, and while I loved it, Henry did *not*. We would be in tears laughing at how mad Henry would get. We would always stay until both Henry and I caught a fish. It didn't matter how small it was, Dad would act so excited.

Anyway...yeah, I would come out here and remember what it was like for him to be proud of me... what it was like for him to love me..."

Breaking out of his grip, I turn in his arms to face him, wiping the tears from his face while I fight back my own. "Oh Ledger...I'm so sorry...I..."

A half smile forms on his face as he tucks a strand of loose hair behind my ear. "It's okay, sweet girl. I'm not telling you this to make you sad. After years of therapy, I'm starting to come to terms with things. I know he loved me in his own way. I just want you to know that I understand that parents can suck sometimes."

His masculinity has never been so apparent as he pours his heart out to me, crying shamelessly in my arms. I'm caught between wanting to ride him or confront him until sadness flashes in his eyes again, making up my mind for me.

I gently run my fingers through his hair before caressing his face. "What is it?"

"It's going to sound silly...because I know your relationship with them is rocky, but you not wanting to bring them around hurt in a way I wasn't expecting. I've never had a woman before, and I'm so proud of you, baby. I'm proud of our house and our life. I want to show it off to everyone I've ever met...and I'm having a hard time not thinking you're ashamed of me when you don't want to do the same."

"I'm not ashamed of you," I say, taking his face in my hands. "I love you so much. I...I'm just trying to manage these changes at a reasonable pace for my parents' sake."

"I know, love. And I want you to know that I understand and that I'm here for you. But I still believe that any parent should be happy to see their daughter loved and provided for. Because I will take care of you. I'll love you and cherish you every day. I promise you that. And when we have kids of our own, I promise that I'll love and cherish every one of them as well."

I nod as he wipes the tears now falling freely down my face before kissing me on my brow and turning me around in his arms. "I know that this will be difficult for everyone involved, but it's going to be okay. We'll get through this together. I'll do whatever you need me to do."

"I love you so much. Thank you so much for sharing this," I whisper, laying my head against him again as he holds me tight.

"I love you too."

We sit out on the deck for what seems like both an eternity and only a moment, wrapped in each other's arms as the sun sets. Something shifted today. I know that this week will be difficult, but I'm ready to face it. I'm ready to face anything with Ledger by my side.

Chapter Twenty-Five

Ledger

Even in my wildest dreams, I don't think I could have imagined what a comedy of errors this week would be. It started with Sloane ripping the bandage off and telling her parents the morning they arrived that she and Dean had broken up. She and I had planned on brunch the next day for my introduction as his replacement, *although it's hard to call me the replacement when he should never have been anywhere near what's cosmically mine in the first place.* Her mom apparently lost her shit at the news of their breakup and spent the evening and most of the next day on the phone with Dean's mom while her dad tried to smooth things over from a business perspective with the Christensens. Then, a kitchen fire at Rendezvous kept me in the city all day. Luckily, no one was injured, but it will affect our operations for at least the next two weeks while construction crews are in and out. Thankfully, I have Jack to handle most of that shit show.

Our new plans for a group dinner on Wednesday were once again thwarted by Sloane's mom, who decided they needed a "girls' shopping day" even though, according to Sloane, she absolutely hates shopping.

Which brings me to my current situation, which is far from fucking ideal. Thanksgiving fights have been a tradition at the arena for as long as I can remember, and although I've never participated, I'll attend to support friends in high-profile bouts. This morning, some fuckers from out of town thought it would be a good idea to crash the action and start a melee involving not only scheduled fighters but spectators too. Shit got out of hand quickly... and before I knew it, I was fighting one asshole while another sucker punched me from the side.

Things wrapped up quickly after that, but it doesn't change the fact that I'm about to show up *barely* on time to Sloane's apartment for Thanksgiving lunch on my bike, dressed in jeans, boots, and a T-shirt showing off both sleeves of tats. *With a fucking swollen, split lip* from the asshole's cheap shot. Sloane has already told me about her mom's pet peeve for punctuality, if only with people she doesn't like. Based on how she took the news of my existence when Sloane finally told her, I'm squarely on that list.

I pull into the complex as quietly as possible on the bike, hoping to avoid her parents seeing it as a part of the first impression. Turning the final corner with a bit more throttle than I meant to, I immediately draw the gaze of three people standing around a turkey fryer. Which can only mean that I'm looking at all three members of the Johnson family, and my first impression is officially fucked.

Since the cat is already out of the bag, I might as well go ahead and dive right in. I pull into the nearest parking spot, pop my kickstand, remove my helmet, and head to see my angel for the first time in five days. God, she looks beautiful. She's dressed a little more modestly since her parents are around, but her Thanksgiving outfit is still so fucking cute. I knew about her embroidered turkey sweater since I was with her when she squealed in excitement and ordered it while online shopping, but I didn't know she would pair it with a miniskirt and ankle boots. *Delectable.* Before I know it, I'm standing in front of her, holding her face tightly with both hands, and kissing her like a starving man. And I am. It's been days since I've seen her, days since I've eaten that perfect pussy, and I'm officially over it. I have my hands around her waist, ready to throw her over my shoulder and carry her off to my cave, when I'm finally startled out of my Sloane-induced stupor.

"Ledger!"

Blinking, I realize Sloane is glaring up at me like she's been saying my name repeatedly, and she's officially had to resort to yelling to get my attention. Oops.

"Hi, Angel," I manage, still trying to escape her thrall. I reach back down for a chaste kiss, but she turns so I hit her cheek instead. *Shit.* I've already upset her. I'm officially on my back foot here, and it's gonna take every bit of my charm to weasel my way out of this one. Not that I've ever tried using my charm on anyone's parents, but surely it'll translate at least a little.

Giving myself one more mental kick in the pants, I straighten up and turn to face the scowling Johnsons, giving them a winning smile. Reaching out to shake Janice's hand first, I immediately remember the bouquet I was planning to bring so as not to show up empty-handed. Nothing for it now, I suppose.

"Mrs. Johnson, it's so nice to finally meet you. I'm Ledger Sinclair."

Her hands and eyes are ice cold as she replies, "It's lovely to meet you too, Mr. Sinclair. Although I can't necessarily say 'finally' since we've only known about your existence for a few days."

My smile fades, but I soldier on, shaking Sloane's dad's hand and receiving a grunt and a glare before he turns back to the turkey. "Janice, I think it's almost ready if you'll bring the pan out. Sloane, go ahead and make sure the table is set for four now that Mr. Sinclair has arrived."

"Yes, sir," Sloane mumbles, grabbing my hand and pulling me into the apartment. She pulls me into the hallway while her mom piddles around in the kitchen. "What the actual heck, Ledger? What happened to your lip? Why are you dressed like this, and on your bike? It's like you want them to hate you."

It's already been a hell of a morning, and this is *not* the welcome I expected from Sloane.

"It's nice to see you too. I've missed the hell out of you. Sorry that I'm not up to your standards today for meeting your parents."

I sound like a whiny bitch, even to my own ears, but I feel like I'm going crazy without her at home, and she's clearly under a ton of stress here. Frustrated, I run a hand through my hair, realizing it's getting a little long on the top, and I could have used a trim and a shave. Maybe she has a point that I didn't bring my A game today.

"I can't even believe you went to the fights this morning. Could that not have waited? Are you okay, or are you hurt worse than just the lip?" she asks, and seeing tears beginning to form in her eyes has me feeling guilty as hell.

"I'm sorry, baby," I say, pulling her in for a hug and giving her a kiss on the top of her head, sniffing her coconut shampoo to ground me. "I don't have any excuses for the fight. All I can do is put my best foot forward from here on out, okay?"

She takes a deep breath and plasters on an artificial smile. "You're right, we need to be a united front or they'll take us down. Come on, it's time for Thanksgiving with the Johnsons."

I wish I could go back to an hour ago when I thought this week couldn't get any worse, because *holy fuck*. I'm wracking my brain trying to remember if my father was *this* bad, and while I'm almost certain he wasn't, it's been long enough that I really can't be sure.

Our lunch started off polite, if a bit stilted, with Sloane's parents asking what I do for work before heavily insinuating they didn't believe me. Particularly in light of the expense of Sloane's car.

Things rapidly took a negative turn when Mrs. Johnson decided to rehash embarrassing tales of Sloane, starting all the way back to when she began to walk.

"I'd love to see pictures of Sloane as a baby, Mrs. Johnson," I say, assuming that she would jump to reminisce over how cute her child was growing up.

"Ugh, she wasn't much to look at as a baby, I'm afraid. She didn't grow into her ears until she was around four, and she closely resembled Scott's father for almost a year."

I see Sloane blush a deep red and cast her eyes downward to fiddle with the napkin in her lap, and I can feel my blood pressure rising. I really thought I could be the bigger person here, but hearing her mom continue with this derogatory bullshit about my angel is severely testing me.

"I find it hard to believe she's ever been anything but absolutely perfect," I say, in a quiet but even tone that immediately has all eyes on me. Reaching for my glass of tea, I continue matter-of-factly, "I certainly hope all of our babies look just like her."

Time seems to slow as I sip my drink, with Scott growing redder in the face than I've ever seen a human and Janice looking like she's seconds from passing out. I'm too scared to look at Sloane, knowing that she probably wishes I hadn't said more than two words during this meal, let alone uttered a sentence implying I'm going to fuck their daughter at some point. *If only they knew what I've done...*

"Mr. Sinclair! Is that why you've suddenly appeared in our lives, stealing Sloane from Dean and buying her fancy cars with what's obviously drug money? Is my daughter pregnant?" Janice is out of her chair now, so I guess we're fully fucking doing this.

I remove my napkin from my lap and gently pat my mouth, remaining seated and refusing to meet her aggression.

"Sit down, Janice," Scott says, pulling his wife back into her seat. Now we're all just looking at each other in a triangle of anger while Sloane puts her elbows on the table and her head in her hands.

"What exactly makes you think I sell drugs, Mrs. Johnson? And please call me Ledger. I'm thirty years old, not seventy."

Even this was the wrong thing to say, apparently, because Janice lets out a disbelieving squeak and almost bursts my eardrums.

"Thirty?" she screeches. "Sloane Johnson! You told us this man was twenty-three and had just graduated last year! Is anything you've told us true?"

Sloane's forehead is now on the table, completely at a loss for how to proceed. I hate that I'm making her life an ounce more difficult today, but I'll be damned if I'm going to continue to sit here and listen to these assholes trash the love of my life for one more moment.

"Sloane likely tried to soften the news of our relationship for your sakes when she told you, and assumed taking our age gap out of the equation might make me more palatable to you. I understand why she would do so, but please allow me to dispel any more false, frankly insulting assumptions you may have about me. I will admit that during my difficult teenage and young adult years, I was a nuisance to my parents, and I caused them no small amount of grief, yes including drugs. I hate to say I have indeed done many drugs in my life, but not for years, and I do not nor have I ever sold them.

"As far as Sloane's car is concerned"—*and her house, and her wardrobe and every single damn thing she will ever want for the rest of her life*—"I purchased it through my very legitimate business. I'm not sure how much she's told you about my family, but my father left us with quite the legacy. While my brother Henry runs the successful company he left behind, the rest of us have used our platforms to create our own businesses to channel our interests."

I look over to see my girl is starting to calm down. It seems I'm finally saying the right things. "And no, she is not pregnant." *Yet.* "I just like to mess with her. You've met my mom, Blanche? Well, the first time my mother saw us together, she immediately commented on how beautiful our babies would be, embarrassing poor Sloane." To my dismay, the condescending words about their daughter seem to lighten the air. "Of course, I think we can all agree what a blessing babies are."

Mrs. Johnson finally speaks up. "Within the confines of marriage of course."

"Of course." I agree with my most innocent smile, squeezing Sloane's hand under the table to portray my true feelings. I finally feel the tension in the air dissipating, giving me the confidence to continue. "Also, I categorically deny 'stealing' Sloane from Dean. He was cheating on her throughout their relationship, as well as doing drugs and committing various other crimes, which I've, to date, avoided going to the authorities about but am happy to do so if I see fit."

Both of Sloane's parents look at me in disbelief as her mom speaks up. "That just doesn't sound like Dean. We've known the Christensens for years. He and Sloane practically grew up together. In fact, if you want to see, we have darling pictures all the way back to when they were in the nursery at church together. There must be a mistake with your findings. I just refuse to believe Dean would do those things. He just comes from such good *stock,* you know how that is?"

My snob comes out as I internally roll my eyes. Both of their families are upper-middle class at best.

Her dad nods in agreement. "Janice is right. He comes from too good a family to do any of that mess. You know, golf has always been his best sport, but he was a great football player as well. A stand-up quarterback. Took the team to state all three years he started."

"Unfortunately, Sloane didn't lose enough weight to cheer until her senior year, and by that time, he was already in college. Can you imagine just how perfect *those* pictures would have been?" *Janice* interjects.

I want to take their heads and knock them together like the *idiots* they are, but a glance at my girl, who's not shaking anymore, reminds me to behave. I ignore her mom's statement and go in for the kill with her dad. "You know, my brother Henry was a quarterback. Played here years ago."

I can see the gears turning as her father puts two and two together. "Henry...Sinclair...Your brother is *Henry Sinclair*?"

"The one and only, sir."

I watch Scott's allegiance shift from Dean to me as we spend the remainder of dinner talking about my brother. Janice, however, is just as much against the idea of Sloane and me, maybe now more than ever since her husband seems to have jumped ship.

Her passive-aggressive comments escalate until she flat-out asks me to leave, asking Sloane to see me out. Once we're outside, I sit back onto my bike while Sloane stands between my legs, gnawing again on her bottom lip.

"I'm sorry, Angel. I know you didn't want me to make a scene. It took everything in me not to throw you over my shoulder and take you away from those horrible people. They don't deserve to breathe the same air as you, baby—"

I'm cut off by Sloane's soft lips on mine once, twice, and a third chaste kiss before she pulls back.

"Thank you," she whispers, "for toning it back so much." She wipes her eyes on her sweater sleeve and scoffs. "I know they are a bit much. I wish I had the nerve to stand my ground, but it would just make everything so much worse."

"Hey." I press a kiss to her forehead. "Don't do that to yourself. One day, we'll talk more about all my shit with my dad, and you'll see that only being *old* and having years of therapy give you the balls to stand up to awful parents."

That finally brings a smile to her face. "You're not old."

"Yeah, well, tell that to Janice." I chuckle, and she finally gives a small laugh. "Can you please come back with me?"

She deflates, and I already have my answer. Running a hand through my hair, I try to calm down and see things from her point of view, but now that I've actually spent time with these assholes, it's a lot harder. Her parents suck, but she doesn't need them anymore. Does she doubt that I would take care of her? Doesn't she realize she has no need to rely on them for anything?

Before I can ask, the apartment door opens, and Janice is calling out, "Sloane, dear, your favorite cinnamon rolls are coming out of the oven. Come back in and let's eat them while they're hot."

Sloane rolls her eyes and gives me a sad smile. "No, I really have to go back in, but they'll be gone soon."

"They'll be gone this time, but what about next time? Are you going to let them continue to make you feel this way forever?" I try and fail to keep a hint of displeasure out of my voice.

She shrugs it off and moves away, backing toward the apartment. "They're my parents, they aren't going away. It'll blow over. At least you've won my dad over. Maybe you can write a devotional or something and get my mom on board too. I love you. I'll text you soon."

And she's gone. Putting on my helmet and very safely coasting out of the parking lot, I hit one of my favorite winding backroads and fully intend to open her up and let the speed carry my troubles away when I remember I have Sloane to consider and ease off. *Fuck.* No drugs, no daredevil bike rides, no Sloane, no fights tonight...none of my vices are available anymore. *What the fuck am I supposed to do now? Deal with feelings like an adult?* Just as I'm contemplating setting Sloane's apartment building on fire so she and her parents will *have* to leave, a text arrives from Jack.

Jack:

> Problem with the kitchen contractors. One of them is married to a city councilwoman and is bragging about how she's running for mayor on a family-based ticket, including ridding the city of "filth like this fucking club."

Feeling a different kind of rage, the kind I can actually do something with, I reply, "Thank fuck. Be there in an hour." Until I get Sloane home where she belongs, this is exactly what I need to keep busy. Hopefully, her parents leave soon. I refuse to wait much longer until she's legally mine.

Chapter Twenty-Six

Sloane

Thanksgiving went about as smoothly as it could, considering my heavily tattooed new boyfriend showed up on his motorcycle shortly after I broke the news that Dean was officially out of the picture.

I'm sitting in the living room of my apartment listening to my parents go on and on about how Dean will probably take me back if I apologize for everything, discounting the fact that they just met Ledger yesterday.

I can't listen to them any longer. "I'm not going back to him. Don't you understand that he *cheated* on me? I'm with Ledger now, and I'm *happy.*"

They look at me in shock before Mom speaks up. "Oh please, Sloane, I'm sure he has a perfectly good explanation for his behavior. As for Ledger, you know better than to date a guy like *that.*"

"A guy like what, Mother?" I ask.

"A hoodlum riding around on a motorcycle, getting all those tattoos, fighting," Mom says, putting her hand over her heart for emphasis. "And he's thirty, Sloane. I cannot believe you thought you could lie to us about that. As if we wouldn't have found out!"

I turn around and roll my eyes. I wonder what they would think about him if they knew he was a millionaire many times over.

"Anyway, that leads me to the great news! The company your dad and Mr. Christensen work for is hosting its annual Christmas party here next weekend, so we'll be staying in town for another week. Isn't that great? As always, family is encouraged to attend. I'm sure Dean will be there, so it's the perfect opportunity to patch things up with him!"

Next weekend? *No.* That's the weekend Ledger and I were supposed to go to New York. There's a huge event at one of the most prominent sex clubs in the country, and he was invited to attend as a business partner. We were going to spend Friday night enjoying the club and the weekend eating our weight in food and spending our nights on the town.

"I have plans for next weekend, Mom. I can't go to the party, and I'm *not* getting back together with Dean!"

This must get my father's attention because he snaps around from whatever TV show he's watching to yell at me. "You *will* be attending this party with us, and if I ever hear you talk to your mother like that again, I'll pull you out of college, and you'll be taking online classes from our house. Do you understand?"

I hang my head and reply with a defeated, "Yes, sir."

I'm able to make it to the bathroom before the tears start falling. I pull out my phone and send Ledger a long text explaining why I won't be able to join him this weekend.

He's been so understanding this past week about my parents, but I can tell it's been bothering him, and I'm afraid he's going to show up guns blazing and cause a scene. *All I want to do is make everyone happy.*

To my astonishment, he replies calmly.

Devil:

> I'm so sorry, love. I know you were looking forward to this as much as I was. This is the last time you'll have to put up with them treating you like that. When I get back, I'm making you mine. Legally. Fuck, I'm going to miss you.

Me:

> Wait, are you still going?

Devil:

> As long as it's okay with you. I would really hate to back out after I've committed to attending, but say the word and I'll stay. It's probably best I'm as far away from your parents as I can be right now, though.

My heart drops in my chest. Ledger has been nothing but devoted to me, yet the thought of him there without me makes me doubt everything. I have to remind myself how irrational my jealousy is. In fact, I know if I told him how I felt, he wouldn't go. *I mean, I'm pretty sure he just insinuated he wants to marry me.* This is a huge opportunity for him, so I need to take a deep breath and get it together.

Me:

> No, that's okay. I'll miss you too. So much. I'll be fine as long as you promise we can go back sometime soon!

Devil:

> We can go anytime you want, baby.

"Sloane!" my mom calls. "Are you just going to hide out in the bathroom all day?"

Me:

> Ugh, I'm being summoned. I'll call you when they leave tonight. I love you!

Devil:

> I can't wait. I love you most, Angel.

I rinse my face with cold water in an attempt to hide my tears and put my game face back on before heading back into the living room.

The week feels like it drags by. My parents insisted on driving me to and from class because I "don't need to be driving a car bought with drug money". If I wasn't in class, they found any reason possible to occupy my time, no doubt in order to keep me from seeing my "gangster boyfriend."

When my parents drop me off at rehearsal, I jump out of the car and run into the church to see Ledger. We've been having group practices since Blanche discovered we were officially a couple, so there won't be much one-on-one time, but I'll take anything I can get at this point.

I find him immediately, standing at the front of the church talking to Blanche, and I take a moment to admire the muscular planes of his broad back. I do my best to sneak up on him, but as soon as I'm within an arm's length, he turns and greets me by lifting me into his arms. My legs instinctively wrap around his waist as I lose myself in a kiss that's extremely inappropriate for church.

Blanche clears her throat, bringing us both back to the moment, and he gently puts me down, but doesn't let go. "I've missed you, Angel," he says before placing a kiss on the top of my head.

Before I can reply, Blanche starts practice, and we sit down at the table where our "date" takes place.

Between our lines, he hardly takes his hands off my thigh. Going from daily, multiple orgasms to nothing has my body igniting with every touch. I have to remind myself it's only four more nights. I'll be back in our bed by Monday. The two hours of rehearsal are almost over, and I'm debating whether I should risk it all and climb him in front of God and everyone when I see my parents walking through the front doors.

Ledger must notice the change in my posture. "Relax, baby," he whispers in my ear. "You aren't doing anything wrong."

I want to believe him, but one glance over at the look on my parents' faces tells me all I need to know about how the rest of my evening is going to go.

"I love you, I'm so sorry, but I have to go," I say when Blanche announces practice is over. I give Ledger's hand a squeeze, fighting the tears welling up in my eyes, and sulk over to my parents before they can confront Ledger.

The thought of them saying something offensive to him is bad enough, but imagining his mom getting involved terrifies me. I turn back to get one last glimpse of my beautiful man before I walk out the door and can see the hurt in his eyes from across the sanctuary.

Me:

I'm so sorry. I just didn't want them to cause a scene. Especially in front of your mom.

Devil:

It's fine. I'm going to go ahead and take the jet to New York tonight. I set up some additional meetings since you aren't coming with me. I'll text you when I get there. I love you.

Me:

I love you too.

I can feel the defeat in his text, and it kills me. Instead of listening to my parents' discussions about the Christmas party, I stare at our text thread waiting for a response that I don't receive until three o'clock in the morning.

Devil:

Just got to the hotel. Gonna get some rest. Wish it was with you.

It's nine in the morning when I see his text, but I reply as soon as I do.

Me:

So glad you made it safe. I wish I was there too!

Ledger wasn't lying about the additional meetings. I've hardly heard from him all day. His last message was at ten o'clock, letting me know he was at the club.

Any ounce of confidence I had about him being there is gone, so I do what girls do best. I lie on the couch with Allie, scouring the internet for pictures of tonight's event in hopes of catching a glimpse of Ledger.

"Got some!" Allie yells, shoving her phone in my face. "Look, I told you there was nothing to worry about. Here are like ten pictures of him just standing beside some other men, fully clothed. Unless he's into men, you're good to go."

I think about him telling me he had occasionally messed around with men in the past and shiver.

Well, that's *something to unpack.*

"Let me see," I say as I take Allie's phone from her. We spend the next thirty minutes zooming in on every photo to make sure nothing seems suspicious.

"I'm sure you have nothing to worry about, Sloane. That man is devoted to you with a capital D. Here, let me make you a sleepy-time cocktail or you'll never fall asleep tonight."

She's right. I could have a live stream video of him the whole night, and I would still feel this pit in my stomach.

He's been to that particular club before. He gave me a whole speech about the possibility of running into someone when we originally planned our trip.

"It's much less likely than me running into someone at Rendezvous, but if it happens, please don't let it ruin our fun. Remember, baby, they are the past, but you are my entire future."

Now all I can think about is him running into someone there and forgetting about me. He's treated me like the queen of his world for the past couple of months, but that doesn't negate the twenty years I spent never being enough.

The first thing I do when I wake up is look to see if I have any messages from Ledger. Sure enough, there are several messages describing his evening. I respond, letting him know how much I can't wait to go with him, then go about my morning.

A good night's sleep really did wonders for my jealousy. Allie was right. Ledger hasn't ever given me a single reason to doubt his devotion to me.

As the day goes on, my assurance in our relationship ebbs. I have nothing to do but monitor my phone for a message from Ledger while I wait for my mom to pick me up to get ready. I haven't spent this much time with my parents in months, and even living at home, it's usually in smaller doses than this. I'm on edge, and I feel like I haven't had one second of happiness since they arrived.

It's close to one o'clock in the afternoon when my phone starts to ring. I don't even check to see who it is in my enthusiasm to answer. "Hello?"

It's Ledger, and his voice is strained and hoarse. "Good morning, Angel."

"Morning? It's one in the afternoon."

"Damn, you're right. I can't believe I slept so late. I guess that's what I get for staying out until four in the morning. These thirties are hitting me hard." He chuckles.

I'm trying my best to remain calm. I've barely ever stayed out past midnight, and the thought of him out that late, in a sex club no less, doesn't sit well with me.

"Wow. You must've really been enjoying yourself." And just to add insult to injury, I add, "I guess that explains why you've lost your voice."

"Not at all, baby. I stayed late to see how their shutdown compares to ours. And as for my voice, conducting business conversations in a club is not easy on your vocal cords."

"Oh," I say, with way more sass than I intend.

"Sweet girl, I could never have a good time without you. *Especially* in a damn sex club. Why do you think I haven't been to Rendezvous without you? I would've never agreed to go last night if we weren't supposed to go together."

I'm feeling every bit of our age difference in how eager I am to jump to conclusions, so I try to reel my attitude in a little. "I'm sorry. It's probably my period causing me to be so emotional."

I swear I can *hear* the disappointment in his voice. "Now I feel even worse for leaving. You weren't supposed to start until Monday. I should be there to take care of you."

My instinct is to believe him, to be rational, and let go of any mistrust I have. Then I think about Dean and how I believed him for years, even though he was messing around behind my back. Insecurity floods my brain. I'm about to beg him to leave right now and come home when I'm reminded of the reason we aren't together in the first place. "Ugh, my mom's here. I'll text you when I can, but she hates when I'm on my phone, so you might not hear from me much today."

We exchange goodbyes, and I prepare myself for the rest of my day, still unable to shake the pit of doom building in my stomach. *Fuck it.* Nothing to do but put on my best Johnson smile and try to get through this party without screaming, crying, throwing up, or all three.

The party is in full swing. The first hour was spent eating the same boring chicken and green beans while listening to upper management give the same mundane speeches about how amazing their employees are.

Luckily for me, we're seated at a different table than the Christensen family, so I haven't had to deal with Dean yet. At this point, I'm just biding my time until I'm forced to interact with him. I haven't seen or heard from him since the night we broke up, so I don't have a good gauge on how he will react when my mother inevitably forces us together.

For the moment, I enjoy my peace. My parents left to mingle after the speeches were over, and it's the first bit of alone time I've had since Mom picked me up to get ready.

As I assumed, I haven't been able to look at my phone much today. I take the opportunity to respond to the message Ledger sent me a couple of hours ago, letting me know he was heading to a gala with some potential partners for the new club he'll be opening next year. Tears well in my eyes when I think about the fact that I was supposed to be with him tonight.

Me:

Can you tell me what you had picked out for me to wear since I didn't get to go with you? It has to be better than this stupid ruffled dress my mom insisted I wear.

I don't expect him to text back anytime soon, so I give in and start scrolling social media. Ledger doesn't update his socials often, but the Rendezvous marketing team always posts, so I click on their profile and immediately watch through their new stories. The first several are just advertisements for upcoming events and new member specials, but eventually, I land on a series of reposts from attendees of the gala.

I'm feeling déjà vu as I scour every photo for details of the night I'm missing out on. Unlike the images from the club last night, these include women. Lithe, beautiful supermodels surround him in almost every picture. Other men are around him as well, but it's clear that the women are interested in Ledger.

My mother's words from earlier start pouring into my mind.

"You didn't tell me you've gone up a dress size. I see you've really let yourself go since your breakup with Dean. Let's hope he can overlook that tonight. Maybe we can spin it as if this is a result of your heartbreak from not being together."

"Mom, I've told you countless times, I'm with Ledger now and I'm happy. I'm not getting back with Dean."

"Hmm, well, I'm sure Ledger *wouldn't mind you losing a few pounds either. Where did you say he was this weekend? New York? I would have kept myself in shape if my boyfriend was going to be traveling to a city with so many beautiful women. Especially a man of his...nature. He certainly looks like he spends time in the gym, probably has to be fit in case any of those drug deals go bad..."*

Actually, Ledger has been the one fattening me up. Suddenly, it doesn't matter that he seems to love the way my curves are exaggerated from the few extra pounds I've gained. My insecurity gets the best of me, and I don't know if I'm just searching for a compliment or what, but I send Ledger another text.

Me:

I just saw some pics from the gala. I'm a little relieved I didn't go. I would stick out like a sore thumb beside those supermodels surrounding you.

Again, he doesn't respond, so I go back online to see if there are any new stories. That's when I see it. Until now, there haven't been any pictures of him touching another woman, but the latest story boasts a photo of Ledger and a tall beautiful brunette. A brunette who favors *Lenora*. Her hand rests casually on one of his arms while his rests on the small of her waist, and they're engaged in one of those *I'm fancy and come from money* cheek kisses.

Red-hot rage hits me, and I'm once again fighting back tears that threaten to fall. I sit shaking in my seat, blind to anything going on in the room as I stare at the image that seems to be stealing my future away from me. After a minute, a text notification pops up on my screen from the devil himself.

Devil:

> I have no idea what you're talking about, love. But regardless, what's a supermodel to a goddess?

The part of me that wants to respond is heavily outweighed by the jealous, petty, and irrational gremlin living in my brain, so I start taking screenshots of everything and sending them to Allie instead of replying to Ledger.

I'm midway through my flood of texts when I hear a familiar voice from the chair beside me.

Dean.

I knew I'd have to talk to him at some point tonight, but this is really not the time. *Or is it?* Ledger is mistaken if he thinks he can go off and do God only knows what with other women while I wait on him like a desperate little girl.

To my surprise, Dean isn't a total asshole. "Hey, Sloane. How have you been?"

"Good," I say as I try my best to forget about my current crisis. "What about you?"

Dean runs a hand through his hair. "I've been better. Actually, that's what I wanted to talk to you about. I'm really sorry...for everything. I was kinda the worst boyfriend."

"Yeah, kinda."

Dean shakes his head in shame. "I know I don't deserve it, but I hope you can forgive me one day. This is probably a long shot too, but...I miss you. Do you ever think we could be friends again?"

I almost shut him down then and there, knowing for a fact if Ledger ever caught wind of us having any type of relationship at all, he would go full caveman. But *screw* Ledger. "Sure, we can be friends."

That puts a smile on his face so contagious I can't help but return it with one of my own.

We spend the next hour retelling old stories from both prior to and during our relationship. When the band starts playing one of our old songs, Dean stands up and holds his hand out, requesting a dance.

We make our way to the dance floor, and his arms wrap around my waist, but they aren't large enough. I place my hands on his shoulders, but he's a few inches shorter than I expect, so the angle seems off. When he pulls me close to him, I catch a whiff of his cologne. It's citrusy and clean, and *wrong*. One look in his *not smoky-gray* eyes is all it takes for me to realize I can't do this. It doesn't matter what's going on in New York.

I head back to my table, where I see the texts from Allie start flooding in.

Allie:

> **Oh shit…**

Allie:

> **Okay look, let's not jump to conclusions. I'm on a date right now, but I'll leave as soon as I can. Just try to get home, and we can rehash everything together.**

Mom is sympathetic when I lie and tell her I've been throwing up. I didn't drive tonight, so I call a rideshare and head home to an empty apartment. Allie isn't back yet, so I wash my face and climb into my cold bed alone. I should wait for her to get home, but I honestly don't feel like talking about it. Regardless of her advice, I am absolutely jumping to conclusions. Like taking a running jump off a one-hundred-foot cliff into the river of conclusion itself. The last thing I remember is seeing a text from Ledger, but I don't open it. I turn my phone off and let sleep carry me away.

Chapter Twenty-Seven

Ledger

It's almost midnight when I pull up to Sloane's apartment complex. I look down at the picture on my phone that had me prematurely leaving New York as if it's somehow changed since I got off my jet. It's still the same stupid picture of Sloane wrapped in that fucker Dean's arms with her mom's same stupid caption: *We've been watching this beautiful couple for three years now. Can't wait to see more.*

On my way back to my hotel after dinner, I tried calling Sloane, but she didn't answer. In fact, I haven't heard from her since last night. My heart rate spiked with fear before I could pull up her apartment's security footage. Thankfully, I could see that she was safe, lying in her bed reading. Her parents left earlier, so I knew that wasn't the issue anymore, and I could see she was in her apartment alone. I started digging for any clue as to why she would be ignoring my calls when *the picture* popped up on her social media. That's when I lost all rationality and arranged for my jet to leave immediately.

I grip my phone with almost enough force to break it as I march up to her apartment and start banging on the door. In my rush to get here, I forgot my key.

"Sloane!" Nothing. "Sloane, you either open this door right fucking now or I'm kicking it in."

Before I know it, the door swings open and my perfect girl is staring up at me with those beautiful eyes of hers while wearing my goddamn T-shirt.

We stand there staring into each other's eyes, and as I rake mine down her body, I notice her nipples pebbling under her shirt. All of my anger is pushed aside by how much I need this woman.

I wrap one hand around her neck while the other finds her waist in a bruising grip. I walk her back into the apartment, never breaking eye contact, and lock the door behind us before leaning down to kiss her.

Her back is against the wall, and my hand trails up her thigh to see if she's wearing anything under that shirt, when she suddenly shoves me away.

"Stop it, Ledger! You don't get to storm in here and touch me like nothing is wrong."

I give her some space, but I still have a hold of her. "Oh no? And who gets to do that now? Dean?" I say, gripping her hips to emphasize his name.

"No? Why would you say that?" The look of confusion in her eyes is genuine enough, but something is going on here, and I'm going to get to the bottom of it.

"I don't know, maybe this?" I pull my phone out of my pocket and show her the picture her mother posted a few hours ago. "What the fuck is going on here, Sloane?"

I don't know exactly how I expect her to react to my dramatic show of evidence, but pulling out her phone with a photo of her own is definitely not it. "I don't know, *Ledger.* What the fuck is this?"

She always throws me off when that sweet mouth of hers talks like that, so it takes me a moment to realize what I'm looking at. "That would be yours truly greeting the mayor of New York's *wife.* The same mayor who finally signed off on our new club, by the way."

The fire leaves her eyes as her whole demeanor changes. "Oh, I didn't...I'm sorry."

"Now your turn, what is this about?" I ask, holding up my phone again.

She looks between me and the picture several times before hanging her head. "I saw that picture of you last night and thought the worst. Dean came to our table, apologizing for everything. We talked for a little while, and when he eventually asked me to dance, the only thing I could think about was how you were probably dancing with one of those gorgeous women."

Gorgeous women?

Sloane places her hands tenderly on my shoulders and looks into my eyes. "It didn't last a minute, though. Everything about it was wrong. I left him on the dance floor, told my mom I had been throwing up, and got a ride home. I'm so sorry, Ledger, I..."

"Baby, stop." I take her face in my hands and kiss the top of her head before resting my forehead against hers. "I'm not thrilled about what happened, but I understand firsthand how irrational things like that can make someone. I mean, I'm here right now instead of in my hotel bed because of a stupid picture. You've got my entire heart, Sloane, and I think I have yours as well. At some point, we're going to have to start trusting each other with them."

"It's hard for me..."

I scoop her up in my arms and carry her to the couch. "I know, sweet girl, I know."

She squeals as I drop her onto the couch, her shirt riding up in the process. To my dismay, she is, in fact, wearing panties. *She's on her period. Of course she's wearing panties.* The thought comes barreling through my mind like a train. "You know, I haven't had anything to eat in hours," I say, shimmying the pink cotton panties down her thighs, and she moans. "And it just so happens that my favorite meal is sitting right in front of me."

Sloane's eyes go wide when she feels me gently tugging on the string of her tampon, no doubt just now remembering why she was wearing one in the first place. "No! I'm still bleeding like crazy."

She tries to close her legs, but I keep my grip firm. "Mmm, even better." Finally, I pull her tampon free of her body, and it's glistening with not only blood but also her arousal, showing me that she's just as excited as I am that I'm finally home. Seeing her blood reminds me of the first night we were together. I have to resist the urge to suck on it like a lollipop and toss it aside.

I gently fuck into her with my pointer finger until it's coated with blood, then bring it to my mouth and make a show of licking it clean. "Fucking *delicious*." I haven't broken our eye contact the whole time, and her pupils that have been gradually dilating are now completely blown.

Her moans fill the air as I dive back between her legs and feast on her like the starved man I am, alternating between her swollen clit and her bloody opening. When her hands find my hair in an attempt to pull me closer, I move my mouth to her clit and use two fingers to fuck into her pussy, stroking that sweet spot of hers fast and hard as my tongue rims her swollen bud.

I feel her orgasm building as her legs start to tremble and she flutters around my fingers. When I suck her clit into my mouth, she *explodes.* She squirts onto my face and chest as her body arches off the couch. I look down, and the image of just how much bloody cum I'm covered in has me *feral.* To the point I'm afraid to fuck her.

My restraint is short-lived when she sits up and starts frantically trying to remove my clothes. "More. Please...I need you."

In the blink of an eye, we're both completely naked, and I'm lining up at her opening with my fist around the base of my dick. "Is this what you want, you little slut? Was my mouth not enough for you? You need me to fuck this bloody cunt with my cock too?"

"Oh God yes." She moves her hips to force the head of my dick inside her. "Please fuck me. Please."

I pull back to flip her around so that her ass is in the air and bury my entire length inside her in one hard thrust, ripping a scream from her mouth. "*Goddamn,* I missed this pussy," I growl.

My pace starts slow as I indulge in what I've been dreaming of for the past two weeks, but the harder she grips me, the more I lose control. I lean over her, kissing and sucking a trail from her spine to her neck. "Does this satisfy my little slut, or do you need more?"

"More, harder. Fuck me harder."

"God-fucking-dammit, Sloane," I say before losing every ounce of control I have. *Well, almost every ounce...*I fuck her like an *animal.* My hands alternate between her breasts and her ass, but it's not a good enough grip. I move one hand to her throat, holding her steady, while the other grabs her hips, giving me the perfect leverage to fuck her harder than I've ever fucked anyone before.

It doesn't take long for her body to start shaking again in that telltale sign that her orgasm is on its way. "Does my good girl like being fucked like a whore tonight? Is this what you wanted when you asked me to fuck you harder? Did you want me to abuse your perfect little cunt like I'm paying for it?"

I can feel her pussy fluttering around my cock, and I'm so close to going with her. I move my other hand so that both are wrapped around her throat as her orgasm crashes into her so hard she passes out.

I'm chasing my own release when I happen to look up and see someone standing not ten feet from us. *What the fuck is Dean doing in her house at one in the morning?* I'm sure I look like a savage, holding an unconscious Sloane up by her throat and covered in blood. *Good, he should know who he's fucking with if he doesn't leave her the fuck alone. I'm worse than savage when it comes to her.* I make eye contact with him, smirk, and wink before my own orgasm hits me. Throwing my head back with a guttural growl, I thrust *deep* into Sloane one last time and fill her up with so much cum that I can feel it leaking out around my dick.

When my post-orgasm haze clears, I look up to find we're alone again. I don't know how long that asshole had been standing there, but he definitely got a show. I'm sure he's never seen someone getting fucked that hard. I've never experienced anything so intense. I know I should be furious that he got to see what Sloane looks and sounds like when she comes, but the caveman in me is beating his chest.

Bringing my mind back to the woman beneath me, I slowly pull out of her, earning me an adorable little grumble.

"Come on, baby," I say, scooping her up. "Let's go get cleaned up."

Sloane isn't out cold, but she hardly says anything to me as I wipe up the mess we made, bathe us, and settle us in bed. As soon as I get us both under the covers, she cuddles up to me, and everything feels right in the world again. I know there are things we need to talk about, but right now, all I want to do is enjoy lying here with my angel in my arms.

Chapter Twenty-Eight

Sloane

I wake up to an empty bed, and if it wasn't for the ache between my legs, I would be inclined to believe last night was just a dream. The last thing I remember was the tsunami of an orgasm that came crashing into me as Ledger fucked me relentlessly. Just the thought of last night has my pussy weeping for more. *Good Lord, that man can fuck.*

The smell of frying bacon brings me back to the moment, and I quickly brush my teeth and wash my face before following the scent into the kitchen. The sex god himself is standing over a skillet wearing nothing but a pair of gray sweatpants that hang low on his hips. He's absolutely delectable and all *mine*. I walk up behind him and wrap my arms around his waist before peppering his back with kisses.

"Mmm, good morning, Angel." Ledger turns the stove off and removes the skillets from the burners, then spins around in my arms and picks me up. My legs are wrapped around him as he carries me to the counter, sets me down, and steps between my legs. "God, I missed you."

Moving one of his hands from my hips to cup my face, he leans in and brushes his lips against mine softly. I part my lips to allow him entrance, and he takes it without hesitation. We remain lost in each other until the oven beeps and Ledger breaks our kiss to pull out a pan.

"Cinnamon rolls?" I ask as the smell of something sweet fills the air.

Ledger places the pan on the counter beside me and grabs the frosting, dipping out a bit with his finger and holding it up to my mouth for me to taste. "Orange rolls, baby, your favorite."

"Ooo, did you use that recipe from my book?"

"Nope," he says, holding up a cardboard wrapper. "These are from a can. Now go sit down. I'll bring you a plate."

I hop down from the counter and hug him tight, looking up into his eyes. "With an extra orange roll?"

Ledger wraps his arms around me as best he can with his hands full and kisses the top of my head. "Two extra orange rolls, sweet girl."

I make my way over to our table and take a seat, shortly followed by Ledger juggling two plates of food and two glasses of orange juice. We eat in silence, pretty much devouring our breakfast. When we've both finished, I start to stand to take our plates to the sink, but Leger beats me to it. "Sit back down, love. I've got it."

When he's rinsed off our dishes, I notice him making another plate of food and shoot a look of absolute confusion his way. "For Allie," he says, putting the dish in the microwave.

Ledger walks back to the table, but instead of sitting beside me like he was earlier, he takes the seat across from me. *Okay, this is weird.* He lays his arms out on the table with his hands in the air, an invitation for my own. One that I accept gladly. No matter how many times I touch this man, taste him, or *have him inside me,* I still feel fireworks with the brush of a finger.

"Angel, I think we need to talk. We should've had this discussion last night, but, well, you know how that went," he says, smirking at the reminder of the animalistic way we ended our night.

"Um, okay." There is no way this is going to be a good conversation. I know I reacted like an immature, jealous brat for the second time since we've been together.

I'm waiting for him to tell me that our age difference is just never going to work out when he responds. "I know you have a hard time believing me when I tell you, *and show you,* just how much you mean to me, but at some point, I need you to understand. You do not and will not *ever* have to doubt my complete and utter devotion to you. I need you to tell me what I can do going forward to avoid these feelings you've been having."

Ledger squeezes my hands when I don't answer. It's not like I haven't been trying to think of an answer. It's just, there really isn't one. "I don't know."

"Baby..."

"No! I really don't know. You've been absolutely perfect. You've never once given me a reason to doubt you, and I know that. I guess I'm just terrified to lose you. I mean...you've been the best thing to happen to me in my entire life, and I've never had a reason to think I deserve someone like you."

He pulls my hands toward him and gives them a kiss. "*I'm* the one who doesn't deserve *you.* Not the other way around.

It's pretty evident that you didn't receive the affection you needed growing up, which may have contributed to a lack of confidence in yourself. We briefly discussed it before, but would you be open to going to therapy? It's worked wonders for my childhood trauma."

Wow. Okay, so this wasn't the talk I thought I was about to get. *Of course he wasn't going to break up with me. Why can't I get it through my thick skull...*

"Yeah, that would be great actually," I say, fully smiling for the first time since we started this little *talk* of ours. "You know what's funny? I've never felt this way before with anyone else. I definitely never got jealous of Dean."

"Hmm, speaking of Dean, I understand your reasoning for dancing with him"—he narrows his eyes—"even though I would prefer you not to do that again. But is there a reason he showed up in your apartment in the middle of the night last night?"

Okay, that was completely out of left field. "Huh?"

"Dean. *In* your apartment. Around one in the morning. Why? How?"

"Ledger, I have no clue what you're talking about. Dean was never in my apartment yesterday. Besides, you were here by then. Around one, we would've been..."

"Correct. Does he have a key?"

"Um, he used to...I guess I never got it back from him."

"I'll get someone to come out and change the locks. It doesn't matter for you so much since you won't be leaving our house again, but I don't think Dean should have access to Allie's residence," he says, grunting in disapproval.

"Ledger, please tell me what you're talking about. Explain it to me like I'm a toddler."

A smirk forms on his face. "Oh, I would *definitely not* tell a toddler this story. It's simple enough. Last night, while I was fucking your brains out, I looked up, and Dean was standing in the hall. You had just come, so it's no wonder you didn't see him."

He has to be joking. There's no way Dean saw us. *This is a joke. Ledger is about to start laughing and tell me he's just messing with me, getting back at me for that dance.*

He doesn't start laughing.

I'm shaking with fear when he finally breaks the silence. "What's wrong, baby?"

I rip my hands from his grip and shoot up out of my chair, sending it crashing to the floor. "You're lying."

Ledger remains seated as I begin to pace back and forth. "Sloane, what's going on? What's wrong?

"What's wrong? You just told me that my ex walked in on us having sex, and you have the audacity to ask me what's wrong?"

Ledger slowly stands up and walks over to where I've paused my pacing. "I didn't realize you would be so upset with someone watching. You seemed to enjoy it in the club. I'm sorry, I really didn't think you would mind. I truly had you pegged as an exhibitionist."

I bring my hand to my head, massaging my temples. "It's not just *someone* watching. It's *Dean*."

"And what about that asshole seeing just how much you belong to me is so upsetting to you?" he asks calmly, but I can tell by the way his breathing has picked up that he's barely keeping his composure.

"It's not about him. It's the fact that he's going to tell my parents what we were doing. It wasn't vanilla crap either! We were covered in blood, and you were fucking me like an animal," I say, folding my arms across my chest and rubbing up and down frantically as my panic starts to set in. "Oh my God, they are going to think we were doing something satanic."

Ledger grabs my arms and pulls me in for a gentle hug. No words are spoken for several minutes while he holds me close to him, allowing my tears to fall onto his bare chest. I revel in the comfort of his skin against my cheek until his embrace grounds me enough to stop my tears. "So what, sweet girl? We weren't doing anything wrong. You have no reason to be afraid of them," he says, breaking the silence.

I snap at his inability to understand my concerns and pull back in his arms to look up at him. "So what? So they are my *parents!*"

"And who gives a fuck?" he says, raising his voice to match mine.

"How can you not possibly understand why this would bother me? They are going to be *furious!*"

"Because you don't like confrontation? Guess what, baby, sometimes we have to grow up and deal with uncomfortable things."

I try to pull away at that comment, but he won't let me go. "No, you asshole, because they will take everything away from me. They'll make me go back home."

Ledger's grip on my arms tightens. "Sloane Olivia Johnson. How many times will I have to tell you that *nobody* will *ever* take you away? I will give you the entire world on a silver platter, Angel. Nobody will take anything away from you, and nobody will take you away from me."

I look into Ledger's eyes as tears are welling up again in my own. "They're my *parents*. They've been there my entire life. And...and I've only *known* you for what, four months?"

At that, he finally lets go of me and steps back, fisting his hands at his sides. I reach for him, but he takes another step back. The tears are rolling down my face now, and I see one fall from his eye as well.

"Ledger..."

"Best thing to ever happen to you? Isn't that what you said earlier?" He interrupts.

Before I can say anything else, he storms away, slipping on his shoes at the entrance before grabbing his keys and walking out. I stand frozen as the door slams behind him, and his car revs up.

It's not until Allie rushes out of her room that I break, falling to the floor in a puddle of tears. "Oh God, Sloane, honey? Come here." She sits behind me and scoops me into her arms as she rocks us both back and forth on the floor.

"I...I...told him. And he...he left...and...I ruined everything," I say between sobs.

Allie continues to rock me back and forth. "Shhh, I know. I heard everything from my room. It's going to be okay, sweetheart. He loves you. You haven't lost him. He's just hurt right now. Shhh. It's okay. It's okay."

We both skip our classes for the day, and she continues to try to soothe me, but it doesn't work. Eventually, the tears stop, but what's left in their place is a numbness I've never felt before. I go from the couch to Allie's room to my room, just trying to find some semblance of peace, but none ever comes.

I just want to go home.

Chapter Twenty-Nine

Ledger

I'm sitting in my office, staring at my favorite picture of Sloane, when I hear a knock on the door.

I've been living in this office the past week, only leaving to train for the championship fight tomorrow night. The first night I left Sloane's apartment, *the night after she broke my heart,* I didn't get any sleep. I'm on the verge of a mental breakdown.

"Come in."

"Hey, Boss," Jack says, closing the door as he walks in.

Flashbacks of all the debauchery the two of us have gotten into over the years start running through my mind. "Jack, how many times am I going to have to tell you to stop calling me that? I've known you my entire life."

He shrugs. "Doesn't make you any less my boss."

"Touché, asshole."

"Are you ready for your big fight tomorrow?" he asks as he sits on the couch.

Am I ready for the fight tomorrow? This guy is legit. Like all my opponents, I use my skills to find out everything about them, and whatever unhinged tendencies I thought I had pale in comparison to this guy. Not that he doesn't have his weaknesses.

"He won't be a shoo-in like they usually are, but I've been training like a madman. If I play my cards right, I should be able to take him. He's solid, but he doesn't have discipline. The problem with that is he's even crazier than me. Reminds me a lot of myself ten years ago. Which is how I know that if I can get in his head, I'll have the advantage."

"Well, you know I'm going to be there if there's a chance someone will finally beat your ass." Jack shifts his body to lie sideways, propping on the arm of the couch with his legs sprawled out along the length of it.

"Hey, fucker, get your dirty shoes off my bed!" I say, throwing a wadded-up piece of paper at his face.

He catches it and smirks as he stands and sits down in one of my desk chairs instead. "Anything you say, *Boss.*"

We've spent more time together this past week than the entire two months Sloane and I have been living together, and it's both reminded me how much I miss my friend and how much I want to throttle him.

Rolling my eyes, I pull up my emails to see if there's anything I can devote my mental energy to, but just like the other ten times in the past thirty minutes, nothing.

"Tell me again why that's your bed," Jack says, grabbing a handful of Sloane's favorite gummy bears out of a container on my desk and popping one in his mouth.

"Sloane and I had a fight."

"And she kicked you out of your own house?"

The insinuation that she's just a visitor gets my attention, and I finally look up at him. "*Our* house," I growl out. "And no, she's at her apartment."

Jack throws his hands up in an act of innocence. "My bad, I guess you just lost my invite to the wedding."

"Not married yet."

Jack stares at me in confusion before bringing his hands to his face and rubbing his temples. "Look, brother, I'm just trying to figure out what's going on with you right now."

Where to even fucking begin.

Letting out a deep breath, I decide to just go for it. I tell him all about how I became obsessed with her the moment I first saw her, how I stalked her like a psychopath, renovated my house, rearranged my entire life, how I fell madly in love, and how I offered the world to her on a silver platter. All for her to throw it back in my face the moment her parents stepped into the picture. "*I've only known you for what, four months?*"

He stands and walks over to the beverage cart in the corner of the room, pours two glasses of scotch, then sets one in front of me before taking his seat. "Well, she's not wrong. You *have* only known her for four months. So are you going to get back together?"

"I want to...I love her. The past two months have been the happiest of my *life*. And this past week...I don't know what I'll do when this fight is over and I'm not spending eight hours a day training."

"Hmm," he says, taking a swig of his drink, but I can tell he's holding back.

"No, say what's on your mind. Please."

There is a melancholy expression in his eye as he leans forward in his seat and places his glass on my desk. "I'm going to be honest with you. I like Sloane a lot. I mean, sure, she's young, but I think she's good for you. That being said, it doesn't mean that dating a twenty-year-old won't be without its issues. You're going to have to be the bigger person some of the time. But from everything you've told me, that doesn't seem to be a deal breaker...so what *is* the problem?"

"She *hates* her parents. I mean, she loves them in a, *they're my parents,* kinda way, but they suffocate her. And she chose them over me."

Jack shakes his head. "Do you remember what you were like ten years ago? I think you're forgetting how much your own father's opinion mattered...and you even had the rest of your family to lean on when he was being a dick. She doesn't have anyone."

"She has me...I've done everything I can over the past few months to show her that—"

"You're an idiot." He cuts me off. "Women talk through their emotions, dude. The only reason she would do that in front of you is because you're the only person in her life who's made her feel comfortable enough to speak her thoughts out loud."

Well, fuck me.

"Why don't you just ask her to marry you? I mean, you added her to the fucking deed to your house, so what's a ring?" Jack continues. "It's obvious you want to eventually, and I'm sure that would make her feel more secure."

Why *have* I been waiting to ask her? I had a ring custom-ordered before she moved in. "Where did you get all this knowledge about women from anyway? You'd have to actually talk to the women you fuck to learn something about them."

I swear I see something like sadness flash across his eyes. "I don't know, man. I just know that if I loved someone as much as you love Sloane, and there weren't a million things keeping us apart, I'd never let her go."

He's right. I can't let her go. I've given her space this week, but after tomorrow's fight, I'm getting her back. Whatever it takes.

Jack changes the subject, lighting the mood for what seems to be both of us. "Alright, now that we've cleared your love life up, tell me about New York."

We'll be renovating a building in a different part of the city than the club I visited, but even then, we're planning to collaborate to avoid creating too much competition between us. That means we get to be a little more creative with our offerings than Rendezvous. And by we, I mean Jack. Hopefully, he'll stop with all the "Boss" shit now that he'll have his own club to run.

"Our real estate agent wanted to make sure there weren't any better options before we moved forward with the spot we found online, but seeing it in person only solidified my opinion. You're going to *love* it. Everything about it screams to me, from the location to the layout to the price. It's old enough to have a little character of its own, but not so old that we'll have to jump through a million hoops for renovations."

"That sounds great! When do you need me up there?" Jack asks.

"The sale went through, so we can get started as soon as you're ready to go." As much as I want to get started on the new club, I'll miss my friend. This is the opportunity of a lifetime for him, and he will have a field day coming up with ways to make this club unique. It's not like I see him much now that there's a five-foot-five blonde monopolizing my time.

"I have the staff ready, so I'll work on getting my own things in order so I can get started ASAP," he says.

I extend my vulnerability from our earlier conversation into this one. "You know you don't have to go, right? We can get someone else to do this if you'd like. In fact, I'm tempted to keep you here regardless. I've never been so far away from you, man, and I'm going to miss your crazy ass."

With that, a small smile breaks his solemn face. "I know, brother, I'll miss your crazy ass too, but we both know this is where I need to be. Plus, you're all boo'd up now anyway."

With the mention of my girl, I stand and start to gather my things. "Grab your stuff. You're coming home with me," I tell Jack.

"Anything you want, *Boss*. What's the plan?" he asks, following me out of my office.

"We're going to plan my wedding. I'm getting married tomorrow after the fight."

"Um, you know you're going to be beaten to a pulp, right? I'm sure Sloane will love those pictures."

I elbow him in the side as we walk down the hall. "Shut up, I'll look better than you'll look in your wedding pictures, roughed up or not. "

"Yeah, right, like I'll ever have any of those." He chuckles, elbowing me right back. He continues to tease me about my plans, but as long as he's helpful tonight, I don't care. I've only got one thing on my mind. *Getting my girl back.*

The world around me is quiet as I sit in the locker room, staring at the engagement ring in my hand. *All I have to do is get through this fight, and she'll be in my arms before I know it.* My mind wanders down a rabbit hole of my angel and all the ways I'm going to make this up to her when I hear a knock on the door.

"Five minutes."

I shut the little black velvet box and lock it up along with my thoughts of Sloane. If I don't get my mind right, this fight will be over before it's started. A splash of cold water from the sink and a few soft punches to my jaw have me amped up and ready to go take weeks of frustration out on this bastard.

Walking through the crowd, I take notice of Margot and Jack in two of the four front row seats I had reserved and give them a slight nod. During our planning last night, Jack coordinated with Allie to make sure she got Sloane here tonight. We haven't talked since our fight, but I was hoping there was a sliver of a chance she'd come. The two empty seats beside them momentarily discourage me before I remember the fight is starting a bit earlier than planned.

By the time I enter the cage, I'm locked back in. I stand in my corner, shifting from one foot to the other to keep my blood pumping as I watch this young cat make his entrance, giving me a psychopathic smile as he enters his side. *Cameron Lee.* I size him up because no matter how much I've studied him on screen, it never compares to seeing exactly what I'm working with. I watch as he slightly favors his right side when he throws some air punches. He's almost as tall as me but much slimmer, which may give him an edge on speed, but it leaves him with less muscle padding around those left ribs.

We wait as the announcer introduces us and gives the whole pre-match rule spiel, and before I know it, the starting bell has rung. Just as I anticipated, he charges forward to land the first punch. He's fucking athletic, and his stamina allows for his aggressive style, but I've noticed after watching film that he slows a little after the first few rounds. For rounds one and two, I just dodge his fists, letting him chase me, only throwing a punch of my own when the perfect opportunity presents itself. Both of us are able to land a hit or two but nothing serious.

The next two rounds are not as gentle. While he's slowed enough to make this a level playing field, he's still quite a bit quicker than I am, meaning I'm more banged up than I have been in a while. Not to say he doesn't have just as many wounds. The years of experience I have on him are working in my favor, and I can see it's getting to him exactly like I hoped.

Round five is going in my favor. I think I've finally gotten the leg-up I need to finish him off when someone in the front row by Margot catches my eye.

Sloane.

Time stops as I study every detail of my sweet girl. The expression of fear on her face is almost enough to throw in the towel and tap out right here. Before I can so much as smile her way, a heavy fist lands on my cheekbone, knocking me back into reality.

As Lee hits me with punch after punch, I know what that moment cost me. I can't even get an arm up in defense, much less attempt a jab of my own. I'm pushed up against the cage on the side farthest from Sloane, and pain is radiating across my body when I'm finally given a reprieve.

Lee stands behind me with his arm around my neck in a submission hold as he tilts my head toward Sloane and whispers in my ear, "Is that your girl over there in that delicious black leather get-up? Mmm, she's a sexy thing. I bet she's got a sweet little cunt to have *The* Undefeated Ledger Sinclair so distracted." I try my best to get out of his grip, but he tightens his hold on me, almost cutting off my oxygen in the process. "After I've knocked you out, how about I see for myself? I bet that bitch's big tits will bounce real nice as I fuck her over your bloodied body. I hope for your sake she's on birth control...it doesn't really fucking matter to me either way."

My pain and fatigue immediately disappear. I slam my head back against his as hard as I can, catching him off guard and allowing me to break out of his grip. Before he can regroup, I attack him relentlessly with punch after punch, backing him across the cage until we are directly in front of where Sloane is sitting.

My hits fall *hard* across his body, but I know that if the referee calls time, I may lose this adrenaline and advantage going into the next round. I have to knock him out, and I have to do it *now*. I land several jabs on his ribs, and when a crack on his left side momentarily catches him off guard, I put all my strength into a punch aimed at his temple.

His body falls back before sliding down to the ground at my feet, and my attention shifts to Sloane. I expect her to be running for the doors after watching me take this man down, but to my surprise, she's still there. She's sitting in her seat, staring at me, but it's not fear in her eyes. It's hunger.

Chapter Thirty

Sloane

"I don't even think he would want me there, Allie. You heard what I said. I've never seen such a devastated look on his face, and I don't think I can handle it if I show up and he ignores me or seems upset to see me."

I pinch the bridge of my nose to stop myself from crying, and really, it's annoying that I even have a single tear left to cry at this point. I should have dried up days ago.

Allie continues to tighten my leather corset top, purchased weeks ago when I was excited to watch Ledger in his championship match.

"I love you like a sister, sweetie, but we have reached the 'tough love' portion of this whole episode. You were emotionally fragile and said shit you didn't mean. He went all caveman and didn't fully listen to your concerns. Both of you were wrong and both of you were right, in different ways, okay? I mean, he sent someone to change the locks on our door, for crying out loud. I let you be angry, then sad, then depressed, and now we are going tonight so you can support him, and you can both move past this. I know for a fact he misses you and has been going crazy without you. Jack said so." She finishes lacing me up, and I can barely breathe.

"Jack? Since when do you talk to Jack?"

Allie gives me a smirk. "Don't worry about me and Jack. We're going to be late if we don't leave right now. And I'm driving that dreamboat you call a tank. Let's go."

Taking as deep a breath as I can manage, I glance at myself in the mirror and wonder what Ledger will think of this outfit. My boobs are always impossible to minimize, but tonight they're their own main event, pushed up higher than I thought possible in this corset. Tight leather pants complete my look. Sighing, I lock the door behind me and follow her to the car. *You've got this, Sloane. Failure is not an option. Go out there and get your man back.*

Parking and walking into the building, I realize this is a different caliber of event than the one I had attended previously. There are at least five times more people here, with security everywhere and professional lighting trained on the main cage. Thank God for Allie, who seems to have been texting Jack, because he comes to get us near the entrance to lead us back to our seats.

He glances at Allie, then at me. "I'm glad you're here. Ledger has been pretending not to look toward our seats during the fight, but he's a terrible actor."

"We're late?" I ask, horrified that Ledger thinks I've abandoned him on the night of his biggest fight of the year. We might not have been speaking, but I know his training regimen has been brutal in the lead-up to tonight.

"Some head of something blah blah insisted on moving up the main card so he could fly out early tonight to be in Europe by morning, made some big charity donation in the fighter's names, so Ledger agreed to it. They're in round five now, and I think he's finally got this guy where he wants him. He's pretty fucking good, honestly. The best Ledger's faced since..."

Jack continues, but I'm no longer listening. Ledger, *my* Ledger, is beat to shit in a way I've never seen before. Clearly, his opponent, Cameron Lee, is on a totally different level than the fighters I saw Ledger take down with no effort. We lock eyes the way we always do when we're in a room together, and I see happiness and sadness and relief and love flit across his eyes as mine fill with tears. *Holy shit,* I hate seeing him like this. I want him out of the cage and back home with me, soaking in the bath and cuddling up in bed...

I'm thinking of ways to convey to Ledger that we need to get the hell out of here when the eye contact that means so much to me costs him. A heavy blow lands on his cheekbone, and I scream.

Jack pulls me into my front-row seat. "Sit, Sloane. He's happy to see you, but he needs to get his head out of his ass. Sit and watch. That's the best way you can help him right now."

I know he's right, but I feel like I'm going to throw up and die from the adrenaline coursing through my body right now. Lee lands blow after blow, forcing Ledger into the far side of the cage, then gets him in some sort of headlock, where he can't move at all.

Clearly, it was a mistake to be here. All I'm doing is distracting him. I'm getting ready to stand again and bolt out when Jack puts a hand on my arm.

"Stay. He's going to need you after this either way."

I sit back down in time to see Lee saying something into Ledger's ear. Whatever it is transforms him. He lashes out, slamming his head back into the other man's nose and breaking free from his grip. He's turned the tables, pushing back our way and raining down blows on the other man. It's obvious this fight is over, but technically, he's still on his feet, so Ledger doesn't stop. It's vicious, and I wince as I see teeth go flying. His nose is now basically a diagonal instead of a straight line, and he's barely even got his hands up anymore to defend himself. Ledger hits at his ribs, and they're close enough now that I hear cracks from the force. As Lee sways on his feet, Ledger makes the briefest eye contact with me, and...that's not *my* Ledger. I've only ever seen that look in the movies—when a man is out for blood and vengeance, and he doesn't care who he hurts to get it. *Holy fuck.* I assumed that actors exaggerated, but...I've never seen anything like Ledger at this moment. He's covered in blood, bruised, and has to be exhausted, but he's standing tall, as if he could take on an army of Lees and win.

After a moment that feels like it lasts an eternity, he sends Lee to the floor with one more punishing punch. He's out cold, and medical staff immediately approach to tend to him.

The referee briefly lifts Ledger's arm above his head in victory. The crowd is in pandemonium at this point, but it doesn't matter. His fiery gaze is locked on mine, and people are smart enough to part for him as he exits the cage and comes straight for me. I don't have a chance to even say hi or congrats or whatever you say to your Viking warrior of a man after he's won a bloody fight before I'm unceremoniously picked up and thrown over Ledger's shoulder.

He walks down a dimly lit hallway before opening a door with a code and shutting it behind us. He gently puts me down on the far side of the room, then immediately takes two large steps back, standing with his hands on his hips and his chest heaving. His gaze remains on the floor in front of him, not on me. As I glance around, it looks like we're in a locker room. There are lockers, an open door to a small bathroom area, a fridge, a narrow dining table, and a couch...maybe this is for championship participants. At least it seems clean.

I'm trying to decide what I'm going to say to break the silence when he beats me to it.

"You need to leave."

He's still heaving, breathing heavier than when we entered, and the hands that were on his hips are now clenched into fists at his sides. I can't tell if his nails are drawing more blood from his palms or if the blood was already there. "You need to leave. Now, Sloane."

Usually in a confrontation like this, my first emotion would be hurt, and I would sadly capitulate to whatever the other person wanted just to remove myself from the situation. But something in me snaps. I love this man, I'm a grown woman, and I'm *so done* letting anyone tell me what to do, even Ledger.

"Fuck. Off," I snarl as his gaze finally snaps to mine. His stormy gray eyes are blown black as he zeros in on me. He's opening his mouth to say something else when I stop him with a hand in the air. "I said fuck off. I don't want to hear it. I'm not going anywhere. I don't care about our fight. We can figure all that out later. But you just got the shit beat out of you, then beat the ever-loving fuck out of that guy, and my place is here with you. I'm not. Fucking. Leaving."

We stand locked in a staring match for what feels like forever before Ledger takes a few slow steps, stopping just short of touching me. I look up into his eyes and see him struggling with himself. He looks awful, like he hasn't been sleeping or taking care of himself beyond the bare necessities to get ready for the fight. I'm going to beg him to come home with me and soak in a tub, but I don't get the chance.

My beautiful, bloody warrior bends down, wincing, and kneels at my feet, hands unclenched and resting lightly on the backs of my thighs. He's shaking as he leans forward and puts his forehead against my lower stomach.

I run a hand gently through his hair and press a kiss to the top of his head.

"Angel, you have to go."

"I already told you..." I sigh, ready to try my best to overpower him and get him to the car.

"No, Sloane." He pulls his head back and stares up at me, with a crueler glint in his eyes than a moment ago. "I am beyond fucking happy to see you. You have no idea. I love you, endlessly. And I want you. But if you stay in this room right now, I'm gonna fuck you, baby. Hard. And I really, really don't think I'll be able to stop myself from hurting you."

I release a breath I didn't realize I'd been holding. "Ledger, you would never—"

"Yes, I would." He interrupts. "I would hurt you. I *want* to." He tightens his grip on the backs of my thighs, and I suck in a breath. "I want to punish you for leaving me alone these fucking awful days, for making me miss you, for not giving me a chance to apologize for being wrong in our fight, and for being burrowed so damn deep in my heart that I don't get a goddamn moment of peace when you're not with me. I want to make you scream my name so that every single person in this building knows exactly what I'm doing to you. I want you walking out of here covered in hickeys and bruises from my grip so that anybody who didn't hear can see that you're mine. I can't decide if I'm mad enough to not let you come, or to make you come until it fucking hurts. So please. Leave before I hurt you."

Time stands still, granting me absolute clarity on what I want. What I *have* wanted. What I've tried to bring up as we've played and explored, but Ledger's held back. This part of himself that's so perfectly depraved and dirty, a perfect match to the last part of myself I've been desperate to make unclean.

"Hurt me," I whisper into the space between us, gripping his hair tight enough in my hands to force his head back enough for me to lean down and press my lips to his. "Make it hurt." I trace his bottom lip and stand back up, ready to finally experience the mixture of pain and pleasure that I've read about but that my sweet devil has been too deferential to give me. We've discussed it, but he always comes up with an excuse before we make any plans.

His face clearly shows his warring emotions, but I can see the outline of his hard cock through his shorts. *Damn, have I missed that.*

I see the moment he decides he's not going to do it, and I'm already pulling my hand back before he can even say it.

"Sloane, no. I'm not going to…"

Slap.

The sharp sound of my hand against Ledger's cheek echoes throughout the room as his head whips to the side with the force. *Fuck, that hurts.* My hand tingles as Ledger slowly stands, twisting his head to the left, then to the right, methodically popping his neck.

"Safe word," he says, giving me a look so loaded I can't even begin to know if I've won the lottery or fucked up. Maybe both. Almost certainly both.

"Crimson." No matter what he thinks, I do want this and have for a while—enough to have done my research. *At least, I hope.*

Before I know it, I'm being tugged back from the windowsill and laid on my back on the table. I feel something around my ankles, then wrists, and I realize he's used the curtain tiebacks and something else to secure me. I'm not going anywhere. My head hangs off the end, and I see Ledger approach upside down. He's naked and still smeared with a considerable amount of blood. "Stay still."

I do as I'm told when I feel cool metal against my upper arm, then the left strap of my corset falls away. The right follows soon after, and Ledger, clearly unable to be bothered to untie me, slices right down the front of my top until I'm naked from the waist up.

He's less controlled now, as if seeing me topless and at his mercy has unlocked a new level of possessiveness. His hand settles across my throat, and he gives me a moderate squeeze, enough to have my full attention. He puts something cold and jingly in my right hand.

"I'm fucking this throat that you've denied me for nearly a month, and you're going to lie there and fucking take it. You won't be able to say anything, so drop the keys if you need to stop. If you're lucky, I will."

Before I can say I understand, his dick is as far back in my throat as it can go, and I immediately gag around his piercings. I've improved since I started sucking his cock, but I'm by no means an expert. Ledger is unbothered, simply pulling out and pushing back in as tears start to stream down my face. Just as I think I have a good breathing pattern down, and I'm focused on breathing through my nose, he reaches across my body to slap one of my breasts as it bounces from the force of his thrusts. I scream around his dick, causing him to groan and his pace to falter for a thrust before picking back up.

"That's my bad girl. Scream for me, Sloane." He rains down slaps, alternating breasts until I can feel the heat from my blood rushing to the surface of my nipples as they turn red.

I whine at being called his bad girl, not sure if I love it or hate it because I'm so used to being good.

"Do you not like that? That's what you are, though, isn't it? I hate to break it to you, Angel. But good girls don't love having their throats fucked. Only bad little whores do. So it looks like that's exactly what you are."

Fuck me, I'm dripping. *Maybe I am his bad girl.*

As I wiggle and try to find any nonexistent chance at relief for my throbbing clit, he reaches a long arm over my torso and gives me a slap there too through my leather pants. I scream and choke more around his dick, his pace now more feverish and uncontrolled.

"None of that wiggling. That's bad-girl behavior. Do you know what else a bad girl would do?"

I try to shake my head.

"A bad girl would come from me sucking on her raw nipples."

He leans forward to suck my nipple into his mouth, then *bites it,* and that's all it takes. I let out a muffled scream as I come *hard.*

"That's my fucking girl. My Sloane might just be a perfect little pain slut, aren't you? Here's your reward that I promised you. Do. Not. Swallow."

His dick pulses as he comes down my throat, groaning my name with his head thrown back. He pulls back at the last second to give me a mouthful to keep before stepping to the side and untying my limbs from the table. Grabbing around my waist, he sits me up and positions me on my heels. I whine as I realize he isn't going to let me come, and he laughs, coming back around to face me at the head of the table and giving each nipple a harsh pinch as he does so. More tears fall onto my already wet cheeks, and he watches, fascinated, as one trails all the way to my jaw. I'm beginning to think he's forgotten about my uncomfortable mouthful of cum when his eyes snap to mine.

"Show me."

My cheeks flush as I open my mouth and stick out my tongue, cum dripping from the tip down onto my breasts below. His gaze follows the drops until he leans down and licks them up before capturing my mouth in a searing kiss. I recognize immediately that this is the first real kiss we've had in over three weeks, and I'm crying again, this time from happiness at having this connection again. I'm so caught up in how right I feel and how *at home* I feel that I don't notice Ledger's hand trailing up my back to wrap my ponytail around his fist. He tugs on my hair as he breaks our kiss, keeping my bottom lip in his teeth and biting *hard*. I'm surprised when he lets go that I don't taste the coppery tang of blood, and by the looks of it, so is he.

"Naughty girl," he says, before he leans down and *bites* into the fleshy underside of my left breast. I scream, loudly and unmuffled, this time without a dick in my mouth. This is definitely all pain and no pleasure. I writhe, but his grip is strong. When he pulls back, I see that he succeeded in drawing blood this time, and he's licking me off his bottom lip.

He pulls me off the table and carries me to the couch, bending me in half over the edge and holding my forearms together behind my back. He steps back, and I immediately miss his warmth. The longer I stand here half naked in my stupid, sexy leather pants, the more I realize how silent and cold this room is. I want to turn and see where Ledger is, or open my mouth and ask, but both of those options feel like losing the game before we've even started to play.

I'm lost in the sensation when he breaks the silence. "Why do you think I didn't let you come just now?"

"Umm..."

He brings his hand down *hard* on my right cheek, followed immediately by the left.

"You're more eloquent than that. Don't 'umm' me. I know you know the answer. Tell me."

He's pulling at my waistband now, and I finally catch up and realize he's mad at the pants.

"The pants! I'm sorry. I'm sorry for the pants. I'm sorry you don't like the pants."

He chuckles darkly, and it makes my blood run cold. "I love the pants, baby. They hug your perfect curves in all the right places. You look like a delectable little slut, showing off what she's got and waiting for someone to take it. What I don't love is that you wore them out of the fucking house for every man in here tonight to see. And they all looked. I saw them. Lee certainly looked. Do you know what he said to me to make me snap?"

He's cutting my pants from my body in a much more civilized manner than he did my top.

I shake my head.

"He wanted to fuck you, Angel. He wanted to see your titties bounce in his face. *He wanted to know if you're on birth control.* Are you on birth control, Sloane?"

I shake my head again.

"No, you're not, are you? Because you're mine, and you give me that perfect little cunt raw anytime I want it so I can put a baby in you. Yet you can walk around anywhere, looking like a fucking goddess among men, and no man would have a single indication that you're taken, would they? Rest assured, we're fixing that tonight, baby. In more ways than one. Now. Don't move a muscle. Bite down on this if you need to, but *be still,*" he says, handing me my balled-up leather top.

With that, Ledger stands back, and I barely have time to feel the coolness from the blade hitting my skin before he's cutting into me. I bite down on the leather in my mouth as he continues carving into my skin. My body tries to buck on instinct, but he uses his other hand to hold me down on the couch. He's already done before I realize he's carved his initials into my ass. Any pain I was experiencing is immediately replaced by the overwhelming euphoria of being claimed so savagely.

"Much better. Now anyone who sees your ass will know who you belong to, Angel."

He grabs one of my ass cheeks and squeezes, and I feel the warm stream of blood dripping from the fresh cut. I gasp as the hot, piercing pain shoots straight to my clit. *Fuck,* I was hoping it would be like this. Despite my best efforts to be good, I smile, and he sees it.

He kicks my legs out wider with his feet, and my head hits the couch cushion when I feel his body heat on mine. With no warning, he slides into me in one thrust, his heavy balls slapping my clit as he settles in to the hilt. His rumbling groan is exactly how I feel, but my relief sounds more like a strangled whine into the couch cushion. Ledger fucks me steadily and deeply, with every one of his piercings feeling as good as I remember. Time has no meaning for me as I float, feeling his ladder tug on my entrance with every thrust, his thighs hitting my raw, sore ass, my nipples chafing against the fabric of the couch...I come back to myself a bit when he wraps my ponytail around his fist again, and I feel the angle change as he bends one of my knees onto the couch arm.

"Ledger...please..." I beg because at this point, I think any pressure on my clit will push me over the edge, but if I don't come soon, I'm going to die.

"Is your little whore cunt tired, baby? We can move on."

I'm too tired to scream, but I let out a pitiful gasp as he drops my head back to the couch and my leg to the floor before pulling out of me completely and leaving me feeling devastatingly empty.

"I don't keep lube here for obvious reasons, but I think we can get enough blood dripping from where I carved my initials in your skin to provide what your ass is going to need."

I tense up and immediately try to stand from the couch, but a heavy hand keeps me in place.

"Good girls get cum in their pussies, baby. But we've established how bad you've been, haven't we?"

For some reason, this makes me panic. Ledger has always treated coming inside me with such reverence and as such an honor, and now he's denying me. It's all I want, and it feels incredibly wrong. Before I know it, I'm full-on sobbing. *Fuck, I read about the emotional release, but this is brutal.*

"Tell me, Sloane," he says, rubbing soothing circles up and down my back.

"I love you," I scream. "Please. I love you, I'm sorry, but you promised. You *promised* you wouldn't come anywhere else, and I *need* it. I don't want it anywhere else. You said you wouldn't...until I was...and I'm not...unless you're tired of me?" I can't do anything except sob with my entire body at this point, but I feel myself being gently picked up and turned to straddle Ledger's lap.

"Shh...my sweet girl. I'm sorry. You're right. Forgive me. You're right about where it goes. I would never deny you that. I could never be tired of you. Put me back in and ride me, baby."

I'm still hovering somewhere between a dream and reality, but I'm aware enough to know I've just been given permission to take what I want, so I do. Rising on shaky legs, I guide Ledger's thick head to my entrance before sinking down inch by inch until my hips are flush with his.

Ledger's head falls back onto the couch as I ride him, my rhythm steady. "Mmm, fuck yes. Faster, baby."

I try my best, but I can barely pick up the pace without it hurting where I've been cut open.

"Sloane, faster. I need you *faster,*" he growls, his whole body tensing up.

"Help me," I whisper. My entire body radiates pain from his punishments, and I'm not up to the task of riding this man how he wants right now.

"I'll always help you." With a kiss to my forehead, my fighter, who went five hard rounds not even an hour ago, puts his hands under my thighs, lifts me, and slams me down on his dick. My scream only encourages him, and he continues the motion, thrusting up to meet me each time.

When I don't think I can take anymore, and I'm about to say crimson...I look into Ledger's eyes. His thumb finds my clit, and I explode into black.

Waking up, I put my forehead against his and open my eyes to find tears streaming down his face. "I'm yours. I promise I'm yours. Everything I have is yours. You have to know that now, baby. Please tell me you know."

"I know," I say, realizing that I do. I fully, irrevocably, believe deeply within myself that this man is mine. I'm done fucking around and questioning it, and I'm *so* done not living life how I want.

Chapter Thirty-One

Ledger

I could count on one hand the number of times I've cried as a grown man, but Sloane provokes deeper emotions than I realized I was capable of. Deeper *love* than I thought I was capable of.

When I feel her shivering, I find a blanket and wrap her up like a burrito, keeping her in my lap with her head tucked into my neck.

Both of us seem to be cried out for now, with a pregnant silence between us. It's less tense than earlier but still so different from how things usually are, and I can't take another second of it.

"Sloane..."

"Ledger..."

I smile as we speak at the same time. Shifting, I bring Sloane up to straddle my lap, keeping my soft cock from rubbing her swollen, abused pussy. I just want her close. Once she settles back, the soft blanket protecting her ass from the rough hairs on my thighs, I gently kiss the top of her nose and look into her eyes.

She's wrecked, but she looks sated, and her eyes are clearer than I've seen since before her parents arrived and shattered our perfect bubble of bliss. This is how she deserves to feel all the time, and I'm done allowing anyone, even herself, to stand in the way of that. Today was our line in the sand.

As I look at her marked with blood from both of us, I realize she's covered in the very thing she chose as her safe word. *Crimson.* She never said the word. Instead, she let me cover her body in it.

The trust she placed in me tonight, to see exactly who I am at my most unhinged, was...*fuck.* Sublime. Transcendent. Impossible. She makes me feel seen and worthy in ways I never knew I needed or dared to hope for. And she's mine. It's high time she had every single piece of me and the reassurance she needs to know exactly where she stands.

Giving her one more forehead kiss, I pick her up and carry her to the shower, standing with her body glued to mine, just letting the scalding water rinse us. I watch as the stream of water changes from deep red to clear, and I can't help but think about the symbolism of how Sloane has cleansed every part of me. How she's erased my past and given me a bright and shining future. And how I intend to do the same for her, making sure she wakes up every day knowing how cherished she is.

Setting Sloane on her feet, I soap up my hands and wash her body, cleaning it like the temple it is. When I'm finished, she does the same to me, neither of us saying a word throughout the process.

Once we're clean, I dry us both off, bandaging where I've carved my initials into her, and place her gently on the counter. "Stay here, Angel."

Moving to the locker where I left my hopes and dreams earlier tonight, I take a deep breath and enter the code. First, I reach for my phone and send Jack a quick text letting him know I'm activating plan A. At this point, I think he's due for his fifth raise in three months. *Maybe I should just sign the club over to him. Then I could stay home and be Sloane's full-time house husband.* Tabling that thought for later, I grab the box that hopefully represents my future and palm it, my hand large enough to hide it as I come back to stand between Sloane's knees.

My hands are shaking, so I cage her in with my arms and set the velvet box on the counter behind her, out of sight. I try to open my gaze and allow her to see every ounce of what I'm feeling, but the enormity of it is impossible to share with a look.

"Angel...I've had too long to think about our last interaction. Our fight has been on a nonstop loop, and I need you to know that I've come to realize I was wrong. I understand your hesitancy, and as much as we both know that we're it for each other, it has been fast. Your parents are important figures in your life, and I should never have insinuated otherwise. I promise to try my best in the future to think more carefully of your perspective before I bulldoze all over your feelings. You don't deserve that."

Her eyes glisten with tears, but if I don't get this all out now, I'm afraid I never will.

"I forget sometimes that you're so much younger than me because I've been an immature piece of shit for so long, only caring about myself and not being considerate of how my actions affected other people."

She gives me a watery chuckle at that, and I kiss her nose, unable to keep my lips off her for very long.

"I'm learning to be better about that, and you've been patient with me, which I appreciate more than you know."

I take a deep breath, grab the box from behind her, and drop down to one knee.

She lets out a half sob, half gasp and covers her mouth with one hand while reaching for my cheek with the other. I nuzzle into the inside of her knee and give her a quick kiss before pulling back.

"Sloane. My angel. You have come into my life like a whirlwind of happiness and contentment and turned my idea of joy upside down. Any inkling of pleasure or love I ever thought I felt before I met you was a sad imitation of what you've given me, and all I want for the rest of my life is to try to make you happy. I can't stand being parted from you, and I need you to know that I would do anything to make your days perfect. We can live anywhere in the world that you want, have no kids or a ton, travel in an RV, live on a sailboat, open a bookstore—whatever you want, baby. Anything for you. Please just let me be by your side for it. I want to respect you and your family and make all of your fears about whether or not I'm yours disappear. So please. Please, Sloane. Will you do me the honor of being my wife?"

Tears stream down her face, and I really fucking hope I haven't misread this. A piece of my soul broke off and gifted itself to my angel tonight, and I hope she'll give me a piece of hers in exchange.

She gently strokes my cheek, and when she lowers her hand from her mouth, there's a sweet smile on her beautiful face.

"Yes," she says, breaking into a fit of giggles. "Yes, you ridiculous, perfect man. Of course, I'll marry you."

Letting out a relieved sob of my own, I stand and pull her into my arms as she wraps her legs around my waist. I can't catch my breath, laughing and crying and trying to plaster myself so closely to every inch of her skin that she can never get rid of me. Pulling back, I place my forehead to hers.

"You didn't even look at the ring."

"Ledger, I couldn't care less what that ring looks like. It could be a candy ring, and we could live in a shitty apartment, and I would be just as ecstatic to be your fiancée."

I know she's telling the truth, but fuck, it feels good to know that she's about to get every single one of her whims catered to, forever.

"Humor me. I spent a great deal of time designing this for you."

Picking the box off the floor where I dropped it in the rush to get my hands on her, I open it and hope that she loves it and sees that I've tried to encompass as much of her personality as I could in the design. It's elegant but whimsical, perfect for my vibrant Angel.

She's been staring wide-eyed at it for so long that I'm tempted to hide it and tell her we'll design whatever she wants when she bursts into tears all over again and throws her arms around my neck.

Hoping this is a good sign, I kiss her temple. "Do you like it?"

Sloane pulls back and wipes her eyes on her fluffy blanket. "Ledger. If you don't put that beautiful ring on my finger right now, I think I'll die."

Laughing, I oblige my fiancée. *Fuck, that's nice. Too bad it won't be for very long.* Reaching for her left hand, I slide her ring onto her finger, hoping it never leaves.

"It's a perfect fit," she whispers, giving me a blinding smile.

"Of course it is. Do you think I didn't measure your finger before I designed this ring?"

A quirk of her lips tells me she's not at all surprised by my attention to detail. "How long have you had this ring, exactly?"

"Longer than I care to admit."

Swaying her softly in my arms, I bask in the rightness of how this feels. "What do you think, fiancée? Do you want a big white wedding? Something small on a beach? Vegas with Elvis?"

Sloane sighs in contentment. "I would marry you here and now, wearing nothing but this blanket. I've never really wanted a big wedding, and as hot as it is to call you my fiancé, thinking of you being my husband makes me feel crazy with how much I want it."

Fucking jackpot. My girl is on the same page. Glad I texted Jack about plan A.

"Well...what do you say we get married tonight? But maybe not here. It smells a little, and the lighting is awful."

"I wish, but I'm pretty sure there are papers to fill out and you have to wait a few days and get things notarized..."

"Sloane, if you think I haven't been renewing marriage licenses since about two weeks after we met, you must not know me at all. Everything is ready. Jack is ordained, and we have all the papers. If you really want to do this, it would make me the happiest man in the world to make you Sloane Sinclair tonight."

I think I've stunned her again until she gives me another one of her gorgeous smiles, shifting my world on its axis as only she can.

"Yes!"

A few hours later, we're watching the sun rise with champagne in our hands, gently swaying back and forth on our balcony hammock at home.

She's back home, and she's never going anywhere without me again. She'll be lucky to ever have six hours alone, let alone weeks...she'll want a girls' trip at some point, but surely, I can make it if I go and just kinda follow at a safe distance, just to make sure she's got everything she needs...

"What are you thinking about?" my *wife* ponders, and I'm hard, already thinking of her new title. But there's no way she's ready to go again, so I kiss her nose and tell her a partial truth.

"You."

Our ceremony earlier was perfectly simple, with Jack, Margot, and Allie transforming our home into a romantic space to begin our forever. Allie helped Sloane into a simple white silk midi dress that I *may* have had made for her with this evening in mind. I wore black slacks and a white shirt, with my sleeves rolled up and the top three buttons unbuttoned, just the way my angel prefers. With her hair pulled back into a messy chignon, as Allie called it, and minimal makeup on, Sloane looked...ethereal. Unreal. *Mine.* I can't wait to stare at her every day for the rest of my life.

"My wife," I whisper, feeling tears forming in my eyes again. I've probably cried more tonight than any other day of my life. Maybe more than every other instance of my life combined. "You've made me so indescribably happy, Sloane. I'll spend forever thanking you."

"My husband," she breathes against my lips, and as the sun rises, words leave me, and all I know is her.

Chapter Thirty-Two

Sloane

"Wake up, Angel," I hear as I open my eyes.

Squinting, I look up into the beautiful eyes of my *husband.* "Mmm, good morning again."

"It's two in the afternoon." Ledger chuckles, brushing my wild hair out of my face before placing a chaste kiss on my forehead. "We have to leave for rehearsal in an hour, or I wouldn't have woken you."

Ugh. Practice is early today since most of us are students, and we're officially out for Christmas break. I make a scene of stretching and sigh before I notice the new additions to my ring finger. *I wonder when I'll ever get used to wearing this beauty.* "You're the one who kept me up until six in the morning." I try to add some sass to that, but another glance at the extraordinary man I'm now legally tethered to has me smiling from ear to ear. *I wonder when I will ever get used to that as well.*

"Come on, love. Let's get you dressed before I say fuck it and keep you in this bed instead."

My body is still sore from the way Ledger ravaged me after his fight, but the way he made love to me last night, gentle and slow, worshipping every inch he decimated only hours before, has me wetter than I'd like to admit.

"Okay, I vote we stay," I say as I fall back down onto the bed.

He picks me up and walks me to my vanity. "Sloane Sinclair, if we don't show up for the last rehearsal, we will *both* reap the wrath of my mother."

Oh right. Blanche. My now mother-in-law, who has no idea we are married and who will be finding out in roughly an hour and a half. "Are you sure we should tell her tonight? Don't you think we should get through the play and tell her on Christmas Eve when we tell my parents?" I half yell at Ledger as he walks into the closet.

He walks back out holding a matching set of tacky Christmas sweaters. "My love, you have absolutely *nothing* to be worried about. *Trust me* when I tell you, she's going to be thrilled." With that, he hands me one of the sweaters as well as some leggings and leaves me to get ready.

"Okay, you're sure you want me to keep the rings on?" I ask Ledger as we walk up to the building.

Ledger opens the door with one hand, the other resting on the small of my back as he guides me through the church. "Yes, just act as normal as possible. As soon as she sees it, she's going to freak out, and then I'll tell her she's got another daughter. It's perfect, trust me."

"Do you want to take bets on what she'll notice first? The ring or these freaking marks you left all over my neck," I say, recalling how much concealer I used to try to cover my bruises, to no avail.

Ledger only smirks and gives my still sore butt a little love tap.

To no one's surprise, the hickeys and bite marks are the first thing my mother-in-law notices.

"Ledger Sinclair, *what have you done?*" Her smile quickly turns to a scowl as we approach. "I don't typically judge one's bedroom activities, but *really, son?* Our play is in *two days!*"

I look at Ledger beaming with pride, a complete contrast to my absolute mortification. The moment of awkward silence is only broken by Blanche's squeals when I bring my hands up to cover my beet-red face.

Her mouth drops open in surprise as she yanks my hand to her face. "You mean to tell me...wait a minute, *two* rings." Her eyes go wide as she looks down at Ledger's left hand to see a matching wedding band adorning his ring finger.

Ledger holds up his hand in question. "Yes, ma'am, we are very much married. I'd like to introduce you to your new daughter, Sloane Olivia Sinclair."

Blanch looks between Ledger and me for a moment before nearly tackling me in a hug so aggressive I almost topple over. When she finally pulls back, tears are welling up in her eyes. "Oh, my darling, I'm so, so happy for you." She stops to pull her son in for a three-way hug. "I'm so happy for you both."

She pulls back a second time, still holding on to an arm each. "Welcome to the family, dear. Oh, and I take it all back. It wouldn't be a good wedding night if you were any less marked up than you are," she finishes with a wink.

I give her a shy smile, blushing at her insinuation. "Thank you so much, Blanche."

"You are very welcome," she says, glancing down at her watch. "I'm afraid I'm going to have to wait until after this rehearsal to hear all the details." The sadness in her eyes morphs into delight as she exclaims. "Oh, I know! Come over to my house after we're done here! I'll fix a nice dinner, and you can tell me everything."

"Well, actually..." I pause to look up at Ledger. "We're going to be decorating the house for Christmas."

Blanche slaps her son on the arm, pulling a groan from him. "You haven't decorated for Christmas?"

"Ow! No, *Mother*. Sloane and I were going to do it together, but her parents came into town, so we weren't able to."

She rolls her eyes. "Fine, I'll come over tonight with Margot, and we can have a little decorating party to fix everything up." With that, she gives us one last hug and begins our final rehearsal.

We've only been home long enough to change into some matching Christmas pajamas and pull out the ungodly amount of brand-new decorations Ledger ordered for us when Blanche comes trudging through our side door. She's followed by Margot and Jack, all loaded down with food and *more decorations.*

"Jack! This is three nights in a row you've wound up at our house. Not that I don't miss the days of us living together, but I like to keep Sloane with as little clothing on as possible, and I'm afraid I'd have to kill you if you saw her naked," Ledger says, giving Jack a hug.

My already blushing cheeks redden as Blanche responds, "Oh, Jack was at the house when I got home to pick up Margot, and I recruited him to help with the heavy lifting. No worries, dear, you'll have your new bride to yourself before too long." With that, she wraps her arm around my shoulders and squeezes. "Plus, the more this lovely lady is scantily clad, the more likely I am to have a grandbaby."

"Jesus, Mother, she's not a cow," Ledger says, pulling me from her grip into his warm, strong arms before leaning down to whisper into my ear. "But she's not wrong, you know I can't wait to fuck a baby into you."

Apparently, my vagina is in agreement with Ledger. My entire body ignites, and arousal floods between my legs as I lose my balance, collapsing into his arms. Luckily, everyone has moved into the living room where all the decorations are strewn about, listening to Blanche delegate tasks.

Christmas music plays throughout the house as I put cookies in the oven, and the festivities begin.

It doesn't take very long to put up a whole store's worth of decor when you have five sets of helping hands and a decoration overlord organizing everything.

We're finished in no time and have congregated in the kitchen when Blanche hands us all a glass of champagne. "To Sloane and Ledger," she says as we all clink our glasses together in a cheers. "And to grandbabies," she says as we cheers a second time, this one laced with laughter. The guys grab a plate of cookies and sit at the table while Blanche, Margot, and I stand around the island.

"So tell me everything," my mother-in-law requests. "I will forgive you for not inviting me, but you better not leave out a detail."

Ledger chuckles from the table beside us, and I cover my face with my hand as Margot responds, "Oh, for the love, Ledger. *Please* leave out *those* details."

He just shrugs his shoulders, winks, and goes back to his conversation, leaving Margot and me to discuss the more savory details of the night I got engaged *and* married, including all the pictures from both our phones.

Blanche is in a lover's daze when we finish, but snaps back quickly to direct her attention to Margot. "You better include me in *your* wedding plans, missy, or I will absolutely never forgive you."

Margot rolls her eyes at her mother. "Don't worry, Mom, you've got plenty of time to prepare. I've made it through four years of undergrad and am almost through my master's without any prospects, so I doubt there are any wedding bells in my near future."

"All the more reason to spend some time abroad!" Blanche exclaims.

"I know, I know. I have two internships lined up between New York and Paris. I just haven't decided yet," Margot explains, her eyes darting briefly in Jack's direction.

"If I were a single twenty-three-year-old, I would try to find the sexiest Frenchman I could and climb him like a tree," Blanche retorts, fanning herself for dramatic effect.

I glance over at the boys. Ledger is in the middle of talking about something, but Jack seems to freeze at Blanche's words.

"*Mother!*" Margot whisper-yells.

"Oh, you're a boring bunch," Blanche says, rolling her eyes.

At this, Ledger chimes in, getting out of his chair and walking toward me. "Trust me, nothing is boring over here," he says, cocooning my body in his from behind and wrapping his arms around my waist.

"Ledger!" Margot and I practically scream at the same time.

Blanche elbows her in the side. "Well, *you* give me a grandbaby, then!"

Ledger squints his eyes at his sister. "Oh no, you don't. You're not allowed to date until you're thirty, remember? Don't think I won't make good on my promise to beat any fucker who lays a hand on you."

Margot and Blanche both roll their eyes as Jack chokes on his cookie.

"Speaking of grandchildren, let's show your mom the room you had put in for the nursery."

The baby-crazed pair follows me up the stairs without question, leaving Margot and Jack behind. What I thought would take five to ten minutes turned into a long ordeal.

I eventually leave my husband and his mother alone, feeling like a bad host for abandoning our company, but as soon as I reach the kitchen, I freeze. Margot and Jack hide their appearance well with their champagne flutes, but their lips are slightly swollen, and Jack's hair is disheveled.

"Alright," Blanche says, following Ledger back into the kitchen. "Let's give these two newlyweds some privacy."

We walk them outside and exchange our hugs and kisses before they climb into Blanche's SUV.

Ledger stands behind me with his arms wrapped around me and his chin resting on the top of my head as we wave them off. That is until Blanche hangs her head out the window and yells, "Grandbabies!" to which my husband responds by giving a thumbs-up, throwing me over his shoulder, and running up to our room, making good on his promise until the early hours of the morning.

Chapter Thirty-Three

Ledger

The play was a resounding success. Even more successful was my ability to keep my hands to myself. The professional makeup crew my mother hired for this production managed to cover Sloane's bruises and hickeys, and it was all I could do not to drag her into a broom closet and add more. For Mom's sake, though, I kept it together, and based on the audience's reaction, everyone was moved by her modern take on the Christmas story. As thankful as I am for this play and my mom's scheming for bringing Sloane and me together, I'm ready to have my wife to myself for Christmas. Well...not just to myself. We've decided that an after-party at our house tonight is the perfect opportunity for Sloane's family to meet mine and for us to announce our marriage to her parents. She's nervous but hopeful that once they see that I've made an honest woman out of her, they'll come around. I'm not convinced that will be the case, but it's objectively better to go ahead and get everything out in the open so that, regardless of what happens, we can all move forward.

Luckily for me, my mother's vision of Lucifer favors the same cut and style of custom suit as I do, so I'm already dressed and ready to head home for the party. I'm just waiting for my wife to finish changing.

My wife. Fuck, that has yet to get old. I'm not convinced it ever will. I have our rings in my pocket, waiting to put them back on later this evening once we've made our announcement. Just as I'm at the end of my patience, Sloane emerges from the dressing room with my mother in tow.

God, she's beautiful. I'll never get over the effect her presence has on me, like my entire body is attuned to hers on a cellular level. She's wearing white for me again—a silk, corseted midi dress with fur trim around her calves. With her blonde hair and minimal makeup worn for the play, she truly looks like my personal angel. *Which she is. Legally. Forever.* She's also wearing a white faux-fur coat that I recognize as my mother's, and they're chatting animatedly as they finally approach.

"Darling, it looks better on you than it ever did on me. And since you two skipped all the usual parties and events associated with a wedding, it's my right to continue with all my little gifts. Isn't that right, Ledger?"

Smiling, I pull Sloane into me and kiss the top of her forehead, determined to have skin-on-skin contact for the rest of the evening. "Whatever my wife wants, Mom."

With a wistful sigh, Mom winks at me and moves toward the church entrance. "Are the Johnsons riding with you?"

"We've got to figure that out. Either way, you'll all probably beat us there. Just use your codes for the gate and door. Call me if you have any problems."

"Alright, dear. See you soon." With a kiss on the cheek, Mom leaves us alone to try to find Sloane's parents in the hustle and bustle.

"You were wonderful tonight, Angel. I couldn't take my eyes off you," I say, nuzzling into her neck and wondering if we have time for a bathroom quickie before we leave. Knowing that everyone will be at the house all evening has me feeling like a whiny child with my favorite toy just out of reach.

"You were a pretty handsome devil, yourself." Sloane giggles. "Maybe we should re-enact our scene later but with fewer clothes and a spicier ending."

"That's it, you little temptress, we're not going home tonight. I'm going to find the most isolated cabin I can, and we're not coming up for air until…"

A throat clearing startles both of us, and we look up to find Scott Johnson watching me fondle his little girl in the vestibule of a church on Christmas Eve. Well. I've never claimed to be an angel, so I'm not sure what anyone expects.

"Hi, Dad," Sloane says, giving him a stiff side hug.

"Mr. Johnson, it's very nice to see you again. Merry Christmas Eve. If Mrs. Johnson is ready, I can pull the car around, and we can head to the house."

Shaking my hand, Scott seems less testy with me than before. Maybe he's thinking about my brother. Can't wait to see his reaction when Henry arrives for our family soiree tonight.

"She had an errand to run. I'll ride with you both, if that's alright."

Sloane frowns, and like her, I wonder what Janice could possibly have to do on Christmas Eve.

"Of course, I'll bring the car around, and we can head out. Sloane, make sure your mom has the address, please."

I'm a little surprised that we arrive home without any major drama in the car, although Janice's absence likely accounts for that. The only tense moment occurred when Scott assumed he would be sitting in the passenger seat beside me, and I had to remind him that Sloane gets carsick and would therefore be in the front. I'm also surprised to see that we're the first three back to the house, and my mother hasn't arrived yet with any of my family.

"Home sweet home," I say, giving the back of Sloane's hand a kiss and coming around to open her door for her as Scott stares up at the house. I've parked in the circular drive in front, and with the landscaping and Christmas lights we've added, it truly is a place I'm proud to bring my wife home to.

"Quite the place you've got here," he says, noting the security system and the large garage around back.

"Thank you, sir. I've had it for a few years, but I've just finished some fairly extensive renovations. This one here"—I chuckle, giving Sloane a little squeeze—"has quite the refined taste. My bachelor decor wasn't to her liking, so we've changed almost everything."

This earns me a thoughtful glance from Scott, like he's confused as to why I would go to all the trouble, but I'm saved from my initial desire to punch him in the face by my mother pulling up behind us.

Scott immediately notices Henry, and I breathe out a tense breath of air I hadn't realized I was holding. *Sorry, Henry, but you're going to be babysitting him all night, if only to take some pressure off Sloane.*

"Darlings! We had to make a little pit stop. I hope you don't mind that we didn't beat you here," Mother says, coming straight to Sloane and hugging her like we didn't see each other less than an hour ago at the church.

"You're fine, Mom. We only beat you by about thirty seconds. This is Sloane's dad, Scott Johnson." I make quick introductions all around between Margot, Jack, Henry, my mom, and Scott. Once we're all acquainted, I usher everyone inside out of the cold.

Luckily, everything was already set up to host, including a spread for way too many people. Sloane and I were fortunate to have our housekeeper, Mrs. Smith, recommended by my mother. We still cook together, but having meals prepped and not having to worry about cleaning the house has given us more time together for *newlywed* activities. She's also discreet, and after an unfortunate incident involving her finding us naked in the foyer, whenever the security system alerts her to our arrival, she makes herself scarce. *"Just for the honeymoon phase, dear,"* she said when I was mortified that Sloane and I couldn't control ourselves. But it's worked out in my favor.

With Henry and Scott deep in discussion about football seasons past—*I really owe him one for this*—and Margot, Jack, and my mom discussing the play, I nurse my spiked eggnog and feel surprisingly sentimental. With the huge tree in the living room, all the Christmas decorations, and the delicious smell of food wafting from the kitchen, I feel more at peace than I ever have.

A knock on the door reminds me of exactly who hasn't arrived yet, and just like that, my peace shatters.

"I'll get it!" My mother is already moving to the front door, likely still convinced that *she'll* be able to charm Janice Johnson and be best friends with her future co-grandmother. She hasn't quite gotten the full picture of why I'm certain that will never happen...but I have a bad feeling she's about to.

"Sloane's darling mother has arrived, everyone, and she brought a surprise! One of Sloane's very best childhood friends!"

I glance up to see who the fuck is in my house and feel goose bumps rise on my skin. *Fucking Dean Christensen.* In *my* fucking house. Why is he in my fucking house?

I can't help myself. "Why are you in my fucking house?" I snarl, barely holding on to the facade of being a decent human being that I try to keep in place around Sloane's parents.

"Ledger!" my mom and Sloane hiss in sync. *Come on! This asswipe is in my house, and I'm supposed to be civil?* I'm clearly not going to win this one.

Deciding to keep my mouth shut, I grip my drink even tighter and pull Sloane into my side when she moves past me toward her mom. Taking a deep breath of her coconut scent that I love so much, I try to find my peace in this rapidly devolving situation. God bless both my mom and Jack, who are trying to distract our new arrivals with discussions of the play and church and golf. Henry still has plenty of material to keep Scott preoccupied for hours, if not days. Maybe we can get through this dinner unscathed, and Janice's little stunt will be for nothing.

Now that everyone is here, and we've found an extra place setting for our unwelcome surprise guest, we can finally sit down and eat. A full mouth of food will surely prevent anyone from causing too much drama.

The meal is delicious, not that Mrs. Smith has ever made anything that wasn't. Thanks to my mother's frankly ridiculous life story, she's been able to regale everyone with tales from her youth that take some of the heat off Sloane and I. Scott has laughed a few times, and Janice has had a few glasses of mulled wine (although I think my mother told her it was mulled juice, so I'm not sure she realizes exactly what she's been drinking). I'm gathering the courage to finally make our announcement when everything promptly goes to shit, thanks to the asshole who I should've kicked out of my house before he even crossed the threshold.

"I gotta say, Ledger, I expected a lot more black paint and red leather in your house," Dean says, before downing the rest of his glass of wine and sitting back in his chair. The smirk on his face tells me he knows exactly what he just did, and my urge to snap his neck hits an all-time high. That won't help this situation, though, and it won't help Sloane, so I take a deep breath and decide it's time. It's time to ascend to the final plane of being the bigger person. Nothing is going to rattle me tonight. My wife needs me to be calm and in control.

"Sloane's perfect taste drove the design for the interior," I say, hoping to deflect from the underlying accusation he just leveled at me. Kissing the back of her hand, I keep our fingers laced and place our hands on her thigh, noting that she's as tense as a board. "We plan to tackle the exterior next, with a pool and sundeck—"

"It's just," Dean interrupts, "I would have thought that your aesthetic would have carried over at *least* a little. Or do you keep all the whips and chains and mirrors confined to the bedroom? Or do you have a red room? When I think of the interior of a sex club owner's bedroom, French country chic just doesn't really fit, ya know?"

Everyone at the table sucks in a quick breath through their teeth, and then...silence. You could hear a pin drop. I'm not convinced any of us are actually breathing.

"You own...a *sex club?*" Janice whisper-screeches, saying the word sex like it's a curse word, which, to her, it probably is. Scott is standing now, and his face is approaching nuclear levels of redness, to the point I briefly think that tonight might actually be the night he has an aneurysm or heart attack, or both. "Is this true, Sloane? You're dating a *deviant* who not only does drugs and rides motorcycles but owns an entire sex club?"

I can feel Sloane trembling in her seat next to me, but that's okay. I've never felt more in control than at this moment. Sloane is my priority, followed by my family, and the Johnsons can get fucked for all I care.

Turning, I face my mom first. "Mom, I'm sorry that you had to find out about this in this way. I haven't been entirely truthful with you, and while the security business is legitimate, it has become largely self-sustaining at this point. I do operate a club in the city dedicated to exploring pleasure, and it's been one of the most fulfilling creative endeavors of my life."

My mother gives me a soft smile before sweetly sipping her wine. "Honey, if you think I didn't know about Rendezvous within a week of you applying for the permits, I'm not sure you know me at all."

That gets everyone's attention, and Jack chokes on his own drink. "Don't be dramatic, Jack. I'm old but not dead! I'm just surprised you boys haven't seen me there, although I do usually bring a mask and stick to the people I know. Some things a mother *does not* need to see."

"You *own and operate* a sex club..." Janice is starting to shake now, and I begin to think maybe a couple of ambulances should be called, just in case. "You have corrupted our daughter!"

"Well, he owns *a majority* of it, technically, but a large portion of the shares are mine as well. And I'm not sure you can characterize him as *running* it anymore, at least not in the past few months. He's been way too busy staying locked up here with Sloane and...ow!" Jack exclaims. I'm thankful Margot smacks him on the side of the head to stop before he can describe any more of what I've been doing to Sloane over the past few months.

Dean is standing now, still nonchalant and smirking like he's not done dropping bombs on our Christmas Eve gathering. *Fuck.*

"I'm *also* surprised you have so much light colored furniture here. Do you have secrets for getting them clean after you fuck her bloody in your little perverted satanic rituals? Or is that just in her apartment living room and not here?"

Jack is clearly still trying to defuse this situation, but it's too far gone. He doesn't realize, blabbering on, "Hey, I've never seen him take part in a satanic ritual! Perverted, I mean that's pretty subjective, I'd say. A few years ago, I had two nuns who..."

"Jack, that's enough," I grind out, pinching the bridge of my nose. "Dean, it's time for you to go."

"Is what he's saying true, Mr. Sinclair?" Scott breaks his silence. "Dean, how would you even know these things?"

I sigh, knowing that at least a partial truth is necessary here. "Mr. Johnson, it is true that—"

"I know because I saw it, Scott. With my own eyes." Dean is sorely testing my patience right now.

"You broke into a residence in the middle of the night, where you had no right to be!" I refuse to be blamed for this asshole breaking and entering when he knew he had no business.

"I had a key!" Dean shouts. "I had a key, and I wanted to check on Sloane and explain that this has all been a misunderstanding and a nightmare, and I couldn't sleep without telling her how I felt! So of course I let myself in to surprise her, and instead, you were fucking her! Covered in blood! And you didn't stop even when she was unconscious!"

Well, *this* is an even silencier silence than the silence earlier.

Janice has tears of anger trailing down her face, and Scott has sat back down and drained his wineglass.

"Well, I've been fucking around Ledger for a long time."

I groan internally, willing *anyone* to stop Jack again, but nobody does. "And I know damn well he wouldn't do anything like that without consent, so whatever you saw still isn't your business, asshole. Time to go," he says, trying to help but completely unable to read the room.

Before Jack can toss Dean outside, Janice snaps.

Her voice is low as she steps toward Sloane, still seated beside me. "You. Little. Slut. Or are you a whore? He certainly seems to be paying you enough between the house and the car. I knew you would spread your legs before you were married, but for this *godless deviant?* I've never been so disappointed to call you my daughter!"

Janice is screaming by the end of her outburst, and when I see her raise her hand as if to backhand Sloane, my calm snaps back into place, and I decide we're done here.

Stepping in front of Sloane, I block Janice's slap with my forearm. "Do. Not. *Ever.* Raise your hand. Against *my wife.* "

In the drawn-out, tense stillness that follows, Janice stares me down as I block her from even looking at Sloane. My mother manages to herd everyone else out, leaving us alone with the Johnsons.

Finally, Janice turns and crosses the room to stand beside Scott.

"You have *ruined* our daughter. She was such a good girl, and I don't know how *you* managed to pull her away from God and defile her," her mother says, glaring at Sloane as if she doesn't even recognize her.

I pull Sloane to her feet and hold her face in both of my hands. "I love you, Angel," I murmur, giving her a small kiss and trying to see any hint of how she's feeling in her eyes. She's obviously sad, but her tears have seemingly dried up from earlier, and her glint of determination makes me grin. "That's my girl," I whisper.

Standing proudly in her beautiful dress, she breaks her silence. "Give me my rings back, please, Ledger. I feel naked without them."

"My pleasure, baby." I slide mine on first, then retrieve hers from my jacket pocket and reverently place them back on her finger with a kiss. I move to stand behind her, where I belong, with one hand on her hip. *Unless she's in danger. Then I'll be in front of her, shielding her from the world.*

"Mom. Dad. I'm sorry that Dean's crass announcement is how you found out that I'm married. It's not how we had planned to tell you, and I hope you can see the kind of person he is, to try and ruin a lovely evening."

She takes a deep breath, and I am *so fucking proud* of my girl. I give her hip a little squeeze, and she continues.

"I'm not discussing any intimate details with you, but I love Ledger and I am by far the happiest I've ever been. This is my life, and I choose him. This is where I'll be." She sags slightly back into my chest, and I give her a kiss on the temple. It's been a long-ass day, and I know how much energy it takes to stand up to your parents like this.

Surprisingly, Scott is the first to speak. "Sloane, I don't understand how you could do this. We've given you everything you needed, and this is how you repay us? This isn't you."

"He's obviously using you, sweetie," Janice continues. "There must be some ulterior motive here. Men who have money like this don't just dote on women for nothing. All of this is going to come right back around and bite you, I'm afraid."

My wife is tired, so it's my turn to try, one last time, to make these awful people understand.

"This is the last time you're going to be welcomed into our home if you are so blind to your daughter's brilliance that you feel the need to continue to insult her. She is a kind, generous, intelligent young woman who clearly tries to please you but is doomed to fail. You both fail to see her for who she is, but I don't. She's perfect. She helps me see the good in the world, the joy in little things, and the multitude of ways to be happy as a human. If you would stop putting her down for failing to meet your asinine expectations, you would see that. I will not apologize for taking care of her. She's meant to be mine, and the years of life I've had without her were joyless but not wasted because I have everything I need now to make sure she has whatever she wants."

I keep my eyes on her and try to make sure she can see how much I mean every word.

Finally breaking eye contact with Sloane, I turn back to the Johnsons. "My wife is a wonderful woman who has utterly captivated me, and I hope both of you open your eyes and get to meet her one day."

With one more kiss to the top of Sloane's head, I decide to reveal what I really hope is the last surprise of the evening.

"As far as anything coming back around to bite her, let me reassure you on that matter. There's no version of reality in which I would ever grow tired of Sloane, but if she decides she's had enough of me, we have no prenuptial agreement. She has plenty of properties and portfolios already in her name, and she's a millionaire in her own right as of the transactions I finished up earlier this week."

Sloane gasps next to me, and I give her a smirk. "Sorry, baby. I knew if I told you, you'd try to stop me."

"Ledger! I don't want half of your money! We aren't getting divorced!" she hisses, and her cheeks are already flushed the pretty shade of pink that I love so much.

"I know we aren't, baby," I whisper. "I would track you down wherever you tried to go, regardless. But this way, if you decide to, you'll have enough starting capital to make the chase interesting. And now it isn't half of my money, it's just yours."

I straighten back up and grin again at the Johnsons. "But if she does divorce me, she can have half of the half I have left, and we would still both be millionaires."

Sloane pinches the bridge of her nose. "I had no idea you had that much money, you know."

"I do know. It's so cute when you're exasperated with me. Have I ever told you that?"

A scoff from Janice reminds me we *still* aren't alone in our house.

"I think both Mrs. Sinclair and I have said everything we have to say for the evening. If you'll excuse us, we're very much looking forward to our first Christmas as a family."

Thankfully, they seem chastised enough, or maybe just dazed enough, to realize I'm not asking them to leave. I'm telling them to get the fuck out. My mother appears and takes charge of leading them out the door and hopefully *out of our fucking lives*. At least for a while.

I pull Sloane into my arms and use a finger under her chin to bring her gorgeous green eyes to mine. She looks a little tired, but the spark I saw earlier, when she so beautifully put her parents in their place, is still there.

"Hello, Wife," I say, kissing the tip of her nose.

"Hi, Hubby." She giggles, the sound pulling a wide smile to my lips.

"I'm so proud of you, baby. I don't think I've ever been prouder or more impressed with anyone in my entire life than you standing tall and stating your truth to your parents. I'm sorry the evening was ruined, but I—"

Sloane pulls back, arching an eyebrow at me. "Ruined?" She scoffs. "It's only ten o'clock. I'm hungry, and I expect to open at least *one* of my presents tonight. Your family is here, and we have a whole dessert table laid out. Nobody is ruining our first Christmas Eve. I refuse."

Goddamn, I'm so proud of her. "My strong wife." I nuzzle into her neck. "You can have whatever you want. *Except—*"

Shocked, she pulls back to meet my eyes. "Except?" It's obvious I've never denied her anything because she can't even believe the word came out of my mouth.

"Well, baby, there's only one way to do Christmas. We open *all* presents on Christmas Eve. Christmas morning is for Santa and stockings, you silly goose!"

"Hmm…well, I suppose I wouldn't mind Santa *coming early* tonight."

We tease each other about the *proper* time to open presents as we make our way back to the kitchen. Margot, Jack, Henry, and Mom all sit around the kitchen island, picking through the trays of food that had been left by Mrs. Smith. They all look up tentatively when we come in, but Sloane gives them a big smile.

"I need to eat! Then I hear we apparently open presents *tonight?*"

Everyone laughs and moves to put another glass of wine in Sloane's hand and help her fix a plate, while my mom moves over to me.

"Is she really okay, darling?"

"I really think she is, Mom. She's been through a lot recently, but she's so strong, and I think she finally realizes it."

Mom smiles and gives me a hug. "I think you had a lot to do with that, son. She would have gotten there on her own, I hope, but having you in her corner helped give her the strength to do it. I'm sure of it."

"I hope I've given her even half of the support she's given me…I…" God, now I'm choking up talking to my mother on Christmas Eve. "She saved me, Mom. I've been searching for peace for years, and she just feels like…home. Like my personal redemption. Like I'm enough and she wouldn't change a thing."

"I wouldn't."

I was so focused on my mom that I didn't see my wife crossing the kitchen to stand in front of me with two champagne flutes in her hands. She has tears in her eyes, again, but these look happy, and I know she sees the same thing in mine.

Handing me one of the flutes, she reaches on her tiptoes to give me one soft kiss.

"I wouldn't change a thing," she whispers, just for me. "Now come on, *Husband*. I have a feeling one or two of these presents *might* have my name on them, and I'm awfully impatient to see what Santa's brought me."

Watching her lead my family into the living room and standing in the soft glow of the Christmas tree, I realize, for the first time ever at Christmas, I don't want a single thing. I have everything I need right here. My wife. My *Angel*. Home.

Chapter Thirty-Four

Sloane

My body shivers as Ledger takes my hand and helps me out of the car into the cool night air. "Are you *sure* you're ready for this, love?" he asks, running his hands up and down my arms to warm me. "We don't have to go here tonight. If you're set on a club, I can fly us to another before the ball drops. We can ring in the new year anywhere you want."

I snake one of my arms around his chiseled waist, relishing in the hard muscles beneath his dress shirt. "No, I want to go to ours."

Just as I assumed, the acknowledgment that Rendezvous belongs to both of us brings a smile to my husband's face. I want him to know that I am just as proud of what he's built as he is. I want him to know I am proud of *him*.

"Besides," I continue, "it's Jack's last big event before he leaves, and I want to see what he's done with the place."

"Ugh, on that note, maybe *I'm* not ready to go. I don't like the idea of that bastard seeing anything we might get up to tonight."

The thought of this god-like man being jealous over *me* makes me laugh. "Oh, I don't think Jack will be looking my way anytime soon."

I listen to Ledger rant about how I'm the most beautiful woman in the world and how I should be more confident than I am as we walk through the back halls to the front of the club. He finally stops when we get our first glimpse of the winter wonderland Jack has created tonight.

The white decor sparkles like freshly fallen snow. Tonight is an upscale evening, and we live up to the dress code with Ledger in his black suit and white dress shirt and me in my navy-blue floor-length, sleeveless dress.

The event is exclusive to top-tier members, with the focus being a traditional New Year's Eve party. That being said, there are still options for those who want to lean into more promiscuous proclivities, including open access to the exhibition stage for anyone interested. There's also what Ledger described as basically an orgy room, one he made very clear we would *not* be visiting.

Ledger leads us to the bar in the exhibition lounge and orders us each a glass of champagne. *I guess when you own the bar, it doesn't matter that you're only twenty.*

"Well, I'm in luck tonight," he says as he steps behind me and pulls my body flush against his own. "It looks like Jack isn't coming."

"That's a shame. He really outdid himself with all of this," I say, wrapping my arms around his and nuzzling into him as best I can from this angle. "You should really consider giving him a raise."

"Absolutely not. That would be like six raises in three months."

"Well, fine, I guess I'll have to do it." I wink up at him, then turn my gaze back into the crowd, moaning at what's heading our way. "Ugh, looks like you're the only lucky one tonight."

I watch as Lenora struts toward us with a gaggle of other women, all looking at my husband like he's a piece of meat. "Ledger, a pleasure as always," she purrs as she approaches us. "And, girls, this is Ledger's new *girlfriend.*"

Ledger makes no move to greet her. Instead, he wraps his arms around me tighter and kisses the top of my head. "*Wife,* actually," he corrects, holding up my left hand to show off the stunning rings adorning my finger.

I watch all four women visibly pout as Lenora speaks up. "I suppose congratulations are in order. Oh my, I don't remember your name, dear."

I recall a time when this would've made me feel inferior, but with my husband's arms wrapped around my waist and his ring wrapped around my finger, I know my place. "Sloane. Sloane Sinclair," I say, holding out my ring hand to shake hands with the other ladies as they introduce themselves. "I'm afraid I don't recall yours either."

"Lenora," she says, pursing her lips.

I raise an eyebrow and smirk, reminding her from my expression alone that she is, in fact, *Lenora not-Sinclair.*

In a last attempt to dig her claws in, she moves her attention back to Ledger. "That is a mighty fast turnaround. I hope there haven't been any *accidents.* You know, babies alone don't make for a good marriage."

My perfect husband chuckles and holds me tighter. "There are no babies *yet*. Not for my lack of trying, though." He moves his gaze from the girls to me as he tilts my head toward his. "I'm sure it won't be long, though, Angel, considering how much of my cum is constantly inside your sweet little pussy."

Lenora's face turns bright red as jealousy paints all four of their expressions, and I'm reminded of being the first woman Ledger has fucked without a condom. Suddenly, I feel like a queen.

As Lenora and her posse stomp away, I turn in Ledger's arms and look into his eyes. "How many of those women have you had sex with?"

His demeanor shifts. "Baby..."

"Tell me!" I demand.

"All of them," he admits with a sigh as he prepares himself for my wrath.

"Follow me," I say as I down my flute of bubbly and lead him to the empty exhibition stage in the center of the room.

His eyes search mine, trying to figure out what's going on inside my head. "You're going to fuck me raw and fill me up with so much of your cum, it drips out of my pussy for everyone to see."

Desire ignites in his eyes as he kisses me, pulling back to ask, "Clothes on or off?"

"Off. I want them to see what they will never be able to have," I say as I start unbuckling his pants, pulling a growl from him in the process. Ledger removes his jacket and freezes at the top button of his shirt. "*Sloane,* how much of us do you want them to see?"

"Are you embarrassed?" I taunt, walking him backward toward a large leather chair in the center of the stage. "It's not like half the crowd hasn't already seen everything you have to offer."

By the time we reach our destination, the two of us have managed to strip him naked. "Sit," I say, pushing him gently down into the chair.

He's looking up at me, chest heaving, muscles tense, pupils blown, dick at full mast, like a king on his throne waiting to be pleased. And *God*, I can't wait to sit on his lap, sink down onto his beautiful, decorated cock, and do just that. My mouth waters at the thought of feeling each ring of his ladder pull against my entrance until his magic cross hits my sweet spot when he bottoms out *so deep* inside me.

I make a show of removing my dress, knowing the lacy lingerie I have on underneath will drive him crazy. The strapless bodysuit connects to my stockings, giving everyone a view of only my ass cheeks. As much as I talk a big game, I don't think I'm ready to go full nude yet on stage. The way Ledger's dick jerks when he looks me up and down confirms that he's okay with my choice of wardrobe as well.

I straddle my husband, move my thong to the side, and sink down onto him while we both get momentarily lost in the sensation. Ledger's hands explore my body while I adjust to his size. "Jesus *fuck,* baby, what are you doing to me? I thought you wanted *me* to fuck *you.*"

I bring my hips up and back down, riding him slowly. "I wanted them to see your initials carved into me, and this was the best angle. Plus, we *both* know you can fuck me like this if you want to."

Ledger squeezes both of my breasts through the lace that's barely covering them. "Is that what you want, dirty girl? Do you want me to fuck you like this?"

He groans when my pussy grips him, a result of the effect his words have on me. "Actually, I want to show everyone exactly why you only need me from now on."

"Fuuuuck, Sloane," he says as he lays his head back against the chair, his hands finding my hips to no doubt leave a fresh set of bruises. "Ride me then, baby. Show them why you're my *wife.*"

With my ass healed from the night we got married, I'm able to ride my husband like he deserves. I worship his body as I grind my hips into him, taking his length in and out of my dripping core with each movement. My hands roam his body, reveling in the feel of how hard he is beneath my softness.

The melody of our moans and breaths, combined with the sound of our wet skin slapping, will always be my favorite composition. Ledger's filthy words, its lyrics.

My speed increases as that fire in my core starts to rise, letting me know a wave of pleasure is about to wash over me.

"Fuck, Angel, you have to come soon. Grind your clit against me, sweet girl. Show them. Show them how you milk my cum out of me."

His words mixed with the pain from the increased intensity of his hold on me are more than enough to send me over the edge. "Thank *fuck,*" Ledger grunts as he holds my shaking body down onto his dick and pulses jets of cum into me.

We sit interlocked together for what seems like both a moment and an eternity before Ledger breaks the silence.

"What do you think, love? Are you ready to show them just how much you please your husband?"

Before I can even register what he means, he cups my ass and slowly pulls me off his cock, making a dramatic show of just how his uncovered piercings pull against my pussy as he unsheaths himself.

"Let them see exactly how much cum I keep in this pussy."

As soon as the words leave his lips, I feel the warm liquid leaving my body. Some runs down my thighs while the rest drips straight to the floor. My eyes widen, and regardless of the fact that I just had sex in front of a room full of people, my cheeks begin to blush.

"It's okay, baby. I hate to waste it too. I'll fuck some more into you soon. Don't you worry."

I can feel my pussy flutter around nothing at the promise of his cock. "Take me home?"

"Are you sure? You were so excited to come tonight. Are you okay?" His concern makes me fall a little more in love with him.

I look out at the crowd of voyeurs, noting how the only ones in attendance who don't look pleased are the ones who are just mad they can't be in my position right now. *Can't ever be in my position.* "This has been so much fun," I assure my sweet man. "I just want to be alone with you."

We both throw our clothes back on before Ledger picks me up and carries me through a door at the back of the stage. "Me too, Angel, me too."

"Ugh, I really don't want to put those heels back on," I groan, holding up the stilettos I wore tonight.

"Hop on my back, baby," Ledger says, turning around and bending over to help me up for a piggyback ride.

He walks us through the back hall, but I need him to get me home faster. "You know they say to bring in the new year the way you want to spend every day, so how about we make sure you're balls deep inside me when the clock strikes midnight?"

Before I can hold on tighter, he speeds up to a running jog, his strong arms the only thing keeping me from falling on my ass. "God, I love you, Angel."

"I love you too, Devil. I love you too."

Epilogue I

Ledger

Two years later

Sloane and I lounge on a hammock bed, slowly swaying back and forth in the shallow, crystal-clear water. Our children are building sandcastles beside us, and she's reading her fifth new book in as many days. I have a book of my own in my right hand, and my left arm is wrapped around her shoulders with my hand resting on the swell of her stomach. *She looks so beautiful.* She places her left hand on mine, our shining wedding bands clinking against each other, then turns to smile up at me and opens her mouth to speak when...

I'm jolted awake by the beeping of my alarm blaring on my nightstand. Groaning, I reach over to turn it off before covering my face with my hands. *I could've used another few hours of dream bliss.* Damn, that was by far the most peaceful I've ever felt in a dream. Perfection. Smiling to myself, I remember that my real life has been just as peaceful lately and just as perfect.

I gave her *almost* two years. She never went on birth control, but I knew she wasn't really ready to have a baby, so I kept up with her cycle and strategically avoided as many close calls as I could. I'm only a man. I wasn't ready to share her yet either.

I waited until she officially graduated with her BA in Business. I begged her to forget about classes, assuring her she was already richer than God and didn't need a degree. Her compromise was to transition to online classes, which allowed us to spend the past two years traveling the world.

Her true passion has been documenting our travels. What started off as a fun project for her to keep up with all our stops by posting a video of us at each destination has turned into a following of almost a million people across her various socials.

I roll over to find my angel's side of the bed empty, but before I can question where she is, I hear her singing from the bathroom and smile again.

Chuckling, I make my way to the bathroom to enjoy my girl's shower concert. Sloane's hair is soaped up and twisted on top of her head as she shaves her legs, pausing every few seconds to gesture along with her song.

I can't keep my snickering to myself anymore at her adorable noises, and she squeals when I startle her with my presence.

"Ledger! You scared the crap out of me. I thought you were still asleep," she says, picking up the razor she flung down when I startled her.

"And miss this performance? Never," I say, pulling off my boxers and stepping into the shower with her.

Kissing her deeply, I move to help her rinse out her hair with the handheld attachment.

"Happy New Year, how did you sleep?"

"Happy New Year to you *again*. Mmm," she moans, as I use my fingers to massage her scalp while I rinse. "Overall, pretty well, I think. How about you?"

I finish my rinsing and pull her back into my chest, wrapping my arms around her waist and resting my chin on top of her head.

"Incredibly well, until I woke up and you weren't in bed with me. Please don't make a habit out of that, baby. I like cuddles in the morning. You know this."

Sloane's giggles are infectious. "Well, I hardly ever beat you getting up, but obviously you were having some good dreams—you were smiling in your sleep. Care to share with the class what was so lovely?"

I nuzzle into her neck and smile, placing one hand across the span of her swollen lower stomach. "Just dreaming about our future, Angel. That's all. Now hurry up or we'll be late to our own party."

"What do you want it to be?" she asks, as we make our way to my mom's house for the gender reveal party.

"Human."

"Ledger, seriously!"

"What? I am serious! With all the monster and alien smut you've been reading, I can never be too sure."

Her cheeks blush that beautiful shade of pink, "I, uh... I didn't know you knew about those."

"I know *everything,* dirty girl. You know that."

Sloane gasps as I pull into my mom's driveway, and I follow her gaze to see the Johnsons' car.

"It's okay, baby. They can't hurt you," I say, squeezing the hand of hers already on my own and bringing it to my mouth to kiss.

My brave girl takes a series of deep breaths and sits up straight. "I know. Let's do this."

Before we can knock on the door, we are greeted by my mother, blocking us from entering the house. "Sloane, darling, I know you're probably going to be royally pissed at me, but I had a little talk with your parents and ended up inviting them over."

"Mother, what is this about?" I grit out, interrupting her confession.

I'm leveled with a glare only a mother can give her child as she turns her attention from my wife to me. "This is about Sloane and her parents making up for the good of this baby."

I'm about to march us both back to the car, gender be damned, when Sloane speaks up. "Ledger, it's okay." She places a hand on my chest and uses her other to bring my own to her swollen belly. "Blanche is right. This is for the best. It's been two years. It's time."

Mom finally lets us through, and we're greeted by our whole family. I can tell Sloane's parents want to say something to her, but they just sink into the background as more of the others crowd around us.

"Alright, everyone, I had all kinds of games for us to play before we did the reveal, but *I just can't wait any longer*!" Blanche announces to the room. "Jack, dear, can you do the honors?"

Jack disappears into the kitchen before rolling out a black punching bag until he stops in front of me. "We thought this would only be fitting considering the night you, um, got married," he says, glancing at the Johnsons. "Sloane, you're welcome to do the honors, I suppose, but I think this was designed for our dad-to-be."

Sloane steps back in a clear sign that she wants nothing to do with this.

"I haven't fought since that night either, but I'll give it a go."

The material rips with one punch, sending blue powder flying into the air, and before I can make sense of *literally anything,* I hear the collective screams in the room. "It's a boy!"

I turn to my wife, whose beautiful eyes glisten with unshed tears as she wraps her hands around her womb, before picking her up, careful to avoid any harm to our baby and spinning with her in my arms. "A boy, baby!" she says as her tears start to fall down her face. "We're having a boy!"

I set her back on her feet and lean down to rest my forehead against her, placing my hands over hers on the swell of her stomach as tears begin falling from my eyes as well. "I know, Angel. I know, a boy."

"Hey! A little Ledger!" Jack says, pulling me out of the universe where only my wife, my unborn son, and I exist.

"Oh *Lord,* let's hope not, for everyone's sake," my mom responds, making her way over to Sloane and wrapping her up in a hug. "Congratulations, sweetheart. You are going to be the best mother." My mom looks at me with tears in her eyes as well. *Tears all around it seems.* "*Both* of you will make fantastic parents." Removing an arm from my wife, she cups my face, wiping a tear as we lock eyes. "I'm so proud of you, son."

Margot and Henry congratulate us, leaving Sloane's parents for last. I'm already on the defensive in case one of them, *her mom in particular,* decides to say something to ruin this beautiful moment.

Her dad approaches first with his arms open for a hug that she reluctantly accepts. "Congratulations," he says before stepping back to shake my hand. "To both of you."

"Um, thank you."

"Thank you, sir."

Sloane and I say at the same time, respectively.

"I've been keeping up with your travels. You seem happy. I'm glad."

His words allow us both to relax a bit in preparation for her mom's greeting. "Congratulations to you both. You were correct about one thing, babies are a blessing..." She pauses, and I see her hand hesitate to touch her daughter's baby bump, but she just holds her hand out for a shake instead. Sloane wraps her arms around her mom for a hug, catching her off guard. I can see her mom sink into the hug only for a moment before pulling back and telling us all they have to get going.

My mom is by my wife's side the minute they walk out the door. "They will come around, sweetheart."

"I know." My strong girl smiles, then surprises us all. "Um... Blanche... Please tell me there's cake."

"Cake, then games!" my mom announces as the rest of us celebrate our little guy.

"Soooo do you have any names picked out?" Margot asks.

Sloane looks up at me. "Well, I think Ledger Jr. would be perfect."

I shake my head in disapproval as Henry interjects. "You know Henry the fourth is always an option."

"Ew, you weirdo, it's not *your* son," Jack says, making a gagging motion.

Henry uses his hands to massage his eyes. "It doesn't *have* to be a direct father-son succession, you buffoon. But I doubt I will have any children of my own, and it would be a waste of a fourth."

Mom hits the back of Henry's head. "Oh hush, you will absolutely have some of your own. All three of you will," she says, pointing at Margot and Jack in the process.

Margot turns a deep shade of red as Jack chokes, bringing our attention away from our little argument. "You alright, man?" I ask, hitting him harder than necessary on the back.

"Yeah, yup...just all this talk of babies. I think I'm going to go get some air," he says, drawing laughter from all of us.

Jack wanders off, and I sense my opportunity to steal Sloane away and give her a gift I've been keeping in the back of my sock drawer for over two years now. Handing her a tiny white gift bag, I give her a sheepish grin as she raises an eyebrow.

"Ledger, I think you've bought the baby at least a hundred outfits at this point, not to mention all my gestation presents, pre-push presents, mommy-to-be presents."

"And don't think for a second I'm anywhere close to being finished, Angel. But this one is probably the most special one yet."

I'm not even pretending to hold back the tears as Sloane pulls out the motorcycle onesie from early on in our love story.

She gasps and her own tears begin to fall, although it doesn't take much for her to cry these days.

"Ledger...is this for our baby?" she sobs, echoing my words to her from so long ago.

I laugh out a sob, thrilled that she remembers that night as clearly as I do, and so fucking excited to see our tiny little guy finally wearing this in a few months.

"Yeah, Sloane. This is for our baby. I promise not to let him on a dirt bike until he's at least four, though," I joke, as she slaps my arm and wipes her tears.

"Don't even tease about that! He's not getting on anything motorized until he's a teenager at least!"

Laughing at Sloane's momma-bear attitude, we head back inside to the party, which is still in full swing.

After hours of playing games, eating, laughing, and celebrating my son with those I hold closest to my heart, I wrap my arms around Sloane, resting my hands on her bump. "You ready to go home, love?"

"Hmm, as long as we can take some cake."

"I'll have a whole damn bakery built on to our house if you ask."

"Promises, promises," she says with a smirk on her face. "Come on, let's go say our goodbyes."

Epilogue II

Sloane

"I can't believe we're having a boy," I say, holding the sonogram in my hands, cuddling with Ledger in our hammock.

"I'm still relieved it's not a minotaur," Ledger says, earning a slap across his chest.

Of all the places we've traveled to, I swear my favorite is in this hammock watching the sun set. It reminds me of the morning we watched the sunrise after getting married. Ledger reminded me that I could watch the sunrise any time I wanted, but we both know I'm not getting up before the sun does.

Sitting here, curled up with my husband...I'm not convinced life could ever be any better. But when our little guy arrives, I know it will. I've already been referring to him as LJ in my head, for Ledger Jr., but his dad isn't on board with that plan. *Yet.* Sighing, I shift to try to get a little more comfortable, and I already know this is nothing compared to what's coming as I get bigger.

"I already can't get comfy. I don't know what you're going to do with me once I'm huge."

Ledger smiles into the crook of my neck. "I'll carry you around, baby. And I'll give you massages all day, every day. We need to ask the doctor if it's possible for you to be massaged too much."

"Well, we can cross that bridge when we come to it, I guess. But for now, I need to get out of this hammock."

He helps me to my feet, and we head inside. I feel...horny. That's the problem. So freaking horny.

He looks a little nervous, which is rare for him, so I try to stay calm and prepare myself for *whatever* he's got up his sleeve. He leads me toward the nursery, then opens a door to what's been a catch-all room. As he steps inside, I see the space is dominated by a narrow padded...chair? I'm not really sure what I'm looking at because it looks like a plush chaise lounge and a gynecology chair had a baby. I'm seeing back support, adjustable head and neck support, soft-looking fabric...

"What is this, Ledger?"

I turn to find him looking sheepish. "I know it looks weird, but I had the idea that something where you can sit and relax in multiple positions might be necessary at some point. So we drew it up with the idea that everything is adjustable...you can basically change the angle on anything, and even the padding for the cushions can be changed out depending on if you want it softer or firmer. I had several different covers made, so if you don't like this material, there are others..." He lets out a long breath, and I see his cheeks are pink. "The idea was a massage chair, but then I couldn't stop imagining it as a sex chair. So it's...both?"

Now that he mentions it, I can see his vision. Looking around the room, I see shelves holding massage oils, toys, lube, and dozens of flameless, flickering candles, all adding to the ambience. Lavender fills the room from a diffuser, and spa music is playing from a hidden speaker. There are no windows, but a few lamps cast the room in a soft glow.

"Ledger, did you make me a pregnancy sex room?"

He can tell I'm in awe of what he's done with the place, and his confidence is clearly back. He stands behind me and wraps me in his arms. "Pregnancy *massage* room, Angel. If sex happens here, well, that's just a bonus. *But* given how much we're both enjoying you being pregnant"—he nips at my neck—"I figured it was a wise investment to go ahead and have all this built out."

Looking at the chair and seeing how comfy I'll be able to sit with my legs fully supported but spread wide, any happy tears I was about to cry are replaced with hot need shooting straight up my spine.

"I can't believe you did this. Are you going to give me a massage?"

"Well, that's the other part of your surprise, baby. Since you wouldn't let me stare at you during your online classes..."

"That was weird!"

"Fully disagree, but I digress. I had to do something with those hours every day. So for the past year or so, I've been training to become your personal massage therapist. I just finished my prenatal certification this week."

Okay, I have to face him for this. I turn around, and he has a wide smile that's one of my favorites. He looks so pleased with himself and carefree, and I wish I could eat him with a spoon.

His smile turns into a dirty smirk. "A spoon, baby? You can just suck straight from the source, you know."

I squeak. "I did not mean to say that out loud."

Ledger laughs at me before beginning to unwrap my robe and my braid. "You've been doing that a lot lately, and it's amazing. Until we can develop technology for me to read your mind, it's like the closest I can get to your inner monologue. I thoroughly enjoy it, but I didn't realize I've been such a bad influence on you. You swear *a lot* in your thoughts these days, baby," he says, spinning me to face him naked. His hot gaze sweeps from my head to my feet, before coming back to my eyes, and I gasp, seeing the raw emotion there. Placing a hand on my belly, he rasps, "You have *no idea* what it does to me, knowing that I did this to you. The pleasure of seeing you like this...it's almost more than I can bear some days."

He rubs my stomach for another few seconds before seeming to shake himself out of it and leading me to my chair...although it feels more like a throne, all things considered. I'm naked, but the temperature in here is perfect.

Once I'm melted into the chair, which is possibly the most comfortable thing I've ever had the pleasure of sitting on, Ledger produces a plate of sliced fruit from a fridge in the back of the room and some chocolate sauce for dipping. "Is this an okay snack, baby?" I open my mouth in answer and let him feed me until the entire plate is gone.

Now that I'm not hungry, I'm just horny as I wait to see what my husband has up his sleeve next.

"What do you say, Angel? Let me put all those hours of massage training to the test?"

"Yes, please." I sigh, as he adjusts my chair to be at a more relaxed angle, with my arms on rests comfortably to my side, and my legs extended and parted in a natural V, just enough for him to stand between.

My eyes are closed, waiting for him to start rubbing me into oblivion, when I feel silk brush over my eyes. *He's blindfolded me...yes. Freaking finally.* I've been asking for the return of the blindfold for months, but he's been denying me and keeping me on my toes. Worth it, to be surprised now and sink into the bliss of not knowing where he's going to touch next.

"Now, Mrs. Sinclair," he begins, and my pussy clenches on nothing, just like it does every time he calls me that. Which is often. "You'll tell me if I'm using too much pressure?"

"Yes."

"Yes, what?"

"Yes, *Daddy,*" I moan, as his massage-oil-coated hand makes its first touch on my instep. He groans at the word, and for a second, I hope he abandons his massage plans and shows me how well this thing can function as a sex chair. Ever since we found out I was pregnant, he's insisted I call him that. "For practice."

"That's a good fucking girl," he growls. "I'm gonna make you feel so good, baby."

And then, for what feels like ages, all I know is his oiled touch. He pays attention to every muscle in my feet and up my calves before switching to my arms and hands, gently relaxing me until I feel like I'm truly one with the chair. An adjustment leaves my head and neck supported but my scalp available to him, and he rinses the oil off his hands before giving me the most thorough scalp massage of my life. I'm so relaxed when he finishes that I don't even realize he's tucked my head fully back onto the table and moved again between my thighs.

"I think I missed some spots earlier, baby. Are you okay if I get them now?"

"Mmm," I reply, until I feel an oiled hand start working on my thigh. I noticed he skipped them earlier but didn't think much of it because everything felt so good. But as he gently works on my muscles with the same diligence as he has every other body part, I can't stop wishing he would move his hand just a little to the side and massage my pussy instead. As he finishes the top of one thigh, he glides his fingers lightly over my clit on the way to the other, and I can't help the gasp that escapes.

"Are you alright, Mrs. Sinclair?"

"Yes," I whisper. "Please don't stop."

He gives my other leg the same treatment, working my inner thigh and coming as close as he can without actually touching my pussy. I've never been so simultaneously wound up and relaxed in my life. Finally, he speaks again.

"I need to adjust your chair to continue, if you're okay? Do you want more?"

"Pleeeasseeee. Please more," I whine, not even sure if I'm fully awake at this point or in some half-dream trance.

He chuckles. "As you wish."

The panel of the chair underneath my bottom is shortened, and my legs are angled so that my position now much more closely resembles a chair from my OB appointments. I'm fully spread to him now, and I really, *really* hope this means what I think it means.

Ledger starts back in with warm oil on his strong hands, catering to the underside of my thighs that he couldn't get to before. It feels so good, but his fingers are now drifting closer and closer to my center. Finally, he gives up on all pretense and starts including my pussy lips in more and more of his passes. Tiny brushes against my clit send fire through my veins, and my breathing picks up as he plays with me more and more. I can feel myself opening up for him as I become more aroused, and I know before long I'll start dripping.

"There it is. Didn't take you long at all once I really started. What a good wife you are, dripping for me when I've barely even touched you," he purrs, trailing his long middle finger all the way up my slit. I can feel how wet I am, and it definitely will run down to my ass in this position. He finally puts pressure directly on my clit once, twice, three times, and I'm gone, screaming my orgasm and feeling it in my bones.

I'm expecting the blindfold to come off and Ledger to fuck me in this perfectly positioned chair, but he keeps playing with my pussy like he has all the time in the world. Finally, I hear him step back and shuffle things around on the shelves.

His voice is raspy when he speaks. "You have no idea how hard it is not to bend down and lick up every bit of what you just gave me, baby. But we're going to need all of it for what I have planned."

I hear a specific, familiar click and let out a low moan as I finally realize what's happening. I'm practically a noodle, as relaxed as Ledger could possibly make me, because he's going to *fuck my ass.*

He gives a good-natured laugh now. "Yeah, you're a smart girl. You've wanted this, and now you're going to get it, baby. You've got my baby in you, which means for a few more months, I can put my cum wherever I want it. And tonight, Sloane, I'm coming in your ass. I promise you'll love it."

I whimper, and I've never been so glad to have a husband obsessed with my comfort. We've been on a whole "anal sex prep" plan for almost a year now. Ledger was so confident he would knock me up soon after I graduated that he insisted we be ready. Plugs have been a part of our play for a while, and he acquired some slightly smaller jewelry for his piercings, to ensure I'm comfortable during our first time. I didn't even notice he had swapped them out earlier...so tricky, my man.

"I'm going to remove your blindfold, but it shouldn't be too bright."

Blinking back into the present, I barely see Ledger standing over me before his lips are on mine, claiming my mouth with an intensity proving just how affected he is by my massage. *Glad it's not just me.*

"What do you think, baby? Are you ready?"

I smile at him and settle back into my throne. *It's definitely a throne; chair is too simple a word to describe the magical properties this piece of furniture possesses.*

"Yes, please."

He preps me gently with his fingers and then with my favorite dildo, slowly opening me up for him the way we've been practicing. With his other hand, he keeps constant teasing touches on my clit and in my pussy, making me a squirming mess, begging for more. Finally, he pulls everything free and squeezes what feels like an entire bottle of lube onto my asshole and his cock.

"Tell me if anything hurts. I'll go slow."

Pressing into me, he does go slow, and *now* I can tell that he's definitely downsized his jewelry, but *fuck me, he's bigger than the dildo.* I whine, and he stops advancing to spit on my clit and rub tight circles in my favorite spot. It feels so good that he sneaks in another inch, and the feeling *morphs.* The uncomfortable pressure is still there, but what was initially pain has been accepted by my body and transformed into something else entirely. Pleasure, yes, but the fullness is so foreign, and I feel so connected to Ledger that all I can do is take deep breaths and accept this feeling.

"You okay, Sloane?"

"Yes, please, it's getting good...more. Please," I whine, watching Ledger's eyes roll back into his head as he mouths, "*Fuck me,*" and gives me another couple of inches. God, watching him lose himself to pleasure when he's inside me is just as good as experiencing it myself.

His eyes pop back open and meet mine as he pushes in slowly until his hips are flush against my ass. He looks down at where we're connected, jaw clenched and nostrils flaring, before leaning his head back to look up at the ceiling. I can see his muscles tensing, and I briefly worry that he's hurt himself somehow when his thumb starts again, rubbing circles on my clit.

"You have to come, Sloane. Please," his voice cracks, and I realize he's not hurting. He's trying not to come. Fuck, I love doing that to him. And it's not going to take much, so he's lucky that I'll be able to do as he says.

As I feel myself tightening like a rubber band about to snap, I give him a warning.

"Ledger...Daddy...I'm going to..." He immediately moves, sensing that I'm right there. He plunges two thick fingers inside my pussy while his thumb continues working my clit, and he gives in and starts thrusting. I feel his ladder drag in and out, and that's what shoves me fully off the cliff. I don't fall...I'm just floating, a million tiny pieces of myself caught in a sparkling net of pleasure, drifting in the wind. I vaguely get a sense of Ledger yelling his release, but I'm not fully conscious anymore, certainly not fully in my body. Finally, I wake all the way up as I'm being rinsed off in the shower.

"Hi, baby," he whispers, tears streaming down his face.

"Hey, hey, it's okay. What's wrong?"

Ledger has my face cupped in both his hands, and if I didn't see a blinding amount of love every time he looked at me, I might be caught off guard by the adoration I find in his gaze.

"I just love you so much. You've given me so much of your love and your trust, and today was such a gift, to be able to worship you and share that with you." He takes a deep breath. "You're my whole world. You and LJ. I wish I could marry you again and again just to celebrate what you mean to me."

I give him a soft kiss. "I love you too. And LJ, huh? Have I been saying that one out loud accidentally, too?"

His smile is everything, maybe the sweetest I've ever seen from him. "Yeah, Angel. You have. When you're awake and when you're asleep, you talk to him, and that's all you ever call him. You'll be the best mom ever. And you can name him whatever you'd like."

I don't have any more words for now, so I just rest in Ledger's arms, this beautiful man who has given me a world I hadn't known could exist. As we finish our shower and do our nightly routine and fall into bed exhausted, I think of how perfect the day was. I know tomorrow will be even better, because regardless of what happens, I'm his. Regardless of what anyone else thinks of me, or what the world throws at us, I'm Ledger Sinclair's. Forever.

Missing the Sinclairs already?

Sign up for our newsletter for an exclusive *Redeemed in Crimson* bonus chapter and find out how Ledger spoiled Sloane for her birthday!

https://dl.bookfunnel.com/4b8ymo4tlt

Be the first to know about T.K. Drake's new releases and receive exclusive content!

www.tkdrake.com

Instagram: @tkdrakeauthor

Also By T.K. Drake

Masked in Deception
Book Two in Sinclair Affairs Series
Coming October 2025

Margot

When he was a cute little boy with curly golden hair, I wanted him to hold me every time I fell and kiss every scratch. He grew into a heart-throb teen, lanky from getting tall so fast but with washboard abs that glistened in the summer sun. I was still a little girl filled with fantasies of being a princess and was convinced he was my prince charming. Somewhere along the way, he grew into the man he is today. And somewhere along the way, every lover of mine morphed into Jack when I closed my eyes.

He's been the axis my world spun around. Always in the back of mind. Always in my heart. And God have I wanted him.

Jack

I should have more reservations than I do or at the very least consider the reason I've been keeping my distance for the past week. There should be some concern about the consequences of taking things past the point of no return. There is no illusion that this would only be for one night. That we would be able to wake up tomorrow morning and carry on with our lives like nothing ever happened. But a world doesn't exist where I could ever tell her no.

Acknowledgments

Thank you, Universe, for giving two best friends the chance to live out a dream. Thank you, childhood obsessions, for leading us into the arms of all of our book boyfriends. Thank you, small town oppression, for forging us into unapologetic adults who are aggressively pursuing happiness.

If you're reading this, thank you. You've already changed our lives.

About the Authors

T.K. Drake is a dynamic duo of best friends who couldn't find the perfect romance novel and decided to write it themselves. As only children, they spent their childhood entertaining each other with elaborate stories and games. Reuniting as adults has inspired them to unleash their creative energy into contemporary and dark romance, bridging gaps in the genre and writing books they longed to read. Based in the Southeastern United States, when not writing they are usually reading, lounging on the beach, or planning their next international vacation.

www.ingramcontent.com/pod-product-compliance
Lightning Source LLC
Chambersburg PA
CBHW030335120726
47901CB00007B/1804